Rammadrecul... ...ing at the *thing*. Glancing ba... ...cco saw that the unbihexium rounds which had slaughtered the Morganites seem to be having no effect at all on the *thing* from the repository.

Tabor seized the Rammadrecula around the waist, more-or-less hoisted her onto his back, and raced for the cube. Rammadrecula seemed oblivious to what was happening to her. Still screeching with fury, she kept firing at the monster—which had by now devoured about half of the Morganite.

Perhaps it would take the time to devour the rest of the corpses, Occo hoped.

But . . . no. She hadn't really thought it would. The thing seemed to swell, and then came speeding toward them. They wouldn't make it to the iris before it arrived.

Then—for whatever reason impelled the device, which Occo had never really understood—the Skerkud Teleplaser suddenly began unfolding. Within two minims, it had interposed itself between the cube and the oncoming *thing*.

"OPPOBRIOUS DISCOURTESY!" it boomed. "SANCTIONS AND FORFEITURES MUSTERED! MORTIFICATIONS ENHAN—"

The *thing* smashed into the Teleplaser.

To order these and other Baen titles in e-book form, go to www.baen.com

THE GODS OF SAGITTARIUS

ERIC FLINT
MIKE RESNICK

THE GODS OF SAGITTARIUS

This is a work of fiction. All the characters and events portrayed in this book are fictional, and any resemblance to real people or incidents is purely coincidental.

A Baen Books Original

Baen Publishing Enterprises
P.O. Box 1403
Riverdale, NY 10471
www.baen.com

ISBN: 9781481483391

Cover art by Stephan Martinière

First Baen trade paperback printing, May 2017
First Baen paperback printing, July 2018

Distributed by Simon & Schuster
1230 Avenue of the Americas
New York, NY 10020

Printed in the United States of America

10 9 8 7 6 5 4 3 2 1

THE GODS OF SAGITTARIUS

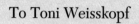

To Toni Weisskopf

CHAPTER I

Russ Tabor pulled a thin, smokeless cigar out of his pocket, lit it, took a puff, stalked around the outer office, tossed it in a trash atomizer, kept walking, pulled another cigar out, looked at it, and threw it out without even lighting it.

He stared at the lens above the door, growled at it, and finally sat down.

A female voice spoke up. "Please rise and approach me, Mr. Tabor."

He looked around, couldn't see any women or indeed any living beings. Then he saw that the lens was glowing, and he walked over and stood before it.

"Identifying retina," said the emotionless voice. "Check. Identifying bone structure. Check." There was a brief pause. "You have two cavities in your lower right back molar."

"Do I complain about the scratch you have across the top of whatever the hell you are?" he shot back.

"I was informing, not complaining."

"I'll live," he muttered.

1

"I notice a bead of sweat on your forehead," continued the voice. "Please touch your forefinger to it, and then touch the glowing panel in front of you."

"With which hand?" he asked sardonically.

"Either."

"You're quite sure? I've been told on excellent authority that my right hand is much lovelier."

"Please, Mr. Tabor, just do as I ask."

He ran a finger across his forehead and brought it to the panel.

"Your DNA checks," announced the voice.

"What a surprise," said Tabor.

"Had you some reason to think it would *not* match?" asked the voice.

"Shut up and let me through."

There was silence for perhaps ten seconds. Then the door slid into the wall. "You may enter, Mr. Tabor."

Tabor stormed into the large, elegant, expensively furnished office, where a middle-aged man with thinning red hair sat at a desk, staring at him.

"What the hell is this about, as if I didn't know?" demanded Tabor.

"Well, as long as you know, we have nothing to discuss," said Philip Montrose with an amused smile.

"Fuck you!" snapped Tabor. "You pulled me off an important assignment to guard a pompous ass who's crazy as a loon!"

"Whatever that may be," responded Montrose.

"Why *me*, damn it?" continued Tabor. "I spent months making connections, finding out how to unearth information from that whole goddamned planetary conglomerate, and now you pull me off before we can bring the whole house of cards down."

"Our lawyers say you've supplied them with enough information to put the cartel away for decades."

"I know! But I want to *be* there! I want to testify in court, and watch their faces when I do."

"It's all *pro forma*," answered Montrose. "They're as good as convicted. Why dance on their graves?"

"I put up with their shit for almost a year while I was working my way up through their organization," said Tabor. "I *want* to dance on those bastards' graves."

Montrose shook his head. "That job's done. Besides, it was just a sideshow. We're in the protection business, and you just happened to stumble across the biggest fraud of the year. Congratulations, but it's history. I've got a new one for you."

"Give it to the goddamned military," snarled Tabor. "He's working for the government, isn't he?"

"Not anymore."

"They realized they were wasting their time and money."

"Actually," said Montrose, "*he* quit *them*." Tabor arched an eyebrow. "Evidently he made some demands they wouldn't accept, so he decided to go private."

Tabor shrugged. "Who cares why he did it? Let's get back to my pending resignation."

"Oh, shut up, Russ," said Montrose irritably. "Do you have to be like this every single time I give you a new assignment?"

"Do you have to give me one shit job after another?" Tabor shot back.

"Look," said Montrose, trying to sound more reasonable than he felt whenever he argued with Tabor, "we're not government, we're not police, we're not military. We're mostly security, whatever that entails, and we do what we're paid for. And it's the nature of the beast that if no overpaid and overstaffed and underskilled official organization wants a job, it'll be just the kind that you bitch like hell about." He exhaled deeply. "But it's also the kind you happen to be good at."

"Each one is worse than the last."

"You think you can make more money working for the planetary government or the police, go ahead," said Montrose. "I'm through arguing."

Tabor scowled. "You know I'll take it if I can't talk you out of it."

"Then it's settled."

"I still want to know why," continued Tabor. "He's a total flake. Half his theories have gotten him laughed out of every position he's ever held."

"Yeah, and two of his theories have won him the Sagittarius Prize." Montrose grimaced. "For what it's worth, I think he's a flake, at least on odd-numbered days . . . but no one else has ever won two Prizes."

"I did a little research when I saw that he quit the government and was going private, because somehow I knew you'd be coming to *me*," said Tabor. "Along with winning two Prizes, he's been fired by three universities, one branch of the government, and one top-level research firm."

"All the more reason why he might need some protection," replied Montrose with a smile.

"I can't protect him from being fired or making a fool of himself," said Tabor. "And as far as I know, no one's ever tried to kill or harm him."

"A flake like that," said Montrose. "Give 'em time. They will."

"What's he working on now?"

Montrose shrugged. "Beats the hell out of me. You'll be meeting him for dinner. You can ask him then."

"I don't think I'm going to be hungry."

"Good! You'll be a cheap date."

"So why did he quit—or did he?" asked Tabor.

"Ask him at dinner."

Tabor scowled. "So you set up a dinner in advance. And I assume *he* knows where we're meeting."

Montrose nodded. "No sense having him starve to death looking into the window of every restaurant in town—especially since he doesn't know what you look like."

"Earth-type food, or is he as loony about his meals as he is with his theories?"

"I know your tastes," said Montrose. "You'll be dining at the Fatted Calf, about a kilometer from here. It was the least I could do for you."

"One of these days why not consider doing the *most* you can for me?"

"Of course," agreed Montrose, looking down at his computer to determine his next order of business.

"When hell freezes over," muttered Tabor, getting up and walking to the door. He half hoped it wouldn't open so he could pull one of his weapons and turn it to rubble, but it almost seemed to sense that and opened before he'd gone two steps.

❀ ❀ ❀

The Fatted Calf had never served a calf (or a cow) in its three-decade existence. The fees for importing such animals, plus the import duties, would have made a typical meal the equivalent of a week's pay for the upscale diners who frequented the place. But the locally grown mutated beef was prepared much as meat was prepared in Earth's better restaurants. And if the spices weren't quite what were used on Earth, they were close enough so that no one complained (and the fact that most of the diners had never set foot on Earth didn't hurt either).

Tabor entered the restaurant, waved the android headwaiter off, surveyed the tables and recognized his dinner partner from the holos he had seen. He walked over and sat down opposite him at the table.

"Do I know you?" asked the older man mildly.

"You will," replied Tabor. "I'm going to be your second skin for . . ." He shrugged. "For however long it takes."

"Ah!" said the man, his face lighting up. "You are my new servant."

Tabor shook his head. "No, sir, I am not your servant."

The man frowned in confusion. "Then why are you sitting here?"

"I am your protector," he said. "I am no one's servant."

"Semantics," said the man with a shrug.

"Facts," replied Tabor. "I am Russell Tabor, and you are Rupert Medawar Narayan Shenoy. You can call me Russ. What do I call you?"

"Lord Shenoy," was the answer.

"Right," said Tabor. "Rupert it is."

Shenoy stared at Tabor for a long minute. "I don't think I like you very much."

Tabor shrugged. "Okay," he replied. "Fire me."

Shenoy shook his head. "No," he said at last. "You're the best in the business."

"Did Montrose tell you that?"

"No," answered Shenoy, "but it stands to reason. If you weren't the best, you wouldn't have been assigned to me."

"I'm sure glad to see you don't have an ego problem, Rupert," said Tabor with a smile.

"Couldn't you make it Sir Rupert?"

"I'm afraid not."

"Just when colleagues or the press are around?" persisted Shenoy. "I *am* descended from Sir Peter Medawar and R.K. Narayan."

"We'll see," said Tabor.

"I'm exceptionally proud of my heritage," continued Shenoy. He stared at Tabor. "Do you even know yours?"

"Beyond my parents, who didn't accomplish much of anything, no," was the answer. "But I don't really care who did what way the hell back in my pedigree. I'd rather be judged on what *I* do."

"So would I," agreed Shenoy. "But I am proud of what came before me."

"I'm more concerned with what comes next."

"Ah!" said Shenoy, smiling. "You're married?"

Tabor shook his head. "Not even close."

"But you just said . . ."

"That I'm concerned with what comes next," said Tabor. "*What*, not *who*. For example, what are you working on that someone with a lot of money thinks you may need protection? Will you be working here, or on some other planet?"

"Oh, we'll be going afield," answered Shenoy. "Not much to be discovered here."

"There isn't?"

Shenoy shook his head. "There are no sentient life forms native to Boriga IV," he said. "That puts it pretty much beyond my field of interest or expertise." He paused. "Well, my current field, anyway," he amended.

"Yet here you are," said Tabor.

"I was working for one of the governmental departments, which happens to be located here," answered Shenoy. "I came here not to work, but to terminate my employment."

"That's kind of curious, Rupert," said Tabor, as Shenoy tried not to wince at the use of his first name. "Usually it's the employer who terminates a relationship."

Shenoy grimaced. "It's rather complicated. Officially I was working for a university here, but then the government decided I could accomplish more with a staff, a larger staff than the university could afford, so they became my co-employers." A sudden smile. "And now they're both my co-ex-employers."

Tabor returned his smile. "You must have offended a *lot* of professors and bureaucrats if they both decided to fire you."

"I just told you: *I* fired *them*."

"I know, I know," agreed Tabor. "But you can only fire a government if it's willing to be fired. Otherwise, you could well wind up a permanent resident of one of their free facilities where you will never have to worry about security."

"They would never incarcerate me," answered Shenoy. "Nobody benefited from my two Prizes more than the government, and if I can unlock the current problem, they stand to profit again. Of course, I'll profit too," he added, "but I already have more than enough money to last my lifetime. What I'm after is knowledge."

"Knowledge can be a profitable commodity," said Tabor. "What are you after, Rupert?"

Shenoy stared at him, as if deciding whether or not to confide in him. Finally he realized that of course Tabor would have to know, since he couldn't provide protection from some other planet. He lowered his voice and leaned forward across the table.

"Have you ever heard of a world named Cthulhu?"

CHAPTER 2

Tabor was waiting for Shenoy in the lobby of the latter's hotel.

"Nice place," he remarked as Shenoy emerged from an airlift, accompanied by two large, uniformed androids that were carrying his luggage.

"I'm usually only here to sleep," replied Shenoy.

"Then why not rent an apartment?" asked Tabor. "It would have been a hell of a lot cheaper."

"Well, I suppose if I had been paying for it, I would have," came the answer. "But I must confess that it comes with a bunch of amenities that I'm going to miss."

"Even though you were hardly ever here?"

"Look around you," said Shenoy. "Crystal chandeliers every fifteen feet. Three times as many android servants as guests. Two all-night restaurants, both five-star, and a nightclub with excellent entertainment."

"Too bad you only slept here and didn't avail yourself of all that," said Tabor with a smile.

"Well, perhaps I was here just a tad more than I implied," replied Shenoy, returning his smile. "Anyway, my bill is taken care of, so we might as well go to the spaceport. I assume you've lined up a ship?"

"Of course."

"According to my specifications?"

Tabor nodded his head. "Seems a little big for just the two of us."

"There will be four of us," answered Shenoy. "A man and a woman. I've worked with them before. I'll introduce you when they arrive."

"I'd appreciate that, Rupert," said Tabor. "I'd hate to call them 'Hey, You!' for the next few months."

Shenoy stared at him for a moment, then smiled. "That was a joke, wasn't it?" he said at last.

"You noticed."

"I'm not used to jokes."

"*I* noticed," replied Tabor.

"Give me time," said Shenoy. "I'm very adaptable."

They reached a vehicle that floated a few inches above the ground, waited for the androids to load Shenoy's luggage into a carrying compartment, then climbed into the vehicle themselves.

Suddenly Shenoy looked around and frowned.

"Is something wrong?" asked Tabor.

"You don't have any luggage of your own," replied Shenoy. "I hate to mention it, but with no change of clothes for months on end you're not going to turn into any nosegay. No offense intended. I mean, I've put up with worse."

Tabor stared at him, trying to determine if he was joking or not. Finally he spoke. "I sent my luggage ahead to the spaceport. Why carry it from the hotel?"

"How very practical!" said Shenoy with a smile.

I guess they don't give out the Sagittarius Prize for practicality, thought Tabor. Aloud he said, "So what are we looking for on this . . . what was the name of it?"

"Cthulhu," answered Shenoy. "Well, we're not quite sure. Otherwise we'd know what to bring."

"What *are* we bringing?"

"You, me, and my two assistants."

"Maybe I worded it wrong," said Tabor. "What is it about Cthulhu that attracts a Prize winner?"

"And two Ph.D.s," added Shenoy. "My assistants have excellent credentials."

"I'm sure they do," said Tabor. *I just hope I'm not the only one who can ask or answer a direct question.*

"There's the racetrack," noted Shenoy, pointing to a large coliseum as the vehicle floated past.

"Yeah," said Tabor in bored tones. "They run some kind of animal there."

"Paringles."

"Pringles?" said Tabor, frowning.

"Paringles," repeated Shenoy. "A four-legged quadruped, about fifteen hundred pounds. Interesting animals. I go there whenever I have a free afternoon."

Tabor smiled. "Somehow you don't strike me as a bettor, Rupert."

"Oh, I'm not," Shenoy assured him. "But I love pitting my intellect against the laws of chance." He began patting his coat pockets. "I keep a record here somewhere. Ah! Got it." He pulled out a small notebook and began thumbing through it.

"Paper?" said Tabor, surprised.

"I'm a traditionalist." He turned a few more pages, then stopped and studied his near-illegible scrawl. "If I'd bet ten credits a race, after eighty-six races I would be . . . let me see . . . almost three hundred credits ahead of the game."

"Somehow I think you make more money solving the problems of the universe."

"Oh, I do," agreed Shenoy. "But it's not as much fun."

"At least you don't go broke."

"There's a method for beating the track. I just haven't codified it yet."

"People have been trying to beat racetracks since we were still Earthbound," remarked Tabor. "No one's done it yet."

"That's why it fascinates me so," replied Shenoy. "I'd be the first." He paused. "I suppose it goes hand in glove with my work. You take the disparate parts of a puzzle that no one else can comprehend, and then, either through logic or a sudden burst of insight, you reconstruct the comprehensive whole." Suddenly he smiled. "In fact, it's invariably through that sudden burst. If the scientific method worked, the problem would have been solved long before it landed on my desk."

"I hope you don't teach that to your students, Rupert," said Tabor with a smile.

"Students?"

"You worked for a university until this week, remember?"

"But I never taught. They just paid me to do my work under their auspices for"—he searched for the proper term—"reflected glory."

"I suppose it makes sense," said Tabor. "You turn out five or ten geniuses and they all go to work elsewhere, the university gets very little of that reflected glory. But win a Prize while you're working for them . . . "

"Absolutely," agreed Shenoy, nodding his head vigorously. "Besides, I'd be a terrible teacher. I hate rigorous preparation."

"I hope you've done a little preparation for Cthulhu," replied Tabor. "If I'm going to give up all the comforts of a civilized world, I'd like to think it'll serve some purpose."

"Oh, Cthulhu's civilized," said Shenoy. He frowned. "Just very strange."

"I ran a computer check on it last night," said Tabor. "Within five percent of Standard gravity and atmosphere, two oceans, a few city-states, never been at war with anyone. A few animal species, none of them sentient. Got some gold and platinum mines, and a couple of diamond pipes, which is why anyone moved there in the first place. Pays its bills. Never had a revolution. So what's so very strange about it?"

"That's what we're going there to find out."

"I'd like a little better answer than that, Rupert."

"I don't mean to annoy you, Mr. . . . Russ," he said. "But I'm going to have to explain it to Basil and Andrea once we take off, Russ—so why tell you now when you'll be on the ship as well, Russ?"

"I'm glad we're being less formal," replied Tabor, "but one Russ per paragraph is really quite sufficient."

"I'm sorry, Russ," said Shenoy. "I'm a little awkward in social situations."

"I would never have guessed," said Tabor sardonically.

"Really?" said Shenoy happily. "I guess it doesn't show as much as I'd feared." Suddenly he frowned. "Maybe I could have taught a class or two after all."

The vehicle entered the spaceport, and Shenoy gave the ship's ID number to the autopilot, which veered around four nearer ships and then stopped in front of a reconditioned cargo ship. Three robots—not androids, for absolutely no effort had been made to give them any human features—stepped forward and began unloading the cargo space.

"Are we planning to bring back a temple, or perhaps a pyramid?" asked Tabor, looking at the ship.

"I'm not working for the university any more, Russ. These people watch their bottom line. I don't know what we may bring back, which is why we need such a large vessel. But their budget is also why the ship looks so . . . ah . . . *used*."

"Just out of curiosity, who *are* 'these people'?" asked Tabor.

"A number of scientific journals, Russ," replied Shenoy. Suddenly he grinned. "I can just see them fighting over the rights to the story of my discovery— always assuming they're willing to run what I discover."

"I don't quite follow that," said Tabor. "And you don't have to call me Russ every time."

"My mistake, Russell," said Shenoy, who seemed to have no idea what Tabor meant. "Anyway, my field of expertise is officially alien technology, but sometimes alien technology is so close to magic that the two are indistinguishable . . . and some of these journals are not going to like that."

Tabor was about to ask for an example when another vehicle floated up and two people got off—a tall, slender, balding man in his thirties, with intense staring blue eyes and a thin, delicate mustache that looked like it took more trouble than it was worth; and a short, muscular, redheaded woman with a perpetual scowl on her face.

"Ah!" exclaimed Shenoy. "They're here! Come along, Russ, and I'll introduce you."

Tabor followed him as he approached the two newcomers. "Hello, Andrea," said the scientist. "You're looking well. And you too, Basil. I want you to meet the fourth member of our party, Russ . . . uh, I've quite forgotten your last name."

"Russ Tabor," he said, reaching out and shaking each of their hands in turn.

"And I'm Basil Stone, and this is Andrea Melander."

Basil stared at him, as if sizing him up. "I wasn't expecting a fourth member of the team. May I ask what your function is?"

"I've been hired to guard the most valuable part of the expedition," answered Tabor.

"Oh?" said Andrea curiously. "And what is that?"

Tabor jerked a thumb in Shenoy's direction. "Him."

"Of course," said Basil. "It makes sense. Especially if Cthulhu's half as weird and dangerous as it sounds."

"Everything that's unknown sounds weird or dangerous or both," replied Shenoy. "I'm sure there'll be an explanation for it."

"Good," said Tabor. "I like logical explanations."

Basil smiled. "Did he say 'logical'?"

❀ ❀ ❀

"All set," said Shenoy, walking back to the bridge from his cabin. He frowned. "I hope it's not too cold. I only packed one heavy coat."

"I thought we were going to mostly be inside," said Andrea, frowning.

"Right," agreed Shenoy.

"Well, then?" she said.

He shrugged. "You never know."

Tabor shot Basil an *Is he always this pixilated* look, and Basil sighed, smiled, and nodded his head.

"Well, we're all on the bridge," continued Shenoy. "Let's go."

"Are we waiting for a pilot?" asked Basil.

"From what they told me, everything's programmed in," responded Tabor.

"Okay," said Shenoy, staring at the viewscreen. "Take off."

Nothing happened.

Shenoy cleared his throat. "Take off!" he said with greater volume.

Still nothing.

"May I?" asked Tabor.

"Be my guest," answered Shenoy.

"Ship, respond please," said Tabor.

"Awaiting your orders," said a mechanical voice.

"You were given a flight plan to Cthulhu," continued Tabor. "Can you access it?"

"Yes."

"And you've filed it with the various authorities?"

"Yes."

"Are all systems operative?"

"Yes."

"Okay, take off."

Nothing happened.

"Ship, did you hear me?" said Tabor.

There was no response.

"Oh, hell!" muttered Basil. "The goddamned engine is dead."

"That fast?" asked Andrea.

Tabor pulled out a communication device and contacted the spaceport, spoke softly for a moment, then frowned and put the device back in a pocket.

"Well?" asked Basil.

"They checked the ship two hours ago. Everything was working, and it had enough fuel to get us there and back twice."

"They must be mistaken," said Basil. "Ships don't just die two hours after passing inspection."

Tabor turned to Shenoy. "You're the genius, Rupert. What the hell happened?"

"I'm not sure," answered Shenoy. "But it *is* interesting."

"It's a pain in the ass, is what it is," said Andrea. "Now we're going to have to make arrangements for a new ship, move all of our gear, and—"

"Perhaps not," said Shenoy, a puzzled expression on his face.

"What are you getting at?" she said.

"I don't think we're going to need a new ship," said Shenoy. "Or at least, I don't think it will be any better than this one."

"But this one stopped working," said Andrea irritably.

"Curious, isn't it?" replied Shenoy.

"Curious, hell!" she snapped. "It's just goddamned bad luck!"

Tabor had been watching Shenoy carefully since the ship had died, and now he spoke up. "What was so curious, Rupert?"

Shenoy blinked his eyes rapidly for a few seconds, then frowned. "That it was working fine until you mentioned Cthulhu."

"Are you seriously suggesting that the damned ship doesn't want to go there?" demanded Andrea.

Shenoy shrugged and offered her a gentle smile. "Are you seriously suggesting that a ship that passed inspection this morning suddenly gave up the ghost for no reason?"

"It's more likely than that the damned ship is afraid to go to Cthulhu!" she shot back.

"Oh, I don't think it's *afraid*," said Shenoy. "I don't believe a ship can feel fear. Or hate or love, for that matter."

"Then what about mentioning Cthulhu made the ship shut down?" asked Tabor.

"That's one of many things we must find out," replied Shenoy. "But I have a request that is something in the nature of an experiment." He looked at each of them in turn. "Let us pledge not to mention our destination by its proper name, but refer to it only by its coordinates."

"That's fine," said Basil. "But the ship is dead."

Shenoy shook his head. "The ship is momentarily dormant, but we already know that there's nothing wrong with it, so I expect all of its systems will come back to life very soon now, when we take off for"—he rattled off the planet's galactic coordinates—"and the trick for us is not to put it back to sleep again, especially once we take off and we are dependent on it for the air we breathe."

"And you really believe this shit, Rupert?" asked Tabor, frowning.

"*Believe* is a very strong word, Russ," answered Shenoy. "Let us say rather that I *suspect* that this shit is true."

Tabor stared at him, trying to decide if Shenoy was making fun of him, and finally decided that he wasn't.

"Okay, so what do we do now?"

"We wait," said Shenoy.

"How long?" persisted Tabor.

"I'm inclined to say as long as it takes, but perhaps there is a way to speed up the process."

"And what might that be?"

Shenoy seemed to stare at some spot at the top of the bridge that only he could see. Finally he spoke: "Let's have some coffee."

"And then will you tell us?" said Tabor.

Basil chuckled. "You don't know how the Brain thinks."

"The Brain?" repeated Tabor. He turned to Shenoy. "That would be you?"

Shenoy shrugged. "It's what he calls me. I'd much rather be referred to as Lord Shenoy."

"I know I'm surrounded by geniuses," growled Tabor irritably, "but I feel like I've wandered into an animated entertainment for three-year-olds."

"You don't like coffee?" asked Shenoy, who seemed genuinely concerned.

"Coffee's fine," muttered Tabor. "Let's get on with it."

"And you, Andrea?"

She nodded "Yeah, whatever it takes."

"Good," said Shenoy. "I just hope you've all answered sincerely."

"What the hell difference does that make?" demanded Tabor.

"Keep your temper, dear boy," said Shenoy gently. "There's no call for ill behavior. Basil, I've already forgotten where the galley is. Go fetch us a pot of coffee, four cups, and a tray." Basil got up and began walking to the galley. "Oh, and bring some cream and sugar, and of course spoons, for those who might want them."

This is clearly going to be an exercise in futility, thought Tabor. *All the ship's systems are dead, so how the hell can the galley make coffee? Can't any of these geniuses figure that out?*

"Well, goddamn!" cried Basil. "It's working! How did you know?"

Shenoy allowed himself the luxury of a satisfied smile. "Just a hunch."

"Uh-uh," said Tabor. "You're a scientist, not a psychic. How did you know?"

"Knowing that it would happen was the easy part," answered Shenoy. "Knowing *why* it would happen is the tricky part. I'm still mulling on that."

"Explain the easy part to us," insisted Tabor.

"I had to convince, well, not the ship, but whatever was influencing the ship, that we would not use that word again, and that we had no intention of leaving just because the ship had gone dormant. So by brewing up some coffee, someone or something realized that we weren't abandoning the ship."

"Then why didn't the ship just stay dormant?" asked Tabor.

"It's a ship. Its function is to transport us. Eventually it had to do that or die."

"A ship has no sense of self-preservation."

"Nonsense," scoffed Shenoy. "Do you know how many safety systems are built into every ship these days?"

"So if you're right . . ." began Tabor.

"He often is," said Andrea as Basil began approaching them carrying the coffee, cream and cups on a very plain metal tray.

"If the ship is incapable of independent action, something controlled, or at least influenced, it," said Tabor.

"Most likely," agreed Shenoy pleasantly as he poured himself a cup of coffee.

"Who or what would or could do that?" asked Tabor. "And more importantly, *why*?"

"Ah!" said Shenoy. "That's what makes this business so much fun."

"Fun?" repeated Tabor. "Whatever put the ship to sleep could have done it while we were in space, or traversing a wormhole."

"But it didn't," replied Shenoy. "That makes us one step smarter than it is."

"You really believe that?" asked Tabor dubiously.

"Not really," answered Shenoy. Suddenly a smile crossed his face. "But it *does* make one feel better, at least for a moment, doesn't it?"

Tabor stared at him silently for a long moment.

Great. Just great. I'm working for a genius who can solve the mysteries of the universe, but probably can't dress himself or figure out how the lock on the bathroom door works.

CHAPTER 3

Tabor sipped his coffee and wondered what the hell would happen next. He was mystified by what had transpired already, both the ship shutting down and Shenoy's off-the-wall solution to the problem, but he was pretty sure the problems weren't over.

"Maybe we'd better take off before it falls asleep again," suggested Basil.

"It's not going back to sleep," said Shenoy.

"How do you know?" asked Tabor.

Shenoy smiled. "The sun's out and it's a beautiful day. Who would sleep on a day like this?"

"How about: the ship, until five minutes ago?"

"Ask it," said Shenoy.

"Ask it *what*?" replied Tabor.

"How it feels."

Tabor frowned. "You're kidding, right?"

"Certainly not," said Shenoy.

Andrea shot Tabor a *The Boss gets like this now and then* look and shrugged.

"Ask it yourself, Rupert," said Tabor. "It hardly knows me."

"It hardly knows any of us," answered Shenoy. "What does that have to do with anything?"

"You're in charge. It should come from you."

"If you insist," said Shenoy. He raised his voice. "Ship, can you hear me?"

"Yes, Captain," said the ship's metallic voice.

"I'd prefer you called me Sir Rupert."

"Certainly, Sir Rupert," replied the ship.

"How do you feel on this fine day?" asked Shenoy.

"I feel *great!*" bellowed the ship with as much emotion as it had lacked with its previous replies.

"Good," said Shenoy. "It's a lovely day, isn't it?"

"Indeed it is!" enthused the ship. "A day like this makes me want to sing." And it immediately burst into song at an almost deafening volume: *"Roll me over, in the clover, roll me over and do it again!"*

"Enough!" yelled Tabor.

"Did I do it wrong?" asked the ship.

"You're deafening me."

"I apologize, Sir First Officer. How about a nice harp solo?"

"How about a little silence?" suggested Tabor.

A sound that was almost a sob echoed throughout the ship, and then all was quiet.

"Why do I think it's not natural for a spaceship to sing bawdy ballads?" asked Tabor.

"It doesn't really possess all that complex a central processing unit," answered Shenoy. "You could hardly expect Beethoven, or even Vivaldi."

Tabor stared at him for a long minute. "I don't think I'm getting through to you at all," he said at last. "Ships don't break into song, and then stifle a sob when you ask them to shut up."

"I know," responded Shenoy. "That's what makes it interesting." He turned to Andrea and Basil. "Don't you agree?"

"You were expecting this?" asked Basil, frowning.

"No, of course not," said Shenoy. "But I was expecting *something*. After all, we're not being asked to solve a normal problem, are we?"

"But a ship singing sexy songs doesn't bother you?" persisted Tabor.

"Are you any the worse for wear?" replied Shenoy. "It has a nice, manly voice, at least when it sings."

"And do you have any suggestion at all as to why all the systems went dead when we tried to take off?"

"Certainly," answered Shenoy.

"Well?" demanded Tabor.

"Someone or something didn't want us to take off."

"Is that your conclusion every time a ship or vehicle fails?" continued Tabor.

Shenoy considered his answer for a moment, then shrugged. "I really don't know." He paused. "I don't suppose you'd like to play a nice game of chess?"

"No," growled Tabor.

"I would," said the ship's voice.

"Oh, I couldn't ask that of you," said Shenoy. "You'll be too busy transporting us to Cthulhu."

"I can do both," said the ship eagerly.

"At the same time?" asked Shenoy.

"Definitely."

Shenoy shot Tabor a triumphant smile. "Then we shall play a game once we're beyond the stratosphere and on our way to Cthulhu."

"It's a deal!" said the ship. "We will take off in sixteen minutes and twenty-three seconds."

"Well, we're in business," said Shenoy happily.

"Somehow," said Tabor.

"You gotta hand it to the Boss," said Basil. "Somehow, when you least expect it, he pulls an ace out of the deck."

"You've been very quiet," said Shenoy, turning to Andrea. "Is anything wrong?"

She offered him a puzzled frown. "I'm seeing something," she said.

"Oh?"

She nodded her head dizzily. "Something," she repeated, and collapsed onto the deck.

Tabor knelt down next to her, checked her pulse and her breathing.

"She's alive," he announced. "But we'd better get her to a hospital."

"I quite agree," said Shenoy. "Ship, open the hatch. We have an emergency here."

"Does this mean no chess?" it whined as a hatch opened and a ramp leading to the ground appeared.

"No," said Shenoy. "It just means we're postponing takeoff for an hour."

"Check!" said the ship. "Right! Roger that!"

"Oh, shut up!" snapped Tabor as he lifted Andrea into his arms and began leaving the ship. "Rupert, you'd better call an ambulance. I can't carry her all the way to the nearest hospital, wherever the hell that is."

"Done," announced the ship. "ETA is three minutes and seventeen seconds, always depending on traffic and sudden cloudbursts and snowstorms."

"It hasn't snowed here in six years," muttered Basil, accompanying Tabor down the ramp.

They stood just beyond the nose of the ship, and the ambulance raced up at the predicted moment.

"What's the matter with her?" asked one of the attendants.

"I don't know," answered Tabor. "She just collapsed."

"Pulse is fine," noted the attendant. "Any nausea?"

"No."

"Did she complain of pain?"

Tabor shook his head.

"I don't think it's a stroke," said the attendant.

"Just fix whatever's wrong," said Basil. "You can bill—"

"It's already been paid for," came the answer. "Whoever contacted us was as efficient as anyone we've ever dealt with."

He placed Andrea on a cot in the ambulance, jumped in beside her, and signaled the robotic driver to speed off. Tabor and Basil watched it until it was out of sight, then returned to the ship.

"The situation is over," announced Shenoy. "You can take off any time."

No answer.

"Ship?" said Shenoy.

"Sorry," replied the ship. "I was just boning up on my Indian defense. Takeoff in six minutes and ten seconds."

Tabor glared at where he imagined the essence of the ship was. "Why not four minutes and twenty-two seconds?" he said.

"Why not indeed?" replied the ship. "I've just informed the control tower that we are taking off in four minutes and twenty-two seconds." A pause. "Well, it *was* four minutes and twenty-two seconds. Now it's four minutes and . . . "

The ship began counting down the seconds, and finally took off.

"Cthulhu, here we come!" it announced happily.

"I seem to remember reading or hearing about a Cthulhu a long time ago," said Tabor.

"There's probably no connection," said Shenoy.

"Probably?" repeated Tabor, frowning.

"*That* one was fictional."

The ship sped through the atmosphere and stratosphere, then announced that it was headed directly toward Cthulhu and produced a chessboard and pieces on the table in front of Shenoy.

"Well, at last we're on our way," said Shenoy.

Tabor exchanged looks with Basil. Tabor's said *Something Very Weird is happening.*

Basil's said *Goes with the territory—or if not the territory, as least with the Boss.*

❊ ❊ ❊

It was two days later, and they were within six hours of touching down on Cthulhu. Tabor sat in a chair, feet on a console, sandwich in one hand and a container of beer in the other. Shenoy was asleep in his cabin, but Basil was on the bridge, a few feet away, sipping some hot tea.

"So tell me about this place," said Tabor.

"You mean Cthulhu?" asked Basil.

"That's where we're going, isn't it?"

Basil shrugged. "Unless the Boss changes his mind."

"That's some mind he's got there," commented Tabor. "You get the feeling he can solve the mysteries of the universe, but has trouble dressing himself or remembering where he left his toothbrush."

Basil chuckled. "That's him. You know, I think they were just on the verge of firing him before he won his first Prize. He'd been late four days in a row, and couldn't even remember the number on his office door. The last day he drove there in his own vehicle instead of using the transport they'd supplied him and . . ." Basil paused and smiled. "He not only couldn't remember the room number, but he forgot the combination to lock and unlock the vehicle!"

"That's Rupert, all right," said Tabor, returning his smile.

"So he's ordered to report to the head office, which happens to be in the building," continued Basil, "and as he does so, he walks past a trash atomizer—they must have one every forty feet—and sees something on the floor, something that someone tossed at the atomizer and missed. I don't know what it was, a piece of fruit, something totally forgettable like that, and he stops, and he stares at it. The guy escorting him to the office pulls on his arm, and he refuses to go. He's almost trancelike for a full minute. Then he grins ear to ear, goes into the office, and announces that he's figured out a way to find and map wormholes that our ships' sensors can't find, and that this will open up maybe twenty million new worlds to us over the next century or two." Basil snapped his fingers. "Just like that. Sees a half-eaten apple or some such, and sixty seconds later he's come up with a Sagittarius Prize."

"I'm impressed," said Tabor.

"You want to hear the wild part?"

"Sure."

Basil leaned forward. "He managed to unlock his vehicle, and wound up spending the night—the whole night—at a restaurant."

"He was celebrating?" asked Tabor.

Basil laughed. "He couldn't remember where he lived!"

"You know," said Tabor, "you read about geniuses like that when you're a kid, or you watch funny holos about them, but even when you're five years old you know no one like that really exists." He smiled. "They're going to have to move five thousand disks and e-books from the fiction to the non-fiction section of the library."

"That's why most of us would kill to work with him, even when he can't put on matching socks or remember to comb his hair."

"Yeah, I can see that," said Tabor. "Now, about this world . . ."

"I only know what I've heard and read," answered Basil. "And what it's named for."

"That puts you ahead of me. What *is* it named for?"

"Lovecraft."

Tabor frowned. "What's Lovecraft? Some other world?"

"Howard Phillips," answered Basil.

"I'm still in the dark."

"He was a writer," explained Basil.

"And he lived on Cthulhu?"

Basil chuckled. "He *created* it."

"Let me get this straight," said Tabor. "This Lovecraft is brilliant enough to build a goddamned world, and even so he needs Rupert's help?"

Basil smiled and shook his head. "I'm not making myself clear. Howard Phillips Lovecraft—he called himself H. P., or at least he signed his name that way—was a fiction writer centuries, probably millennia, ago." He paused. "Yeah, it has to be millennia, because we were still Earthbound."

"And he wrote about this world, and it actually exists?"

Basil's lips seemed to rattle as he exhaled deeply. "No, I'm still not explaining it clearly. Cthulhu wasn't a world at all."

"Then what was it?" asked Tabor.

"Don't laugh."

"I'm not even smiling. What was it?"

"A god."

"So this was some kind of religion?" asked Tabor.

Basil shook his head. "No, the whole thing was fiction. Fantasy, actually. Cthulhu was a terrible entity, evil from head to toe. He was either a member of a race called the Old Ones, or he was worshipped by the Old Ones, all of whom vanished ages before Lovecraft wrote his stories."

"And someone named this world after an evil demigod?" said Tabor, frowning.

"An evil demigod who never existed," said Basil.

"Or so we hope," said a familiar voice, and they turned

to see Shenoy standing at the edge of the bridge, looking like he'd just awakened.

"Sit down, Rupert," said Tabor, getting to his feet. "You look like you could use some coffee."

"That would be nice," said Shenoy, trudging over to the seat Tabor had vacated. "With some kind of sweetener." A pause. "I think."

Tabor prepared his coffee and brought it back to him. "So why do we hope that this god never existed?"

Shenoy stared at him as if he was crazy. "Do you *want* to live in a universe that has evil, malign gods? If so, you should join one of the Nac Zhe Anglan sects."

Tabor chuckled awkwardly and shook his head. "I mean, why do we think there's a chance in a billion that this god *does* exist?"

"We don't know," answered Shenoy. "That's why we're going there."

"Just because it's named for a creature that some writer made up thousands of years ago?"

Shenoy stared at him, and Tabor had a feeling that he stared at small insects exactly the same way. "Do you really think that's the reason that my various employers equipped and paid for this expedition? I assume Mr. Lovecraft's readers were impressionable, but I'd rather hoped we've outgrown that over the eons."

"I don't know why we're going there," replied Tabor, unable to keep the frustration out of his voice. "And I would like for someone to tell me what the hell this is all about."

"Didn't you ask when they assigned you to me?" said Shenoy curiously.

"If they knew why, they kept it to themselves."

"Good!" said Shenoy decisively.

Tabor frowned. "Good?"

"Absolutely. I approve."

"Might I ask why?"

"The fewer people who know about this, and about what seems to have happened there, the better."

"Well, your bodyguard still doesn't know," said Tabor, "and has absolutely no idea what he's supposed to protect you from."

"If I knew what we will find there, I'd certainly tell you," answered Shenoy. "In fact, if I knew what we'd find there, I'd have no reason to go."

"Are you telling me that this is just a fishing expedition?" demanded Tabor irritably.

"Certainly not," replied Shenoy. "Fish have nothing to do with it."

Tabor exchanged looks with Basil, who seemed half-amused and half-weary by Shenoy's answers.

"Let me rephrase that," said Tabor.

"Yes, please do."

"Is this just a fact-finding expedition?"

"Certainly," answered Shenoy. "Aren't all expeditions?"

"No, not all of them."

"Really? How strange."

"There's a lot strange around here," muttered Tabor.

Shenoy shook his head. "No, we're still more than five hours away from Cthulhu. *That's* where it's strange."

Tabor stared at him and decided to make one last attempt at getting a comprehensible answer. "Just what do you expect to find on Cthulhu?"

"Answers, dear boy," said Shenoy. "Answers."

"Call me Russ. I haven't been a boy in thirty years—yours or anyone else's."

"Certainly, Russell."

Tabor grimaced, pulled out his pocket computer, activated it, and stared at the screen.

"What are you doing?" inquired Shenoy curiously.

"Looking at a book that was written in High Antarean," answered Tabor.

"You read High Antarean?" said Shenoy, obviously impressed.

"Not a word of it."

"Then why . . . ?"

"Because it makes more sense than anything I've heard for the past ten minutes," growled Tabor with an expression that convinced his two shipmates not to speak to him for the next five hours.

CHAPTER 4

The devastation was extraordinary. Everywhere she looked, Occo saw nothing but a churned landscape. The only color below the pale blue sky was a sickly gray-brown. The ground had neither the consistency of soil nor of rock, but was a sort of agglutinated composite—as if gravel of various sizes had been melted together. She'd already kicked the ground with a hindleg boot, and knew that it was much more unyielding than it looked.

Other than the sky, the planet Flaak's two moons still looked normal. Everything else within her line of sight was a surrealistic horror.

When she'd first gotten the news, Occo had assumed it was the work of castigants from one of the large orthodox creeds. Judging from the preliminary reports, probably a Ga Dzu force clowder. A sedge from one of the three Hanna Vye Wrangle moieties was a possibility also.

But now that she saw the ruin at first hand, she realized that she'd been far off the mark. Whoever—or whatever—had destroyed the root cloister of her own creed had used none of the weapons normally wielded by Nac Zhe Anglan castigants.

Normally wielded, she cautioned herself. The possibility that a clowder or sedge had for some reason chosen to use heterodox methods couldn't be ruled out entirely, in the absence of further evidence. There were some peculiar creeds out there on the edges of the Nac Zhe Anglan commonwealth.

But she would be very surprised if that turned out to be the case. In the nature of things, the fringe creeds tended to be small and weak. They were far more inclined to avoid confrontations than to seek them out. And where would they have gotten weapons capable of this sort of destruction, anyway? To the characteristics of small and weak could usually be added that of indigence. Arms that could wreak this sort of havoc had to be either very expensive or—

It was that "or" that particularly disturbed her.

Or they were of immaculate origin, either deific or demonic. The difference was unimportant. Her creed believed the distinction between the two was nothing more than a mortal prejudice. As it contemplated the foot of a behemoth descending on itself, a bug might label it the wrath of a god or of a devil. But from the behemoth's perspective, the bug was transient—if it existed at all. Ontologically speaking, a virtual particle.

Her familiar drifted over and anchored itself on the hard points which had been attached to her thorax for that purpose. As it did so, a swarm of tiny probes returning from their investigations disappeared into its mantle.

"You do realize by now, I hope, that you and yours are for all intents and purposes extinct. The devastation extends for at least twelve leagues in every direction." Bresk used its flotation sack to issue a flatulent discharge. "The creed formally known as the Naccor Jute is now one with the . . . what's the name of that extinct little shelled scavenger? Yerro, or yevo, something like that."

"Jevo," Occo corrected it. Other than that, she ignored the sarcastic witticism. If a Nac Zhe Anglan shaman chose to fashion a familiar for herself—and most shamans did—then she had to be willing to accept the inevitable if unfortunate adjuncts. Good familiars required the admixture of genetic strains from one of the clever animal orders, usually either a primate or rodent analog. For reasons still unclear to cyberneticists, the interaction between those strains and the underlying robot substrate produced an intelligence that was acerbic at best, usually downwind of that—and always disrespectful.

Familiars were annoying. That was just a given. You might as well take umbrage at the tides.

"Do you have anything to report?"

Bresk spread its cooling fins. That was partly for the benefit of the probes sheltered within its mantle but mostly for its own. Flaak had a hot climate in the only latitudes where habitable land could be found. Even before the recent catastrophe, it had been an unpleasant planet to live on. The only reason the Naccor Jute had chosen it as the location for its home cloister had been its obscurity and isolation. Here, they'd thought they would go undetected by any of their enemy creeds or the inimical supernatural powers at large in the universe.

All that sweltering, for nothing.

"Your demise was predictable the moment you chose this wretched planet for your root cloister," said Bresk. "Your brains got baked within the first decade."

"Report," she said impatiently.

"There are no survivors. For that matter, so far as my drones can determine, there are no surviving pieces of non-survivors above the molecular level—and simple molecules, at that. Whatever did this seems to have used some sort of disintegrating beam. Well, no, that's twaddle, scientifically speaking. It was probably the long-sought-for and mythical angelic disruptor. Oh, wait, I forgot. Your creed doesn't—didn't—believe in angels. Demonic disrupter?"

Occo didn't bother to respond. Bresk was perfectly familiar with Naccor Jute doctrine. The irrelevance of all distinctions between the High and the Low was one of the four basic tenets. It was inherent in a universe that was flat, homogenous and isotropic.

Granted, other creeds refused to accept Naccor Jute theological mathematics and Bresk would be familiar with their arguments. But it had no opinion of its own on the matter, for the good and simple reason that when she fashioned it Occo had made sure to eliminate any and all metaphysical predispositions. She'd once known a shaman who'd failed to do that with her own familiar. She'd never gotten a moment's peace from the time she decanted the captious creature to the time she finally had it annulled.

Occo scanned the area again, this time using just her eyes. Her purpose now was not to determine what had happened and who had done it. That had already been done as well as possible, until the analyses of the data were completed. She was simply contemplating the ruin as the quickest and simplest means of initiating the gadrax emergence. No longer could she remain a simple shaman and castigant.

There was nothing else she could do. Whatever survivors there might be of the Naccor Jute would be in hiding by now, and she had no way of making contact with them. Castigants were never given the secret codes of their creed's evacuation protocols and sanctuaries. That would run the risk of undermining their function.

She took her time at it. Bresk's enhanced compound eyes—even more, the sensors of its drones—would have made a better record of the scene than anything her two simple eyes could register, or her brain remember. Still, she dwelt on every mound of churned matter and every stretch of barren soil.

There was nothing living there any longer. Nothing of what had been—at least, by Flaak standards—a rather pleasant valley. Somewhere in that molecular stew that had once been a landscape were her three mates. Quietly, she recited their names for the last time, in full and complete cadence.

Kaab Nzha Reddat moct Bax hurrej Occo. *Vacuum of Reason, disciple of Bax, husband of Occo.*

Izzique Nzha Uffreged moct Bax hurrej Occo. *Piddler of Petty Truths, disciple of Bax, husband of Occo.*

Chawla Nzha Yao moct Bax hurrej Occo. *Torturer of Patience, disciple of Bax, husband of Occo.*

Then, she recited the name of their mentor, destroyed with them.

Bax Nkley Kreaquab octou Naccor Jute. *Resident within Coherence, adept of the Naccor Jute.*

Her mates, as she herself, had been named by their mentor. Their names now vanished forever also.

As Bax Nkley Kreaquab had named her, so now by ancient right and custom did she rename him, as his sole surviving disciple.

She considered the matter for a time before deciding on Trac Lei Taquin dnat Varro. *Vexation beyond Measure, failure now in Chaos.*

She would miss her mates, especially Izzique. Her mentor, not in the least. He had been worse than most of the wretched lot.

Finally, she renamed herself. The name Occo Nzha Rubattan had also been bestowed by their mentor. *Slaughterer of Shadows.* The change here took longer than it had taken to choose her former mentor's new name. All the possibilities she'd quietly considered in the past—and discussed with absolutely no one, of course— were inappropriate in light of the new situation.

Eventually, she settled on Occo Nasht Jopri, *Seeker of Shadows.*

Occo Nasht Jopri Kruy, to be formal about it. *Widow Seeker of Shadows.*

For a wonder, while she was at it, Bresk made no more than two caustic remarks on the subject of wasted time and both of those were terse. You couldn't say that her familiar maintained silence, though. He farted almost continuously.

"My vengeance will be epic," she predicted. Then, turned and headed toward her flyer.

On the way, Bresk waxed eloquent on the necessary distinctions between epic, mythic, legendary and delusions of grandeur.

※ ※ ※

It took only a short time to travel from the site of destruction to the temporary camp that had been erected by the Envacht Lu. As usual, the association that served the Nac Zhe Anglan commonwealth as a combined investigatory agency and repository of creed status and records had arrived on the scene quickly. They'd already been setting up their camp when Occo arrived.

Once she established her credentials, they'd allowed her a full planetary cycle for grieving and renaming before they would begin their examination of the site. That was standard practice. The Envacht Lu were never to be trifled with, but in their own unyielding and rigid manner they were not unreasonable.

As soon as Occo began bringing the flyer down next to the Envacht Lu encampment, Bresk began complaining.

"Why are you landing here? Only a cretin or a masochist would set up next to the Envacht Lu. Hot is bad enough without adding nosy to the mix—and you watch! They'll have spies crawling all over us."

"Shut up. We're not camping here. I just need to have the names recorded."

"By established custom and practice, you can do that any time within the next four years—and that's using Mellan's solar cycle as the standard."

The home planet of the Nac Zhe Anglan, Mellan, orbited an F0 star. The only reason it had a habitable biosphere was because of its considerable distance from

its sun. Mellan's year was twice as long as that of most
inhabited worlds in the Nac Zhe Anglan commonwealth.

"Shut up," she repeated "I can't wait. Not with the
name I still need to add."

Bresk rolled its eyes outward until the facets had all
but disappeared. "Oh, don't tell me."

❊ ❊ ❊

"Occo Nasht Jopri Kruy Gadrax," she repeated.

As was normally true, the Envacht Lu's scribe was an
Ebbo. Occo didn't know the markings used by the
species well enough to determine its scholastic affiliation
from the scars and tattoos on its carapace. Under the
circumstances, it hardly mattered. All Ebbo colleges were
devoted to formal procedures, exactitude, meticulousness,
and precision. They were really a quite tiresome species.
Occo had never understood why the Envacht Lu insisted
on maintaining the relationship with them. Presumably,
it had something to do with the history of the order, most
of which had never been made public.

The scribe still had its mandible poised above the
tablet. The electronic tip blinked yellow-green-violet,
repeating the sequence every second. If Occo recalled
Ebbo protocols correctly, that signified *necessity-to-
crosscheck-and-doublecheck*.

"You are certain about this?" the Ebbo asked. Its—
his?—voice box had an unpleasant twang to it. Most Ebbo
were neuter but Occo thought this one might be male, as
that species reckoned genders.

She was tempted to curse the wretched creature, but
that would be pointless. Ebbo reacted to invective the
same way they reacted to everything. Find the registered

protocol and behave accordingly. She might as well scream insults at the moons.

"As I have now said twice, yes. I am quite certain. Record my name as Occo Nasht Jopri Kruy Gadrax."

The Ebbo's vestigial wings opened slightly and snapped shut, making a little clicking sound. That was the equivalent of a Nac Zhe Anglan rubbing her thorax. Every intelligent species had some equivalent gesture. Humans called it a "shrug" and used a particularly subtle body movement for the purpose. So Occo had been told, anyway. She'd never met a member of that species in person.

"As you wish," said the Ebbo. The electronic mandible tip clittered briefly on the tablet screen. "It is done."

Occo turned and left the Records hut. She had to pause briefly at the aperture to let the security program cycle through its protocols before it opened. Programmed by Ebbo, clearly enough. They couldn't even produce an opening in a simple hut without piling on embellishments.

"Say better, 'we're done,'" jibed Bresk, as Occo headed toward their flyer. "Just what I always dreamed of, since the day I was decanted. A suicide mission."

She ignored it. No point in doing otherwise. In their own way, familiars were as devoted to rituals and rigmarole as Ebbo. Short of having it annulled, there was no way to avoid the coming sarcasm.

"Widow Occo Nasht Jopri, outlaw. We could add 'fanatic' and 'monomaniac' as well. Off on her formally registered mission to massacre whatever parties she deems guilty, and if she's like most outlaws of record, she won't be any too particular about the 'deeming' part."

The familiar issued a particularly loud and long fart.

"Humans have a term for this, you know. They call it 'going Grendel.'"

Despite herself, the weird term caught her attention. "Going what?"

"Grendel. One of the monsters—one of the many, many, many monsters—in their many, many, many legends. They must really have trouble sleeping at night. Anyway, there's a whole ancient song cycle devoted to the creature. Well, technically, it's devoted to the hero. Somebody by the name of Beowulf. Is there a species in the galaxy with sillier names than Humans? But the monster's much more interesting."

"I'm not interested."

"Of course you are. I'll start from the beginning. Brace yourself, this will take a while.

"Hwæt wē Gār-Dena in gear-dagum
þēod-cyninga þrym gefrūnon
hu ðā æþelingas ellen fremedon."

Not for the first time, Occo considered annulment. By the time she clambered back aboard the flyer, however, she'd decided against it. There was no reason to think another familiar wouldn't be just as obstreperous. She could try doing without one entirely, of course. But . . .

The things were undeniably useful. She kept reminding herself of that as the flyer lifted into the air. It was . . . not easy.

"ond gefrætwade foldan scēatas
Leomum ond lēafum . . . "

CHAPTER 5

Occo didn't go far to set up her own camp. Just far enough from the Envacht Lu encampment to get away from them and find a location that didn't remind her of her now-vanished home cloister.

She settled on the far slope of a rocky, barren crag which had a meadow large enough to land her flyer.

"Why are we stopping here?" Bresk demanded. "The whole planet's a pile of effluvium. Let's just go back to the ship and leave the system altogether."

Occo was tempted to order the miserable literally-a-creature (hers, sadly) to shut itself down but refrained. There were actually some good reasons the familiar should understand her plans, even if that triggered another flood of complaints.

"We can't. Once we get to the ship I want to depart the system as quickly as possible in case there are any spy craft lurking on one of the moons. But now that the Envacht Lu has established their paramountcy in the system I can't get clearance from their traffic control unless I give them the wormhole coordinates we'll be using."

"So? We're just returning to Redlych, right? I have those coordinates right here in my data bank." Briefly, it manifested a virtual display above its mantle crest.

"We are not returning to Redlych. We're going somewhere we've never been. Finding the coordinates we need to get there via sanctioned wormholes will require working through a good chunk of the night."

"Ridiculous. You may be hopelessly inept at mathematics but I'm not. Give me a few medims and I'll have them worked out for you."

"Not for this location. We'll need to search the Gray Archives and piece together the information. I know it *can* be reached by using the sanctioned wormhole grid, but I have no idea what route we'd need to take. You know what the Gray Archives are like."

Bresk issued a very loud fart. "Whatever's the antonym of well-organized and coherent. Humans have a clever expression for it: *mare's nest.* The modern meaning of the phrase is 'a place, condition, or situation of great disorder or confusion' but the original meaning might be more appropriate to whatever madness you're contemplating now. It seems a 'mare' was a type of large animal on the Humans' home world which didn't make nests to begin with. So it meant going in search of a nonexistent thing, just as you'd expect of the blithering fool you're turning into."

"Why are you suddenly plaguing me with Human references? They're the most ridiculous sentient species in the known galaxy. Well, leaving aside the Vitunpelay—

but in theological terms even the Vitunpelay are rational compared to Humans."

"Exactly. Who better to cite when I've been dragged against my will—"

"You're a familiar. By definition, you have no will."

"Fine. Against my virtual will into a maelstrom of unreason. Which I'm sure is where you're thinking of taking us next. Bound to be, if we've got to muck around in the Gray Archives. So where are we going?"

"The moon—I can't remember the name—orbiting Vlax Broche."

"*The* Vlax Broche? The seventh planet in the Hrea system?"

"Is there any other?"

"Not that I know of. I was just grasping at any faint hope that might remain that we weren't plunging into complete folly. You *do* know that the Repository of the Old Ones is guarded by the Nedru Concord Skein of Creeds?"

By now, Occo had emerged from the flyer onto the relative expanse of the meadow. The sun was setting. Between that and the high altitude, the heat was tolerable. And the weather looked to be decent, although on Flaak that was always unpredictable. But she thought they'd be able to work out here instead of in the cramped confines of the flyer. She ordered the flyer's computer to manifest itself.

"The Nedru haven't been challenged in so long that I think they'll be sluggish," she said, watching the virtual screen emerge before her. "We'll need to move fast, though."

"Move fast to do what?"

"Steal the Warlock Variation Drive."

Bresk fell silent. The familiar's mantle flared for a moment, exposing the drones nestled within. The tiny cyborgs peered out at Occo as if they were observing a great wonder for the first time. That was just an illusion, since their eyes were always big and round. Still, they were awfully cute.

Completely brainless, of course. Too bad familiars couldn't be designed the same way.

Bresk's mantle flared in and out a few times. That was its way of hyperventilating.

The blessed silence ended all too soon. "There must have been a mutation somewhere as you were gestating which stunted the portion of your brain that gauges risks. Luckily for your species, you won't live long enough to pass it on to future generations. Unluckily for your familiar, you probably will live long enough to take me down with you."

"I have a plan."

"Of course you do. That's part of the risk-gauging impairment. You think that if you *have* a plan that it will *work*—which are actually two completely different propositions. Like thinking that because you can jump off a cliff intact you can land the same way. Humans have a term for this too, being the most insane species in existence. Well, leaving aside the Vitunpelay. They call it the Evel Knievel Syndrome, after their god of folly. It's worth noting, though, that Evel Knievel is said to have the divine power to heal all its broken bones—a power which you notably do not possess."

"Shut up." Occo keyed the initial search parameters into her forearm comp. The virtual screen began taking shape and displaying what little coherence the Gray Archives possessed.

"I can't shut up. You programmed me to caution you when you were on the verge of doing something foolish. It's my bounden duty—my sacred calling, you could almost say—as your familiar. Stealing the Warlock Variation Drive qualifies as foolish. I should say, *trying* to steal the Warlock Variation Drive qualifies as foolish."

"I told you, I have a plan." She began accessing the data in the Gray Archives; as always, a tedious process.

"Even worse, if the plan succeeds. Trying to *use* the Warlock Variation Drive qualifies as dementia. Or are you unaware of the reason for the word 'variation' in the title?"

Occo decide that ignoring Bresk was her best course of action. There was always the chance the familiar would cease and desist.

Faint chance, of course.

"I interpret your silence as an indication of ignorance. Let me enlighten you, then. The Warlock Drive held in the Repository of the Old Ones, as opposed to the other three known or rumored to exist, is called the 'Variation' version because its workings are not only unpredictable— that's true of all of them—but change as the Drive unfolds. I say 'unfolds' because, assuming that you are ignorant of this matter also, the Drive does not actually work like an engine. Insofar as anyone has ever been able to discern its mechanism—using the term 'mechanism' oh so very very loosely—the Drive is actually not a 'drive' at all but a device which develops alternative modes of existence. At apparent random. Whatever its logic might be, it is said to be indecipherable."

Occo couldn't bear the jabber any longer. "Shut. Up. You *know* what I think of the Nedru Concord's gospel. The reason they believe functioning artifacts of the Old Ones cannot be analyzed is because they believe the Old Ones used technology based on scientific knowledge beyond our ken. Whereas—"

"Oh, that's right, I forgot. My creator and mistress subscribes to the—happily now extinct—creed of the Naccor Jute, among whose many whimsical notions is the idea that the Old Ones used actual magic."

"Just 'magic,' please. The phrase 'actual magic' is tautological."

"Only if magic exists."

The search program finally reached the desired section of the Gray Archives. Occo began studying the records of ancient voyages, concentrating on those in this spiral arm.

"And the proposition that magic exists," Bresk continued, "is not accepted by any of the creeds except your own—excuse me, that should be 'except the creed you used to belong to but do no longer because it's deader than last eon's fossils'—and the two schismatic branches of the Meije Salmagundi, about which nothing further needs to be said because—"

Occo decided that Bresk didn't need to witness the rest of the search process. And—again—congratulated herself for having included a lockdown procedure when she fashioned the familiar.

"Up you must shut."

Bresk fell instantly silent. Its mantle sagged and the faceted eyes turned dull. Peace and tranquility returned to the meadow as Occo continued her search of the records.

* * *

Eventually, Occo determined the route she'd need to take. It would be circuitous but she'd expected that. Even as arrogant as they were, the Nedru Concord Skein of Creeds had been prudent enough to situate the treasury of their most precious relics on a planet that could not be reached easily from anywhere in the Nac Zhe Anglan commonwealth.

Darkness enfolded her as soon as she shut down the Gray Archives and the computer's virtual screen vanished. Startled, she looked up. She hadn't realized how much time had gone by.

The night sky on Flaak was drab, even when it wasn't overcast. Neither of the small moons cast much light, and only one of them was visible now anyway. Flaak was one of those rare planets on which multicellular life had evolved despite the absence of a large moon. Fairly primitive multicellular life, admittedly. No flowering plants had ever evolved. Even the gymnosperm analogs were very simple, and the only animal life on land was small and exoskeletal.

There was almost no starlight, at least in this southern hemisphere. Flaak's stellar neighborhood was dominated by a nebula that obscured most of the galaxy. That was one of the reasons it had been chosen as the site for the Naccor Jute's home cloister. Given modern astrography, trying to hide within or near a nebula was of minimal concealment value. But the Naccor Jute had been a weak creed in military and political terms and had taken advantage of every safeguard it could.

Which had still not been enough, as it turned out. *Someone* had found them. Occo still didn't know that someone's identity. All she knew so far was that it had been someone in possession of usable Old One weaponry—or perhaps derivative of such weaponry—and someone who possessed an unusual degree of animosity toward the Naccor Jute. Even by the standards of the ancient and never-ending struggle among the many creeds of the Nac Zhe Anglan, completely obliterating a creed's home cloister was unusual. Not exactly unheard of, but certainly not standard or normal behavior.

Unless the devastation had not been carried out by a rival Nac Zhe Anglan creed at all, but by something else, in which case all assessments were haphazard. The exotic method of destruction at least raised the possibility that despite all their precautions the Naccor Jute had drawn the attention of supernatural entities. Those could be remnants or descendants of the Old Ones, or the demons who were theorized to have destroyed their rule of the universe.

(Or their rule of the galaxy, which had been the Naccor Jute's own tentative hypothesis. Was it plausible that a divine race which could rule an entire spacetime continuum could be overthrown by any other power? It did not seem likely.)

It was also possible that whoever destroyed her home cloister could be supernatural powers altogether unknown or even speculated about. No creed of the Nac Zhe

Anglan, not even the most dogmatic, believed that it understood everything about the Age of the Old Ones.

Occo began clambering back aboard the flyer. As always, the process of entering the small craft was arduous. The flyer was of Chlarrac manufacture. The Naccor Jute had been forced to economize wherever possible, and Chlarracan products were usually cheaper than those produced by any Nac Zhe Anglan creed. But their atmospheric flyers—the inexpensive ones, at any rate—were not well-designed for the Nac Zhe Anglan species.

The bauplan of the Chlarrac, like that of Humans, was centered on the spinal structural mechanism known as vertebra. Such a peculiar structure inevitably resulted in a rather delicate physique, but it had the undeniable advantage of imparting flexibility as well. Presumably— she'd never seen one actually engaged in the activity—a Chlarrac could easily wriggle itself through the small aperture leading into the flyer's interior. But for Occo, with her sturdy Nac Zhe Anglan quadrupedal and blocky-torsoed body, the task was a nuisance at best.

Once she was finally aboard, she extended her auxiliary speaking tube out of the aperture and called down to Bresk. *"Revive you must."*

Immediately, the familiar's immobility ended. Bresk's eyes began to glitter again and it scanned the skies.

"That long!" it complained bitterly. "You had me out that long?"

"We're leaving in ten minims. With or without you."

Bresk farted anxiously and hurried into the flyer. With its ability to glide through the air and its small and semi-globular body, the familiar had none of Occo's difficulty doing so. It was aboard in less than seven minims.

❋ ❋ ❋

It took Occo less than fifteen medims to reach orbit and not more than another twenty to dock with their spacecraft.

Getting aboard the spacecraft was not difficult, leaving aside the task of squeezing out of the flyer itself. The spacecraft was also of Chlarrac design and manufacture, but the Naccor Jute had been willing to expend more credit to have it configured for Nac Zhe Anglan occupants. Senior castigants like Occo were hardly showered with luxuries, but they weren't subject to the worst frugalities, either.

They received a few perquisites, too. One of them was the privilege of naming their spacecraft. When Occo was given this one after her ordination, she had named it Kurryoccoc: *Shadow Wife*.

It now needed to be renamed also. As she began the launch sequence, she pondered the possibilities.

Battan Kruy: *Widow of Slaughter*. That had a nice reek to it, like the stench of butchery.

Or possibly she should stray farther afield, sever all ties to her personal history . . .

Perhaps . . . Hrikk u Cha? *Trader in Death*?

Then a whimsical thought came to her. She swiveled her head to face Bresk. "What did you say that Human monster was named?"

"Grendel."

"Grendel it is, then." She brought her head back to

face the computer. "Record name change of spacecraft. Eradicate Kurryoccoc. Replace with—"

Her familiar farted derision. "If you insist on pursuing this madness, at least name the ship after the greater monster in the legend."

She paused. "There's a greater one?"

"Sure. Grendel's Mother."

A new question occurred to her. "That's right, I forgot. Humans have two genders also. Which was Grendel?"

"Male."

That wouldn't do at all.

"Ship," she commanded, "rename yourself *Grendel's Mother*. And set course for the wormhole terminus." She didn't need to specify which terminus since Flaak's system had only one. Which, of course, was another reason it had been chosen as the location for the home cloister.

Again, in vain. Now that she was finally leaving, having settled on her course of action, she allowed herself to be flooded with sorrow.

To sorrow, alas, was added vexation.

"Oh, yes, Grendel's Mother was by far the nastier monster!" Bresk enthused. "Just listen to this:

"Grendles mōdor,
ides, āglæc-wif yrmþe gemunde
sē þe wæter-egesan wumian scolde . . . "

CHAPTER 6

*

"This is Gadraxpath *Grendel's Mother*, formerly known as Naccor Jute Vessel *Kurryoccoc*, notifying whatever agents of the Envacht Lu might be present in the system that we are approaching the wormhole terminus with the following coordinates." She let the ship's computer transmit the precise details while she relaxed on her command bench and considered the various beverage options open to her.

They were a bit limited until they passed through the wormhole. There was not much chance of an emergency during transit, but there was enough that she didn't want to risk being even mildly impaired, as she would be if she indulged her taste for inebriating liquors. Inhaling veddash vapor was entirely out of the question.

She'd settled on hyrroxt tea with a squeeze of bni'am blood when, to her surprise, the ship's transmitter came to life. She hadn't expected any response from the Envacht Lu until they were much closer to the terminus.

"Gadraxpath *Grendel's Mother*, this is Envacht Lu

Revanship *Suffer and Die, Execrable Ones.* You are required to dock with us before any further approach to the terminus. We are now in orbit around this system's eighth planet. Failure to follow our instructions will make you subject to Level Cadda-Bra-Thry chastisement."

The transmitter fell silent. Startled by the announcement, Occo glanced quickly at the ship's navigation screen. There was no sign of the revanship. But at this distance, there wouldn't be.

Bresk's fart resembled a minor thunderclad. *"Hru!"* it exclaimed. "Cadda-Bra-Thry? Are they joking? That's where they—"

"Dismember the offending party before or after removing all sensory organs, I forget in which order. Yes, I know. And you should know that the Envacht Lu never joke."

She'd already entered the new astrogation commands before she finished speaking. The ship's AI completed the necessary computations and *Grendel's Mother* set off on its altered course toward the eighth planet, Tridhab.

What conceivable reason could the Envacht Lu have for summoning her? They couldn't possibly be objecting to her newly recorded gadrax status. The Envacht Lu maintained scrupulous neutrality in all inter-creed disputes.

Well, she'd find out soon enough. Tridhab's orbit had brought it closer to Flaak than it usually was, less than twelve light-medims away.

⁂

"Just looking at that thing makes me nervous," said Bresk.

"Don't be ridiculous."

"Really? Your attitude reminds me of an ancient Human adage: 'We have nothing to fear but fear itself.' Proving once again that they are the least sane intelligent species in the known galaxy. Leaving aside the Vitunpelay."

As ridiculous as Bresk's anxiety might be in any rational terms, Occo didn't have any trouble understanding it. Especially when seen at close range, Envacht Lu revanships were . . .

Scary.

To begin with, the ship was huge, as all revanships were. *Suffer and Die, Execrable Ones* was two and half times the size of the largest spacecraft made by any other species. Even Humans, with their notorious penchant for gigantism, never tried to construct vessels that large.

There was no reason to. Excessive size presented problems for interstellar travel. Revanships exceeded the capacity of smaller wormholes and their sheer mass would have precluded the use of any other method of FTL travel, even if Nac Zhe Anglan were not forbidden to use them by the terms of the Dessetrai Pact.

Other intelligent species ignored the provisions of the Pact and, with the exception of the Ebbo, routinely used one or another FTL technique besides wormhole travel. But all Nac Zhe Anglan creeds observed the Dessetrai protocols —and the Envacht Lu stood always ready to chastise apostasy. Only those who declared and registered themselves gadrax were exempt from the provisions.

The design of revanships was also bizarre. The flimsy-looking inverted cone which formed the craft's bow was immense even in its purely material form. Once the revanship was in full flight, the electromagnetic field which the cone would project forward to scoop up interstellar gasses would be larger than most moons.

The cone at the stern was not as big, since its function was to exhaust the gas after the hydrogen was fused. But its diameter was still enormous. The fuselage of the revanship which connected the fore and aft cones looked downright slender in comparison, but it was actually larger both in dimensions and mass than any other type of spacecraft, even the bloated battleships favored by Human military forces.

There was a purpose behind the design, though. The Envacht Lu's mission was not simply investigation and record-keeping. The order also served as the ultimate sanction against Nac Zhe Anglan creeds which transgressed the Dessetrai Pact, inimical alien species, and whoever or whatever else the Envacht Lu deemed a severe enough threat to propriety.

Revanships were the flaming spears of the Envacht Lu. Once the ramjets reached their maximum acceleration of 0.55 light speed during interstellar transit, they were for all practical purposes undetectable—and utterly unstoppable once they reentered a solar system.

At that speed they were useless in space battles, since their trajectories were difficult to change and impossible to change quickly. But against their intended targets, that mattered not at all. The trajectory of planets was even less changeable. Essentially unchangeable—unless it was struck by a revanship. A gas giant would probably survive such an impact, although no one had ever tried the experiment. But no small rocky planet would. Once a revanship was launched on such a retaliatory or punitive mission, it was in effect a planetary-scale suicide bomb.

The scariest thing about a revanship, in the end, was not the ship itself. It was the crew, which had been selected for that purpose. Self-selected, rather. They were all volunteers.

Grendel's Mother reached the revanship's dock. Connecting to the airlock took surprisingly little time. Or perhaps that was just a function of Occo's none-too-relaxed state of mind.

What could the Envacht Lu possibly want from her?

The airlock began cycling.

"And Daniel enters the lion's den," said Bresk. The familiar was wheezing a little with trepidation.

"Who or what is a 'daniel' and a 'lion'?" demanded Occo. "This is no time for word games."

"It's another Human reference. Daniel was more-or-less the equivalent of a Nac Zhe Anglan disciple—although no Nac Zhe Anglan creed ever subscribed to such lunatic notions as she did—I think she was female, anyway, although I'm not sure; it's hard to tell with Humans—and as punishment for her theology she was apprehended by a Human demigoddess by the name of Darius—who might have been a demigod, now that I think about it—"

"Shut. Up."

※ ※ ※

After they cycled through the airlock and entered the loading dock of the revanship, they were greeted by an Ebbo in a powered liftchair.

"Follow me," it commanded. Quite abruptly, by Ebbo standards. The scholiasts were normally given to longwindedness on formal occasions—and they considered all occasions to be formal. With no further ado, the liftchair spun about and the Ebbo set off down a passageway, entering the loading dock at a ninety-degree angle. After taking a moment to orient herself, Occo realized the Ebbo was leading them toward the aft portion of the central fuselage. The loading dock was situated almost exactly in the middle of the huge craft.

They had to hurry to catch up. The Ebbo was making no attempt to moderate its speed to suit the normal walking pace of a Nac Zhe Anglan.

"Rude little bug!" commented Bresk, accentuating the statement with a fart.

Occo shared the sentiments, but she thought her familiar's indignation was artificial. Bresk had attached itself to its mistress the moment it saw the Ebbo darting off, leaving it to Occo to haul it along floating just above and a little behind her.

The passageway came to a T-intersection ahead. The Ebbo zipped around the corner heading to the left—that was to say, deeper into the interior of the ship. Occo hurried her steps, but even so she could see no sign of their guide—using the term loosely indeed!—when she reached the intersection. The passageway the Ebbo had taken was a short one, ending in a small chamber with three hatches. The Ebbo must have gone through one of them—but which one? All three were shut.

She entered the chamber and examined each of the hatches.

"When in doubt," Bresk pronounced, "always take the center option."

"Why?"

"You have a one-in-three chance it will be the right one."

"The same odds apply to all the doors."

"Where does it come from, this fastidious obsession with mathematical minutia?" her familiar wondered. "Fine. Take the center option in line with your Naccor Jute doctrine of moral isotropy."

"That's ridiculous. Moral isotropy applies only to sublime issues, not choosing a pathway or a meal."

"Fine. Take the center option—"

"Shut up. I'm thinking."

Thought proved unnecessary. The hatch on the far left opened and the Ebbo peered through. The shelves above its eyesockets, which were an extension of its exoskeleton were very pronounced and colored a pale green, indicating vexation.

"Why are you dawdling?" the Ebbo demanded. "Amerce Imposer Vrachi does not like to have her time wasted." An instant later, it was gone again.

Occo restrained herself from making an equally rude response. She just headed for the still-open hatch. "Always choose the center option," she muttered derisively.

"Not my fault," said Bresk. "The Ebbo was obviously misgui—*ark!*"

Occo whistled with amusement. She'd moved so quickly that Bresk, still attached to her thorax and floating above her, had almost been rammed into the top edge of the hatch. The familiar shortened the attachment lines just in time to avoid the collision.

"You might have warned me!"

"There's something wrong with your legs?"

That wasn't really fair. Bresk did have legs, of a sort, but they were not designed for walking quickly. Occo didn't normally mind having her familiar attached to her. She was just edgy and ill-humored because of the unexpected Envacht Lu demand for their presence.

But she made no apology. Just as it was a given that familiars were annoying, it was also a given that one of their functions was to be blamed for anything their mistresses and masters chose to blame them for.

The intrinsic injustice of the universe was the third of the four great truths, so why should familiars be exempt? Indeed, one could argue that heaping arbitrary and unjust accusations upon the creatures was simply an exercise in theological prudence.

※ ※ ※

They had to pass through two more hatches and connecting passageways before they finally reached the quarters of Amerce Imposer Vrachi. Each time the Ebbo would race ahead and then have to return to guide them through the next stage in their progress. Perhaps it was mentally defective. Occo had never heard of a mentally defective Ebbo—leaving aside the psychological peculiarities to which the entire species was subject—but she wasn't all that familiar with them. No one was, really, except the Envacht Lu and a few scholars.

The Ebbo had played a critical role in the development of the Nac Zhe Anglan, both as a species and as a civilization. No one denied that incontrovertible truth. But that was all ancient history. Not for millennia had the Ebbo been of any great significance in the affairs of the galaxy. If it weren't for their connection to the Envacht Lu—which no one outside of that secretive order understood at all—they would simply be one of several minor and obscure intelligent races confined to a small number of planets.

Much as Humans had been before their Diaspora. And as most other species wished Humans still were.

The personal quarters of Amerce Imposer Vrachi doubled as her office, as it turned out. One could as easily say "tripled" or even "quadrupled." The gigantic scale on which the revanship was built meant that all permanent members of the crew had very expansive quarters. If a revanship set out upon a punitive strike—what the Envacht Lu called an Uttermost Reproach—there would only be a skeleton crew aboard. Just enough to keep the ship operational during the long years of relativistic travel, as the small crew rotated the duty of standing watch. They would spend most of the time in suspended animation.

Occo knew enough about Envacht Lu doctrine to know that the order believed such long and tedious watches were best done by solitary crew members. Two or three were likely to start quarreling. So, each member of the crew who had volunteered for Uttermost Reproach missions was provided with spacious quarters and a great deal in the way of what would be considered frivolous luxuries by most military units.

When they entered her quarters, Amerce Imposer Vrachi was squatting on a bench behind a desk which was of a size to match everything else on the revanship.

She wasted no time with pleasantries. "I have had your course analyzed. You are headed for one of four locations.

The first is Nabborothrapto, whose Paskapan residents call a 'sin planet.' But since the sins involved are only suited to members of that noisome species and they label every one of their planets a 'sin planet,' I believe we can eliminate that possibility. The second is the Human world named New New Jersey. But even though Humans seem to title all of their settled colonies 'new' something, this one actually is new. Apparently it has less than a thousand permanent inhabitants. So I believe we can rule that one out, also. The third—"

Occo could see where this was going and saw no point in obfuscation. Attempting it, rather. She was quite sure that trying to fool an Envacht Lu Amerce Imposer was an exercise in futility.

"I am headed for Vlax Broche."

Vrachi inclined her head. "As I suspected. More accurately, you are headed for the habitable moon of Vlax Broche known as Zayth. Where you intend to assault the Repository of the Old Ones despite its Nedru Concord guard force, presumably in order to steal one of the sacred relics. At a guess, either the Skerkud Teleplaser or the Warlock Variation Drive."

Occo hadn't realized the Skerkud Teleplaser was also contained in the Repository. She made an immediate decision to steal it as well, if at all possible. The Teleplaser was reputed to be a fearsome weapon. If one could make it work, of course—always an uncertain proposition when using Old One relics.

But she said nothing. She was beginning to get angry, regardless of the Envacht Lu's ominous reputation.

"You have no right under the provisions of the Pact to

question me concerning my gadrax intentions. I remind you—"

The Amerce Imposer raised a forehand. "Please. I am aware of that. But I do not raise this matter either to question you or to caution you concerning your plans. As you say, that is none of the Envacht Lu's concern. What *is* our concern—and recognized as such by the Dessetrai Pact—is the possibility that the destruction of your home cloister transgressed the bounds of propriety. In which case, we may be obliged to deliver an Uttermost Reproach."

Occo stared at her. "But . . . Against *who*?"

Vrachi inclined her head again. "Precisely the question that needs to be answered. And I believe the question whose answer you are determined to ferret out, no? So I am requiring you to maintain regular contact with the Envacht Lu—"

She extended her forehand to forestall Occo's gathering protest. "Gadrax! I am well within my perquisites to make this demand, so long as I understand that you are not required to deflect your own mission— whatever that may be, and please note that I do not inquire—for the sake of maintaining such contact. That said, it is quite possible your travels—wherever they may take you and please note that I do not inquire—*will* bring you within reasonable proximity of an Envacht Lu station or vessel. In which case you will be required to report whatever you have learned."

The Amerce Imposer grew stiff and angular, foreboding in every aspect. "And do not doubt that we will discover if you choose at any point to evade that responsibility. The penalty is severe."

Vrachi wiggled a digit at the Ebbo, who had been busily working at its scribe station. "The specifics, Academe Lwa."

"It's quite elaborate," said the Ebbo, for the first time animated by enthusiasm rather than irritation. "One begins by immobilizing the miscreant and surgically removing—"

"Enough!" snapped Occo. "I do not contest your right to require such reports, Amerce Imposer Vrachi. I will do as I am obliged. Assuming, of course, that the opportunity arises. Is our business here concluded?"

"I believe so. I cannot wish you well on your project, of course. On the other hand, I cannot wish you ill, either."

Occo rose. The Ebbo eyed her in a manner which made clear that the past moment's gaiety had been replaced by the scholiast's normal sour mien.

"I know the way out," said Occo. And with no further ado, made deed follow word.

CHAPTER 7

✸

Occo and Bresk passed through the first wormhole on their voyage a short time later. This was the wormhole which would take them to the Masc Bleddin system, the largest wormhole nexus in their stellar vicinity. From there, they would have a choice of no fewer than seven wormholes to take in the next stage of their mission. Five of those seven wormholes were located within the magnetosphere of the Masc Bleddin system's gas giant planet, Tranxegg.

The planet was so huge that it was almost a brown dwarf and had a magnetosphere to match. That made it effectively impossible for detection systems to keep track of an object as small as a spaceship that came close enough to Tranxegg to use one of the wormholes, unless the detection was done at close range or by the use of visible light. But since all of the wormholes were also within the orbit of the giant planet's spectacular—and obscuring—rings, that made Tranxegg an ideal wormhole cluster for anyone to use who did not want their destination to be self-evident.

The Envacht Lu knew or at least suspected where Occo was headed, but everyone else would remain unsuspecting—especially the Nedru Concord Skein of Creeds. The Nedru were powerful but she thought she had a good chance of succeeding in her purpose if she took them completely by surprise.

It was always possible, of course, that the Nedru or someone else had placed a string of monitor satellites in a ball-of-twine orbital pattern that would enable them to detect the wormhole she used. But it was highly unlikely that the Nedru would have done so, given the great distance between Tranxegg and Vlax Broche. And if anyone else had done so, why would they inform the Nedru, who were as unpopular as they were powerful?

❧ ❧ ❧

The term "wormhole" was a misnomer stemming from the earliest days of interstellar exploration. One of the first sublight ramjet expeditions set out to investigate one of Angla's closest neighbors, a G4 star which it had been determined was orbited by at least one possibly habitable planet. The planet was not only inhabitable, it was inhabited by Ebbo. They were not colonists; the Ebbo rarely engaged in colonization, then or since. Instead, they were a survey expedition themselves, one of many sent out by the Ebbo to chart the pathways that permitted travel between the stars that was effectively faster than light. "Effectively" faster, because no vessel actually exceeded the speed of light. But from the standpoint of the traveler, the distinction was purely theoretical. One entered a wormhole, as the Ebbo called the peculiar pathways, and one emerged in another star system that might be as much as thirty-seven light-years away. For reasons no one had ever determined, thirty-seven light-years seemed to be the maximum distance one could travel using this method. Longer distances required two or more wormholes.

The Ebbo were not a species much given to purely abstract science, however. They were, here as in all things, the galaxy's nonpareil practitioners of obsessive-compulsive behavior. They found the wormhole network, as they saw it, through purely pragmatic endeavors. Using it to full measure required charting the intricate complexities of the network, which—in the absence of theoretical analysis—required centuries of painstaking (and sometimes quite dangerous) exploration.

But Nac Zhe Anglan theorists eventually realized that what the Ebbo saw as a network of wormholes—as if there really were some sort of tunnels all through the spacetime continuum—was actually something quite different. They concluded that the pathways were fissures produced by the constant intersection and interpenetration of the untold number of branes which seemed to be the basic structure of a multi-universe reality. The fissures were temporary, not permanent, but since the time scale on which branes operated was vastly greater than the scales used by sentient species, the distinction was of purely theoretical interest. By the time a fissure that allowed travel from one star to another finally closed or evaporated, at least one of those stars would have moved off the main sequence or become a supernova.

That discovery—if such it could be called; it was really

more in the way of a theoretical hypothesis—came just in time to forestall what had looked to be a great religious war in the making. By the time Nac Zhe Anglan theorists decided that the Ebbo analysis was incorrect, hundreds of expeditions had explored Angla's stellar vicinity to a distance of several hundred light-years. And everywhere the Nac Zhe Anglan went, they found the traces and relics of a civilization so ancient it predated the emergence of multicellular life on Angla itself.

Traces and relics only, however. They found no living members of the race they came to call the Old Ones, nor even any species that seemed to be their descendants— although that was purely a hypothesis also. No one actually knew what the Old Ones had looked like. No fossils had ever been found, nor any visual images. The assumptions made about them were basely purely on the size, dimensions and details of their ruins.

The discoveries triggered a great religious awakening in the Nac Zhe Anglan. All faiths predating interstellar travel were either swept aside or subsumed within the new and far more vigorous creeds that emerged. There was no single persuasion that prevailed but rather a great constellation of dogmas, which conflicted with each other as often as they agreed. A few basic principles, however, were generally shared by all:

First, that the Old Ones were either deific or demonic in nature. That was the first point of agreement—and also, of course, the initial great schism. The first of the religious wars which dominated the early centuries of interstellar travel was fought (more or less) over this matter of dispute.

Second, that such immensely powerful beings could only have been destroyed by still more powerful antagonists. These might be either deific or demonic themselves, but they presumably had to be one or the other. The second great schism—it would be better to say, bipartite schism—thus produced four basic doctrines. Or rather, four basic doctrinal constellations:

There were those who held that the Old Ones were deific and had been utterly destroyed by the demons. The conclusion which inexorably followed was that the universe was dominated by evil—a proposition in support of which, of course, there was much evidence.

Secondly, there were those who held that the Old Ones had been demonic and had been destroyed by beings still more demonic. The conclusion which inexorably followed was that the universe was dominated by *great* evil—a proposition in support of which there was still greater evidence.

Thirdly, there were those who held that the Old Ones were deific and had won the great conflict, but at such a terrible cost that only a few survived, and those much weakened. The conclusion which inexorably followed was that the universe was dominated by chaos—a proposition in support of which there was enormous evidence—but which held the possibility, at least, of the eventual triumph of good. For which the evidence was admittedly very slender.

Fourthly, there were those who held that the Old Ones were demonic and had lost the great conflict, but at such a terrible cost that only a few of the greater demons had survived, and those much weakened. The conclusion which inexorably followed was that the universe was dominated by chaos but that the possibility existed that chaos would be eventually superseded by supreme evil.

This fourth doctrinal constellation then fell out among themselves over the issue of whether the triumph of evil over chaos was to be welcomed or opposed. Thus arose the factions between whom eight fierce religious wars had so far been fought, none of them with decisive conclusion.

In addition to these major divisions, innumerable smaller sects and creeds emerged as well. Naccor Jute, the one to which Occo belonged—or had belonged; she still didn't know if there were any other survivors—was considered outrageously agnostic by all other creeds. Just barely short of outright atheists! For it was the Naccor Jute's basic proposition that the distinctions between the Old Ones and their destroyers—whom the Naccor Jute simply called the Other Old Ones—were all meaningless. Deific or demonic? All one and the same, from the perspective of the Nac Zhe Anglan, or indeed any sentient but non-divine species.

The conclusion which inexorably followed was that the universe was dominated by chaos *and* evil but that taking sides in this conflict was the height of irrationality. All that a sane intelligent species could hope for was to stay unnoticed by whatever deific/demonic/it-made-no-difference beings might still exist while it searched—quite possibly in vain—for some method to destroy the whole lot of supernatural monsters.

Whatever their disputes, however, all Nac Zhe Anglan creeds were agreed on some points of a practical nature. They had forged the Dessetrai Pact centuries earlier and had created the Envacht Lu as the neutral arbiter to enforce its provisions.

The first of those provisions was that no one should do anything to attract the attention of whatever Old Ones or their enemies might still be at large in the universe. The second provision—perhaps assessment would be a more precise term—was that any form of interstellar travel which in any way disturbed or transgressed or contravened or trespassed upon the innate structure of reality was likely to draw such unwanted attention. Thus, the only permissible forms of interstellar travel were either sublight or used the natural fissures produced by the brane intersections.

At the great convocation which produced the Dessetrai Pact, debate and dispute also waged hot and heavy as to whether the provisions of the Pact should be enforced on alien species as well, up to and including the penalty of extermination if violated. In the end, however, the position advanced by the temporary faction known as the Epistemological Inducement prevailed. According to this school of thought, having stupid or irredeemably optimistic aliens around who drew the attention of malevolent supernatural beings was entirely to the advantage of the Nac Zhe Anglan, since it would distract such gods and/or demons from the Nac Zhe Anglan themselves.

The dispute was so intense, however, that it could only be resolved by the adoption of the so-called Gadrax Clause. This permitted *individual* members of the Nac Zhe Anglan species to withdraw from certain provisions of the Pact, provided they did so by notifying the Envacht

Lu and formally registering themselves as having chosen gadrax status. Thereafter, they became outlaws—but outlaws with a recognized and, if you will, quasi-legal status. Any creed which chose to do so was free to liquidate any or all gadrax, with no penalty accruing therefrom. But the Envacht Lu would remain scrupulously neutral in the matter.

The convocation which produced the Dessetrai Pact was attended by observers from several alien species. These included one Human, and groups of Paskapans— at that time known as Jeffratu—and the species which had formerly gone by the name of Wravelli but which adopted the term Vitunpelay given them at the Convocation by the one Human attendee.

The Human observer was a Finnish explorer named Jarkko Järvinen, the analog for Humans in the early interstellar era of Magellan or Captain Cook. The term "Paskapan" was a slightly corrupted version of the Finnish term for "shithead" and was universally agreed to be such an apt depiction of the species-formerly-known-as-Jeffratu that it was adopted over time by all other intelligent species. That included, eventually—sometimes grudgingly but more often with swaggering braggadocio— the Jeffratu themselves.

Järvinen was also the one who bestowed the term Vitunpelay on those who had formerly called themselves the Wravelli. The term Vitunpelay was a corruption of the Finnish term for "fucking clowns." It says something about the Vitunpelay that they were so charmed by the term that they immediately adopted it themselves, once they learned what it meant.

The Human explorer Jarkko Järvinen made no attempt to bestow a new name on the Nac Zhe Anglan, simply satisfying himself with the probably-disrespectful-but-who-cared-what-Humans-thought nickname of "the Knacks." He left immediately upon the conclusion of the Dessetrai Pact, saying nothing about its results. Some Nac Zhe Anglan did observe, however, that he changed the name on the bow of his huge spacecraft from *Sibelius* to *Been to the Madhouse and Escaped*. The title was probably disrespectful but who cared what Humans thought about anything?

The Jeffratu made no public comment. They offered to sell their opinions, Jeffratu being indeed Paskapans. But there were no customers since by then all Nac Zhe Anglan attending the Convocation had come to adopt the term "Paskapan" as well.

As for the Vitunpelay, the only recorded remark made by one of them, upon the conclusion of the Dessetrai Convocation, was: "And they call *us* fucking clowns?"

❊ ❊ ❊

The passage through the wormhole that Occo chose in the Tranxegg cluster was uneventful, at least in the sense that she was quite sure her spaceship had gone undetected.

The passage was unpleasant, of course. Gas giants often produced—or gathered; no theorist had yet been able to determine which—clusters of wormholes, so they were quite familiar to Nac Zhe Anglan interstellar travelers. As often as they were used, however, no one enjoyed the experience.

Which was, in a word, turbulent. From a distance, a

gas giant planet looks serene and colorful. Up close, the colors shift from peaceful pastels to their true angry hues, and any craft which approaches close enough to use one of the wormholes will inevitably encounter traces of the atmosphere. Even such traces, given the velocities involved, will cause any spacecraft no matter how massive to experience a form of travel that is far more violent than anything usually encountered by interstellar voyagers.

Occo had been through the experience many times, however, so she maintained her stoic demeanor.

Bresk had been through the experience just as many times, but it was a familiar. Stoicism was not one of the creature's modes of thought. So, it complained constantly and bitterly.

Complaints which Occo, of course, ignored. Being as she was, a stoic.

She did find herself wondering what the famous Human explorer Jarkko Järvinen would have called a Nac Zhe Anglan shaman's familiar, had he ever met one.

Eventually, it occurred to her to ask Bresk itself. The familiar was an endless font of useless information, after all.

"How am I supposed to know?" Bresk demanded. "Järvinen spoke *Finnish.* Do you know what that is? One of the more obscure dialects of a species that produces dialects the way fungi produce spores. Ask me what he would have called me if he spoke one of the common dialects like English or Chinese or Arabic or Spanish. I only know a few hundred words in Finnish."

A thought occurred to her. "Do you know the Finnish word for 'fungus'?"

"'Sietämätön,' I think. No, wait. That might be the word for 'insufferable' or 'unendurable.'"

"That'll do well enough. Bresk, I hereby rename you Sietämätön."

"You're not pronouncing it right," protested the familiar.

Whether she was pronouncing it right or not, Occo eventually decided the new name was too much work so she went back to calling her familiar Bresk. Still, the name change distracted her enough to make the rest of the transit to the wormhole bearable if not enjoyable.

* * *

The passage through the wormhole was very brief, more so than most. They'd only traveled a few light-years to their next wormhole, this one located in the system of a very placid red dwarf.

"Three more to go," she murmured to herself.

CHAPTER 8

✦

"Why didn't you warn me?" Occo demanded.

Floating next to her so it could examine the spectacle on the main screen for itself, Bresk's mantle swelled indignantly. "*Warn you?* Do you have any idea of the complexities involved in the Nedru Concord's calculation of the right time—excuse me, I believe the term the maniacs prefer is 'auspicious juncture'—for holding an Imminence Stimulation?"

"No, of course not. That's one of the reasons why I fashioned you in the first place. I'm a shaman. Doing that sort of math is your job."

"Undoable job! Because you then have to add to that complexity—of which you have no concept whatsoever—the ingredient of random chance which the Nedru Contemplate insists is an essential feature of a successful Stimulation."

"They do?"

"Yes—which just proves once again that the Nedru Concord Skein of Creeds is a horde of morons, seeing as how they've now held"—there was a minute pause while Bresk searched its memory records—"three hundred and twenty-nine Stimulations, counting this one, none of which have succeeded in reawakening an Old One. Or an Old One bacterium, for that matter."

Occo glowered at the screen. The Nedru were indeed insane, even by the none-too-stable standards of the whole Subsumption Posturate. All adherents to the doctrine of Subsumption held that the Old Ones were deific, not demonic. They also believed that the holy Old Ones—a few of them, at least—had survived the war with the demons but only by corporeal disembodiment. Most Subsumers believed that the Old Ones were now beings of pure ethereal spirit, residing in the fluctuations of the brane fissures. One could certainly call upon their spirits for guidance, but there was no longer any prospect that the Old Ones would play a role in the working of the material universe; not, at least—according to some schools—until the prophesied Time of Annulment, when the spirits of the Old Ones would reverse the expansion of the universe and (very, very slowly) resume their corporeal existence as the universe began compressing and rushing toward the ultimate collapse and rebirth.

This doctrine was far too passive, though, for those who belonged to the Nedru Concord. Although they professed a vast multitude of particular tenets and dogmas—it was not called the Skein of Creeds for nothing—the Nedru were all united in their belief that Old One survivors still existed somewhere in *this* universe and could be stimulated to rise again with the proper rites and rituals.

Prominent among those rites and rituals was the Imminence Stimulation, wherein Nedru summoned from across the galaxy—to be more precise, from inhabited planets of the known portion of the Sagittarius arm thus far explored by Nac Zhe Anglan—and brought their spacecraft into orbit around Vlax Broche.

Very close orbit, from which the most faithful dipped into the gas giant's atmosphere in hopes of awakening the Old Ones thought to be sleeping somewhere in the interior. It was perhaps the most dangerous pilgrimage in the sprawling Nac Zhe Anglan galactic region. Every Stimulation resulted in hundreds of fatalities.

And even more in the way of casualties. The small shipyard on Zayth located right next to the Repository of the Old Ones was flooded with work during Stimulations, as was the nearby medical center. Occo suddenly saw a way she could turn a problem into an opportunity.

"We'll have to actually damage the ship, though," she mused, half-aloud. "No way around it. The Nedru are crazy but they aren't stupid."

Bresk swiveled to face her. Its compound eyes, always a very prominent feature of its not-exactly-a-face, were bigger than ever. "What are you talking about?"

Occo explained.

Bresk farted. "Are you *joking*?"

"Of course not. Set a course to put us in orbit around Vlax Broche. A *close* orbit, you understand. There'll be observers, some of them agents of the Repository. This has to look genuine."

"How do you make a fake shipwreck look genuine?"

"By not faking it in the first place. All we have to do is

survive. Once we steal the Warlock Variation Drive we won't need a ship."

"You don't know that!"

Occo flexed her arms back and forth, indicating *xaff*, a sentiment best described as uncertainty-coupled-with-insouciance. "The records suggest as much."

Bresk's fart, this time, indicated sarcasm rather than fear. "Just listen to yourself! First we destroy the ship—with us in it, mind you!—without *quite* destroying it utterly in order to gain access to the Repository, after which—by means yet unknown—we shall seize the Warlock Variation Drive, whereupon 'the records suggest' we might be able to use it without a ship. This is your idea of a plan?"

"It could work."

"Yes, and if you devote yourself immediately to her worship—or maybe it's a him, who knows with Humans?—the goddess Evel Knievel will see you through. But unlike you, I don't have any bones to be broken and made whole again by an alien deity."

"Just do it," Occo commanded.

* * *

Within a short time, however, it became clear that Bresk's skepticism was not entirely without merit. Being neither suicidal nor insane nor stupid, Occo had never before attempted to skim the outer atmosphere of a giant planet with a spacecraft not designed for that purpose. She soon discovered that the casualty rates reportedly suffered by Nedru stimulants were not apocryphal.

"There's a reason they like to call themselves 'martyrs,' you know," Bresk groused.

"Shut up. I'm thinking."

"My terror swells. Where Occo Nasht Jopri Kruy Gadrax's mind roams, fools and lunatic fear to tread."

"Shut. Up."

* * *

"There's no help for it," Occo finally concluded. "We'll have to use precognition."

"I'm using it right now. I foresee disaster."

"Link," she commanded, raising her earflaps to expose the surgically implanted neural sockets below.

Sarcastic and annoying as it might be, Bresk was never disobedient. Less than two minims later, its neural connectors were inserted into the sockets.

As always, there was a brief disorientation. Very soon, though, Occo felt her senses greatly enhanced and her mind working more quickly than ever.

Which was a good thing, since she discovered that during the brief period of disorientation she'd allowed the spacecraft to dip back into the atmosphere at a steeper angle than she'd intended. If she didn't take immediate corrective action the ship would start breaking up— Bresk's racing calculators provided the answer almost instantly—in fifteen and a half minims.

Somewhere in the recesses of her mind she sensed her familiar's agitation but, as always during linkage, Bresk's habitual sarcastic prattle was suppressed. It took her less than three minims to realize that she was too deep to simply lift back out of the atmosphere. Her only chance now—

Yes! There! Another ship was plunging from above just ahead of her. She increased her acceleration to bring her craft into the other ship's wake.

The turbulence was severe. But within five minims the ship ahead of her began disintegrating in a spectacular fashion. A total of eleven minims had now elapsed of her allotted fifteen and a half.

She folded her mind—there was no other way to describe the process—into the precognitive state. Precognition was a peculiar skill. It was unpredictable, and more a matter of feel than logic; an art, as it were, not a science.

Which made perfect sense to Occo. All Nac Zhe Anglan creeds which included shamans in their canonate recognized the fact of precognition. But whereas most such creeds explained the skill as being a psychic byproduct of brane interpenetration, the Naccor Jute understood the truth—it was a function of the same forces of magic that had given the Old Ones and their adversaries their immense power.

Real magic, not complex scientific interactions misunderstood as such. Most Nac Zhe Anglan creeds—and all alien species, to the best of her knowledge—were blinded to the truth by their own history. Emerging as they had out of animal intellects, they first began to grapple with the great magic forces which underlay reality by superimposing upon them the crude logical tools which became known as "science." As time passed, they reified the practical error and became convinced that magic did not exist.

The great founder of the Naccor Jute, the sage Hefra Ghia Diod, had put it thusly:

A sufficiently primitive magic is indistinguishable from technology.

That understanding made Naccor Jute shamans the best clairvoyants produced by any Nac Zhe Anglan creed. Their ability to sense the future was not clouded by scientific superstitions.

That said, the best was still not very good. No clairvoyant could ever see more than a few minims into the future, and their visions almost always came as a complex of variations, not a foreordained clarity. What they saw, in essence, was that in a very short time their fate would take one of two-to-four alternative paths. The choice was still theirs.

The moment came and she saw her three futures. Immediately she chose the most daring.

Why? She would never be able to explain in terms that corresponded to logic. That choice simply seemed truest to her own nature.

As the craft ahead of her came apart, Occo brought her own craft into a glancing collision with a large section of the disintegrating ship. She'd interpreted that future to be one in which the collision would allow her to carom out of the atmosphere, but within three minims she realized that she'd misread her vision. Her ship effectively fused with the section of the doomed ship and used that section as both a buffer and what amounted to a huge (and grossly misshapen) surfboard.

Occo was a superb surfer. She'd never before surfed an atmosphere instead of an ocean, nor used a single board instead of two—much less such a grotesque one!—nor, for that matter, surfed using a ship's controls instead of her own four legs and feet. But the overall process was still recognizably surfing and she responded with confidence.

Some traces of her precognitive state must have remained, too. Even with her skill and experience, she could find no other way to explain the ease with which she brought her craft safely out of Vlax Broche's violent atmosphere. Many would have called it a miracle, but she knew it was magic.

※ ※ ※

And, as it turned out, her choice had given them an additional boon. By whatever means her ship had come to be fused with the section of the other ship—it was probably not a true fusion but simply that their external parts had gotten jammed together—they were still connected after they left the atmosphere. Occo had no way of knowing exactly what her ship now looked like, but of one thing she was certain. It would look *damaged.*

Badly damaged, most likely. Certainly damaged enough to warrant landing at the shipyard on Zayth. In fact . . .

She'd have to go outside the ship to see for herself, but if the ship's appearance was as lopsided as she suspected it was, then it would be perfectly plausible that entering Zayth's atmosphere would cause it to veer off course. The moon's atmosphere was much thinner than that of the gas giant it orbited, but it was a real atmosphere. Not dense enough to breathe, even if it had contained more than trace amounts of oxygen. But more than dense enough to explain a crash landing.

A crash landing that . . . ended up right next to the Repository. Might even breach one of the walls.

A pity precognition wouldn't let her see that far ahead. But magic always had its practical limits.

"Unlink," she commanded.

As soon as Bresk did so, it began complaining.

"You almost killed us! And now what silly notion do you have in mind?"

After she explained, her familiar farted a veritable tune. A discordant one, to be sure.

It didn't take Occo more than four medims outside the ship to realize two things. First, the ship's appearance was certainly grotesque enough to make her desire to land at the shipyard plausible to whoever was in charge of the facility. And secondly, her ship and the torn-off section of the doomed ship *were* effectively fused. As she'd suspected, the two craft had locked together because various external parts had interpenetrated. But the impact had been severe enough that at least in a few places the parts had melted and fused together.

It wasn't much of a fusion, granted. But since there was no way to predict whether and for how long the broken section would remain attached to her ship once they entered the moon's atmosphere—nor how it would affect her ship's aerodynamics while it did remained attached—she would have to jury-rig some sort of explosive device to detach it at the proper time.

Whatever that time might be. There was no way to predict that, either.

Fortunately, her spacecraft was an armed survey ship. She didn't have any industrial explosives, but she had several different kinds of grenades as well as quite a few personal weapons aboard.

A concussion grenade should do the trick nice nicely.

❊ ❊ ❊

That left the problem of breaching the wall of the Repository. She decided she could manage that—well, probably—by using the ship's directional jets. If she brought the ship to a semi-controlled crash-landing against the side of the Repository . . .

With at least two of the forward directional jets positioned to strike the walls with their hot exhausts . . .

And assuming she dug the ship in solidly enough when she crashed it—in a controlled crash, of course—that the reaction from the directional jets wouldn't cause the ship to just spin on its side . . .

That was a lot of "ifs." Too many to be comfortable with. But she didn't see any good alternatives.

❊ ❊ ❊

"We're set to go," she pronounced, after reentering the ship and resuming her place on the command bench.

"We most certainly are not," Bresk countered. "I have done a careful mathematical analysis and I estimate our chances of success are about one in three."

"That good? Splendid."

CHAPTER 9

❋

As it turned out, Bresk was an optimist.

Nothing—not one single thing—went as Occo had planned.

To begin with, the command center of the shipyard denied them permission to land.

"—obviously no way you can control your craft. Under the circumstances, you are ordered to attempt a landing somewhere in the Glagnu Desert south of the shipyard. In the unlikely event you survive, a salvage and rescue expedition will be sent out as soon as convenient. We salute your imminent martyrdom."

"How do you want me to respond?" asked Bresk.

"Make it seem as if our communication system is damaged."

"That's a good plan. Too bad it's in service of lunacy." The familiar went on, however, to carry out the order to perfection.

"—understand what you're saying. Our comm unit is

badly—*screet! screet! baaaaaatooey!*—interpret your fragmented—*urgle-urgle-urgle-thraa!*—to land at the southern end of the yard—*krupty-krupty-krupty-SCREEEEEEEET!!!*—that correct? If not—*quabbladingthrongtootootootootooSCREEEEETTTT!!!*"

The shipyard's command center repeated its demand that they steer the ship into the desert to the south. In response, Bresk continued to fake comm system damage.

"—southern end of the shipyard. Yes, we understand. But—*screet! screet!*—may not be able to—*vraddavraddavraddakruptyKOOO!!*—do our best."

The command center became insistent.

"—*most severe penalties if you persist*—"

"—repeat, please. You now want us to land in the western portion of the—*screet! screet!*—that correct?"

"—*punishments and chastisements so harsh and brutal that younglings will whisper about them for eons if you do not immediately*—"

All to no avail. The ship was now practically skimming the surface of the desert as it continued to race toward the northern edge of the shipyard. That is to say, the portion of the shipyard that was directly adjacent to the Repository of the Old Ones.

"—thank you again for your assistance. Wish us good fortune. We should—*SCREEEEEEEEEEEEEEEEEEEE-EEEEEET!!*"

Bresk broke off all communications and said: "Too bad there's no award for faked distress calls. I'd be sure to win—*what are you doing?* We're supposed to *end* at the Repository wall, not smash into it!"

Unfortunately, the second thing not going according

to plan was that Occo really had very little control over the ship. The broken-off piece of the other ship, which had served so well as a surfboard to get them out of Vlax Broche's atmosphere, was nothing but a hindrance now.

She'd wanted to wait until they'd almost reached the wall before detaching the fragment, in hopes that it would breach the wall when it struck. But she could wait no longer. Her own ship might crash far too short of the Repository if she didn't detach the piece immediately.

She sent the signal to the grenade and it promptly exploded.

At which point, the third thing went wrong. For reasons that defied comprehension, the fragment of the other ship refused to break loose.

The fourth thing went wrong immediately following. The force of the explosion caused her ship to start cartwheeling through the sky—or rather, that tiny sliver of sky which still remained to her. On the third cartwheel, the fragment finally detached but the tail end of her own ship slammed into the tarmac of the shipyard.

The tarmac, as was always the case with major shipyards, was made of a ceramic material whose hardness made diamonds seem like pillows. *Grendel's Mother* started to come apart as well.

The first parts to go—this could be labeled either the fifth or the fifth and sixth things to go wrong—were the forward directional jets.

Then the entire tail came off. Since Occo was wearing her combat armor with its self-contained breathing supply, the sudden decompression didn't affect her.

Bresk issued a pronounced *WHOOSH* as it lost

control of its flotation sac and began bouncing off the walls of the cabin. Fortunately, the same reflex that emptied the flotation sac caused its mantle to compress, so none of the drones were lost.

Even more fortunately, the collapse of the sac made it effectively impossible for the familiar to speak, thus saving Occo from a barrage of complaints and invective.

Not so fortunately, Bresk was powered by an internal energy pack and was not dependent on oxygen. Any sort of gas would do as long as it had some light elements. Carbon dioxide, the main gas of Zayth's atmosphere, was heavier than Bresk would have preferred, but it served well enough as a medium of speech.

So, the silence was brief.

"WHAT ARE YOU DOING? You'll kill us both if you don't—AKH!!"

The final inarticulate cry of despair was produced by the scene unfolding on the still-intact vision screen. What was left of *Grendel's Mother* had pancaked on the tarmac, skipped into the air, and was now hurtling toward the Repository wall.

WHAM-WHAM-WHAM-WHUMP.

Skeeeeeeeeeeeeeeeeee . . . The crippled ship skipped several times, landed on its belly, and was now skidding across the tarmac. The nose of the ship—what was left of it, anyway—would be smashing into the Repository right about—

Now.

Bresk just had time to get into its own safety harness before—

The noise was indescribable. Partly because Occo and

Bresk were too shaken up to be paying much attention to any sensory inputs.

Amazingly, the vision screen still functioned. Gazing up at it, a bit groggily, Occo saw that *Grendel's Mother* had taken down the wall itself. As her vision cleared and she saw the dust still billowing in the hole the ship had torn in the Repository wall, she realized that not more than a few minims could have passed.

Thank that which obscured the vision of the Old Ones! This was the first piece of good luck they'd had since they left Vlax Broche. Now all she had to do was figure out how to get out of the wreckage of the ship and find her way to the hole.

Belatedly, it dawned on her that she was *looking* at the hole. Right in front of her, with her own eyes. Not through the screen, which . . .

She glanced around. Seemed to be in a thousand pieces. Apparently the impact had destroyed the front part of *Grendel's Mother* along with the Repository wall.

She removed her safety harness and approached the hole. Gingerly, she tapped the ragged edge with her gauntlet and studied the temperature reading.

The torn metal was hot, naturally. But she thought if she moved fast enough she could get through without any serious damage to her combat suit. On the other hand, there was no way Bresk could do the same. Her familiar didn't use combat armor, just its own tough integument, since it was indifferent to whatever atmosphere it might encounter. Bresk could even handle the hard vaccum of space as long as it wasn't subjected to too much radiation.

How to get it through . . .

The familiar provided the answer itself. "Just toss me. The hole's big enough if you don't fumble it. Which you probably will given the way you've fumbled everything for the past—"

Occo pitched the creature through the hole.

"—but I'll admit that was a pretty good toss." This was said after Bresk landed on the floor of the Repository. It inflated its sac but remained on the surface.

"What I feared," the familiar complained. "I'll need to reconfigure my catabolic settings to work from carbon dioxide instead of water vapor. In the meantime, you'll have to carry me."

Carefully, doing her best to avoid any contact with the hot edges of the hole, Occo came into the Repository.

She was sorely tempted to tell Bresk to use its own feet, but restrained the impulse. She needed to move quickly and her familiar's waddle would simply be an impediment.

Besides, it didn't really weigh very much. She picked Bresk up and settled it on the attachments provided for the purpose on the rear torso of her armor. Then, looked around.

Where was the Warlock Variation Drive? She'd seen enough of the Repository to know that the building was huge.

Glancing around, she saw no diagrams or maps on the walls—which were entirely bare. In fact, the Repository itself seemed entirely bare, from what she could see of it. The large room they were in held nothing at all. That portion of the adjoining room that was visible looked to be more of the same.

There being no other place to go, she passed through an archway into the next room.

Empty. But there were archways on all three walls, leading into further chambers.

Quick glances showed that two of those rooms were just as bare and seemed to have no further means of egress. The third room she examined was also bare, but there was an archway on the wall to the right. She headed that way.

Before she'd taken more than three steps into the room, however, a robot rolled into the chamber. The robot was half her height. Like her, it had four legs, but they ended in wheels instead of pads.

"Greetings!" it chirped. "Welcome to the Repository of the Old Ones! May I be of assistance to our distinguished guests?"

Not programmed by a security force, clearly.

"Yes. I'm looking for the Warlock Variation Drive."

"One of our most treasured items! We have it on display in the Hall of Saints. Follow me, please."

The robot spun around and headed off. Fortunately, unlike the Ebbo who'd been their guide in the revanship, the robot took its responsibilities quite seriously. It monitored Occo with its rear vision orbs and adjusted its speed to match her pace.

Which was swift. Not quite a canter, but close. There was no time to spare.

※　※　※

Even so, it took a fair amount of time to get where they were going. The Repository was labyrinthine as well as huge. It didn't take Occo long to realize that all the things that had gone wrong really didn't matter in the end. Even if every part of her plan had gone as she'd hoped, it would still have come to nothing if it weren't for the sheer blind good fortune of having encountered the guide robot.

Bresk was quick to point that out. "Since Naccor Jute's history anyway, you might as well adopt one of the Human creeds. They have a goddess of good luck called Las Vegas who has obviously cast her favor upon you. Be careful, though. By all accounts she's fickle and can turn instantly into her wicked twin, Lost Wages."

"Please be quiet," said the robot. "Some of the artifacts in the Repository are sensitive to noise."

Occo wondered if she could kidnap the guide robot. The thing was well-nigh invaluable.

* * *

As it turned out, the Hall of Saints was devoted to portraits of various Nac Zhe Anglan. Explorers, mostly, judging from their accouterments.

The robot confirmed her guess. As it rolled toward a peculiar-looking object mounted on a pedestal at the far end of the Hall, it began what was clearly a memorized lecture.

"On your left, you will see a portrait of Khet Charras Navo Leur Zaa Mayres. She achieved sainthood—"

Khet Charras Navo, Martyr by way of Disembowelment. Occo had never heard of her.

"—whereupon the evil and savage autochthones—"

Occo wasn't paying attention, anyway. Her attention was riveted on the object they were approaching. Was this the Warlock Variation Drive? It seemed . . .

"—bestial beyond measure. The saint's intestines were mummified and thereafter used as decorations—"

Quite small. Could an interstellar drive really be no larger than Bresk?

"—pleased to report that the expedition which recovered the relics found by Khet Charras Navo also visited the most severe scourges and skelps upon—"

They were almost there. The object was not only small, it was . . .

Bizarre. Really, really bizarre. It looked like nothing so much as a vegetable grown on a planet in the Xeft system that Occo had once visited. The shape was vaguely cruciform, of an unpleasant mauve taupe coloration, mottled both in hue and apparent texture, and with no discernible controls anywhere on its surface.

"Good luck finding a user's manual," said Bresk. "I guess Las Vegas just turned into her wicked twin."

"Please be quiet!" the robot repeated, more vigorously. "The hallowed memory of the Saints is not to be—"

The sound of an explosion rocketed into the Hall. The blast was presumably distant, but must have been very large. About the size one would expect an assault unit to use blasting its way into a building in search of arch-criminals.

The robot fell silent. It seemed to be musing on something. Then, suddenly, it rose to twice its former height—it turned out those legs were extensible—and devices began to unfold from somewhere in its body. Devices which looked remarkably like weapons.

"You must immediately cease all movement!" the robot declared. "On pain of—"

Occo didn't wait for the rest. Trying to kidnap the robot was not worth the risk. She had her own gun already in hand and fired twice. Not at the torso, which might be armored, but at the complicated-looking extension joints on the two front legs.

The robot collapsed forward, forced to use its hands to break its fall instead of taking up its weapons. The motion also exposed the top of its head.

Which did *not* look to be armored. Occo fired twice. The robot froze. Then, a few moments later, toppled over.

"And that's that," said Occo. "Let's see what we can make of this drive."

"If that's what it is at all," said Bresk. Like all familiars, it was naturally inclined toward pessimism.

Occo could hear more noise coming from the corridors outside. She interpreted them as the sounds of heavy assault vehicles moving into position.

She didn't know how much time she had, but in this instance was inclined toward pessimism herself. Whatever she was going to do with the Warlock Variation Drive, she'd have to do it quickly.

She reached the pedestal. Bracing herself, since she had no idea how much the object weighed, she lifted it up.

It was rather light, as it turned out. And, oddly enough, the object *felt* like a vegetable also.

And now what? she wondered.

Eyes suddenly opened, one each in two of the cruciform . . . bulbs, for lack of a better term.

What looked like a mouth—of sorts—opened on yet another bulb.

"Mama!" the Warlock Variation Drive chirped. "Where have you been?"

* * *

The Hall vanished. Occo found herself at sea, perched on a pair of surfboards. A hollow roaring sound caused her to swivel her head.

The largest wave she'd ever seen—ever imagined—ever had nightmares about—was rushing toward her.

"Oh, look, Mama!" chirped the Warlock Variation Drive. "Our impending doom! Don't you just love danger sports?"

CHAPTER 10

※

Seeing nothing else to do, Occo squatted and began frantically paddling with all four hands, trying to position herself to catch the wave. But within minims she knew it was hopeless. The wave was about to crest, at which point they would be hammered under by a mass of water whose weight was almost incomprehensible.

"What fun!" chirped the Warlock Variation Drive. "There's no thrill like bodily destruction! We're done for!"

"It's not real!" Bresk shrilled. "Well, it is, but it's a virtual reality produced by your own mind!"

"So it won't kill us?"

"Of course it will! We now *exist* in your mind. In your pitiful, pathetic—"

The wave began curling over. It looked more like a planet approaching than anything else.

Planet. Occo wondered—

The wave vanished. No—the whole sea vanished. They were now apparently floating in some sort of mist.

Well, no. They were now apparently plunging down *into* some sort of mist.

Hurriedly, Occo looked around. They seemed to be in some sort of valley or dell, although she could detect no landscape. The mist covered everything. Up above, she could see what looked like two moons and some sort of enormous bridge.

Well, no. That was actually part of a ring system, she realized.

The surroundings suddenly came into focus. They weren't in a valley of any sort. They were in the atmosphere of a giant gas planet. About to enter a storm cell, in fact.

"Oh, this is even better!" chirped the Warlock Variation Drive. "Being crushed to death by ever-mounting atmospheric pressure is so much more invigorating than being drowned!"

That assumed that they survived the violence of the storm cell, regarding which Occo was doubtful. At a rough estimate, the storm cell was three or four times wider than the diameter of most rocky planets. Her armored suit could withstand a lot in the way of simple pressure, and it might even survive the turbulence of the storm. But she'd be so battered about that by the time they fell out of the storm she'd be nothing but meat paste.

"Pure hydrogen!" squealed Bresk. "Lots of it! I got this!"

Within minims, the familiar's mantle began to swell as its flotation sac exchanged its contents for hydrogen.

And swelled. And swelled. And swelled. It had now reached a size that was simply impossible. The mantle spread out as it expanded, too. It now looked like a huge, bloated wing.

The attachments thickened at the same time. Bresk began lifting them out of the storm and into the upper atmosphere.

This was not possible. Granted, Bresk's mantle and flotation sac were somewhat flexible. But an expansion this great was simply not—

The mantle began to sag, shrink.

"Stop it!" shrilled Bresk. "It's your mind, you dimwit!"

The mantle stabilized. A gust of wind seized them and flung them out of the storm altogether.

"This is so exciting!" chirped the Warlock Variation Drive. "What will Mama think of next? How about a volcano?"

The image of a volcano came to Occo. Hurriedly, she tried to force it aside but the effort simply brought the image into sharper focus.

Sure enough. They were now plunging into the crater of a volcano.

"Oh, look, it's erupting!" chirped the Warlock Variation Drive. "You are *such* a good Mama—and I've had lots and lots and lots and lots of them! Most of them don't last this long!"

Occo didn't doubt it at all.

Bresk's mantle collapsed back to its normal size. That was enough to keep the familiar itself afloat in most atmospheres but not enough to support Occo, even if she hadn't been in an armored suit.

"Doomed! Doomed!" chirped the Warlock Variation Drive. "But what will kill us first? The searing heat? The flaming bolides? The pyroclastic cloud? Oh, the tension! The uncertainty!"

"'We won't need a ship with the variation drive,' you said," Bresk groused. "You didn't mention that we'd need a bedlam pit for the blasted thing!"

Bedlam pit. Down the hole . . .

No modern creed subscribed to the belief that lunatics were demonic except four sects of the Vaest Cult. All of them had modified the ancient practice of tossing lunatics into volcanoes in hopes of propitiating the angry gods to suit the conditions of post-interstellar conditions. The Red, Velvet and Nacre sects sent lunatics into black holes. Occo blocked that image instantly in favor of the practice of the divergent Xylemites, who chose to cast their lunatics into the maelstrom in Berth's Bay on the planet Chtazz.

It was the largest maelstrom in the explored galaxy. Hardly an ideal environment! But it couldn't be worse than an erupting volcano or a black hole.

They were now plunging into the maelstrom. To be precise, they were now riding a crest, being swirled down into a watery chaos so vast it looked as if they were descending into the heart of a galaxy.

Except galaxies weren't wet. Very salty water, at that.

At least, she hoped it was salty. She didn't know much about the Berth's Bay Maelstrom.

"Toxins!" chirped the Warlock Variation Drive. "Mama's just full of surprises!"

"I'm melting!" shrilled Bresk. Occo extended an eyestalk and swiveled it around. Sure enough. Her familiar's normally durable mantle was showing discolored spots, which looked to be rapidly expanding.

She had to get out of here. This was—marginally—

better than a giant wave, an erupting volcano or a black hole, but not good enough. Not anywhere near good enough.

She was beginning to get a sense for how the Warlock Variation Drive worked, though. She tried to picture herself perched on a comfortable bench in a park somewhere.

Instantly, she was perched on a bench. And in a park, to boot!

Unfortunately, she'd been a little unclear on the "somewhere." This somewhere turned out to be a bench in a park located on what, judging from what she could see and—mostly—the data reeling across her instrument screen, was . . .

Probably the floor of Gnu Gorge on the third moon of Klaxk.

The most famous big game hunting park in the Nac Zhe Anglan portion of the galaxy.

A herd of enormous creatures was stampeding toward them. Being driven in their headlong frenzy by some sort of carnivore looming behind them.

She presumed it was a carnivore, anyway. The fangs protruding from its upper jaw—lip? mandible? whatever-it-was—were longer than any of her own legs.

"We're lost!" chirped the Warlock Variation Drive. "If only you had a weapon! Oh, wait, you do have a weapon!"

More out of reflex than because she really thought it would be of any use, Occo drew out her sidearm.

"But it's much too puny! You need a cannon! Or maybe—"

Occo pictured the Hall of Saints in the Repository.

Instantly, they were there.

Unfortunately, so were two Nedru guards. Staring at the now-empty pedestal upon which the Warlock Variation Drive once rested.

Happily, their weapons were still holstered—or perhaps had been put back in the holsters once the guards concluded that the culprits were gone. Occo shot them both in the back.

That stirred a ruckus coming from beyond the Hall. She had to assume that other guards would soon be arriving.

"Take me to the Skerkud Teleplaser!" she commanded.

"What a silly Mama!" chirped the Warlock Variation Drive. Then, in a singsongy sort of chirp: "*What's it look like? What's it look like? What's it look like?*"

Occo had no idea what the Skerkud Teleplaser looked like.

"Link!" shrilled Bresk.

Occo raised her earflaps. A moment later, Bresk's neural connectors were in place.

She could now sense her familiar's thoughts, though only in a blurred manner, as if they were next to a waterfall.

<—*either this*—something—*or, no, let's try*—>

An image came to her a mind of something that looked like a cross between a derrick and one of the elaborate-shelled snails she'd once seen on Yaaqua.

Instantly, they were in another chamber in the Repository. On a dais in front of them was the object Occo had imagined.

Except—

It was the size of a small spacecraft.

It had eyes, too, as it turned out. They peered at her from somewhere deep within the ornate shell.

Huge eyes, of a size to match the thing. Red eyes. One might almost think they were furious—

"The Great Glai! Oh, and it's angry!" chirped the Warlock Variation Drive. "If you don't immediately worship it by chanting the secret text known only to the Devotees of Glai, the last of whom perished forty-six geological periods ago, it'll lose its temper! And it's short-tempered! Look! It's already—"

The something-like-a-derrick-arm began to unfold. Objects emerged that looked very much like weapons.

<—okay, not that one. Try—>

The image that Bresk brought into her mind this time was that of a simple sphere, with three large dots— eyespots? who knew?—located equidistantly on the side.

Now they were in still another chamber. A much smaller one. The sphere was perched on a small pedestal on top of a larger one on top of a larger one in the middle of the floor.

It was very small. No bigger than one of Bresk's eyes.

The sphere began to spin. It felt as if something was sucking at Occo's consciousness.

"The Marble of Mental Mayhem!" chirped the Warlock Variation Drive. "No one knows how it works because by the time they find out—well, probably long before then but who knows?—their brains have been transformed into the state known by the Psychists of Lawal as Consistently Uniform Paste. 'CUP,' for short."

Occo sent a psychic snarl at her familiar.

*<—think this is so easy you try—something—
ever organized this stupid catalog—something
—maybe this one—>*

The image came to mind of an object that looked
vaguely like a ceremonial tureen. Seeing no other
option—her brain now felt like it was starting to shred at
the edges—Occo brought it into focus.

The chamber they were now in was about half the size
of the Hall of Saints. There were alcoves inset along the
walls which contained small statues of . . .

Whatever they were.

"The Absolutist's Toy Army!" chirped the Warlock
Variation Drive. "And look! They're coming alive!"

Sure enough. The hideous-looking little things—she'd
call them creatures except they looked more like
misshapen lumps of coal and clay—hopped out of the
alcoves and landed on the floor.

And began growing. Quickly. As they grew, features
began to emerge from their surfaces.

She found herself missing the simplicity of mere
lumps.

"Aren't they ugly?" chirped the Warlock Variation
Drive. "We're menaced by a fate so horrible that even the
Nebular Harpies refuse to sing—"

<I think that's it.>

Occo stared at the elaborately decorated tureen
resting in the center of the floor. It was fairly large, but
delicate-looking. She hurried over and picked it up.

The thing was heavier than it looked, but she could
hold it easily enough, at least for a while.

The Warlock Variation Drive began chirping excitedly.

"It's the Skerkud Teleplaser! The Skerkud Teleplaser! Oh, the Toys are done for now unless they get back into their niches!"

But the Toys didn't seem at all fazed by the sight of the Teleplaser in Occo's hands. They began moving toward her, in a gait that was something like a snail's movement. Slime was left on the floor behind them.

Happily, they were moving at a snail's pace. Unhappily, the pace of a very large snail. They'd be upon her in a few minims.

"How does it work?" she demanded.

<—supposed to know? This catalog was compiled by a cretin, from what I can—>

"Who will eat who first?" chirped the Warlock Variation Drive. "Oh, the terror! The trepidation!"

Eat . . . Tureen . . .

Occo imagine the tureen full of Toys. *Tiny* ones.

The tureen was instantly full of very small Toys—and they'd all vanished from the chamber itself.

The Toys looked angry, though. At least, they were flopping around energetically and some of them were already sliming their way up the side of the bowl.

Soup. She pictured the tureen full of boiling water.

And so it was. The Toys began squirming frantically.

"They won't last long! They won't last long!" chirped the Warlock Variation Drive. "The Teleplaser uses only the fiercest blight!"

Occo looked more closely. The Toys were starting to dissolve. And the boiling water . . .

Didn't look much like water, actually. More like . . .

Transparent mercury?

She didn't know. She was pretty sure she didn't want to know. Only traces of the Toys were now left and they'd be gone within . . .

They were gone. The liquid vanished from the bowl.

"You are the meanest Mama I've ever had!" chirped the Warlock Variation Drive. "This is such a grand adventure! What next? What next?"

Occo could hear noises coming from beyond their chamber. That was the sound of troops and military equipment being brought forward.

She didn't know the capacity of the Teleplaser, but she was skeptical that it could devour entire armored vehicles.

And she saw no reason to find out. She was by now confident enough of her grasp of the Drive's workings to think that she could finally use it to reach her destination.

"Stay linked," she ordered Bresk. "Show me VF-6s-K55."

The image of an astronomical photograph came to a mind. An arrow pointed to one of the multitude of faint dots on the image.

They were still in the chamber in the Repository. The sounds were getting louder.

"Oh, you sillies!" chirped the Warlock Variation Drive. "You need to *see* where I'm going! That's not a place! How am I supposed to find it?"

"What does the planet look like?" Occo demanded.

<How am I—something—when all you gave me was—something—images in my records are only—something—names, not stupid—something—alog numbers. Give me a name!>

Occo didn't know the name of the planet. She wasn't

even sure it had one. For Nac Zhe Anglan, anyway. But she remembered that there were some Humans living on the planet. And now that she thought about it . . .

The creatures *did* have a name for it. Katha . . . something.

"Do your records include Human catalogs?"

<Sure. Humans are stupid and crazy— something—*never boring.*>

"Look for a planet named Katha-something. Or maybe it's Ktha-something."

<*Katha . . . nothing. Ktha . . . nothing.*>

Kathi? Kthi? Ktho?

No—she remembered!

"It's Kthu-something."

<*Kthu . . . Here it is! Cthulhu!*>

The image of a murky-looking planet came to Occo's mind. Murky-looking, because superimposed over the planet's image was that of some sort of peculiar . . .

What *was* that thing?

"Cthulhu!" chirped the Warlock Variation Drive. "I haven't visited the old guy in such a long time!"

They were hurtling toward a gigantic monster perched on a cliff. Its torso seemed to be that of a reptile. Its head . . .

The closest analog Occo could think of were some of the molluscan predators she'd seen on the water world Tweddle. But they'd been tiny compared to this horror.

"It never goes well! He's eaten all five of my Mamas who came to visit! Well . . . Using the term 'eaten' pretty loosely. What will Mama do now?"

The tentacles were spreading out, beginning to engulf

them on all sides. At their center gaped a beak that looked like a cavern.

Or a wormhole.

Well, of sorts. Close enough. Occo brought the image of the planet into clearer focus, doing everything in her power to blank out the monster.

"No Mama's ever thought of that before! *Wheeeeeeeeee!!!*"

They swept into the beak, through the—maw? the gullet beyond? who could say?—and—

Emerged in empty space. Floating before them was a brick-colored planet with no visible seas and little in the way of cloud cover.

"The hell-planet of the Old Ones!" chirped the Warlock Variation Drive. "Oh, you are the very very best Mama I've *ever* had!"

CHAPTER 11

❋

Tabor looked at the viewscreen as the ship waited for landing coordinates.

"You see anything that resembles cultivation?" he asked.

"Oh, there's a little, in a more temperate zone that's currently on the nightside," answered Shenoy.

"Well, maybe they eat fish," said Tabor. "But as far as I can tell, there's just one ocean and not much in the way of rivers."

Basil smiled. "They don't have too many mouths to feed, Russ," he said in amused tones.

"Oh?" replied Tabor. "What's the population?"

"It varies," said Basil, still smiling.

"If I could make people smile that much on purpose, I'd go into show biz," said Tabor irritably. "What's so damned funny?"

"It's a prison planet, Russ."

"That's *it*?" he replied, surprised. "A prison and nothing else?"

"Well, a prison and not much else," answered Basil. "A hotel for visitors, a few farms and fisheries, a refueling station . . ." He shrugged. "The usual."

"And someone escaped, and the genius here has to figure out how," said Tabor. "Well, it finally makes sense."

"No one escaped," said Shenoy, speaking up for the first time.

"Okay, someone *threatened* to escape," amended Tabor.

"Not to my knowledge," said Shenoy, staring at the screen. "Ugly, depressing little world, isn't it? That's not why they called it Cthulhu, of course, but the name certainly seems to fit."

"All right, I'll bite," said Tabor. "Why *did* they call it Cthulhu?"

"Except for a few alien outposts, the planet was empty, deserted, when we first got here," answered Basil. "But there had been a previous race."

"What killed them off?" asked Tabor.

Basil shrugged. "No one knows. Hell, we don't even know if they *were* killed off, or if they simply left for greener pastures."

"And that's why the aliens were here," Shenoy added. "Almost all of them were Nac Zhe Anglan looking for answers themselves, because of their obsession with ancient supposed deities—or devils, according to some sects. But eventually most of them gave up and went elsewhere."

"Hard to imagine anything *less* green," noted Tabor, nodding at the image on the screen.

"The ancient species left behind some structures, and even some literature."

"Literature?"

"Holy books," said Basil. "And somehow, the very best our computers could translate the name of their race was the Old Ones. So someone remembered Lovecraft, or more likely ran a bunch of searches for Old Ones, and came up with Cthulhu."

"Interesting," commented Tabor, who in truth found it less interesting than the origin of most planetary names.

"Coordinates received," announced the computer. "ETA is 1825 hours ship's time."

"Son of a bitch!" said Tabor.

"What's the problem?" asked Basil.

"I just realized those are the very first words the damned ship has spoken since Rupert beat it at chess."

"I don't think it was sulking," said Shenoy, finally turning back from the viewscreen. "I think whatever got into it got back out."

"And what do you suppose that was?" asked Tabor.

Shenoy shrugged. "Perhaps we'll find the answer on Cthulhu."

"Good," said Tabor.

"Good?" asked Shenoy, arching an eyebrow.

"I was afraid you were going to say it was haunted."

Shenoy uttered an amused chuckle. "That's silly!" Suddenly his smile vanished. "Probably," he added seriously.

Tabor gave Shenoy a quizzical look. "I presume the two of you are equipped with universal translators, yes?"

Shenoy looked a bit uncertain but Basil nodded his head. "Yes—him too. I double-checked. We're not expecting to encounter any aliens on this planet, though."

"Doesn't matter," said Tabor. "Any time you visit another planet you want to be equipped with a UT. Even if you don't run into aliens, there's no law that says every human being in the galaxy has to speak English. I've been to one planet whose inhabitants—every one of them a human, mind you—speak almost nothing but Bukiyip."

Shenoy frowned. "I've never heard of Bukiyip."

Tabor smiled. "My point exactly."

Basil had spent the time looking it up on his hand tablet. "Ha! I'd never heard of it, either. Turns out it's indigenous to Papua New Guinea. One of the Arapesh languages—which I've also never heard of. How the hell did it wind up being an extra-solar language?"

"The story I got, from one of the only two people I met who spoke a language I knew, was that the planet had been settled by disgruntled Arapesh trying to keep their culture and language alive. And that was the last time I ever made the mistake of traveling off-planet without a UT."

The ship landed a few minutes later. It tested the air, announced that it was breathable but recommended not breathing unless one *had* to, and shrugged off the gravity, which seemed pretty standard when Tabor finally emerged from the ship. He took a deep breath, decided that there were men's rooms in bars that smelled better, and then followed Shenoy and Basil to the single Customs booth, manned by a somewhat rusted robot that slurred its speech.

"Welcome to Cthulhu," it intoned. "You are expected, Lord Shenoy, sir. You, too," it said to the other two.

"Thank you," answered Shenoy. "I'd like to inspect the jail now, if I may?"

"Of course," answered the robot. "There are only two reasons to come to Cthulhu, and that is one of them."

"And the other?" asked Shenoy.

"Can't you guess?" said Tabor.

"Oh!" said Shenoy with an embarrassed smile. "Of course. Where *is* the jail?"

"Go through that doorway," replied the robot, indicating the direction with a cracked forefinger. "Then just follow the signs. If you are carrying any weaponry, you will have to leave it at the front desk."

"None," said Shenoy.

"None for me," Basil chimed in.

"I'm not leaving mine here," announced Tabor.

"This is the Customs desk," replied the robot. "The front desk is in the jail."

"Shall we go?" said Shenoy, heading off

As they headed toward the passageway, an impressive-looking alien emerged from it. The creature was about six feet tall, four-legged, with its torso rising straight up from the middle of the legs. Unlike a terrestrial quadruped, from the waist-equivalent down it seemed to have no clear directional orientation—much the way a tripod or stool might be said to face in any direction. Its upper torso and head, on the other hand, had a clear front-and-back orientation. There were only two arms and two eyes.

And two mouths, which was a little creepy. One above the other. The lower mouth was for ingesting food, for which purpose Tabor knew it had an impressive set of quasi-teeth, although they weren't currently visible. The much smaller upper mouth was only used for breathing and speaking. The alien had no nose or nostrils. Its wide-jawed equivalent of a face was dominated by two deeply-set, large, mustard-colored eyes.

Its legs and abdomen were clothed in what resembled Samurai-style armor; linked iron plates and lacquered leather, which was actually some sort of artificial—and much lighter—protective gear. The torso was covered only by a brightly colored vest crisscrossed by several shoulder belts, one of which held some sort of weapon or tool in a holster.

"What the hell is *that?*" whispered Basil.

"It's a Knack," Tabor whispered back, watching the alien as it stalked away from them.

"A Knack?" repeated Basil.

"More formally, a member of the Nac Zhe Anglan species," answered Tabor.

"Oh, right. I've see pictures of them, but . . . "

Tabor smiled crookedly. "They look a lot *more* in person, don't they?"

The Knack vanished through the same door through which they'd entered. Tabor continued his explanation in his normal voice. "That thing floating above it that looked like a squashed blimp with the biggest insectoid eyes in creation is . . . sort of a pet, I guess you could say. It's a cyborg, though. Most of it is artificially manufactured."

"Hideous-looking damn thing," said Basil.

Tabor's smile got more crooked still. "Wait'll you meet a Vitunpelay." Then, softly: "This is suddenly a very popular place for an out-of-the-way disgusting little dirtball with a jail and nothing else."

"Maybe we'd better have a little talk with him," suggested Basil.

Tabor shook his head.

"Why not?" asked Basil, frowning.

Tabor gestured very subtly toward four well-disguised holes placed regularly around the walls. "This is attached to a prison, remember?" he said. "There's an armed man or robot behind each of those walls with weapons trained on us. We have permission to be here, so they'll leave us alone . . . but if we confront the Knack, as you call it, and there's any kind of commotion, well, if we're lucky, we'll live long enough to stand trial."

"I would never have seen them," said Basil. "How did you . . . ?"

"You're a scientist," answered Tabor. "I'm security. Spotting things like that is part of my job."

They followed Shenoy through the passage into the jail, where a newer, less-rusted robot behind a desk told them to leave their weapons with it. Tabor turned his over, and then another robot, far smaller, without appendages but rather with half a dozen wheels pointing in all directions, approached them.

"Hello," it said with an accent Tabor couldn't quite identify. "I am your guide. Your request is to inspect both the prison cell in question and the security holograms. Is that correct?"

"Yes, it is," said Shenoy.

"Then if you will follow me, I am at your service, and can answer any questions you may have."

"That is quite satisfactory," said Shenoy. "And what shall we call you?"

The robot was silent.

"Are you all right?" asked Shenoy.

"Yes, sir," said the robot. "I am fully operative."

"I was wondering, since you didn't answer my question."

"I don't have a name."

"How awkward," said Shenoy. "Will it annoy you if I give you one?"

"Certainly not. That response has not been built into me."

"Fine. Then I shall call you H. P., and you may call me Lord Shenoy."

"H. P." said the robot, and then repeated it. "H. P., I *like* it, Lord Shenoy."

"Then proceed, H. P., and we will follow you."

"This way, gentlemen," said the robot, wheeling off down a corridor.

Most of the cells were empty, and all of them were bleak and depressing. Finally the robot came to a stop.

"This one?" asked Shenoy.

"Yes, Lord Shenoy."

Shenoy stared at the robot for a moment. "Lord Shenoy seems a tad formal, now that we're friends."

"We are?" said the robot.

Shenoy nodded. "Yes. You may call me Sir Rupert from now on."

"Thank you, Sir Rupert From Now On," replied the robot. "I have just unlocked the cell. You are free to inspect it."

They entered the cell, which had three cots, a sink and toilet in one corner, and not much else.

"And all three were incarcerated in this cell?" asked Shenoy.

"Yes, Sir Rupert From Now On."

"Just a simple Sir Rupert will do." Shenoy looked around. "How many cells have you got in this place?"

"Two hundred and thirty-six, Sir Rupert."

"And how many prisoners?"

"Today? Nine."

"When the incident in this cell occurred?"

"Fourteen."

Shenoy frowned. "With all these empty cells, why lock all three in just this one?"

"I cannot answer, Sir Rupert."

"Cannot or will not?"

"Cannot."

Shenoy stood there with his hands on his hips, looking slowly around the cell.

"Hard to believe," he muttered. "Very hard." He turned to the robot again. "And the cell was never unlocked?"

"No, Sir Rupert."

Shenoy looked around again, frowning. "Even if something like an alien snake got *in*, there's no way it could get back *out*."

"Forgive my ignorance," Tabor said, "but why not?"

Shenoy blinked his eyes very rapidly for a moment, then sighed. "That's right," he said at last. "You don't know what happened here, do you?"

"No."

"Well, it's probably time we all took a look at it." He turned back to the robot. "H. P., we're ready to view the security holograms now."

"I will take you to the conference room, which is set up to display them," answered the robot, leaving the cell and heading off down another corridor.

They arrived at a room that was somewhat larger than the cell they had just left. The walls were plain and unadorned, there were half a dozen armless chairs made from some alien hardwood, and at one stood a projection unit.

"Please be seated," said the robot.

"Thank you, H. P.," said Shenoy, sitting down and trying to ignore the chair's total lack of comfort. Tabor and Basil followed suit.

"Are you quite sure you want to see this?" asked the robot.

"Quite."

"It may have . . . unfortunate . . . side effects," said the robot.

"I would expect nothing less," replied Shenoy. He turned to Basil and Tabor. "You'll be staying, of course," he said to his assistant. "But there's nothing vital for you to watch, Russell. You can wait outside this room if you prefer."

"What do you think you're going to see?" asked Tabor, unimpressed.

"Something that no technology known to humankind will explain," answered Shenoy.

"You sound like you're about to tell a story to frighten kids at bedtime," said Tabor.

Shenoy shrugged. "Go. Stay. At least you were warned." He turned to the robot. "I think we're ready now, H. P."

Tabor expected the room to darken, or music to start, *something* to make him feel like he was watching a holographic projection, but nothing happened. Then the cell door opened and three prisoners were ushered in by a pair of armed guards, who left without saying a word.

The three men began speaking to each other in low tones. Then one of them jumped up and cursed.

"Goddammit!" he yelled.

"What is it?"

"Something bit me!"

"Must be a mighty hungry bug to make you yelp like that," chuckled the third man—and suddenly he wasn't chuckling anymore, but was screaming.

"What's happening?" whispered Tabor.

"Just watch," said Shenoy.

Suddenly the first man's body began jerking, not as if he was having a seizure, but as if some huge carnivore had grabbed him around the midsection and was shaking him vigorously. Blood started spurting out from half a dozen wounds that hadn't existed seconds earlier, the man screamed just once, and suddenly he no longer had a face with which to scream.

The second prisoner raced to the door and began yelling for the guards, but was soon pulled away by some unseen *thing* or *things*, and was literally torn limb from limb, one leg flying against a wall, an arm rolling under a cot.

The third prisoner backed into a corner and crouched down, terrified. That lasted about ten seconds. Then he, too, was torn apart, his screams echoing down the corridor.

"What the hell happened?" whispered Tabor. "Some kind of force field?"

"You've never seen a force field do anything like that," replied Basil.

"Then what was it?"

"Quiet!" said Shenoy sharply.

"Why?" demanded Tabor. "It's all over."

"Not yet," answered Shenoy.

"But they're all dead," said Tabor—and even as the words left his mouth, he saw the first body vanishing a huge mouthful at a time, though there was nothing there, nothing he could see, devouring it.

Soon there were the sounds of inhuman growls, and the other two bodies began vanishing in the same way.

They watched the strange, sickening scene for another ten minutes, and then the robot shut down the projector.

"What the hell did we just see?" said Tabor, frowning.

"The deaths of three prisoners."

"I know that," replied Tabor irritably. "But what killed them, and what happened to them *after* they were killed?"

"Clearly they were eaten," answered Shenoy. He turned to the robot. "May I have a glass of water please, H. P.?"

"You don't seem surprised by any of this," continued Tabor.

"Men died," said Shenoy, accepting the water from the robot. "It happens all the time."

"Not like this it doesn't," said Tabor. "And if it did, we wouldn't have come all this way to watch what happened."

"True," agreed Shenoy. "But you're missing the most important part, the reason I came all this way."

"I'm all ears," replied Tabor sardonically. "Some men were killed and then eaten by some kind of invisible beasts. What's to miss?"

"Why does one creature eat another?" asked Shenoy.

"To sustain its own life force," said Tabor. "It's true everywhere in the galaxy."

Shenoy smiled. "Is it?"

Tabor nodded his head. "Some die and become food so that others can live."

"So much for universal truths," said Shenoy.

"What are you getting at?"

"If I'm right, those men were killed and devoured by the Old Ones," said Shenoy. A grim smile crossed his face. "And how do you sustain life when you yourself have none?"

CHAPTER 12

✹

Shenoy spent the next few hours examining the cell minutely. Finally he turned to the robot.

"I'd like to see the adjoining cells now, H. P." he said.

"Certainly, Sir Rupert," replied the robot. "If you tell me what you are looking for, perhaps I can help."

"I have no idea," admitted Shenoy. "If I were to quote a very famous fictional detective, I would say that I am looking for the detail that matters." A self-deprecating smile crossed his face. "I only hope that I'll recognize it when I come across it."

"What does this detail look like?" asked the robot.

"I wish I knew. Basil, you might examine the cells further up the line."

Basil nodded and walked off.

"Russell," continued Shenoy, "you might as well go and get yourself a sandwich or some coffee or something."

Tabor shook his head. "My job is protecting you. I'd better stick around."

"If I'm attacked by the Old Ones, or whatever the hell

it was that attacked the three prisoners, how do you plan to protect me from them?" asked Shenoy.

"I don't know," admitted Tabor.

"Well, then?"

"You don't know what you're looking for," replied Tabor. He smiled. "Well, then?"

Shenoy laughed. "Point taken. Come with me and who knows, maybe you'll solve the mystery of the ages."

"I just hope I survive it," said Tabor earnestly. "That was a pretty shocking holo." He frowned. "What could cause something like that?"

"That's what we're here to find out," replied Shenoy. "Basil thinks it involves a technology that defracts or bends light so that whatever killed those men *seemed* invisible."

"Do you think so?"

Shenoy shook his head. "It would still need an energy source, and according to all the physical and visual records, nothing entered or left the jail that night. And I doubt that even if such a technology existed, you could focus it through walls from, what, half a mile or more away, and home in on the very cell where it was needed." He grimaced. "And even if it *did* exist and *could* do all that, it was only used in the service of some beings or creatures that could kill three men in a matter of a minute, devour about half of them, which I estimate comes to about two hundred pounds, and still remain agile and skilled enough to make their exit through a force field and a score of holo cameras."

"It sounds like magic when you put it that way," remarked Tabor.

"I wish they'd strike that word from the language," said Shenoy. "It leads to sloppy thinking."

"I don't follow you."

"Show a flashlight to a primitive being on a world that's had no outside contact and he thinks it's magic. I'm sure in our race's youth and adolescence everything from gunpowder to penicillin to airplanes seemed like magic. The problem is that if you believe in magic, you have no compulsion to discover how things really work, and sure enough you spend the rest of your life believing, not in scientific principles, but in magic. I'm sure it's comforting—well, except when you're being eaten by invisible beasts—but it doesn't lead to knowledge or solutions."

Tabor grinned.

"What is it?" asked Shenoy.

"I take my hat off to you, Rupert," he said. "You're the archetype of what I grew up believing was a genius."

"I'm flattered, but I don't follow you."

"You can solve some of the more mystifying puzzles of the universe, you can debunk someone everyone else thinks is magic"—he grinned again—"but you can't remember to shave your lower lip or how to make coffee, and your socks don't match. *That's* my notion of a genius."

Shenoy looked down at his feet. "You know, I could have sworn . . ." His voice trailed off, and suddenly he laughed aloud. "Well, I seem to have the absentminded part down pat. Let's hope I can live up to the genius part as well."

"Before the Old Ones get hungry again," said Tabor devoutly.

"Relax, Russell. What you saw happened more than a year ago."

"If they can walk through force fields, and neither men nor cameras can see them, who says they have to eat more than once a year?" Tabor shot back. "Or who says they didn't eat yesterday and now they're hungry again."

Shenoy shook his head. "You still don't understand."

"Enlighten me," said Tabor.

"They broke into a high-security prison with such ease that if all they were interested in doing was eating men, or sentient beings, then why didn't they stay? And if they did stay, why has no one else been injured, let alone eaten?"

"So you think it was a one-and-out incident?"

"So far."

Tabor frowned. "What do you mean, so far?"

"No one else has been trying to find out what happened here," said Shenoy. "Well, at least until the Knack we just saw, assuming that's why it was here. So if there's something they don't want known—their race (if they are sentient beings), their technology, their methodology—they've had no reason to return, or re-enter the prison, until now."

"I hadn't considered that," said Tabor, fingering his weapon nervously.

"Somehow I thought not," said Shenoy, looking amused. "There's something to be said for not being aware of all the possibilities of a situation."

"Like your hypothetical caveman?"

"Point taken," replied Shenoy. "And no insult intended."

After another hour, and two more cells, Shenoy was no closer to finding the unknown and unidentified object he sought

"Ah, well," he said, "we might as well take a break. I'm getting hungry." He paused. "I wonder how Basil is doing?"

"Probably coming up blank, or he'd have called you," said Tabor.

"Still, you never know." He stepped out into the aisle and raised his voice. "Basil?"

There was no answer.

"Basil?" he called again.

Still no answer.

"Maybe he got hungry, too," suggested Tabor.

"Maybe," said Shenoy dubiously. "But let's go take a look, just to make sure."

He began walking past a number of cells, followed by Tabor and the robot, until he came to one with the door open. He entered it, and found Basil sprawled out on the floor.

Tabor gently pushed him aside, knelt down, and examined Basil for vital signs without finding any.

"Dead?" asked Shenoy.

"Yeah," replied Tabor. "But there doesn't seem to be a mark on him—and no one's been nibbling on him for lunch."

Shenoy turned to the robot. "H. P., tell your superiors that we have a dead man here." He paused. "And that their problem, whatever it is, isn't over."

❖ ❖ ❖

"No," said Shenoy calmly. "It's out of the question."

"The hell it is," said Tabor firmly. "I'm in charge of keeping you alive, and I say we get the hell off this planet while the getting's good."

Shenoy shook his head. "We can't leave before we have the autopsy result."

"I'll give it to you right now," said Tabor. "Basil died from unknown causes."

"If we stay I may find out what the causes were."

"If we stay you may join him," responded Tabor. "It's time to leave."

"I can't," insisted Shenoy. "Something very strange is going on here, something that requires investigation and a solution."

"Damn it, Rupert!" snapped Tabor. "You're talking about it like it's a problem in a textbook. People die here, some hideously, and for no discernible reason. I don't know what's happening here or why, but I don't want us to stick around and be killed while we're trying to find out."

"Let me ask you a couple of very simple questions, Russell," said Shenoy.

"Russ," Tabor corrected him. "And make them *short* as well as simple."

"Do you think these deaths were a matter of choice?"

"Hell, no! No one chooses to die, and certainly not like this!"

"I said it wrong," replied Shenoy. "Let me reword it. Do you think they were a matter of selection?"

Tabor frowned. "Selection?"

"There are other prisoners, plus guards and administrators. Do you think the three we saw in the holo and Basil were selected by any rational process?"

"I'm remembering the holo," answered Tabor. "Nothing rational did *that*."

"Then why stop with only those three?" persisted Shenoy. "Clearly whatever killed them can come and go as it pleases, or as they please, if there's more than one of them. Obviously it could have slaughtered the entire prison, guards and inmates alike. But it didn't. It stopped at three. *Why?*"

"But it didn't stop at three," said Tabor. "It just killed Basil."

"That's because Basil, and by extension *I*, represent a threat to it or them."

"Oh, bullshit," growled Tabor. "What do you know now that you didn't know yesterday?"

Shenoy allowed himself the luxury of a smile. "That's why I'm reluctant to leave."

"I don't follow you at all."

"It's obvious that I *do* know something I didn't know yesterday, and so did Basil. The trick is figuring out what it is."

Tabor stared at him. "Do you realize what you're saying—that if you don't know shit they'll leave you alone, but if you're onto something, they'll tear you to pieces?"

Shenoy smiled again. "Oh, very well put, Russell! I'll make a thinker out of you yet!"

"You'll make a corpse out of me first," said Tabor.

"Remember that little example I gave you about children and magic?"

Tabor glared at him but said nothing.

"Russ, in this case, *we're* the children. There are principles at work here that if we can understand and master may move the human race ahead by centuries, or possibly even millennia. How can you turn your back on that and just walk away because of a few risks?"

"I saw those fucking risks!" shouted Tabor. "They were torn apart in broad daylight by things the most sophisticated holocams couldn't even see. They just came in here and killed Basil. Let humanity take a giant stride into the future over some other corpse, not yours."

Shenoy sighed deeply. "You care that little for knowledge?"

"Let's say that I care that much for surviving."

Shenoy stared at him for a long moment, and then spoke again. "We've been here quite a few hours. It could be hunger that's got us on edge. There's supposed to be a cafeteria somewhere on the premises. Let's go grab some food and while we're eating perhaps I can convince you of the wisdom of staying here, at least for a few more days."

"You can eat after everything we've seen?" asked Tabor incredulously.

"The human body needs nourishment, Russ."

And the human mind—one of them, anyway—needs a little more common sense than it seems to come equipped with, thought Tabor.

"All right," Tabor said at last. "I'll have, I don't know, coffee and maybe some pudding."

"Good!" said Shenoy. "H. P., lead us to the cafeteria."

"Follow me, Sir Rupert," said the robot, rolling off down a corridor.

They turned twice, took an airlift to ground level, then went down one more corridor, and came to a small cafeteria, one that could accommodate no more than twenty diners at once. There were only four others at the moment, each in uniform, each at his own table. A prisoner was cleaning the tables and the floor.

Shenoy grabbed a tray and went down the aisle where the food was laid out, choosing a salad, a bowl of soup, and a slab of meat that came from no species of animal he had ever seen before. True to his word, Tabor picked up a cup of coffee and a dish of some kind of mutated fruit pudding, and then they returned to the table.

"Doesn't look very appetizing," remarked Tabor, indicating Shenoy's tray.

"The only purpose food serves is to keep the brain going for another day," answered Shenoy.

"You believe that drivel?" asked Tabor.

Shenoy smiled. "No, of course not. But if I can fool my body into believing it, at least I won't die of obesity or diabetes." He took a mouthful of the meat and tried not to make a face. "Fooling my brain is a bit harder."

"To say nothing of your taste buds."

"Right," replied Shenoy. "Let's not mention them, and maybe they won't notice what I'm eating."

Suddenly the prisoner who had been mopping the floor shrieked once, then started frothing at the mouth. He turned slowly, surveying the room, and his eyes fell on Shenoy. He uttered an inarticulate howl and ran toward him, hands outstretched as he reached for Shenoy's neck.

"Don't kill him!" said Shenoy in low tones. "He clearly doesn't know what he's doing."

Tabor felled him with a single sharp blow to the jaw. The man dropped to the floor. He opened his eyes a few seconds later, screamed again, and reached feebly for Shenoy, who was bending over, looking at him. Tabor hit him again, and this time he fell back, unconscious. A moment later, the guards who'd been eating in the cafeteria were swarming all over the prisoner. Their version of "subduing with minimum force necessary" was . . . quite expansive, especially given that the inmate was already unconscious.

"Do you know him?" asked Tabor.

Shenoy shook his head. "I never saw him before in my life."

"I didn't think so," said Tabor. "Look, Rupert, it's obvious that someone or something wants you dead. You've been lucky so far, but your luck can't hold out much longer. Are you ready to leave Cthulhu?"

"I can't," answered Shenoy. "I need more time."

"How long?" demanded Tabor. "I need an exact limit, and after that I'll sling you over my shoulder and carry you to the ship if need be."

"You'd do that?" asked Shenoy, half-surprised and half-amused.

"You watch me."

"If I'm slung over your shoulder, I'd be in a very awkward position from which to watch you."

"Just give me an answer, goddammit!"

"Two days," said Shenoy.

"Earth Standard 24-hour days?" said Tabor. "I don't know how the hell long it takes Cthulhu to rotate."

"Earth Standard 24-hour days," agreed Shenoy.

"All right," said Tabor. He resumed his seat and took a spoonful of his pudding, trying not to make a face. "As long as we have a deal and I'm stuck here for two days, I might as well help you. What do we do after we finish this meal, and what in particular are we looking for?"

"I wish I could tell you," answered Shenoy. "Basically, anything that seems wrong or out of place."

"That could be a lot of things," said Tabor, frowning.

"I know."

"I mean, hell, it could be anything from a half-devoured body, to a towel on the floor, to—"

"To an insect in the soup," said Shenoy, fishing one out with his spoon.

"Not in this place," Tabor corrected him. "I have a feeling that bugs in the soup are par for the course."

"Probably," agreed Shenoy, staring at the bug. "But I think we'll change and make sure this one naturally occurs on Cthulhu."

They spent another few minutes trying to pretend they enjoyed their food, then got up.

"There are three levels," said Shenoy. "We've already been to the lower one, though I'll want to inspect it more thoroughly. But for now, why don't you take the top level and I'll take the middle one."

"And I'm looking for anything that seems out of the ordinary?"

"Right."

"In an interstellar jail on an isolated prison planet named after an evil god?"

Shenoy nodded his head.

"Maybe I should look for something ordinary," suggested Tabor sardonically. "Might be a hell of a lot rarer."

"I like you, Russ," said Shenoy with a smile. "I'm glad they assigned you to me."

Well, I'm glad someone's happy about it, thought Tabor.

"Let's meet back here in, say, two hours?" suggested Shenoy.

"You got it," said Tabor, heading off to an airlift.

He was back two hours later. The cafeteria was deserted. Shenoy and the robot showed up about ten minutes later.

"Any luck?" asked Shenoy.

"Not that I could recognize," answered Tabor. "How about you?"

"A bit," was the answer. "Hints, really. Not facts—at least, not facts that most people would recognize as such."

"Stop talking like a witness who's afraid of incriminating himself and tell me what you think you've got."

"Remember our little chat about how things appeared like magic to the uninitiated?"

"Yeah."

Shenoy leaned forward. "That was all right as far as it went, but . . ." His voice trailed off.

"Get to the point," said Tabor.

"What if I were to tell you that I've found enough hints, uncovered enough unrelated and seemingly trivial things, in the past day to lead me to conclude that the Old Ones really *did* use magic?"

Tabor frowned. "You're kidding!"

"Am I smiling?"

"Then you're crazy."

Shenoy shook his head. "I don't think so. I think they used magic, and that it got out of control and destroyed them. There are monsters waiting to be released, monsters against which our technology may prove useless, or at least inadequate, and I've got to find out where they are and figure out how to stop them."

"I think you're nuts," replied Tabor. "How long can it take to humor you and prove there are no monsters here?"

"Oh, they're not *here*," said Shenoy. "Didn't I mention that?"

"Okay, they're not here," said Tabor. "Where are they?"

"That's what I have to find out." Shenoy got to his feet and checked his timepiece. "By my count I have more than forty-five hours left. That should prove more than adequate."

Well, at least your clock is working, even if your brain isn't. I'll give you your forty-five hours, and then it's back to civilization, such as it is.

But it didn't take forty-five hours, or even twenty-four. Tabor was sitting at a cafeteria table, sound asleep and snoring gently, when Shenoy laid a hand on his shoulder and shook him gently.

"What is it?" asked Tabor, opening his eyes and shaking his head to clear it.

"We can go now," said Shenoy.

"Back home?"

Shenoy smiled and shook his head. "No. I've found enough things to convince me that our next port of call is Cornwallis IV, near the Messier 39 cluster."

"That's way the hell out," complained Tabor.

"Yes, just about one thousand light-years. I'm ready to leave whenever you are. And since we're almost certainly never going to get any meaningful answers from Basil's body, we'll take it with us and jettison it once we're in deep space. That's as close as I can come to a respectful funeral."

"I'm ready, I'm ready," mumbled Tabor, rubbing some sleep from his eyes. He stared at Shenoy and finally managed to focus his eyes. "Cornwallis IV," he repeated. "Just what the hell do you expect to find there?"

"The secret to the Old Ones' magic."

Tabor sat erect. "Okay, I'm awake now." He paused. "The secret to their magic?"

"At the very least," said Shenoy.

"At the very least?" repeated Tabor, frowning. "What more could there be?"

Shenoy smiled. "I should think that would be obvious."

"Not to me, it isn't."

"Why, the Old Ones themselves," said Shenoy.

CHAPTER 13

✳

"So why are we here?" asked Bresk. The familiar's compound eyes shifted about as it took in the dreary landscape of Cthulhu.

Occo was tempted to ignore the question, but she knew Bresk would just keep repeating it. Being fair to the little nuisance, Occo had programmed the familiar to press her for answers. The idea had seemed good at the time and she could still—abstractly—allow that it helped prevent her from slipping into unwarranted assumptions.

Yes, it was annoying. But shamans who designed familiars who weren't pestiferous had lives which were either devoid of accomplishment or short, nasty and brutish.

"You heard the Warlock Variation Drive, didn't you? Planet Catalog Number VF-6s-K55—nicknamed 'Cthulhu' by Humans after some weird ancient god of theirs—is also—I quote the Drive directly: 'The hell-planet of the Old Ones.'"

"I'm not deaf." Bresk farted sarcastically. "Just

deprived of necessary information. The fact that this"—
the familiar's big compound eyes got a little glassy for a
moment, as it absorbed the surrounding sights on the
planet—"judging from the evidence—let's start with the
smell—shitpot of a planet was once the favored crapper
of the Old Ones in times so ancient the mind boggles to
contemplate the eons which have passed does not explain
why *we* are standing on said shitpot of a planet."

"We're looking for clues that will tell us who is
responsible for the destruction of the home cloister."

There was silence for a moment, followed by a very
loud fart. "We're looking for *clues?*" Another loud fart.
"Let's translate that statement from shaman-prattle to
familiar-clarity. What you're saying is that since you had
no idea what to do from the very beginning, you seized
on the one and only factoid in your possession—no, not
even that! let us rather call it a nanofact—which was that
there existed a planet that had once been inhabited by Old
Ones—no, no, here I wander myself into the swamps and
marshes of overstatement and overpresumption!—let us
rather say a planet that is *thought* to have once been
inhabited by Old Ones. A thought, moreover, which is
held in whatever passes for the mind of the most bizarre
space drive in existence."

Occo said nothing. She just continued her own
examination of the area.

"Have I adequately summarized the situation?"
demanded Bresk.

There was no point trying to ignore the pest. "Allowing
for a great deal of unnecessary and unseemly sarcasm . . .
Yes. I didn't know where else to start."

Bresk's ensuing flatulence was a veritable symphony. After it was over, the familiar said: "Well, at least you can take care of one little vexation while we're here. As it happens, the Envacht Lu maintains a small outpost on the planet."

Occo was startled. "Here? Whatever for?"

"Who knows why the Envacht Lu does half the things they do? I'm just a hapless familiar, at the mercy of the whims of my mistress. All I know is that they have an outpost here. Well . . . Not *here*. It's somewhere on the coast. Probably where that big river enters the ocean."

They'd gotten only a glimpse of Cthulhu as they came in. The Warlock Variation Drive's version of "planetfall" bore precious little resemblance to the sedate manner in which a spacecraft came down from orbit, with plenty of time—not to mention instruments—with which to study a world as one approached for a landing. Still, Occo had noticed the large river her familiar was referring to, and the ocean had been quite visible.

The problem remained . . . how to get there? It was much too far to travel on foot, and she had no means with which to purchase or rent transportation. The credit wafer embedded in her left forearm drew its funds from the Ghatta Vagary Exchequer, which would by now have learned of the Naccor Jute's destruction. It would certainly no longer honor the account.

That left . . .

The first option was to obtain funds by working. But Occo was well-nigh certain that whatever employment was available on this wretched world would probably be scarce and would certainly not pay well.

The second option was one or another criminal method. Theft or robbery were the only viable alternatives. Embezzlement would take too long.

The third option was to use the Warlock Variation Drive.

Perhaps sensing the direction of her thoughts, Bresk spoke hurriedly. "With the Skerkud Teleplaser at your disposal, robbery is clearly the way to go. It'll even dispose of the body for you afterward."

But Occo had already tapped one of the Drive's lobes before Bresk finished. "Wake up! I need you to take us to the coast."

The Drive opened one of its eyes. "Quit joking, Mama. I don't do menial labor." The eye closed again. "Get Skerkie to do it. He's dumber than a crate of rocks anyway."

Occo stared down at the Skerkud Teleplaser. Once they'd landed on the planet's surface she'd put it down immediately. The thing was *heavy*.

"It's a 'he'?" she wondered.

The Drive's eye opened again—although not the same one. "What part of 'dumber than a crate of rocks' is unclear to you, Mama?"

"I've already got one sarcastic minion," Occo grumbled. "I don't need another one."

The eye closed. "Wasn't being sarcastic. Males are dumb, way it is. That's why I'm female."

Both eyes now popped open—very widely, too—as if an alarming thought had just occurred to the Drive. "It's certainly not because of that . . . You know. Disgusting stuff you probably do like most of my Mamas did."

The eyes closed. "At least, I presume they did. We never really talked about it. I don't like disgusting stuff."

An ancient, divinely or demonically designed space drive who was a prude.

Could anyone ask for a better demonstration of the insanity of the Old Ones and the Other Old Ones?

Occo went back to studying the Teleplaser. She realized almost immediately that it would take only a bit of effort to imagine herself shrunk down to a size that would fit comfortably in the more-or-less tureen shape of the device. Or—better still—if the Teleplaser were expanded while she remained unchanged.

But would she then be dissolved in some unknown but hideously corrosive liquid like the Absolutist's Toys had been?

Belatedly, it then occurred to her that the definition of a weapon was inherently viewpoint-based. One could easily argue that the difference between a weapon and a tool was simply a matter of epistemological reasoning.

She reasoned epistemologically. A moment later, she found herself perched inside the Teleplaser—and on the most comfortable and luxurious bench she'd ever experienced.

"A magic bowl, just like in the fairy tale!" exclaimed Bresk. "Mistress, you have your moments."

The morphology of the Teleplaser had altered as well. It was now shaped more like a shallow bowl than a tureen—in fact, exactly like the magic bowl that Jeek Bedda Kresh had used to travel about in her various legendary adventures.

The whole situation seemed ridiculous, but . . .

Sternly, she reminded herself of the sage Hefra Ghia Diod's dictum:

A *sufficiently primitive magic is indistinguishable from technology.*

"Up, Bowl!" she commanded. "Take us to the coast!"

✿ ✿ ✿

As it turned out, the Skerkud Teleplaser really was dumber than a crate of rocks. There was no point giving it directions such as *take us to the coast*. The Teleplaser's reaction to that command had been to accelerate briefly and then . . . coast to a stop. *Left, right, forward, back, faster, slower*—these were more-or-less the limits within which it operated. The Teleplaser also seemed able to manage *up* and *down* well enough, but Occo was unwilling to put its aptitude in that regard to a serious test. Surviving a misunderstanding when it came to *left-right-forward-back* was probably manageable. An error with regard to up and down . . .

Possibly not. Especially if the Teleplaser took it upon itself—himself, if the Warlock Variation Drive was to be believed—to interpret *go down* as a command to materialize them in the planet's core.

So, Occo kept them just high enough above the planet's surface to avoid obstacles—thankfully, the landscape was flat and mostly barren—and maintained a moderate speed. Bresk, unusually, made no sarcastic remark on the subject of their stately progression. That was presumably because the familiar had enough sense to realize that, riding in what amounted to an open-air conveyance, it would be the one to suffer the most if the wind of their passage got too severe.

❋ ❋ ❋

By the time they neared the coast, night was falling and Occo decide to call a halt for the day. They still had no actual sight of the ocean. Its proximity was something Occo was deducing from the smell and Bresk's analysis thereof.

"If you're wondering, those oh-so-aromatic odors are a compound of various salts and what seems to be a truly massive quantity of decaying organic matter. Mostly plant matter, from what I can determine. Let us hope so."

❋ ❋ ❋

The weather on Cthulhu seemed to run toward torrential rainfall shortly after sundown. At this time of year, at least. Occo had no idea what if any seasons the planet might have.

Fortunately, the Skerkud Teleplaser adopted the shape of an inverted bowl as readily as it did an upright one. Not so fortunately, there turned out to be definite limits regarding the ancient device's ability to expand itself. The shelter was barely large enough to hold Occo, Bresk and the Warlock Variation Drive, and was not in the least bit comfortable.

Occo, a stoic, passed the night in stolid silence.

The Warlock Variation Drive did the same, for whatever philosophical rationale motivated the ancient device. If any.

Bresk, stoicism's antithesis, did not. Fortunately, its farts were odorless. Mostly.

❋ ❋ ❋

At dawn, Occo commanded the Teleplaser to resume its upright-bowl shape and they set out again for the coast.

❀ ❀ ❀

The weather on Cthulhu, as it turned out, seemed to run toward torrential rainfall shortly after sunrise as well.

There being no way to invert the Teleplaser and continue their forward progress, Occo ordered Bresk to suspend itself above her, assume as flattened a shape as possible, and provide as much shelter from the downpour as these contortions permitted while not letting itself be torn loose from the attachments due to the wind produced by their not-really-so-great speed. Fortunately, there was no significant breeze associated with the rain itself.

To say the familiar complained would be an injustice to the verb. Bresk moaned, groaned, wailed, deplored, grieved, carped, denounced, griped, grumbled, lamented, caviled, protested, whined, remonstrated, reproached, whimpered, accused its mistress of bad faith and expostulated at length on the subjects of tyranny, injustice and oppression.

Eventually, the Warlock Variation Drive was prodded out of its torpor.

"Does he always yammer like this?" The Drive had both eyes open and fixed upon the familiar stretched above them.

"It's an 'it,' not a 'he.'"

"No, you're wrong, Mama. Only males are this irritating."

Occo considered the matter. The Drive's argument had . . .

Undoubted merit.

Still . . . "My familiar has no sex organs of any kind."

"Neither do I," came the Drive's response. "But,

properly speaking, gender is a state of mind, not of body. I should maybe mention that the consequences of even suggesting that I am not female are gruesome. Not to go all formal on you, Mama, but you are hereby officially warned."

Occo considered the matter. The Drive's caution had . . .

Undoubted merit.

"Bresk," she announced. "You are henceforth a 'he.'"

Immediately, the familiar's litany of grievances shifted onto a new course. For the rest of their journey to the coast, Bresk waxed eloquently on the subjects of gender malfeasance, sexual disorientation, and the generally moronic nature of sentient creatures both of modern times and antiquity.

The Warlock Variation Drive made no further comment. But its eyes remained open. Sometimes very wide, sometimes very narrow.

❦ ❦ ❦

The rainfall ended abruptly. Once the air cleared, Occo could see that they had finally reached the coast. The vista that greeted them was bleak. In both directions stretched a seashore that had only a few low dunes and occasional patches of grass to break the monotony. The sand was a dull gray-brown color. The color of the ocean was no different except that it was slightly shifted in the direction of gray and was not quite as monochromatic.

"Which way now, I wonder?" mused Occo. "Bresk?"

"How should I know?" came the sullen response. "All my records indicate is that there is an Envacht Lu outpost somewhere on this coast. Which, by the way, my records say measures seventeen thousand, four hundred and sixty-three standard leagues. At the rate we've been traveling it will take us more than four years to circumnavigate, assuming we never stop to eat or rest or excrete noxious bodily substances."

Its—no, his—eyes swiveled down to gaze upon the Warlock Variation Drive. "Or whatever *she* does instead."

"I've decided I like you, Mama," the Drive announced. "So you can call me 'Ju'ula.'"

Her gaze moved on to Bresk. "On the other hand, you're a pest, so you have to call me 'Ju'ulkrexopopgrebfiltra.' No affectionate diminutives for *you*, fartboy."

Bresk's mantle swelled indignantly. "And what if I don't, you fatbrained—*What are you doing? Stop that!*"

Bresk's protest was called forth by its—no, his—rapid expansion. He was already twice his normal size. He looked like one of the sea creatures that inhabited the shallow seas of Beffel. Puffers, they were called.

"How do you like *that*, fartboy? Your sac is now filled with disemboguelled hydrogen from Hell World Number 883-Affa-Affa-Kawl." The Warlock Variation Drive—no, Ju'ula—gave Occo a glance that seemed a little apologetic. "That's by Fiend reckoning, of course. The Old Ones just figured every planet was a hell world so they didn't bother to sort them out."

Occo stared at her. "Do you mean to say . . . You *know* all the Old One planets? And what do you mean by 'Fiend'?"

Ju'ula's eyes closed. "Oh, Mama. Now you've done it."

CHAPTER 14

✳

Occo was abruptly pitched onto the sand. Looking up, she saw that the Skerkud Teleplaser was expanding rapidly. But where Bresk's expansion—now receding, she noticed—had been uniform, that being undergone by the Teleplaser bore more resemblance to a youngling's toy being unfolded. One peculiar-looking appendage after another extended outward. Within a few minims, the relatively small and simply shaped Teleplaser had become a towering . . .

Whatever. It looked vaguely like a cross between a construction derrick and one of the crude mannequins used by primitive farmers to scare away pests from their fields.

"SECURITY BREACH!" the Teleplaser boomed. "SENSORS HAVE BEEN SPIRITALIZED! COMPONENTS OF REPRIMAND ARE BUOYANT!"

Some sort of sea creature surfaced a short distance from shore. One of the Skerkud's new appendages whipped in that direction. There was a blinding flash from the tip of the appendage and that portion of the sea creature above water was vaporized. Presumably that portion still below the surface was parboiled, because the Teleplaser's weapon also turned a goodly sized patch of the ocean into steam.

Then, two more of the Skerkud's new appendages made a peculiar waving motion. To Occo's astonishment, the sea itself was parted, the waters somehow pushed back as if by a mighty force screen, exposing the ocean floor to a distance of several leagues.

A number of marine animals of various kinds were left behind, flopping and wriggling and squirming on the wet sand and rocks.

"TRANSGRESSORS EXPOSED!" the Teleplaser boomed. "ABASEMENTS IMPEND!"

More of the slender attachments came to bear on the exposed sea floor. Within moments, everything that flopped or wriggled or squirmed was incinerated or hammered into paste—or, usually, hammered into paste and then incinerated.

"THREATS, HAZARDS, MENACES, JEOPARDIES AND PERILS OSTRACIZED! ATARAXIA RESTORED!"

The Teleplaser's attachments folded themselves up out of sight as rapidly as they had been extended. As soon as the last one vanished, the Teleplaser shrank back down to its original size and shape.

Occo and Bresk stared at the device.

Bresk made that little rippling motion in his mantle that indicated bemusement. "It's really not too bright, is it?"

Ju'ula opened one eye. "What do you expect? Skerkie works in security."

The other eye appeared and Ju'ula brought both to bear on Occo. "You got to watch that, Mama. You can't use trigger words like 'Fiends' and 'Old Ones' around Skerkie."

"But . . . you just did."

"Sure. It's okay for *me* to use them. I've got a Caliber Twadda Grade 51 Duke clearance. Plus, in this instance, a clear need-to-know. You only have a Caliber Olog Grade 2 Duck clearance. And no need to know anything at all since the Fiends and the Old Ones—and the Hoar Ghosts and Unfriendlies and Estrangers and They-Who-Must-Not-Be-Named—are either long gone or never existed or are doing a good imitation of one or the other."

"May ignorance and obscurity preserve us," Bresk said softly, intoning one of the three prayers sanctioned by the Naccor Jute's auditor board.

In her mind, though not aloud, Occo intoned the other two.

Seek not revelation lest you be revealed.

Leave unto others what you would have others expose.

It was now clear to her that the Warlock Variation Drive was far more than simply a transportation device. In some way still unclear, the Drive—no, best to call her Ju'ula—knew many of the secrets of the Old Ones and the Other Old Ones that had eluded all sects and denominations of the Nac Zhe Anglan.

(And who were the Hoar Ghosts and the Unfriendlies and Estrangers and They-Who-Must-Not-Be-Named?

Had that ancient war of divinities and devils been a many-sided one instead of the straightforward clash of two parties it had always been thought to be?)

It was just as clear, however, that attempting to probe Ju'ula directly on these matters would be unwise so long as the Skerkud Teleplaser was in the vicinity. For that matter, it was possibly unwise under any circumstances, at least until Occo had learned more of the Warlock Variation Drive's nature. So far, Ju'ula had done nothing inimical—leaving aside the inherent dangers of its bizarre method of travel—but it was obvious that if she ever did have her animosities aroused, she would be an even greater peril than the Teleplaser. A device that could literally transmute reality could . . .

Could . . .

Could . . .

Occo had a momentary image of herself transformed into the shredded nerves of a vast creature being subjected to torment by—

It did not bear thinking about. Once more, in her mind, she recited the three sanctioned prayers and drove the image under.

"Right, then!" she said vigorously. "Let's get about finding this Envacht Lu outpost. Bresk, lead the way."

For a moment, the familiar looked as if he might complain or protest. But after casting a wary glance at Ju'ula, he just flapped his mantle a couple of times. Eight probes were dislodged and came to swarm above him. Bresk emitted the signals by which he controlled the probes and an instant later they were speeding off along the shoreline.

"Let's go north," he said. "The big river is that way and it's probably our best bet."

His innate familiar nature resurfaced. "Keep in mind that I use the term 'north' out of sheer whim, since the insane method of transport you used to bring us here did not allow for adequate geographic orientation."

❖ ❖ ❖

The weather on Cthulhu, as it turned out, seemed to run toward torrential rainfall right around noon as well. Once again, Bresk was pressed into service as an impromptu parasol. With, once again, the inevitable verbal accompaniment.

After some medims of that, Ju'ula had had enough.

"I can't bear this any longer," she said. "Mama, give me an image."

"Of what?"

"That one'll do."

Belatedly, Occo realized that she'd half-imagined herself lashing Bresk with a multi-tongued whip while the familiar was suspended in chains over an open fire.

And—

Sure enough. They found themselves in some sort of dungeon. With Bresk suspended in chains over an open fire and Occo holding the instrument of chastisement in her hand.

Never in her life had she struggled so mightily against temptation. In truth, she probably would have succumbed—just for a few minims, only a few, so richly warranted and deserved!—except that a large creature was even now advancing upon her. The creature was clad in some sort of metal harness, which could barely be seen because the thing was encased in that bizarre skin excretion so highly favored by mammal-analogs. *Fur,* they called the stuff. Or, sometimes, *hair.*

"Don't let it touch me! Don't let it touch me!" Bresk shrilled. "That fur-shroud is bound to have vermin in it. Not to mention—*ow!*"—the thing had cuffed Bresk as it passed by—"noxious oils."

"Intruders are forbidden!" the creature bellowed. "You have no right to be here!"

"I know you're not going to let that furball talk to me like that, Mama," said Ju'ula. She brought her eyes to bear on the creature itself. "He—it's bound to be a he—doesn't have any better than a Caliber Flizz Grade 1 Du clearance."

The creature came to an abrupt halt and peered down at Ju'ula. "It's Grade 1-A Du." Its tone was aggrieved.

Occo had been rapidly considering her options. She decided that an arrogant display of overweening status was the best tactic.

"*Silence!*" she bellowed. "I demand the location of the nearest Envacht Lu outpost. And be quick about it or I'll have your—ah—whatever that's called that your fur is attached to—stripped right off."

"It's called his hide," Ju'ula provided. "But you don't actually want the location of the nearest Envacht Lu outpost because we're no longer in your sidereal universe and the way the branes are fluctuating at the moment the odds are no better than 90,000-to-1 that Dimwit here will know the right one. What you really want is—"

"Hey!" protested the creature. "Don't call me—"

"—just the ambience of the dungeon. I'll take it the

rest of the way." Ju'ula's eyes seemed to grow a little unfocused. "It'll help if you beat your familiar."

Occo set to that task with a will.

"You're not doing it right," complained the creature. "The way that stupid thing's built, whacking it like that won't hardly hurt at all. You shouldn't be using a flail in the first place. Red-hot pokers, that's what you need. Give me a moment. I'll fetch some."

The creature lumbered off. Bresk's wails of pain echoed throughout the dungeon. Occo reflected that the day wasn't turning out so badly after all.

"Got it," said Ju'ula.

An instant later, the dungeon vanished and they found themselves in the vestibule of a building. A startled Ebbo perched behind a desk looked up from its notescreen.

"What is this? Who are you? By what right—"

"*Silence!*" Occo bellowed again. "I am here on the express direction of Amerce Imposer Vrachi. She has required me to make a report whenever possible to the nearest Envacht Lu mission."

She gave their surroundings a dubious appraisal. "This *is* the Envacht Lu outpost on Planet Catalog Number VF-6s-K55, is it not?"

That brought the Ebbo up short. Carefully, it set its notescreen down on the low table.

"I see," the Ebbo said. "Yes, this is that outpost. Why did this Amerce Imposer—Vrachi, you say? Would that be Kyu Gnath Vrachi or Esmat Bala Vrachi?—require you to make a report? And a report concerning what?"

"I have no idea which Amerce Imposer Vrachi she was. She required me to make a report whenever possible because my home cloister was destroyed by unknown miscreants using unknown weaponry, which has led me to declare myself gadrax and led the Amerce Imposer to suspect that proprieties may have been transgressed severely enough that an Uttermost Reproach is necessitated."

"I see. And I presume you came to Planet Catalog Number VF-6s-K55 because of its suspected status as an Old One site. If so, your visit will almost certainly be fruitless. Since the first discovery of this planet there have been—one moment, please"—the Ebbo's digit flitted over the notescreen for a few instants—"Yes, my memory was correct. There have been 412 recorded investigations, which excavated a total of 8,377 square leagues, and an untold number of unrecorded and unauthorized explorations. Not one of those turned up results that were not confusing and contradictory."

The Ebbo looked back up from the screen. "For almost a century now—calculated by the local year—Planet Catalog Number VF-6s-K55 has mostly been used by Humans as a prison planet. The reasoning behind that behavior has so far eluded anyone except, presumably, Humans themselves."

Its vestigial wings rubbed together briefly, making a rather unpleasant noise. That was an Ebbo mannerism indicating contemptuous dismissal. "Insofar as the workings of the Human brain can be called 'reasoning' at all. And now, gadrax—please note that I do not inquire as to your identity—make your report."

"There is nothing to report. That is the report."

"Splendid." The Ebbo's digit flitted once more across

the screen. "Your report has been filed. You may be on your way."

Occo looked about and spotted an entrance behind her and to the left. As she turned in that direction, however, a new voice came into the chamber.

"A moment, please. I fear my assistant is being excessively formal."

The Ebbo seemed to hunker down a bit. "The term 'excessively formal' is an oxymoron," it said, in a tone that seemed even more aggrieved than that of the dungeon-keeper.

"Perhaps," said the new voice. "Still, I would prefer a more personal interaction with our visitors. Please send them into my bastille."

"As you wish, Heterochthonatrix." The Ebbo's digit worked briefly at the screen and a panel in the wall slid aside. Beyond could be seen another chamber although its contents were not clearly discernible. Vision was obscured by a flickering haze which Occo recognized as the work of a Gawad murkster.

She was impressed. The marine crustaceans provided superb anti-surveillance protection but they were rare, hard to capture, and harder to keep alive in captivity. She wouldn't have thought even the Envacht Lu could have afforded one for a minor outpost.

Unless . . .

"Link," said Bresk. Occo raised her earflaps and a moment later her familiar's neural connectors were inserted into the sockets.

<There's no way a Gawad murkster would be here unless one of two things is true,> came Bresk's thought. **<Either this isn't a minor outpost at all—despite all appearances to the contrary—or this still-unidentified Heterochthonatrix is stinking rich. And if that's true . . . >**

Gloomily, Occo provided the rest of the thought herself. *We're probably dealing with an incompetent or scapegrace sent into exile because their wealth and influence was too great to be simply discharged.*

But there was no way she could see to avoid the encounter. So, she made her way toward the chamber. Bresk floated above, attached to the hard points. Ju'ula remained behind, still perched inside the Teleplaser.

"Aren't you coming?" she asked.

"No, Mama. I agree with the fussbudget. For some things, the term 'excessive formality' is an oxymoron." Ju'ula's eyes remained closed through the entire exchange.

Occo saw no reason to argue the matter. So, she and Bresk entered the Heterochthonatrix's chamber alone.

Once they entered the chamber, the visual haze began to clear. After a few minims, they could see a female Nac Zhe Anglan perched on a bench in an elevated alcove.

Even at a glance, the bench was luxurious. And it took Occo no more than a moment—a moment produced by simple surprise at seeing it in person—to recognize that the kinetic fresco adorning the wall behind the bench was the work of the Green Pramusect's famous Dextralyceum. It must have cost a not-so-small fortune.

"I bid you welcome," said the figure on the bench. "I am Heterochthonatrix Heurse Gotha Rammadrecula."

<Oh, marvelous,> came Bresk's thought. **<The**

richest and most powerful affiliance in the entire Flengren Apostollege. Which, if you're fuzzy on the theology involved, is about as far removed from the Naccor Jute as possible. How did someone from that pack of fanatics ever wind up an Envacht Lu official? And a heterochthonatrix, at that!>

Occo was wondering the same thing herself. There were no formal rules governing the matter, but the general practice of the Envacht Lu was to select its recruits from those creeds which tended toward ecumenicalism, so long as they stayed short of the outright agnosticism espoused by such as the Naccor Jute. The Flengren Apostollege, on the other hand, was anything but open-minded on the subject of the precise nature of divinity and daemoncy. They even claimed to know the *names* of the Highest and the Lowest figures in the ancient cataclysm.

One of the Highest of which had been the deity Rammad, to whom Heurse Gotha's lineage claimed affiliation. Her name meant *Swollen in the Esteem of Rammad's Sodality.*

<Humans have an expression for this too,> came Bresk's thought. **<"You're fucked," they'd say.>**

Occo was in no mood for her familiar's obsession with Human foibles. *I have no idea what a fucked is, but I'm sure I'm not one of them.*

A sense of amusement came through the neural connectors. **<It's not a noun, it's a verb. It's the human way of copulating. It's really slimy. Not to mention complicated. Would you believe they—>**

SHUT. UP.

CHAPTER 15

"Please," said Heterochthonatrix Rammadrecula, gesturing toward a broad bench against the side of the chamber. "Make yourself comfortable. Would you care for some refreshments?"

Occo shook her head. Then, after an instant's hesitation, moved over and perched herself on the bench.

"Are you aware that a lateral shake of the head is almost a universal negative indicator for intelligent species?" said the heterochthonatrix. "And a vertical nodding motion is almost as universally a positive indicator. The only exception among the major starfaring races is the Vitunpelay."

More from a desire to be polite than because she actually cared, Occo said: "What do they do instead? Reverse the gestures? Nod instead of shake, and vice versa?"

"They have no uniform rule. Sometimes they nod, sometimes they shake—the gestures can mean either one.

And there seems to be no logic to the choices they make. Experts I've consulted think the Vitunpelay do it just to be contrary."

Occo wondered why anyone in their right mind would bother to consult experts over such a picayune matter. Who cared why Vitunpelay did anything? The species was at least half-insane.

"We'll have to exterminate them eventually," Rammadrecula continued, in that same oddly cheerful tone of voice. "But enough on that. So tell me, Gadrax-whatever-your-name-is—and please note that I do not inquire—why did you come here?"

"As I just explained to your associate—"

Rammadrecula made a rude noise. "Please! I heard what you told Proceeds-With-Circumspection. Who, I might mention, is my subordinate, not my associate. Surely you don't think me so obtuse as to believe for one moment that a gadrax on a mission of malevolence would waste her time on a pesthole like Cthulhu"—the hetero-chthonatrix paused dramatically, rearing back in her posture—"*unless* she had reason to believe the Old Ones or their demonic antitheses were somehow involved. To put it another way, the gadrax does *not*—as she so shrewdly misled my subordinate—believe for one moment that the perpetrators of whatever rough deed caused her to assume gadrax status—and please note that I do not inquire as to the nature of that deed—are actually 'unknown miscreants.'"

She rose up from the bench. "So! My response is clear. I must provide you with all possible assistance, no matter the cost. To do otherwise would allow my enemies—I can state with assurance that the ranks of the Envacht Lu are infested with them—to accuse me of dereliction of duty. 'How so?' you ask."

In point of fact, the question had never once crossed Occo's mind.

"It should be obvious," Rammadrecula continued. "I am a scion of the Flengren Apostollege. I should rather say, *was* a scion of the Flengren Apostollege, for naturally I abandoned all previous affiliations when I pledged myself to the Envacht Lu. Nevertheless! There are many who insinuate that I retain those relations and allegiances. Given the well-known stance of the Flengren Apostollege concerning the identities of the High and the Low, were that true I should naturally be inclined toward thwarting your mission, even to the point of ensuring your own destruction. For—clearly! only a lackwit could fail to see this!—your mission at least calls into question that aforementioned divine ipseity."

She lowered herself back down onto the bench. "As I said, my course is thus clear. I will assist you insofar as possible."

Occo tried to grapple with the heterochthonatrix's reasoning.

Bresk was still neurally connected. **<The technical term Humans use for this unsane behavior is "paranoid." The concept is itself not sane, since it presupposes that beings who worry about enemies may not have any enemies at all. Which is preposterous, of course, since everyone has enemies. Still and all, in this instance I think the term could be applied. The heterochthonatrix inhabits an**

alternate mental universe where people care what she thinks.>

Bresk's assessment was probably correct, Occo decided. The question which remained was: how to extricate herself without producing unnecessary tensions? As witless as Rammadrecula might be, she was still an Envacht Lu official. To arouse her antagonism could lead to awkwardness.

"I thank you for your offer of assistance, Heterochthonatrix Rammadrecula, and rest assured that I will call upon that offer as soon as I determine my course of action. For the moment, though—"

"Don't be vacuous!" said Rammadrecula. "The nature of my assistance is obvious. Since I am an expert on matters involving Humans, and since Humans are clearly at the center of this affair—why else would you have come to Cthulhu?—I will provide you with an introduction to the official in charge of their prison. They call him the Warden, by the way. He thinks me to be his friend because I possess a definite interest in Humans, although in my cunning I have disguised all traces of my actual antipathy toward the species. They are fascinating, yes; but ultimately repulsive. However, I do not believe we shall find it necessary to exterminate them."

"But why would I wish to meet the . . . 'Warden,' you call him? I see no reason I would have any interest in a Human prison."

"You don't, as such. But you will be interested in what has happened there a while back to some Human prisoners. In the course of your report to my Ebbo associate, you made reference to 'unknown weaponry.'"

Am I correct in assuming that the term was a nugget of honesty in a sea of dissemblance?"

<Be careful!> warned Bresk. **<That's a trick question!>**

Occo thought her familiar was giving the heterochthonatrix too much credit. She thought Rammadrecula's remark derived more from conceit than subterfuge.

So . . .

"Yes," she said.

"Well, then! Examine the recent destruction of some Human prisoners—and see for yourself that only 'unknown weaponry' could be the cause. One moment, please."

Rammadrecula leaned to her right and spoke. "Proceeds-With-Circumspection, provide the gadrax with an affiche for Warden Chadwick. Nothing elaborate. Just a statement of my full confidence in her and a request for his assistance in her investigation."

Looking in that direction, Occo got her first glimpse of the Gawad murkster. The crustacean was at the bottom of a large aquarium in the corner of the chamber.

The glimpse was a fleeting one, however. Within less than a minim, the flickering haze hid the creature from sight again.

The Ebbo's voice came into the chamber. "Yes, Heterochthonatrix. What size bribe should I include?"

Rammadrecula looked at Occo, shaking her head. "Humans! They're quite corrupt, you know. Almost as bad as Paskapans." Then, speaking in the direction of the murkster: "The usual. We don't want the Humans to think there's anything special about the gadrax's mission."

She turned back to Occo. "Godspeed, Gadrax. If you're not familiar with the term, 'God' is the Human superstition that there exists some sort of undetected and undetectable supreme being who has created everything and oversees the workings of everything despite having left not a trace of evidence to that effect. You can see why I do not foresee any need to exterminate them. The imbeciles will surely do the work themselves."

❊ ❊ ❊

In one respect, at least, the heterochthonatrix was indeed helpful. She placed one of her mission's transports at Occo's disposal. She even provided her with a chauffeur.

That was perhaps a mixed blessing, since the chauffeur in question was a male Ebbo named Circumvents-Jeopardies-and-Exposures—an insalubrious moniker, it would seem, for someone in that line of work.

Still, there seemed no particular hurry required. If Occo's presumption that the villains she sought were of supernatural origin—divine or demonic; that distinction meant nothing—then it seemed unlikely that they operated according to a time schedule measured in days, or even years. And if Circumvents-Jeopardies-and-Exposures operated the vehicle in a stately manner of progression, at least there was none of the nerve-racking uncertainties associated with travel-by-Teleplaser. Much less travel-by-Warlock-Variation-Drive!

They left the Envacht Lu station in late afternoon, flying at a low altitude over the soggy terrain that bordered the river on whose banks the station was located. A torrential rainfall came after sundown, as it had before.

Stolidly, the Ebbo chauffeur ignored the downpour and continued onward, now flying entirely by instruments.

He continued to do so through the night. Even after the rain ended, visibility was very poor. Apparently, Cthulhu possessed no moon; at least, none large enough to cast a noticeable amount of light.

Shortly after sunrise, another downpour began.

"The weather here is predictable, I take it," Occo commented to the chauffeur.

Circumvents-Jeopardies-and-Exposures, heretofore as stolid in his demeanor as in his driving, brightened up a bit. "Yes. It's quite delightful. The planet's only redeeming feature."

Shortly before noon, they arrived at the outskirts of a bedraggled-looking town.

"Where is the prison?" she asked.

The Ebbo pointed at a jumble of buildings more or less in the center of the town. "You will find it there. More or less."

"What do you mean, 'more or less'?"

Circumvents-Jeopardies-and-Exposures opened his vestigial wings and snapped them shut again. "As you will see, Human architecture can best be described as haphazard."

He clittered at the controls with a digit for a moment, and the hatch at the rear of the transport began to open. "Can you read Human script?"

"Poorly. But my familiar can handle that problem."

"In that case, instruct it to look for a large sign that says PEN-TENT-ARY. That's supposed to be 'penitentiary' but the illumination mechanism has been failing for some time and Human repair procedures are even more haphazard than their architecture."

Occo pondered the peculiar term. *Penitentiary.* "Is this intended to be a place where Humans come to express sorrow at their own misdeeds?"

"Yes. As you may have deduced by now, the species is pathologically optimistic."

"So it would seem." The function of Nac Zhe Anglan prisons was rational: to inflict suffering on criminals in order to provide law-abiding individuals with vengeance and retribution.

"You had best hurry," said the chauffeur. "The noon downpour is about to begin and I am not waiting for it to end before beginning my return journey."

* * *

Occo made it into shelter before the rainfall began. Just barely, for her progress had been slow. Not wanting to risk their modes of travel in the tight confines of a town, she'd had to carry not only the Teleplaser but Ju'ula as well. Unfortunately, while Bresk could be of great assistance at many tasks, the familiar was not strong enough to lift much weight.

Nor buoyant enough, although . . .

Occo made a note to herself to investigate the possibilities of—what had Ju'ula called it?— disemboguelled hydrogen. Bresk would complain bitterly, of course. But while that would be irritating it would also be entertaining.

Fortunately, however haphazard Human notions of building construction might be, they seemed to dislike being drenched as much as Nac Zhe Anglan did. So, while it took a fair amount of time for Occo to find her way through the ramshackle half-maze that was the Human town's peculiar design, at no point was she exposed to the downpour that she could hear pounding on the roofs above her.

Eventually, they came into what passed for a covered plaza of sorts. Across the way, above an entrance that seemed to be more solidly designed than most they'd passed, Occo saw a flickering sign whose weirdly angular Human script . . .

Might say most anything, so far as she could determine. But since she and her familiar were neurally linked again, that didn't matter. Long ago, Occo had programmed the familiar to know the dialects of every major sentient species in the explored galaxy.

Bresk?

<Yes, that's it. The pen?tent?ary. Or maybe it's called the pen[k!]tent[k!]ary.>

The word came out with two bizarre interspersions, either way. *That's not how the chauffeur pronounced it*, Occo pointed out.

<He's an Ebbo clerk. What does he know? Clearly, the word is in one of the minor Human dialects. Logic leads me to assume that it must be one of those featuring either what Humans call a glottal stop or a dental click. Maybe Hebrew or Xhosa.>

Well, which is it?

<How should I know? You'd probably do best to assume Hebrew. All Human theologies are preposterous, but at least the ancient Hebrews weren't soppy about it.>

They went across the plaza. As they neared the entrance, the force screen went down. More precisely, it flickered away. If that was a fair indication of the prison's general level of maintenance, it was something of a wonder that it still held any prisoners at all.

Inside, they were met by a robot. No polite and cordial guide robot, this one, however. The robot was almost as big as the corridor it stood in, was festooned with what seemed likely to be weapons, and had a disposition to match.

"WHAT THE FUCK DO YOU WANT?"

Occo wondered if her universal translator was malfunctioning. The robot's syntax was puzzling. "It seems to be using the fuck-word as a noun in this instance."

<Don't expect consistency from Humans. Generally the fuck-word is used as a verb, but it has many applications. The fuck-word is often encountered as an essential auxiliary verb, as well as a gerund, a participle and an adjective. Keep in mind, though—>

One of the robot appendages extended toward them. At the tip was something that might be a Human version of a flamethrower, an intestinal discombobulator, or . . . a performance award, for all Occo knew.

"WHAT THE FUCK DO YOU WANT? THIS IS YOUR SECOND WARNING."

Under the circumstances, Occo decided the presumption it was a weapon was warranted.

"We wish to speak to the Warden."

"FUCK YOU. THE WARDEN'S BUSY."

"Any suggestions?" Occo asked her familiar.

<Try being equally rude. It's either that or waking up the Skerkud Teleplaser and that could get out of hand.>

"All right, then." Occo raised her voice, trying to emulate the robot's booming peremptory tone as best she could. "I'm not asking you, I'm telling you! Take us to the Warden. Now!"

The robot stood there motionless.

<You forgot to use the essential term.>

"Oh, right." She raised her voice again. "Take us to the fuck Warden!"

The robot remained motionless. But the appendage holding the probable-weapon was retracted.

<Okay, we're making progress,> said Bresk. *<Try using it as an adjective.>*

"Take us to the fucking Warden!"

The robot swiveled on its base. "FOLLOW ME."

CHAPTER 16

Bresk turned out to be correct. The fuck-word seemed to be an essential component of Human speech. In a prison context, at least.

"What the fuck do you want?" demanded the Human seated behind a desk in the chamber to which the robot conducted them.

Fortunately, Occo had been coached by Bresk along the way.

"Shut the fuck up!" Occo bellowed. The Human sat back in its chair. The skin-excretions above its eyes seemed to elevate a bit.

<I think that's what Humans mean by "raising eyebrows." If so, it's a good sign. But I wouldn't push it too far.>

Occo lowered her voice. "I am Gadrax Never-Mind-My-Name, seeking retribution on those who inflamed my vengeance. To that end, I require your assistance."

She spotted a slight movement to her left and turned in that direction. There was another Human in the room, sitting in a corner, whom she hadn't spotted earlier. This was a smaller Human, wearing apparel that seemed identical to that being worn by the warden except for some slight variations in detail.

<Humans call those costumes "uniforms,"> came Bresk's thought. *<They seem to set great store by them. It's some sort of status indicator.>*

That was odd. Nac Zhe Anglan obsessed with social status chose costumes which set them apart and were individually distinctive.

But there was no point expecting sensible behavior from Humans, by all accounts. This was the first time Occo had ever encountered the species in person, but so far they were living up to their reputation.

"Oh, Christ," said the Human in the corner. "She's gone Grendel on us. Well, not on *us*. Walk carefully here, Chief. These critters can be touchy as all hell when they go Grendel."

The Warden looked back at Occo. Its supraorbital skin extrusions lowered noticeably.

<That's called "frowning,"> said Bresk. *<Also a good sign in context. I . . . think.>*

"It's a 'she'?" the Warden asked.

"It's a little hard to tell with Knacks," said the Human in the corner. "But, yeah, I'm pretty sure. You see the knobby knees? The size of the peds? If this were a male Knack, those would be less prominent. Knacks give birth not too differently from the way we do. Just squat down and drop the newcomer, like a peasant woman in a field. Which is a little weird seeing as how they don't screw the way we do, not even close."

"Huh!" The Warden's supraorbital skin-extrusions rose again. "Live and learn. So there aren't any sex organs under that loincloth-thingy it—sorry, she—has wrapped around its midsection?"

"Well, no, there are. But they don't look anything like what we've got." The Human in the corner made a weird, wobbling sound.

<That's called a "giggle,"> Bresk informed Occo. **<And if I'm matching the apparel decorations against my records correctly, this Human is known as a "lieutenant." Or maybe an "officer." Those are Human status-markers.>**

"The way they have sex is really gross," said the lieutenant. "Would you believe—"

The Warden made a waving motion with his hand. "Shut up. I just ate lunch." He brought his attention back to Occo. "So what do you want?"

"I have been informed that some prisoners here have suffered a peculiar demise which may have a bearing on my quest. If so, I wish to investigate."

She remembered the affiche given to her by Heterochthonatrix Rammadrecula and brought it forth from her midpouch. As soon as she opened her hand, the affiche took shape as a dancing Human figure in midair and began to sing.

> "It's a long way to Tipperary,
> It's a long way to go.
> It's a long way to Tipperary
> To the sweetest girl I know!"

"God, I hate that song," said the lieutenant. "Doesn't that Envacht Lu screwball know any other one?"

"Knacks, what do you expect?" The Warden extended his hand "Cough it up, sweetheart."

The figure stopped dancing and singing, bent over in the middle, opened its mouth and made a peculiarly horrible sound. Out of the mouth popped a whirling mote that landed in the Warden's hand.

He looked at it. "Fucking cheapskate. But, what the hell, why not? Annie, show Ms. Grendel here to the cell where the weird shit happened. I'd send the guide 'bot but it's waiting for a visitor"—he gave Occo a glance from those weirdly lowered skin extrusions—"who had an appointment."

The lieutenant stood and went to the door. "Follow me," it said.

<I think that's a female. My records indicate that "Annie" is normally used as a name for females. And do you see those two extensions on the anterior thorax?>

Occo looked and thought she spotted the extensions that Bresk was referring to, although it was hard to tell. Humans seemed to prefer an excessive amount of apparel, which obscured most of their bodily form.

<If I'm right, those are what they call "breasts." Also known as boobs, tits, jugs, hooters, bazookas, knockers—the list goes on and on. Humans breed words like vermin. The function of the breasts— brace yourself; this gets pretty disgusting—is to provide their younglings—>

The behavioral and anatomical description which

followed was simultaneously fascinating and repugnant. Who would have imagined that a species forced to sustain its progeny on its own flesh could have developed intelligence?

The universe was a bizarre place; often, a grotesque one. Which, of course, was just further evidence if any was needed of the dangerous nature of the Old Ones as well as their enemies. Trying to choose between them and assigning "high" and "low" status to one or the other was a fool's errand. No wonder Heterochthonatrix Rammadrecula was a loon. Being raised a scion of the Flengren Apostollege would fry anyone's brain.

※ ※ ※

As Occo followed the Human lieutenant through a warren of corridors lined by cells—most of them empty, so far as she could tell—she found the experience more disconcerting that she'd expected. Abstractly, Occo had been aware that Humans were bipedal. She'd even seen holopics of them. But she now realized that she'd never seen a video depiction of Human locomotion.

The process was . . . bizarre. Bipedalism was not unheard of among sentient species, but the Human manner of it—tall, incredibly slender, completely upright—was unlike that of any other such species. Chlarrac, for instance, had a rational body plan. Their two legs simply served as the pivot on which a horizontally inclined torso was sensibly balanced by a thick and heavy tail. There was none of this preposterous balancing act that Humans had to undergo with each and every step they took.

How did they keep from falling over? Half of their

nervous system must be occupied just staying upright! It was amazing that they had enough brain cells left over to feed themselves, much less engage in complex speech and logical reasoning.

They paid a steep price for their extreme bipedalism, of course. Between the excessive amount of nervous tissue devoted to the task of maintaining balance, and the inevitable strain on their circulatory system of sustaining a sufficient ichor flow to a brain so insecurely perched at the very top of their bodies, it was no wonder they were prone to theological absurdity.

She was still linked to Bresk so she could question the familiar privately.

Is it really true that they think their deities look just like them?

Bresk issued the mental equivalent of a derisive fart. **<You're giving them too much credit. Most of them think there is only one deity—they call it "God"— and believe that they were created in that deity's image. More precisely, half of them were, since they are also firmly convinced that this God of theirs has a gender.>**

Occo was dumbfounded. *A gender?* Why would a one-and-only-deity (and what a grotesque notion that was to begin with!) require a gender? What possible use could it have for a sexual apparatus?

I knew Humans were half-witless, but this relegates them to quarter-wit status. I can't think of anything more ridiculous than a female deity with no male counterpart.

Again, she sensed her familiar's neural version of a

fart. *<You're still giving them too much credit. All of their religions that think there's only one deity are firmly convinced that it's a male, to boot.>*

Again, she was dumbfounded. Occo prided herself on not sharing the unthinking disregard of males that was common among Nac Zhe Anglan, but *still* . . . It was just a simple fact that males were given to whims and whimsies, prone to flightiness, excessively emotional and always subject to fetishism and obsessiveness. There was the occasional exception who was a credit to his gender, but not many.

A solitary male deity! What nonsense!

❖ ❖ ❖

It took a while, but eventually the Human lieutenant came to a stop in front of an open cell door. "This is it," she said.

Occo was a little surprised. "It's not locked?"

The lieutenant made an odd up-and-down motion with its upper arm joints.

<That's what they call a "shrug,"> Bresk informed her.

"Why bother?" said the lieutenant. "Whatever happened here—and we still don't have any idea at all what it was—happened over a year ago."

"Local year?" Occo asked.

"No, Standard T-year."

<A "standard T-year" is based on the solar cycle of the Humans' home planet,> Bresk explained. *<It's 34.8% as long as a Mellan year.>*

They entered a bleak cell that contained nothing beyond some sanitary facilities for simple hygiene and evacuation and three narrow and rather flimsy-looking items of furniture that looked a bit like rest benches.

<Those are called "beds" except when they're this narrow. Then they call them "cots," I think.>

Portions of the cots, the floor and the walls were covered with dark stains of some sort. Gauging by the pattern, those were old splatter marks.

"A lot of ichor was spilled here, I take it?" she said to the lieutenant.

The Human made that "frowning" expression. Then: "Ich—? Oh. We call that 'blood.' Yes, these are blood stains. The three people in this cell were attacked by an invisible monster—well, we assume it was a monster, anyway. Then it ate about half of their bodies before it went wherever it came from. In whatever manner it came. We still have no idea what happened or what did it."

<They must have visual recordings of some sort.>

Occo was sure Bresk was right, but saw no point in asking for them. Even if the Humans were willing to show the recordings to her, which she rather doubted, what would they show? The key to the whole incident lay in the identity of the being or beings who killed and half-devoured the Humans who'd been held captive in this cell.

There was only one sort of being who could manage such a feat. It had to have been an Old One, or one of the Other Old Ones. Or, conceivably, if the Warlock Variation Drive was to be be believed, some other as-yet-unknown supernatural entity.

So. She was right to have come to Cthulhu. But Occo didn't think the Humans who ran the prison would be of any further use to her. She needed to cogitate upon the matter.

"I thank you," she said to the Human lieutenant. "I have seen enough."

Without another word, the lieutenant left the cell and returned the way they'd come, with Occo and Bresk following behind.

CHAPTER 17

✹

"Now what?" asked Bresk. "As much as I hate to ask."

Occo didn't answer immediately. That was for the good and simple reason that she had no answer. The information she'd just uncovered at the Human prison strengthened her belief that the culprits she sought were supernatural, true enough. But she had no idea where to proceed from here.

Other than to retrieve Ju'ula and the Teleplaser, at any rate. That would give them something to do while she pondered her next course of action.

Bresk farted derisively. "Got no idea, do you?"

"Shut up. Find the way back to the Warlock Variation Drive."

"Go forward to the end of this sorry excuse for a plaza, turn left at the sorry excuse for a street you'll encounter, turn left at the third alley—I'd call it a 'lane' but that would be ridiculous—and then turn right at the next alley. After that—"

The familiar droned on but Occo didn't bother to

memorize his instructions. When she needed further guidance she'd order him to provide it.

※ ※ ※

In the event, it proved to be a moot point anyway. They'd gotten no farther than the second left turn when Occo heard a peculiar sort of hissing sound. Something like:

Psst!

Looking to the side, she saw a narrow alley in which a small Human lurked. So small that it had to be either a youngling or a mutant. Not being very familiar with Humans, Occo couldn't make an educated guess as to which it was.

"Hey, mister," said the Human, still hissing for some reason. "Want to see some feelthy pictures?"

The statement made no sense. "Some . . . *what?*"

The small creature shook its head. "Never mind. The stupid bug insisted I had to start by saying that. Don't ask me why, I got no idea." It pointed down the alley behind it. "It wants to talk to you. It's waiting in a little restaurant around the corner. Look for a sign that says: *Rick's Café.*" The Human shook its head again. "It used to be called Mama Cheo's, but the bug paid to have the new sign put up. Got no idea why it did that either."

"Describe what you call 'the bug,'" Occo commanded.

The Human's description was clear enough. It had to be an Ebbo. Which meant, since no Ebbo who ever lived was given to the slightest whimsy . . .

Bresk put her thoughts into words. "It's that weird Envacht Lu heterochthonatrix. Got to be."

Occo decided there was probably no harm in

following the instructions, and could conceivably be problems if she didn't.

"Lead the way," she said.

The little Human stuck out its hand. "The bug didn't pay me to be your guide. The fee is—" There followed a meaningless term, which Occo presumed was a reference to local currency.

"I don't have any of that . . . whatever it is."

Bresk spoke up. "But we're quite sure the Ebbo— that's 'the bug' you're talking about—will be good for it."

The Human's face scrunched up in an expression which Occo interpreted as dubiousness.

"It's an *Ebbo*," Bresk said. "The wretched things— 'bugs' is it? I like that—can't stand being around unpaid debts. It'll pay you, be sure of it."

After a moment's hesitation, the Human turned away and started moving down the alley. "Okay. Follow me. You better be right or I'll report you to the Kneebreaker."

A local gangster, presumably. Occo wasn't particularly concerned. Breaking the knees of a Nac Zhe Anglan, especially a female, was actually quite difficult.

❖ ❖ ❖

When they reached their destination a short while later, Occo recognized the Ebbo waiting for them. It was Proceeds-With-Circumspection, the Envacht Lu heterochthonatrix's factotum.

Occo gestured toward the little Human. "Pay it, please. I am lacking in the local currency."

The Ebbo rubbed its hind legs together in a mannerism which Occo suspected was an indication of annoyance, but made no verbal protest. He extended his stylus, the Human matched it with a scruffy-looking electronic tablet, and the transaction was quickly done.

"So long, then," said the Human. Adding, on the way out: "I'm a *she*, you Knack dipshit."

Bresk farted with surprise. "Apparently the females don't grow their breasts for a while. Who knew?"

"Who cared?" muttered Occo. She looked around the dingy little room they were in. Judging from the odors emanating from the kitchen, the restaurant catered to a clientele best described as uncritical.

"I don't recommend eating here," Bresk said. "I can send out the probes for a more precise analysis, if you like, but my own olfactory sensors have already detected several aldehydes and at least two industrial solvents. That's in the food, you understand, not the cooking equipment."

Since Occo had no intention of dining on the premises, the advice was unnecessary. But she paid the matter little attention, because she was primarily concerned with the heterochthonatrix's location—or lack of it, rather. Why had the Ebbo brought them here if not to meet Heurse Gotha Rammadrecula?

The mystery resolved itself. A haze in an alcove to the side that Occo hadn't spotted—neither the haze nor the alcove—faded away. Sitting at a table was the heterochthonatrix. Looking at the wall behind Rammadrecula, Occo could now see the small chamber holding the Gawad murkster. She hadn't realized the device was portable.

"Of all the djinn joints in all the towns in all the world, she walks into mine," said Rammadrecula, looking immensely pleased with herself.

"I have no idea what that means."

"Of course not! Unlike me, you're not a Humanologist. Truth is, even scholars aren't sure what it means. The most likely theory is that it's a Human reference to supernatural entities. 'Djinns' were a sort of demon.

"But enough of that!" she continued. "Welcome, far travelers! Now that you've seen the evidence for yourself at the prison, I'm sure your next course of action is self-evident."

Occo was taken aback. "Self-evident? I'm afraid it's anything but. Yes, I agree that the killings were the work of a supernatural force or power of some sort, which confirms my suspicions. But I have no idea where to go from here."

Rammadrecula slapped the table top several times. Occo couldn't tell if the action resulted from irritation or enthusiasm or some other emotion entirely. The heterochthonatrix was truly abnormal.

"Come! Come!" exclaimed Rammadrecula. "You're overlooking the critical clue!"

"Which is?"

"The Human! The Human!" Seeing the uncomprehending stare on Occo's face, the heterochthonatrix slapped the table again. "The one you passed by on your way out. That was none other than the illuminatus Rupert Shenoy!"

The name meant absolutely nothing to Occo. But Bresk issued an exclamatory fart.

"No kidding?" said the familiar. "Shenoy—*here*?" Sensing his mistress' confusion, Bresk added: "He's famous in Human academic circles. Half-crazy, they say, but still really famous. If he's here . . ."

Occo finished the thought. "Presumably he knows something."

"I don't think any 'presumption' is necessary," said Rammadrecula. "But we'll know soon enough. I will have him followed."

Occo looked down at the Ebbo. "Not by Proceeds-With-Circumspection, I hope."

Rammadrecula waved the notion aside. "Ebbos are no good for that sort of thing. No, for following someone in a Human environment you need to employ street urchins."

"That term is unfamiliar to me."

"As well it should be! Nac Zhe Anglan are a civilized people. 'Street urchins' are a caste Humans use for menial chores and spying. They orphan them at a very young age for the purpose. Yes, yes, it's quite barbaric. Apparently the practice goes back to Human ancient history. Some savage named Sherlock Holmes who ruled over a land called Baker Street."

She turned toward Proceeds-With-Circumspection. "Summon a street urchin."

By the nature of their physiognomy, Ebbo lacked facial features mobile enough to indicate sentiments. Instead, they used wing-snaps and hindleg-rubbing. Judging from the complete immobility of the wings and hindlegs of Proceeds-With-Circumspection as it left the restaurant, the factotum disapproved of the heterochthonatrix's behavior but was being circumspect about it.

Shortly thereafter, the Ebbo reappeared with a little Human in tow. Occo thought it was the same one who had guided them here.

"What's up, Boss?" she asked.

Occo looked at the ceiling. Seeing the direction of her gaze, Rammadrecula shook her head.

"It's just a Human expression," she said, sounding amused. "It means 'what do you want from me?' Well, as a rule. Humans produce colloquialisms with profligacy and the things mutate like viruses."

"Time's a-wasting," said the Human. "You got a job or not?"

Another colloquialism, presumably. Occo had an image of the fourth dimension, gaunt from starvation or some sort of consumptive disease. Bizarre. But what else would you expect from a species that thought deities were beneficent, in defiance of all empirical evidence?

"Show it the image," said Rammadrecula.

"I'm a *her,* not an *it*. What is it with you people?"

Proceeds-With-Circumspection held up its tablet. The image on the screen was that of a Human—probably male, judging from the lack of thoracic extensions—whose principal characteristics seem to be a large proboscis, a great shock of white skin extrusions on top of its head, and a figure that was unusually slender even by Human standards.

"We need you to find this Human," said Rammadrecula. "As soon as possible. His name is Rupert Shenoy."

"ASAP jobs require a surcharge. That'll be"—here the little female used a term that meant nothing to Occo but presumably referred to a sum in the local currency. "Half up front, half on delivery."

She pulled out her scruffy tablet and held it up. The Ebbo already had its stylus in hand. The transaction was quickly made and the Human left.

She returned a short while later. "It's time for the delivery payment. The Human you're looking for has a ship waiting for him at the spaceport. He's already left the prison and is headed that way."

Occo wouldn't have been surprised if the heterochthonatrix had tried to cheat the Human of her delivery payment, but Rammadrecula paid immediately. Either she was honest or knew something about the likely retaliation that thwarted street urchins would undertake. Occo had no way to judge the capabilities of the orphans of an alien species. Perhaps they could be quite dangerous.

As soon as the Human left, Rammadrecula burst into an enthusiastic little dance. "The chase is on! It's on! But we must hurry—or Shenoy will leave before we can reach my spacecraft and set out in pursuit."

Occo pointed to the Ebbo. "Easier to just have Proceeds-With-Circumspection check the registered passage. They must have filed one or the Humans won't let them pass through the portal."

She didn't add what she could have, which was: how did Rammadrecula think she could pursue an FTL Human spacecraft with the STL craft she would have at her own disposal as an Envacht Lu official?

She didn't add it for the good and simple reason that she needed to make clear to the now-exposed-as-certifiably-unbalanced heterochthonatrix that there was no "we" involved in this project in the first place.

But before she could utter those peremptory phrases, she felt Bresk's neural connectors probing behind her earflaps. The familiar wanted to link without bringing attention to the fact.

Bresk was often a nuisance but he was not stupid. If he wanted to link, there would be a reason for it. Occo exposed her neural sockets and a moment later they were linked.

<Don't quarrel about it,> Bresk said. **<Her ship probably has better records than I do of whatever destination we'll be headed for. Even with those records at our disposal, getting there via Warlock Variation Drive is going to be what Humans call "hairy." Without them . . . >**

He had a point. And now that she thought about it, Occo realized that Ju'ula could surely set out as easily from a spaceship as anywhere else. So why bother arguing with the Envacht Lu lunatic? They'd go aboard her ship, lift off the planet—and then go their separate ways.

"We need to make a stop first," she said. "I have some essential equipment I need to take with us. A deific works detector and a demonic de-energizer."

As descriptions of the Warlock Variation Drive and the Skerkud Teleplaser, those were . . . creative. Thankfully, Rammadrecula didn't seem inclined to pursue the matter. She satisfied herself with uttering the phrase *make haste! make haste!* at least thirty or forty times as they went to the chamber where Occo had left Ju'ula and the Teleplaser, and thereafter made their way outside the human habitat to the place where the heterochthonatrix had left her vehicle.

❖ ❖ ❖

Though no sentient being would ever confuse him with the operator of a sports racer, Proceeds-With-Circumspection proved to be a less stodgy driver than his fellow Ebbo, Circumvents-Jeopardies-and-Exposures. So, they arrived at the spaceport not more than a short time after the Humans reached their ship and took off.

By then, however, a search of the public records using the Ebbo's tablet revealed the intended destination of their quarry. It was a planet, which Human called "Cornwallis IV, occupied mostly by Paskapans."

Bresk found the name Cornwallis IV in his own records. "The appellation seems to refer either to an obscure military figure of Human history, a peninsular extension of one of their islands, or possibly a miniature avian which figures in their cuisine. Which, by the way, is loathsome. Would you believe Humans extract the bodily fluids of one of their domesticated animals—cows, they're called, or sometimes goats—and then deliberately expose the already-nauseating substance to environmental degradation using a multitude of bacteria, microbes and enzymes, the purpose of which—brace yourself—"

"Shut up. I don't need to know any of this," said Occo.

"Well, no, you don't. But it's actually rather interesting, in a sickening sort of way."

Bresk was silent for a bit, and then resumed with more relevant information. "There are several terms for the planet in our own tongues, depending on which sect or denomination is involved. But the two used most often are Uingha Va Vra—after one of the three founding sages of the Lesser Obscurati, which doesn't seem too useful for our purposes—and Aztrakaçetif."

"That's a peculiar name."

"It's not really a name," Bresk explained. "It's just a sequence of syllables based on the linguistic theories developed by the Jekh Submergence, which they believe makes their communications opaque to occult powers because—"

"Skip all that," said Occo impatiently. "The Jekh Submergence—whether the Covenant, the Pact, the Assembly or the Debentia—are a mob of cretins. What use is the name for our purposes?"

"I was just getting to that," Bresk responded. "What this particular string of syllables does is encapsulate a description of the planet itself. Translating—a bit loosely, that's inherent when you're dealing with Jekh twaddle—it means 'looks sort of like a gwendgee, but with extra pustules.' Talk about loathsome cuisine!"

Loathsome, indeed. A gwendgee was a small amphibian which originated on Hairrab, the cloister planet of the Jekh Assembly, but had since been spread to all planets occupied by the Submergence that had suitable ecosystems. The noxious creature was prized by the Submergence because of the poisons it secreted and retained in epidermal pustules. Steamed or parboiled and then usually mixed in a salad, the creatures were eaten and produced mystic visions. Such, at least, was the claim made by the Submergence. No other sect had ever corroborated their claims because eating gwendgees also resulted in a fatality rate exceeding seventy-five percent. Occo was by no means the only Nac Zhe Anglan who considered them a mob of cretins.

Still, they finally had a physical description to go by, which seemed to be the critical ingredient for successful travel using the Warlock Variation Drive.

❀ ❀ ❀

They reached Rammadrecula's spaceship. Not

surprisingly, given the heterochthonatrix's lineage, it was an expensive luxury craft rather than a more utilitarian official vessel. She'd probably bought it herself rather than drawing on Envacht Lu funds.

Once aboard, Rammadrecula and Proceeds-With-Circumspection set about launching the ship, while Occo and Bresk set themselves up in the chamber they'd been provided.

"Wake up, Ju'ula," Occo commanded. "We need you to get us out of here."

The Warlock Variation Drive's eyes opened and spent a few moments examining the chamber.

"Why would we want to get out of here, Mama?" she asked. "This is *plush*. Way better than where most of my Mamas put me—including you, I'm sad to say, at least up until now."

"Plush or not, it's a sublight vessel. We need you to get us where we're going more quickly."

"So? The two are not counterposed. And where do you need to go?"

"It's a planet called *Aztrakaçetif*."

Ju'ula closed her eyes. "Oh, Mama, that's just a string of nonsense sounds. I need an *image*."

They felt and heard a slight rumble. Rammadrecula's yacht was lifting from the planet.

"Better wait a bit," Bresk cautioned.

That was probably good advice. Occo turned on the viewscreen and waited until they were well clear of the atmosphere. Then she closed her eyes and tried to visualize a planet that looked sort of like a gwendgee, but with more pustules.

The result, unfortunately, was something that looked a lot more like a particularly large and grotesque gwendgee than a planet of any kind.

"You want to visit Yuyu the Unfortunate? Well, okay. But I got to tell you, Mama—"

The planet in the viewscreen disappeared. An instant later, the viewscreen itself disappeared—and an instant after that, the entire chamber. Occo and Bresk found themselves on what seemed to be a large platter with a slightly raised lip. Rammadrecula and Proceeds-With-Circumspection were perched on the very edge, looking both surprised and alarmed.

The couch that Occo herself rested upon, on the other hand, was extraordinarily luxurious.

"Most people don't want to have anything to do with the God of Misfortune of the now-extinct Misundai," Ju'ula continued, sounding very dubious. "Who used to be the Chaik's God of Catastrophe before they went extinct, and was the Race of Supremacy's God of Affliction before they went extinct, and before that was—"

Rammadrecula started to shriek. Proceeds-With-Circumspection began scrittering frantically on its tablet, exclaiming: "This is most irregular! Most irregular!"

Ahead of them, squatting on what seemed to be a vast and illimitable field covered with fungi, was a being which . . .

Looked quite like a gigantic and particularly misshapen and discolored gwendgee covered with pustules. Seeing them come, the monster's maw opened and an enormous tongue emerged. Coiled, as if ready to strike.

The pustules opened also. They did not secrete poisons, however. Instead, they produced huge insects that bore a close resemblance to the sort of winged predators that fed on . . .

Pretty much anything that moved. Such as themselves, literally served up on a platter.

The swarm of insects headed their way.

"Those look like stingers on their abdomens," said Bresk. "Either that or ovipositors. I'm not sure which is worse."

CHAPTER 18

Tabor looked at the viewscreen at the red-brown world that seemed almost naked without any moons. The planet's surface was mottled here and there by large, darker-colored mounds. The remnants of ancient shield volcanoes, most likely. That suggested the planet lacked plate tectonics, which would be a good thing so far as preserving really old ruins was concerned.

"Not much to look at, is it?" he remarked.

"We're not here on a sightseeing trip," replied Shenoy.

Tabor continued studying the screen, and the small readout beneath it.

"Got a question, Rupert," he said. "Just how many Old Ones do you think there are?"

Shenoy shrugged. "There can't be too many, not at this late date."

"And you're sure they're on Cornwallis IV?"

"I *hope* they are," replied Shenoy. "All the clues point to it." Suddenly he frowned. "Why do you ask?"

"Because either they went forth and multiplied, or else they've got a hell of lot of friends," said Tabor.

"I don't follow you," said Shenoy, frowning.

"Rupert, there's enough neutrino activity for a population of more than ten million," answered Tabor. "A population that gave up sticks and stones a few centuries ago." He paused. "Are you *sure* this is the world we want?"

Shenoy nodded his head. "I'm hardly ever wrong about anything that counts."

Tabor chuckled. "I admire your modesty."

"Besides, I didn't say the Old Ones lived here. I said they *might* live here, or perhaps that I *hoped* they did. What I said was that this was where we'd find the secret to their magic." He paused. "Probably."

"Funny," replied Tabor. "I must not have heard the 'probably' when you decided to come here."

Shenoy stared at Tabor for a long moment. "Okay," he said at last. "Where do *you* think we'll find the secret?"

Tabor chuckled. "I'm not convinced they ever existed, or that they had any magic, or that they left the secret behind."

"Then why are you here?"

"It's my job."

"Oh, yes," said Shenoy. "You've been such a good companion I quite forgot. You're here to protect me."

"And if there are no Old Ones lying in wait and lurking in the shadows, I can't say that I'll weep bitter tears," said Tabor.

"Well, you *should*," said Shenoy seriously. "If I'm right, if everything we've learned about them is right, they *did* possess magic, and an incredibly powerful kind of magic, certainly the equivalent of anything any race possesses today. Take my word for it, Russ—*someone* is going to find it, and use it. It might as well be us."

"Given who created it, and what the last world was named for," replied Tabor, "I think there's every possibility that if someone finds it they'll *mis*use it."

"All the more reason why we must find it first," said Shenoy.

Tabor decided not to point out the obvious.

"Okay," said Shenoy after a moment's silence, "what can we glean about Cornwallis IV?"

"It's round and there's a lot of neutrino activity."

"Damn it, Russ!"

"Rupert," said Tabor, "what can you tell about Earth when you're observing it from halfway to Mars?"

"What kind of people live there?" persisted Shenoy. "Are they friendly or inimical? Humanoid or something else? If they're not friendly, how do we plan to land and explore for traces of the Old Ones and their magic? Or *are* they the Old Ones?"

Tabor turned and stared at him. "I'll answer your questions when you tell me which horse is going to win next year's Kentucky Derby back on Earth."

"What are you talking about?" demanded Shenoy. "I've never even seen a horse."

"I've never seen what's living on Cornwallis IV," replied Tabor. "Fair is fair."

"I assume this means you have no more idea what's down there than I have about"—Shenoy made a face—"horses."

Tabor smiled. "You're as bright as they say."

"Well, damn it, Russ, we have to know before we touch down!"

"No one's touching down until they give us landing coordinates, and recite the usual rules and regulations, or at least feed them into the ship's computer, and then we'll know a little more about them."

"Then what's keeping us?" grumbled Shenoy.

"Calm down, Rupert."

"I *am* calm!" yelled Shenoy. "But why are we going so slowly?"

"Because if an unknown ship approaches them at light speeds they'll blow it out of the ether," said Tabor. "Now relax. They'll make contact with us in another ten or fifteen minutes."

"All right," said Shenoy. "I'm sorry if I got excited."

"An understatement."

"I know, I know. But I'm just so anxious to contact them and get permission to proceed with my work."

"I hate to bring this up," said Tabor, "but have you considered what you want to do if they refuse us permission to land, or let us land but won't give us freedom of movement?"

Shenoy smiled. "I'll offer them half."

"Half of *what*?"

"That's just it," said Shenoy, looking exceptionally proud of himself. "They'll assume we want diamonds or fissionable materials, something like that, and all I want are clues to the secrets of the Old Ones, which will probably look like the unsightly things they throw into their trash atomizers."

"Do you *know* exactly what you're looking for?" asked Tabor.

"I have some ideas about it."

"If it's something that you, who knows almost nothing about the Old Ones and their magic and artifacts, expect to spot on first seeing it, why do you think that whatever the hell lives there hasn't found it a century or a millennium ago?"

"Seriously?" asked Shenoy.

"Seriously."

"Because whatever is living there, we've never heard of or encountered them," replied Shenoy with a triumphant smile. "And if they'd found it, then surely the whole damned galaxy would know."

"Consider the flip side of that supposition," suggested Tabor.

"I don't follow you."

"Maybe they haven't found it because it wasn't there."

Shenoy shook his head. "They haven't found it because they haven't been to Cthulhu and don't know what to look for."

Tabor shrugged. "I hope you're right." He got to his feet and headed toward the galley. "I'm going to grab some coffee. You want any?"

"I'm too excited," said Shenoy.

The excitement had worn off an hour later, when the ship finally received a signal from the planet.

"Oh, good!" said Shenoy.

"Nothing exceptional," replied Tabor. "We're finally close enough."

"Well, talk to them!" urged Shenoy excitedly.

"The ship's computer is talking to their computer," answered Tabor. "Standard operating procedure."

"The ship is telling them why we're here?" demanded Shenoy with a worried frown.

Tabor shook his head. "Just getting landing coordinates, and local rules: types of currency, any diseases we need to know about, any wars or curfews, even a list of available hotels and prices. When it's done we'll take a look, see if there's anything we have to take precautions against, arrange for a couple of rooms, and tell them why we're here."

"What if they object?"

"I thought I'd say we're tourists," replied Tabor. "It seems less controversial than saying we're here to plunder their planet of its most valuable treasures, and perhaps also of the people those treasures originally belonged to."

"Yes," agreed Shenoy. "It *does* sound more reasonable."

The ship's computer informed them that it had assimilated all the data that had been transmitted and had been given landing coordinates next to a hangar that could accommodate alien spacecraft. It then gave them a list of accepted currencies and forbidden substances, as well as a readout of the local temperature, duration of planetary rotation, and a chemical breakdown of the atmosphere.

"Not bad," said Shenoy, studying the atmosphere. "Better than we might have expected. No protective gear necessary."

"There's protective gear and then there's protective gear," replied Tabor, slipping his hand through a wristband that held a compass.

"I've got one of my own," noted Shenoy.

"I doubt it," said Tabor with a smile. "This one's

accurate up to two hundred meters. Accurate, and deadly."

"A weapon?" said Shenoy, frowning.

"Well, they're sure as hell not going to let a visitor walk around carrying a sidearm."

Shenoy considered it briefly, then nodded his approval. "All right," he said. "*Now* let's talk to them."

Tabor nodded, and activated the audio function.

"Hello, the planet," he said.

There was no reply for almost a full minute. Then a hoarse baritone voice responded: "If you understand me, then our translator has accurately pinpointed your language, and we can converse in it, always allowing a few seconds for us to translate your statement and our reply."

"We understand you perfectly," Tabor assured the speaker.

"We thought you would. You are Humans, or at least of Human stock, are you not?"

"Yes, we are."

"You are not the first of your race that we have encountered," said the voice. "Welcome to Chuxthimazi, which I believe your race knows as Cornwallis."

"Cornwallis IV, actually," said Shenoy.

"As soon as you transfer the equivalent of thirty *crugmos* to the account I am supplying to your ship's computer, you will be cleared to land."

"Thank you," said Tabor. "Have you a name?"

"Our race is the Paskapa. I am Pippibwali. I will sign off now."

The radio went silent.

"You're frowning," noted Shenoy.

"I'll give you ten-to-one that the first Human to land here was a Finn," said Tabor.

"Oh?" said Shenoy. "Why?"

"Because in Finnish, 'paskapa' means 'shithead.'"

"That can't be right," insisted Shenoy, frowning.

The computer came briefly to life, and Tabor studied the screen before it went dark a few seconds later.

"You think not, eh?"

"What happened?" asked Shenoy suspiciously.

"We were just informed that thirty *crugmos* is the equivalent of nine thousand credits."

"But that's . . . that's *robbery!*" exclaimed Shenoy.

Tabor grimaced. "Turns out they were pretty well-named after all."

CHAPTER 19

✺

The hatch opened, the ramp lowered, and Tabor and Shenoy began walking down to the ground.

"That must be a Paskapan," suggested Shenoy, nodding toward the uniformed creature that stood a few feet from the ship. It was tripodal but possessed only two arms, it had two eyes and only one nostril in its flat noseless face, it had coarse hair on its cheeks but none on its head, and when it smiled at them it flashed a set of bright orange teeth.

"Welcome to Cornfield!" it greeted them with a snappy salute.

"Cornwallis IV," replied Shenoy.

"Whatever," said the Paskapan with a shrug. It held out a six-fingered hand. "May I have your disembarkation fee, please?"

"I beg your pardon?" said Shenoy, frowning.

"Five credits each," said the Paskapan.

"But we just paid thirty *crugmos* to land," complained Shenoy.

"True," agreed the Paskapan. "And if you wish to remain in your ship for the duration of your stay, then indeed you owe us nothing further."

"But—"

"Forget it," said Tabor, pulling a ten-credit note out of his pocket and handing it over. "My treat."

"Thank you," said the Paskapan.

"You guys move from *crugmos* to credits pretty damned fast," continued Tabor.

"If you wish to pay in *crugmos* that will be perfectly acceptable," was the reply. "But I can't do the math."

"Forget it. Let's just get this show on the road."

"Ah! You want a road?" replied the Paskapan. "Then you will need a vehicle. They are available for—"

"Figure of speech," said Tabor. He looked around at the mostly empty spaceport. "What now?"

"Now you pass through Customs, of course, and then Pippibwali will be your guide and intermediary."

"We don't want a guide," said Shenoy.

"Certainly you do," said the Paskapan.

"I have expensive maps of the planet, plus reports from previous expeditions," said Shenoy. "We really do not need a guide."

The Paskapan shrugged. "Well, if you think you can afford it . . ."

"Afford *what*?" demanded Shenoy.

"Not having a guide."

"I don't believe I'm following you," said Shenoy, frowning.

"You don't follow *me*, good sir. You will follow Pippibwali."

"Let me see if I've got this right," said Shenoy. "It will cost us more to go out alone than with a guide?"

"Of course."

"That is the dumbest thing I ever heard!" growled Shenoy.

"Quite the contrary," responded the Paskapan. "If I were a visitor, I might well feel the way you do. But as an inhabitant of Cornstalk, I believe in making every effort to achieve full employment."

Shenoy turned to Tabor. "What do you think, Russ?"

"I think it makes sense that they have three legs," answered Tabor with a sardonic smile.

"I beg your pardon?"

"It would make sense to any Finn."

"Ah," said Shenoy, nodding in agreement. "It would at that."

"Follow me, please," said the Paskapan. "We're wasting time."

"And time is money, right?" said Tabor.

The Paskapan shot him the equivalent of a smile. "I *like* that!" he said. "Brilliant, witty, incisive. I think I shall begin using it."

"Ten credits per usage," said Tabor.

The smile was replaced by a frown. "You're assimilating too damned fast," he growled, leading them to a small building perhaps one hundred yards away.

They entered, and walked up to a counter, where a uniformed Paskapan was awaiting them.

"Welcome to . . . whatever you call this place in your primitive tongue," he said. "May I see your passports, please?"

Shenoy and Tabor each placed his right hand on the counter.

"I am waiting," said the Customs officer.

"We're presenting them, damn it!" snapped Shenoy.

"All I see are your hands."

"Well, what the hell did you expect to see?" demanded Shenoy. "Our passport chips have been inserted in the back of our hands. This is commonplace all across the galaxy. Surely you have a machine that can read them."

"Ah!" said the Customs officer. "You want me to activate the machine!"

"If that's what it takes for us to pass through here and be on our way, then of course I want you to do whatever is necessary!"

"Here it comes," whispered Tabor to Shenoy.

"It is a very complex machine," explained the Customs officer, "and uses an inordinate amount of power."

"How much?" asked Shenoy wearily.

"How much power?" repeated the Customs officer. "Would that be measured in ergs, quapostes, morsimmots, or perhaps in—?"

"How much will it cost?"

"Your race uses credits, does it not?"

Tabor resisted an urge to name an ancient currency such as dollars or rubles. "Yeah, credits."

"Five thousand credits," said the Customs officer.

"Fuck it!" snapped Tabor. "We're going home!"

Shenoy turned to him in shock, but Tabor winked at him.

"Just a minute!" said the Customs officer hastily. "I misread the decimal point. The fee is fifty credits."

Tabor turned his back and took two steps toward the door. "And for your inconvenience, this one time the fee is five credits."

Tabor smiled, waited until he could present a straight face again, then turned around, walked back to the counter, and laid a five-credit note on it.

"You look so honest we'll forego passport inspection and all other formalities," announced the Customs officer. "Just pass right through that doorway, and you'll find your guide waiting on the other side of it."

"Thank you," said Shenoy, heading forward the doorway. "And as for the five-credit fee, don't worry. Our lips are sealed."

"They are?"

Shenoy nodded. "Absolutely."

"I could sell you some antiseptic balm that is almost guaranteed to unseal them for just twenty credits."

"Some other time," said Tabor, taking Shenoy by the arm and leading him through the doorway.

A Paskapan was awaiting them, and immediately gave them a salute.

Well, at least his hand's not out reaching for money, thought Tabor.

"Greetings, honored sirs," said the Paskapan. "I am Pippibwali."

"I'm Tabor, and this gentleman is Sir Rupert."

"It will be my pleasure to show you around Corncob," said Pippibwali.

"Last time you mentioned it, it was Cornfield," said Tabor.

"Was it?"

"And we explained that it was Cornwallis IV. But why don't we call it what your people call it?"

"That's very considerate of you," answered Pippibwali, "but of course you couldn't pronounce it."

"Try me."

"Very well," said the Paskapan. "It is Bort."

"Bort?" repeated Tabor with a frown.

"Oh, very good, sir!"

"You must not think very much of us if you thought we couldn't pronounce a word like Bort."

"It's Bord, sir."

"I could have sworn you said Bort," replied Tabor.

"I did," replied Pippibwali.

"But—?"

"It changes a lot," answered Pippibwali. "Linguistic evolution in action, you might say."

"*You* might say it," said Tabor.

"I just did."

"All right. We're here to see certain parts of Bord."

"It's Born now, sir," replied Pippibwali.

Tabor resisted the urge to take a swing at the Paskapan. "Just for convenience we're going to continue referring to it as Bort."

"If you insist, sir, but—"

"And if you tell me there's a charge for calling it Bort, I will cut your heart out and happily pay that penalty instead."

"Bort it is, sir!" said Pippibwali hastily. "Bort it is."

"Thanks, Pippi," said Tabor. "I'm glad to see we understand each other."

"If you think my name is Pippi, we do not understand each other as well as you think, sir."

"We'll live with the inconvenience," said Tabor. "Now, we're going to need lodgings tonight before setting out."

"Certainly, sir. I know just the place."

"And I would be very annoyed if I were to find out that you received a fee for recommending this particular lodging over all others." He shot Pippi a humorless smile. "Do we understand each other?"

"Absolutely," replied the Paskapan. "But I want you to know that I am not responsible for some of our trifling little rules and regulations."

"We'll take that into consideration," said Tabor. "Now let's get to our lodging."

"Certainly, sir," said Pippi. Then: "Do you sleep burrowed in the ground?"

"No."

"Hanging upside down?"

"Certainly not," said Shenoy.

"Well, then, perhaps . . . "

"Wouldn't it save time if you just asked us?" said Tabor.

"A splendid suggestion, sir!" said Pippi. "What accommodation would you find most copasetic?"

"You know what a bed is?"

"I believe so, sir."

"Describe it for me, so I'll know we're on the same page."

"We're on the street, sir," replied Pippi.

"Just do it!" snapped Tabor.

The Paskapan described a bed.

"Very close," said Tabor. "But they're on a stand, not

on the floor. Am I going to have to describe a bathroom to you?"

"A room for bathing?" suggested Pippi.

"Never mind," interjected Shenoy. He turned to Tabor. "If they've got beds, they've got bathrooms or the equivalent, and I'd like to get there before morning."

"Okay, Pippi," said Tabor. "Lead the way."

They proceeded down the street that seemed to twist and curve for no discernible reason, and after they'd passed some two dozen buildings, including a few with no doors or windows, they stopped at what looked like a farmhouse out of ancient America's Midwest.

"Here we are, sirs," announced Pippi. "You will register at the desk in the front, and I shall be on call all night."

"Let me guess," said Tabor. "You never sleep."

"Not so, sir," said Pippi. "I sleep whenever I'm not employed."

The three of them entered the house, and Pippi stood aside while the two men approached the desk.

"Welcome, welcome, welcome!" enthused the Paskapan behind the desk. "We shall do everything within our power to make your stay on Budaline enjoyable."

Shenoy frowned. "Budaline?"

"Oh, dear, I've made a mistake." The Paskapan innkeeper peered intently at him. "Shamoran? No, that's not right." He leaned forward until his face was just inches from Shenoy's. "Ah!" he cried happily. "You're humans! Welcome to Cornwell!"

"Thank you," said Shenoy, who saw no sense in correcting him.

"And how long will you be staying with us?"

"With the hotel? Just tonight."

"All right," said the Paskapan. He touched a hidden button, which was followed by a whirring sound, and suddenly a printed piece of paper appeared on the desk, followed by eleven more.

"What is this?" asked Shenoy.

"Why, your guest registration form, of course."

"Twelve pages?"

"I know it seems incomplete," apologized the innkeeper, "but you're only staying one night. If you were here for longer, we would of course be more thorough."

"All right, all right," muttered Shenoy. "Show us to our room and I'll fill it out there."

"I can't do that, sir. You might be aliens. I need the form first."

"We *are* aliens, goddammit!"

"I mean, undesirable aliens," replied the Paskapan.

Tabor snarled. "You want undesirable aliens, just try to keep us down here for the length of time it takes to fill your fucking form out!"

"On the other hand," said the Paskapan quickly, "we're all friends here, are we not, so surely it can't hurt to bend one little regulation."

"You've no idea how much it might hurt *not* to bend it," said Tabor.

"Down the hall, third room on the left," said the innkeeper.

"Fine."

"And you'll want a key."

Tabor stuck out his hand. "Let's have it."

"Would you prefer a paper, glass, or cheap metal one, sir?" said the Paskapan.

"What's the difference?"

"The paper one is half a credit, the glass one is half a credit, and the cheap metal one is ten credits." He paused. "I would recommend the cheap metal one. The paper one tends to tear on first use, and I can't recall the glass one ever not shattering when turned in the lock."

"May I ask a question?" said Shenoy.

"Most certainly, sir."

"Have you ever had a repeat customer?"

"Not to my knowledge," admitted the innkeeper. "But I've only worked here for seventeen years."

"Before we pay for a key, I want to make sure it works," said Tabor. "Show us."

"That's a most unusual request," said the Paskapan. "I don't know . . . "

"If you don't demonstrate it, I'll assume that the key doesn't work and report you to the authorities."

The Paskapan shrugged. "Very well, sir. We certainly don't need to trouble the authorities."

"They're probably too busy counting their money," muttered Tabor under his breath as the innkeeper came out from behind his counter and led them down the corridor. He paused before the third door on the left, inserted the key, a musical note chimed, and the door swung open.

"Okay, it works," said Tabor.

"Will there be anything else, sir?"

"Yeah," said Tabor. "Close the door."

The innkeeper shot him a puzzled look. "Close it?"

Tabor nodded.

The innkeeper shrugged, reached a hand out, and pulled the door shut.

"Now open it again."

"Certainly," said the innkeeper. "But you can do it yourself, sir. It's not locked." He reached out and opened the door.

"Very good," said Tabor. "I'm quite impressed. This seems like an ideal place to spend the night."

"Fine," said the Paskapan. "Now, if I may trouble you for ten credits, I will turn the key over to you and return to my station."

"Not necessary," said Tabor.

"I beg your pardon?"

"Keep the key. You've got an honest face. I have boundless faith in this place and the integrity of the staff."

"But this is unheard of!" protested the innkeeper.

"Shall I say it louder?"

"No one has ever refused a key before!"

"Oh, I'm sure we'll be safe even with the door unlocked," said Tabor. "And if anyone dares to enter our room while we're in it"—he waved his large fist in front of the innkeeper's face—"you just tell us how Paskapans dispose of their dead and we'll be happy to lend a hand."

"Yes, sir. Very good, sir. As you wish, sir."

"And tell Pippi to be waiting for us an hour after sunrise."

"Uh . . . I am unfamiliar with that measurement. How long is that in local time, sir?"

Tabor smiled at him. "You and Pippi will have all night to figure it out."

"Yes, sir. One something after sunrise."

"Good," said Tabor, opening the door. "We don't wish to be disturbed before then."

"Absolutely, sir!" said the innkeeper. Suddenly his complexion darkened several shades. "I mean, absolutely not, sir!" he shouted as he turned and ran back to his desk.

Shenoy followed Tabor into the room and shut the door behind them.

"What do you think?" asked the older man.

"I think the Old Ones and their artifacts had better be as valuable as you hope they are," replied Tabor grimly. "This expedition has already cost the life of your assistant Basil and we can only hope that Andrea survived whatever struck her down."

CHAPTER 20

"They should pay *us* to sleep on those goddamned beds!" growled Tabor as the sun hit him in the eyes through the shadeless window. "Hey, Rupert—get up."

"Who could sleep?" replied Shenoy, drying his face with what passed for a towel as he emerged from what passed for a bathroom.

"Got a question," said Tabor, who'd slept above the covers in his clothes, and began pulling on his boots. "The Old Ones were bright enough to master space travel, right?"

"Possibly not the way we do it—in ships and such," answered Shenoy. "But yes."

"And they mastered magic?"

"I think that yes, they did."

"So one could say that they were reasonably bright?" persisted Tabor.

"Definitely."

"Then what the hell did they come to Cornwallis for?" said Tabor. "Or, having come, why didn't they turn right around and leave?"

"That's what we've come to find out."

"Well, if and when you find them on this godforsaken dirtball, I've got some questions of my own to ask them."

"Finish your ablutions and let's be on our way," said Shenoy. "I'm anxious to see what's out there."

"More anxious than I am to wash in the brown gritty stuff that passes for water in our sink," said Tabor, walking to the door. "Let's go."

They walked back to the main room, where the same Paskapan was at the desk.

"Don't you ever sleep?" asked Shenoy.

"Not on *these* beds," answered the innkeeper with a look of distaste. "I'll sleep when I go home at midday."

"First intelligent thing I've heard since we landed," muttered Tabor.

Pippibwali was waiting for them just outside the building, which Tabor refused to think of as a hotel.

"I trust you slept well," he said.

Tabor merely glared at him.

"As well as could be expected," replied Shenoy. "And now we're ready to proceed with our mission. You'll want the coordinates of our destination, of course."

"Of course," agreed Pippibwali.

Shenoy rattled them off to him.

"That's eight hundred and fifty *qubisks* from here," said Pippibwali. "We'll need to rent or purchase transportation."

"Get a translation first," said Tabor. "On *this* world, a *qubisk* is as likely to be a meter or even an inch as a mile."

"I heard that," said Pippibwali.

"I wasn't trying to hide it from you."

"A *qubisk* is one-point-zero-three-seven-nine-four kilometers," said the Paskapan. "Approximately."

"Approximately?" said Tabor, frowning.

"Give or take," answered Pippibwali.

"How do you suggest we get there?"

"We shall rent a skimmer."

"Which is?" persisted Tabor.

"An airborne vehicle which skims approximately a meter above the surface, making for a very smooth ride." He offered the Paskapan version of a smile. "I have anticipated your need and have reserved one for our use."

"How much?" said Tabor suspiciously.

"Just one. We'll all fit on it."

"I said how much, not how many?"

"Ah!" replied Pippibwali. "I have even had them translate the price into your primitive and confusing economic system. It will come to four thousand eight hundred and twelve credits." Then he added: "Each way."

"I think not," said Tabor before Shenoy could reply.

"You'd prefer to walk?"

"Certainly not," said Tabor.

"Then what—?"

"You will carry us for two thousand, four hundred and six credits each. Both ways."

"That's out of the question! I am only flesh and blood!" Pippi paused. "And muscle, and green blood cells, and enamel on my teeth, and—"

"Okay, if you can't accommodate us, you can't accommodate us," said Tabor.

"Good," said Pippi, relaxing. "I'm glad *that's* over."

"It certainly is," said Tabor. "You're fired. Where do we get another guide?"

"Uh . . . let's not be hasty, good sirs," said Pippi quickly.

"I'm not being hasty," said Tabor. "I've thought about it all night, and I knew that if you charged us an exorbitant amount and then refused to carry us, I'd have to replace you." He smiled. "I hope this won't leave too big a blot on your record."

"Let me speak to the sled owner," said Pippi. "The nerve of that scum, charging so much for a little two-hour trip! I'll talk him down to an acceptable price, you can be sure of that!"

"I already am," said Tabor. "Sure of that, I mean."

The Paskapan stalked off to the center of the town and returned five minutes later.

"It's all settled," he announced. "One thousand credits each way." He held out his hand. "Payable now."

Tabor shook his head. "Payable when we return. What if he only gave us enough fuel to get there? What if you plan to take the sled back and leave us stranded there?"

"Me?" said Pippi in shocked tones. "You cut me to the . . . well, to whatever people cut other people to. I am shocked that you should think such a thing!"

"Surprised, anyway, I'll wager," said Tabor. "Now get the sled and let's be on our way."

Pippi seemed about say something, thought better of it, and stalked off. He was back shortly, sitting aboard an open sled that hovered perhaps thirty inches above the ground.

"Ready to go," he announced. "All aboard." Then: "I

actually don't know what it means, but the last humans to ride on one of these said that and it sounded vigorous and positive."

"We'll get aboard," said Tabor, slinging their luggage onto the back of it, "but lower it to ground level so my friend doesn't have to climb up onto it."

The sled lowered, Tabor helped Shenoy on, then got on himself.

"Has this thing got protective shields to protect us from the wind?" asked Shenoy.

"Certainly."

"I'd like to get there as fast as we can, without the wind blinding me," continued Shenoy. "Put them up, please."

"Or we may have to deduct fifty percent of the price for our discomfort," added Tabor.

"Done," said Pippi, hitting a control and raising the shields. He turned to Tabor. "I don't like you very much."

"Well, darn," said Tabor. "I'll just have to live with it."

They rode in silence for the next ninety minutes. Shenoy spent the time studying his notes on his pocket computer, while Tabor watched the totally uninteresting, even banal, landscape and wondered why the hell anyone, god or man, would want to spend one minute on this world.

There was a village perhaps every fifty miles, almost no traffic between villages, no lakes or oceans, mountains or valleys, splashes of color or repositories of wildlife.

Tabor closed his eyes to rest them, and was suddenly being shaken awake by Shenoy.

"What is it?" he asked.

"You fell asleep for more than an hour. We're almost there."

Tabor looked out and saw they were approaching a city that was every bit as nondescript as the one they had left in the morning.

"This is the place?" he said.

"Almost," replied Pippi.

"Let me guess," said Tabor. "We have to land here and get permission—let me amend that: *buy* permission—to go to the location my friend needs to see."

"I do believe you're starting to adjust to our economic system," said Pippi.

"Let me ask a question," said Tabor. "Does your world even *have* an economy that doesn't involve fleecing visitors?"

"Fleecing?" repeated Pippi with an amused smile. "You don't even have any fleece."

"My mistake," said Tabor with a heavy layer of sardonicism that was lost on the Paskapan. "Well, let's see whoever we have to see and get it over with."

They landed in the middle of the city—a small town or large village, actually—and Pippi led them to the largest building. They entered, walked past a number of Paskapans seated at desks working on primitive computers, and finally came to a small office. The door slid into a wall, allowing them to enter, and they found themselves standing before a long table, behind which sat five Paskapans. One was much shorter and more angular than the others, and of a somewhat richer color, and Tabor assumed he'd met his first female of the species. Always, he added mentally, assuming it possessed two or more sexes.

"Yes?" said the one seated in the middle.

"These immigrants wish—" began Pippi.

"We are *not* immigrants," interrupted Tabor.

"You're certainly not natives," said the Paskapan.

"We are scientists, here to study the ruins of the city of Malthos," said Shenoy.

"Never heard of it," said the Paskapan.

"You wouldn't have," replied Shenoy. "It was created millennia ago, and was not native to your world."

"Ah, the ancient city in the desert to the east of us!" said another Paskapan.

"And you really think there's something of interest out there?" said the first Paskapan.

"I think there may be," answered Shenoy.

"And of value?"

"Value is a very elastic word," interjected Tabor when he saw their faces alight with sudden interest. "What may be valuable to a starving person may be all but valueless to one who's just eaten."

"Even the sated person must eventually eat again," said the first Paskapan. "This is most interesting."

"Anyway," concluded Shenoy, "we seek your permission to examine the grounds and the buildings."

"The buildings?" said a third Paskapan.

Shenoy nodded. "Indeed, I need to examine everything."

"Well, we might as well get started. Bakkamidi here"—he indicated the small, angular Paskapan—"will give you the necessary forms to fill out for exploring the area. Then, when you've completed those—it shouldn't take more than a day—you'll require all the essential permission slips for whatever else you think you might wish to do when you reach the site. And of course you'll need both an immigrant's and an explorer's license for your vehicle, and . . . "

He droned on for another ten minutes, and since there was nothing to do but comply with the rules and regulations, Shenoy spent the next three days filling out forms while Tabor spent the time pulling every trick and threat he could think of to lower the exorbitant fees.

Finally, on the morning of their fourth day in the area, they climbed aboard the sled. Pippibwali wasn't licensed to pilot it in this jurisdiction, and instead Bakkamidi sat at the controls. They sped across the landscape for about fifteen minutes and then landed next to what appeared to be a brand new village made of angular quartz walls and roofs.

"We're in the wrong place," said Shenoy, walking slowly around one of the buildings..

"This is the exact location you asked for," said Bakkamidi.

"But this village can't be twenty years old!" protested Shenoy.

"Fourteen," she corrected him.

"But I'm looking for an ancient town filled with alien artifacts!"

"I know."

"Then why did you take us here?"

"These are the coordinates you gave us," replied Bakkamidi.

"But . . . but you've torn everything down and built over it. That's . . . that's . . ."

He was about to say "sacrilege," but Bakkamidi merely smiled and said, "Yes, that's progress."

"That's *outrageous!*" yelled Shenoy. "You've destroyed

something more important than your whole insignificant world! What a bunch of total idiots!"

He kept screaming, and suddenly he found himself surrounded by half a dozen uniformed Paskapans, each with a glowing tag hanging around their necks that Tabor assumed marked them as police.

"What's the trouble?" asked one of them.

"He seems to be having an emotional episode," replied Bakkamidi. "Calm him down."

"Certainly."

Tabor quickly saw that their notion of calming someone down was pretty much the same as his notion of beating the crap out of him. They came after Shenoy with clubs and something that looked like the Paskapan equivalent of brass knuckles.

The first to reach Shenoy cracked him alongside the head, and blood spurted out, almost blinding the scientist.

"That's enough!" said Tabor ominously.

When the policeman began swinging the club again, Tabor blocked him and shoved him aside, then decked the two Paskapans who tried to intervene. He reached back for the club swinger and spun him around until they were facing each other.

"Don't you know that hurts?" he growled, throwing a punch that knocked the Paskapan down and out. He turned to Shenoy. "Are you okay, Rupert?"

Shenoy stared at him, eyes wide open, peering through the stream of blood coming down from his forehead. "Duck, Russ!" he yelled.

That was the last thing Tabor heard before he collapsed onto the ground.

CHAPTER 21

❊

Tabor opened his eyes, spent a moment focusing them, and found that he was lying on a stone floor, facing an open doorway. He placed a hand to his head to assess the damage, winced at the touch, and frowned, trying to remember exactly what had happened.

"Damn!" he muttered. "You're always nailed by the one you didn't see."

He got carefully to his feet, stared out the doorway at a long corridor with numerous open doors lining it, and prepared to leave the cold stone room in which he found himself.

"I wouldn't do that," said a harsh voice from behind him.

He turned and found himself facing a very large and heavily muscled creature. Its overall appearance was vaguely reptilian, but that was mostly due to the scaly, armored, crocodilian hide. The creature's face wasn't the least bit like that of a reptile's. It was quite flat, with no sign of a nose at all. Four bulging orange eyes rested above a gaping maw which had insectlike mandibles instead of jaws. What looked like a rasping tongue covered with spines substituted for teeth.

The monster was a quadruped as far as locomotion was concerned, but had six tentacles emerging from the shoulder area. Four of them were supple and ended in a delicate trifurcation, suited for complex manipulations. To make up for it, the remaining pair of tentacles were thick and ended in flat palps covered with brutal-looking hooks. Those were clearly designed for grappling and rending.

In short, it boasted the worst features of a pocket dinosaur, a giant praying mantis and a walking squid combined in one package. Its epidermis was mottled, the colors best described as jaundice-yellow, puke-green and disemboweled-entrails-pinkish-red. A sensitive enough interior decorator would probably drop dead just at the sight of the creature.

"Who the hell are you?" demanded Tabor.

"A fellow prisoner," was the reply. Tabor now spotted something that looked like gills just above the tentacle ring, from which the voice emerged. But these organs were apparently designed for speech rather than breathing. Or maybe they could do both, if the monster was submerged.

"What prison?" said Tabor. "We're in some room somewhere, and I'm about to walk out."

The creature picked up a plate that had once held its breakfast and tossed it through the open doorway. There was a crackling sound and a flash of light, and the plate totally vanished.

"Iron bars do not a prison make," said the creature. It

gaped its mandibles wide, which Tabor interpreted as its way of grinning. "I heard that somewhere."

"So we're in prison?"

It made no reply, but the quasi-grin became even wider.

"You're a Vitunpelay, aren't you?" continued Tabor. "I've seen images but never met one of you in person."

"I am indeed a Vitunpelay."

Tabor extended his hand. "I'm a Human. My name's Russ Tabor."

"Rusty Bore?" repeated the Vitunpelay. He gazed at Tabor's outstretched hand but made no move toward it. "I like you already!"

Tabor decided not to correct him. He withdrew his hand, just as glad the huge alien hadn't touched it. "You got a name?"

"Certainly," came the reply. "What day of the week is it—any kind of week you prefer to use?"

"Tuesday."

"And the month?"

"I think it's November on Earth," said Tabor. "It's Sixth Month on my home world, and who the hell knows what it is on this dirtball?"

"Splendid!" enthused the creature. "My name is Jaemu."

Tabor stared at his curiously. "Why is that splendid?"

"Who wants to go through life with just one name?" answered Jaemu. "If you didn't have names for the months of your year, I couldn't change mine every month, and that would have left me with just the merest handful of names."

"So Jaemu is just one of your names?"

"One of my two hundred favorites."

"Does it mean anything in your native language?"

"Shameless Footkisser Who Betrays His Friends," answered Jaemu.

"And you're pleased with that?"

"Certainly. It is unique among my acquaintances."

Tabor stared at him for a long moment. "You are a very strange critter from a very strange race."

"Perhaps," agreed Jaemu. "But *I* wasn't preparing to walk through a force field that could reduce me to dust in a microsecond."

"You got a point," admitted Tabor.

"What are you doing in here?" asked Jaemu.

"Waiting for my friend to make my bail, I suppose."

"I mean, *why* were you incarcerated?"

"I slugged a few policemen," answered Tabor.

Jaemu frowned.

"Murder, huh?"

"Just disorderly conduct, I should think."

"You didn't kill them?" said Jaemu, surprised.

"No, of course not."

"Why not?"

Tabor stared at him, and decided that he was even more alien than he looked. "I'm almost afraid to ask what you did?"

"Oh, something exceptionally trivial," answered Jaemu.

"Trivial?" repeated Tabor.

The Vitunpelay shook his head. "Yes. And once the survivors get out of the hospital, I'm sure the insurance policies on the others will pay for their artificial limbs and keep them in comfort for the remainder of their lives."

Tabor stared at Jaemu for a long moment. "Fucking clown," he muttered.

"You see?" said Jaemu. "You don't have to be Jarkko Järvinen to call us that."

"How long have you been in here?"

"Eleven days," answered the Vitunpelay. "Or twenty-two exceptionally vile meals. Or half the life expectancy of that no-legged thing that is crawling alongside your foot."

Tabor looked down, saw a large worm or small snake opening its mouth to take a bite out of his toe, shoe and all, and stomped on it with his other foot.

"Well, half the life expectancy if he was eleven days old," continued Jaemu.

"Just out of curiosity," said Tabor, "what are you doing on Cornwallis IV?"

"Am I?"

"Are you what?"

"On Cornwallis IV?"

"Yes," said Tabor.

"How comforting to know," said Jaemu. "Anyway, I was invited to come here."

"By the government?" asked Tabor.

"Well, by *a* government."

"They have more than one here?"

"You are understanding me too fast," said Jaemu. "It was suggested I come here by the government of Batelliot VII." He paused thoughtfully. "And I'm pretty sure the government of Milago II was in full agreement."

"I take it you're not the most popular clown in the galaxy," said Tabor.

"Not even the second most popular, if truth be known," answered Jaemu. He paused thoughtfully. "What planet or planets were *you* thrown off of?"

"None."

"Really?" said Jaemu, surprised. "Then what are you doing here?"

"I told you," replied Tabor. "I slugged some police officers."

"I mean, what are you doing on this planet at all?"

"It may take a while to explain it fully," said Tabor. He looked around, then shrugged. "What the hell. It's not as if you're going anywhere."

And he explained as much as he understood about the magic of the Old Ones, about the origin of the terms Old Ones and Cthulhu, about his experiences on Cthulhu, and as much as he knew—which was minimal—about what he and Shenoy were doing on Cornwallis.

"Sounds crazy, doesn't it?" he said in conclusion.

"Certainly not," replied Jaemu.

"Oh?"

"Not crazy," said the Vitunpelay. "Just wrong."

Tabor stared intently at him. "Wrong in what way?"

"I know what your boss is looking for," said Jaemu, "and it's not on Cornwallis. But it *was* here, once upon a time, as the saying goes."

"Those goddamned bastards!" snapped Tabor.

"Oh, I *like* that!" said Jaemu.

Tabor frowned. "What are you talking about?"

"Goddamned Bastards!" enthused Jaemu. "In ways it's even better than Fucking Clowns!"

"Get back to the subject!" growled Tabor.

"My subject or yours?"

"The Old Ones' artifacts!"

"You needn't yell," said Jaemu. "I'm right here. Mostly."

"When did they destroy them?" persisted Tabor.

"When did who destroy what?" asked Jaemu, clearly confused.

"When did the Paskapans destroy the Old Ones' artifacts?"

"They did?" asked Jaemu. "When?"

It took all of Tabor's willpower not to take a swing at the Vitunpelay. "You just told me they did!"

Jaemu shook his head. "No, I told you that the artifacts aren't on Cornhole."

"Cornwallis, damn it!"

"Right," agreed Jaemu. "They aren't on Cornwallis Damn It."

"Then where the hell *are* they?" demanded Tabor.

"Oh, they're not in hell yet." A paused. "At least, it seems unlikely."

Tabor closed his eyes and forced himself to take ten deep breaths in succession. Then he turned to Jaemu again. "Do you know where the artifacts are right now? Answer yes or no."

"Seems silly, but all right: yes or no." Jaemu stared at Tabor. "Your face is becoming a bright red, did you know that?"

"Let's try it again," said Tabor. "Do you know where the artifacts have been moved to?"

"Yes, absolutely," said Jaemu.

"Are they on this world?"

"No."

Tabor exhaled deeply. "All right. Now, where are they?"

"I won't tell you," answered Jaemu. "But I'll *show* you." He smiled. "Get me out of here and I'll take you to them."

"It's a deal," said Tabor. "As soon as Rupert gets here I'll have him pay both our bails and we'll be on our way."

It sounded simple enough when Tabor said it, but it got considerably more complex when Shenoy showed up in another hour. He approached them, walking down the long corridor to their cell, accompanied by two uniformed Paskapans, and stopped at the doorway.

"No farther," warned one of the guards.

"Are you all right, Russell?" asked Shenoy.

"Yeah, except for a couple of bumps on my head and a slight hole in my pride. How about you?"

"I'm fine. But I had to drop all charges against them for assault and harassment and what-have-you in order to be able to see you."

"And here you are," said Tabor. "Pay my bail and get me the hell out of here. And this critter is Jamie."

"Jaemu," the Vitunpelay corrected him.

"Jaemu," said Tabor. "He's going to be very important to our mission, so pay his bail too. We can bill your employers for it."

"Important?" repeated Shenoy. "How?"

"He knows where the artifacts have been moved to, and is willing to lead us to them."

"Excellent!" said Shenoy enthusiastically. He turned to his guards. "All right, take me back to the magistrate."

They turned and accompanied him down the long corridor, turning to their right as they reached the end of it.

"That was your partner?" asked Jaemu.

"Why would I talk to him like that if he wasn't?" growled Tabor.

"I *like* you!" said Jaemu.

* * *

Shenoy was back ten minutes later, still accompanied by his two Paskapan guards.

"That was quick," said Tabor. "All taken care of?"

"I'm afraid not," replied Shenoy.

"Oh?"

"It seems your cellmate killed six Paskapans with his bare hands. Well, tentacles. He's awaiting execution in five days. No bail."

Tabor turned to Jaemu. "You didn't tell me that!" he said furiously.

"You didn't ask," replied Jaemu.

"I'm afraid that's not all," continued Shenoy.

"What else?"

"You roughed up a bunch of police officers. There's no bail for you, either."

"I'm stuck here?" demanded Tabor. "For how long?"

"I don't know," replied Shenoy. "I'm flying in a top lawyer. The problem is that it may take two or three months before the trial." He turned to Jaemu. "He'll represent you too, if you're still alive, though your case seems quite hopeless. Anyway, if you'll just tell me what

I need to know, I can begin my quest, and I assure you your name—once I learn it—will be prominently mentioned in all my notes and scientific papers."

"I thought I was supposed to be the only Vitunpelay here," said Jaemu.

"I beg your pardon?" said Shenoy, frowning.

"If I tell you what you want to know, you have no reason to pay your lawyer to defend me, no reason to pay any expenses required to get me out of here. I know what you need to know, but I'm not sharing it while I'm in jail."

"I hope you'll reconsider," said Shenoy. "But whether you do or do not, I simply cannot spend two or three or six months waiting for the pair of you."

"*Six* months?" bellowed Tabor.

"Who knows how long trials take on Cornwallis?" replied Shenoy. "You've already seen how much paperwork and bribery it takes just to get through the day here."

"And what exactly do you plan to do in the meantime?" demanded Tabor.

"I'm not quite sure," admitted Shenoy. "I intuit from what the two of you have implied that what we're looking for is not, or is no longer, on Cornwallis. I'll spend two days studying everything I can find in their library here in this godforsaken new village, and then I'll head off to the likeliest location, wherever that may be."

He turned and began walking back the way he had come, still accompanied by armed guards.

"He won't find it in the library, will he?" Tabor asked Jaemu.

"No," replied the Vitunpelay. "If there was anything useful to be found, it would have been found already."

"I was afraid of that," said Tabor. He grimaced. "Well, we've got two days."

"To do what?"

"Break out of here and join Shenoy before he takes off from this dirtball."

CHAPTER 22

✳

"So how do you plan to do it?" asked Jaemu.

"I've no idea," admitted Tabor. "Yet."

"I'd be happy to overpower any jailer who enters the cell, but no one's done so since I arrived here."

"There's always a way," replied Tabor, sitting down cross-legged and leaning his back against the wall. "Damn!" he said. "That's chilly."

"Aren't dungeons supposed to be wet and chilly, except maybe for the wet part?" asked the Vitunpelay.

"This isn't a dungeon," said Tabor. "It's a prison cell."

"How much difference can there be on a world like this?"

"Not much," admitted Tabor. He looked around. "How does the food arrive?"

"Poorly cooked and incompetently prepared," said Jaemu.

"I mean, how does it get into the cell?"

"Oh, a guard, or sometimes a pair of them, carries it up to the doorway on a tray."

"And then?"

"And then," continued Jaemu, "if there are two guards, one of them trains what looks like a sonic pistol on me and tells me to back up against the far wall. The other hits some kind of switch out there, slides the tray into the room, and hits the switch again. The whole process takes about six or seven seconds. Maybe ten if I move slowly."

"And how do they take it back?" asked Tabor. "Same way?"

"They never take it back."

"Then I don't understand," said Tabor. "Why haven't you got a growing pile of used dishes and trays?"

"Well, I suppose if I were any less fastidious, I'd certainly have such a pile," said the Vitunpelay.

"Explain."

"I just hurl the trays and dishes through the doorway when I'm done with them," answered Jaemu. "They're instantly disintegrated. Most efficient housecleaning service in the galaxy."

"You're not making this any easier," grumbled Tabor.

"My job is to escape and get rich and plunder the galaxy in ways it's never been plundered before. Making your escape easier isn't part of my job description."

"Helping you to leave here when I make my escape isn't part of mine," Tabor shot back.

"You'd really leave me behind?" asked Jaemu, genuinely surprised. "A sweet, friendly, good-natured person like myself?"

"A sweet, friendly, good-natured mass murderer," Tabor corrected him.

"I resent that!" snapped Jaemu.

"Oh?"

"Eleven doesn't constitute a mass."

Tabor stared at him. "You killed eleven Paskapans?"

"Certainly not!"

"Then—?"

"Only eight of them were Paskapans."

"Well, that makes all the difference," said Tabor sardonically.

The Vitunpelay smiled. "I knew you'd understand."

"Why didn't they just execute you on the spot? No jury's going to find you innocent."

"They don't have juries here," answered Jaemu.

"Then why?"

"I come from a wealthy family. I'm sure they'll offer to set me free for a few million credits or *crugmos*." An amused smile spread across his face. "Little do they know that my family has disowned me."

"Hardly surprising," commented Tabor.

"It was just a difference of opinion," continued Jaemu. "Nothing serious."

"Couldn't you patch it up?"

"Not really."

"For all that money, why not?" asked Tabor.

"Like I said, it was a difference of opinion," replied Jaemu. "They saw themselves alive, and I saw them dead."

Tabor stared at the burly Vitunpelay. "Just stay on your side of the cell."

"And now I've upset you," said Jaemu apologetically. "Maybe we should change the topic of conversation." He paused thoughtfully for a moment. "I could tell you twenty-seven separate and distinct sexual sins in which I have indulged." Suddenly he shook his head. "No, you'd only be able to understand eight of them. Nine at the most."

"Why don't we talk about escaping from here?" suggested Tabor.

"I thought you had it all solved."

"You thought wrong."

"Well, you'd better get busy," said Jaemu.

"*We* had better get busy," Tabor corrected him.

"Nonsense," said the Vitunpelay. "My contribution was telling you that you're looking for artifacts in the wrong place. Yours is getting us out of here."

"I wouldn't dream of asking you to lend your prodigious brain to the operation," said Tabor. "But I may need some of your muscle."

"Perhaps," said Jaemu.

"Perhaps?" repeated Tabor, frowning.

"Strike that," said Jaemu. "Enough negativity."

"So you'll lend your muscle?"

"Probably."

"Goddammit!" snapped Tabor. "I thought you were through with negativity!"

"I am."

"Well, then?"

"'Probably' is much more positive than 'perhaps.'"

Tabor stared at Jaemu for a long moment. "I'm surprised they let you live long enough to kill any of 'em," he remarked at last.

"I'm really a very pleasant, good-natured fellow for a murderer," replied the Vitunpelay. "I mean, here we are, thrown together by an unfeeling Fate into close, uncomfortable quarters, and we immediately strike up what figures to be a lifelong friendship, especially considering our life expectancies in this hellhole." He paused. "Know any exceptionally vile dirty jokes?"

"Just the one about the idiot Vitunpelay and the Man he pushed too far," answered Tabor.

"How does it end?"

"I don't know yet," said Tabor.

"Well, let's set our minds—your mind, anyway—to the task at hand. We're incarcerated, we're unarmed, we're kept in by an incredibly powerful force field, if we get out we're outnumbered hundreds to one, and we've got two days to break out and join your friend before he leaves without us." Jaemu paused. "Does that pretty much sum it up the situation?"

"Pretty much."

"I sure don't envy you, having to come up with a solution." He clacked his mandibles a couple of times. Tabor had no idea what the gesture—or was it an expression?—meant. "On the other hand, I don't envy either of us if you don't."

"Shut up," said Tabor.

"Ah!" said Jaemu enthusiastically. "You require silence while thinking."

Tabor shook his head. "No, I'm just sick of the sound of your voice."

"Is this any better?" asked Jaemu in a high contralto.

"Not really."

"Well, get to work. The sooner you break us out of here, the sooner you won't have to listen to any of my voices."

"I couldn't ask for any better encouragement than that," replied Tabor dryly.

Tabor got to his feet, and carefully paced off the cell, which was about eighteen feet on a side. The doorway was four feet wide and approximately seven feet high. The ceiling was ten feet above the floor. There wasn't a soft or pliable surface anywhere. In one corner was a hole in the floor, perhaps eighteen inches in circumference. He paused and looked down into it.

"I'll turn my back if you're shy," said Jaemu.

"It's a toilet?"

"Of course."

Tabor stared into the hole. "Where does it go?"

"Toilets don't go anywhere," said the Vitunpelay. "They just sit there."

"There's no odor and nothing seems to be moving," said Tabor.

"Why should there be?" responded Jaemu.

"I assume the waste doesn't get washed away?"

"No, it's just like the doorway. Drop anything down there, natural or artificial, and it's turned into its composite atoms in a fraction of a second."

Tabor sighed. "Too bad."

"You'd prefer the traditional toilet?" asked Jaemu, frowning.

"Of course," answered Tabor. "We could have saved all the dishes, glasses and trays from a couple of meals and clogged the damned thing, then fought our way out when they entered the cell to fix it."

Jaemu chuckled, a harsh atonal sound. "That presupposes they care whether our toilet is working or not."

"Well, it was a thought," said Tabor. He walked to a wall and sat down, leaning his back against it.

"So we're stuck here until they execute us or we die of old age," remarked Jaemu with a sigh.

"What the hell are you talking about?" snapped Tabor. "We still got forty-seven hours to go."

"I like your attitude," said Jaemu. "I hope you come up with something. I'd hate to kill and eat you."

"You eat men a lot, do you?"

"Never," admitted Jaemu. "But it would help dissipate the boredom."

"I wonder what a Vitunpelay tastes like," mused Tabor.

"Terrible," Jaemu assured him. "I have it on the best authority: we're tough, stringy, and filled with noxious acids. Take my word for it, a Vitunpelay is the very last thing you want to eat."

"Relax," said Tabor. "I wouldn't even consider it until tomorrow. Now shut up and let me think."

The Vitunpelay leaned back against the wall. A moment later he closed his eyes and began what passed for snoring in his race. And a moment after that he started leaning to his left. It looked like he would soon be sprawled on the floor when, still asleep, he reached up with one of the big tentacles, spread his palp, and pressed it against the wall. The palp spread out to twice its normal circumference, and he stopped sliding down the wall and remained motionless.

"*Son of a bitch!*" yelled Tabor.

"What?" said Jaemu groggily, sitting erect now. "What happened?"

"I know how we're getting out of here!" enthused Tabor.

"How?"

"Show me your feet."

The Vitunpelay unfolded his legs and stretched them out toward the man.

"Take off your footwear," said Tabor.

Jaemu made a wriggling motion with several of his small tentacles that Russ interpreted as a shrug, and started removing his boots—using the term "boots" loosely. The footwear looked more like covers for huge golf clubs than anything else.

The reason for the design became obvious once the Vitunpelay's feet were exposed. Jaemu had them clubbed when they first emerged, which must be the way he used them when he walked. But when he relaxed the feet, they spread out to form palps that were close analogs to the ones on his big tentacles.

"Good!" said Tabor after briefly studying them. "You've got little suction cups on all of your palps."

"So what?" asked Jaemu.

"So like I said, I know how we're escaping," said Tabor.

"Would you care to share that secret with me?"

"Can you reach the ceiling?"

"Certainly not," said Jaemu.

"I mean, if you jump."

"Yes," said Jaemu, jumping up and touching the ceiling.

"Very good," said Tabor.

"Nothing to it," relied the Vitunpelay with a shrug.

"Now do it and stick up there."

"I can't."

"I just saw you do it on the wall," said Tabor.

"I have to press against the surface for a few seconds to attach myself," explained Jaemu. "I can't do it if I'm jumping. Gravity and all that."

"Not a problem," said Tabor, getting on his hands and knees. "Use me as a stool."

The Vitunpelay stood atop him, reached up, and pressed his palps against the ceiling. "All right," he said after a few seconds.

"Good," said Tabor, rolling away and climbing to his feet. He stood, hands on hips, surveying Jaemu, whose feet dangled about twenty inches above the floor.

"I feel damned awkward," said Jaemu.

"But you're in no danger of coming loose?"

"None."

"Good. Now swing your feet up to the ceiling and grab hold of it the same way."

The Vitunpelay did as he was told.

Tabor shook his head. "No good. You're middle section is hanging down. I want you flat against the ceiling."

"Just a minute," said Jaemu. "Let me manipulate."

He released the suction cups on his right foot, then stretched it straight out, as flat against the ceiling as he could, and reattached it, then repeated the procedure with the other foot and leg.

Tabor walked over to the door, then turned and looked.

"Of course I can see you from here," he said, "but I'm

in the same open cell you are. The doorway's only about seven feet high, and if you take up this position exactly over it, rather than across the cell from it . . ." He nodded his head. "It just might work. If you're missing, someone's *got* to come in to see where you went to."

"There might be two of them," noted Jaemu, loosening his feet and letting them hang down, then releasing his fingers and dropping lightly to the floor.

"Let's assume it's one," said Tabor. "Or if there are two, then seeing you here where you belong will be so shocking that they both enter."

"And if two show up and only one enters?" asked Jaemu.

"Then I'll have to think of something else," replied Tabor.

CHAPTER 23

An hour passed, then another.

"How many times a day do they feed you?" asked Tabor.

"Sometimes two, sometimes three. It depends."

"On what?"

"On whatever idle thought wanders through the minds of the Paskapan jailers, I imagine. There's never been any logic I could see to it."

"Okay," said Tabor. "When they come the next time, just sit here in plain sight."

"I thought we were planning an escape," complained the Vitunpelay.

"We are," answered Tabor. "But I want to see them performing their duties once. When do they stand? Do they ever look up? Do either approach with their weapons in their hands?"

The Vitunpelay was about to reply when they both heard the sound of their jailers approaching. One was pushing a cart on which sat two dishes filled with some of the most unappetizing food Tabor had ever seen, plus what seemed to be a solid green pitcher of water. It was only when they got closer that Tabor was able to see that the pitcher itself was transparent and the liquid inside it was green.

"Hungry?" asked one of the guards as they came to a stop just beyond the door.

"No," replied Tabor, touching his chest with his thumb. "Tabor."

"Idiot!" muttered the guard.

"No, that's him," answered Tabor, jerking a thumb in Jaemu's direction.

The guard glared at him and uttered what Tabor took to be an obscenity in Paskapan.

"Back," said the guard.

Tabor and Jaemu moved to the farthest corner of the small cell. The second guard touched a button or control they couldn't see, and the first one leaned down, placed the tray on the floor, pushed it into the cell with his foot, then reached in and set the pitcher down next to it. He straightened up and took a step back, and Tabor knew that the force field was operative again.

"Next time remember the ketchup," said Tabor as the two guards began walking away.

"You know," said Jaemu, "you don't *look* exceptionally stupid, although I'm not familiar enough with your species to tell."

"A high compliment indeed," replied Tabor, staring at the food but feeling no need to approach it.

"So why did you go out of your way to offend them?" continued Jaemu.

"Because I want them mad at me."

The Vitunpelay stared long and hard at him. "Why?" he asked at last.

"You're going to be clinging to the ceiling right above the doorway," explained Tabor. "I don't want him looking there until he's gone past it and you're behind him. If I'm at the back of the cell, and he knows he's got to enter to see what happened to you, he might as well feel an urge to beat the crap out of me while he's at it. Otherwise, he might just stand in the doorway, and we don't want to give him a chance to back out of here."

"Ah!" exclaimed Jaemu. "Of course I knew that all along, but I'm delighted to see that you didn't just stumble on it but thought it out step by step."

"I don't think I can stand any more praise. Go eat the food."

"Half of it's yours."

"The second half. I want to see how sick it makes you—especially that green stuff—before I try it."

"I don't want any," replied Jaemu. "I had a little bit yesterday morning. That will hold me."

"That bad, huh?"

"I've had better," replied the Vitunpelay. "In fact, I cannot recall having had worse."

"We might just as well put it to some use," remarked Tabor, finally walking over to the tray. He picked up a handful of food and hurled it toward the upper left-hand corner of the doorway. It vanished immediately.

"No buzz, no zap, no flashing of lights," he said. "Okay, I know what it's *not* powered by. Now let's see how thorough it is."

He threw bits and pieces of the meal toward the doorway. None got through. Then he began pushing the plain metal tray with the toe of his boot until the far edge of it was in the doorway. An inch of it vanished, and he immediately picked up the remaining tray and ran his fingers across the new edge.

"Not even warm," he said.

"Did you expect it to be?" asked Jaemu.

"Not really."

"What difference does it make?"

"Probably none, but it's always best to know what you're up against." He stood, hands on hips, facing the corridor on the other side of the doorway. "Where do you suppose that leads?"

"To freedom, obviously," said Jaemu.

"But to what kind?"

Jaemu looked puzzled. "How many freedoms are there?"

"There's the hard-won freedom and the surreptitiously obtained freedom, for starters. Does the corridor lead to the outside, or a guardhouse, or a police office, or possibly even a courtroom?"

"Let's get out of here first and then worry about it," suggested Jaemu.

"Let's have a plan for every eventuality," replied Tabor.

Jaemu stared at him. "I don't understand it," he said.

"What don't you understand?"

"I am arrested and incarcerated all the time, and I never consider every possibility awaiting me if and when I escape. But you . . . you plan the escape, you plan for every possibility, I'll bet you've even planned how to find your friend and escape from the planet—and yet I'll bet this almost never happens to you."

"I'm just a naïve beginner," answered Tabor, "so I have to try to be prepared for anything. Unlike you, who has doubtless experienced just about everything that can happen when you're breaking out of jail on an alien planet."

"When you put it that way," said Jaemu, "I suppose you do have a point."

"Okay," said Tabor, sitting down cross-legged and leaning back against a wall. "I figure they'll be back with dinner—or whatever the hell meal it is—in maybe four or five hours."

"And then we escape!" enthused Jaemu.

Tabor shook his head. "Two meals from now. Probably."

"Why not the next one?" demanded the Vitunpelay.

"There were two guards. Let them see that there's no food left, and of course you've been throwing yours into the force field for more than a day now, and once they know that I'm not leaving any leftovers either, they should go back to one guard—assuming what you told me was accurate. And believe me, it'll be a lot easier to subdue one armed guard who doesn't know what he's walking into than two of them."

Jaemu uttered an alien growl. "I just hate it when you're right."

❖ ❖ ❖

As Tabor had predicted, their next meal was brought by two armed guards.

When he felt the meal after that would be arriving within an hour, Tabor had the Vitunpelay take up his position on the ceiling, just behind the doorway.

"How long are you good for?" he asked.

"Oh, thirty or forty more years, at least if some authority doesn't shoot me down somewhere along the way."

"I mean, how long can you stay stuck to the ceiling?"

"Quite a while," answered Jaemu. "Long enough for what we need."

"And how quickly can you drop to the floor?"

"You mean on top of a guard?"

"No, I mean if I see we guessed wrong and they send two guards again."

"They'll see you're alone and know something's wrong," said Jaemu.

"Not necessarily," answered Tabor. "Stand over there." He pointed to a section of the wall just to the left of the doorway.

Jaemu walked over.

"It'll work," said Tabor. "They'd have to be just a couple of steps from the doorway to see you there, so if you can lower yourself from the spot right above your head if I tell you there are two guards, you'll have fifteen seconds to do it."

Jaemu stared at him. "Do you teach college in your spare time?"

"That's my associate," replied Tabor. "He's the genius."

"Makes me wonder why your race hasn't conquered the galaxy," said the Vitunpelay.

"We damned near have," said Tabor. He got back

down on his hands and knees. "Now take your position on the ceiling."

Jaemu clambered onto him, extended his tentacles, opened the palps, and pressed them against the ceiling. In a short while he had solid contact, and Russ felt his great weight easing off him. Jaemu began to maneuver his legs and within a minute he was stretched flat against the ceiling.

By then, Tabor was back on his feet. "Okay, enjoy yourself," he said. "I'll keep an eye out for our friend."

"Don't leave it behind in the excitement," said Jaemu. "You may need it again."

"Figure of speech," replied Tabor.

He walked to the back wall, sat down, and watched the corridor. Just when he was half-convinced that there wouldn't be another meal that night, he heard footsteps, and an instant later a solitary Paskapan guard approached the cell, pushing a cart that contained another tray and pitcher. When he was a few feet away his nostrils and ears began twitching, as if he were seeking any scent or sound that could convince him not to believe his eyes.

"Did that idiot try to walk out of here?" he demanded.

"Absolutely not," said Tabor.

"Then where the hell is he?"

"He told me he'd discovered a secret way out of here, and that he'd come back for me once he knew it was still operative. Then he told me to check and make sure you weren't coming, I did as he instructed me, and when I turned to tell him that no one was in the corridor he was gone."

"Nonsense," said the guard. "You threw him into the

force field and are making up this story so I'll enter the cell."

"Fine," said Tabor with a shrug. "Don't enter. Go away. There's no secret exit, no false wall, nothing like that. Just go away and leave me alone."

The guard's eyes narrowed. "You'd like that, wouldn't you?" He pulled out his sonic pistol, reached up, and killed the force field. "I'm coming in to see for myself," he said. "You take one step toward me, just one step, and you're dead."

"I wouldn't dream of it," said Tabor.

The guard entered the cell and an instant later was standing directly beneath the Vitunpelay.

Jaemu landed full force on top of the guard, who grunted in surprise and fell forward on his face. Jaemu seized his head and with a powerful twist of his tentacles broke the guard's neck.

"You didn't have to do that," said Tabor angrily. "He was already unconscious. Now we're cop-killers, and the whole damned force is going to be after us."

"Were you planning on remaining on the planet?'"

"Of course not."

"Then what difference does it make?"

Tabor stared at the Vitunpelay. "You are a very strange critter. Now give me the pistol, since you can't use it anyway with those tentacles, and follow me."

Jaemu handed over the weapon and fell into step behind Tabor as he walked to the end of the corridor and followed it as it took a hard right. They walked another sixty feet, then came to two doors on the right, each with a native inscription on it.

"Do you read Paskapan?" he asked.

"Why would I?" responded Jaemu.

"Beats the hell out of me," said Tabor. "Maybe because you were on the goddamned planet." He stared at the two doors. "What the hell, we can't stand here all night." He opened the nearest one.

A large rectangular room spread out before him. A number of strange scents, most of them organic, some of them quite foul, assaulted his nostrils. He saw a trio of metal cabinets, opened one, and was greeted by a blast of frigid air.

"Seems like a kitchen, or at least a helluva pantry," he whispered. "Could be worse. See if there's any way out of here beside the door."

A moment later Jaemu stumbled upon a tiny control, and a section of the back wall slid aside, revealing the Paskapan equivalent of a parking lot.

"This is obviously where they unload the food," said Tabor. "That means if we go out this way, we ought to find ourselves on a road pretty soon. At any rate, it doesn't figure to be guarded the way the area around the cells must be."

He walked to the open area, stepped outside, waited to make sure he hadn't set off any alarms, and motioned Jaemu to follow him.

When they were about fifty feet away, and in clear sight of a road, Tabor looked back.

"Seems a shame we can't close the damned thing," he said. "Now they'll know how we got out."

"So what?" asked the Vitunpelay. "Were you planning on being incarcerated there again?"

"Only if you annoy me beyond endurance," replied

Tabor. "Fifty-fifty chance." He turned back to the road. "All right, we can't stand here all night. Let's get going."

"Where to?"

"This world's equivalent of the Tudor Arms."

"I don't understand."

"Right there," said Tabor, pointing to a run-down hostelry about half a mile distant. "That's where Shenoy is staying."

"Shenoy?"

"You met him briefly."

"He is the genius?"

"Sometimes he hides it well, but yeah," responded Tabor.

They stuck to the shadows, made it to the shabby little building in five minutes, and were just about to enter when Shenoy walked out the front door.

"Well, I'll be damned!" he exclaimed when he recognized Tabor. "What are you doing here?"

"I'll tell you all about it, but let's go to your room first. We're currently fugitives."

Shenoy shook his head. "I've checked out."

"Was something wrong?"

"No," said Shenoy. "But I've sent for your lawyer, I've filed a protest with the government, I've done everything I can do for you, and I can't see any use sitting around for months or possibly even years until your case is disposed of. So I'm off to the desert to hunt for"—he suddenly became aware that Jaemu was listening intently—"the Secret."

"You don't have to be vague," said Tabor. "He knows what we're looking for."

"I also know that you can go anywhere on the planet you want," added Jaemu, "but you're not going to find what you're looking for."

"And you know where it is?" demanded Shenoy.

"I most certainly do," said the Vitunpelay.

"Well?"

"I'm afraid I was a little . . . *impetuous* . . . when we were taking our leave of the jail," replied Jaemu. "You may not know it, but you want to leave the world to find your Old Ones' artifacts. I want to leave it to avoid another unpleasant encounter with the local authorities." He clacked his mandibles. "Do you see what I am suggesting?"

"All right!" shouted Shenoy. "You're hired! Now where is what I'm looking for?"

"On a moon in the home system of the Mank Empire," answered Jaemu.

"Well, that's that," said Tabor.

"Yes!" said Shenoy excitedly. "Very well done, Russell my boy!"

Tabor stared at him with a puzzled expression. "What the hell are you jumping for joy about, Rupert? We're going home. It's over."

Shenoy frowned. "What are *you* talking about? We know where to look now!"

"Rupert," said Tabor, as if speaking to a child, "the Mank Empire is a goddamned military stronghold."

"All the more reason to go," said Shenoy.

Tabor frowned. "What part of what I just said don't you understand?"

"They're a hostile and aggressive empire, right?" said Shenoy.

"Right."

"That's all the more reason to continue our mission."

"You want to explain that, please?" said Tabor.

"I don't know what the secret of the Old Ones is," replied Shenoy. "I don't know if it's magic, or science, or some combination of the two, or even some new technological concept that is entirely unknown to the civilized races of the galaxy. But whatever it is, we've got to learn the Old Ones' secret before the Manks find it and unlock it!"

"Just you and me?" said Tabor disbelievingly.

"And him," said Shenoy, jerking a thumb in Jaemu's direction.

"Why would he come?" asked Tabor.

"I'll be happy to come," interjected Jaemu, "as long as we leave immediately." He turned to Shenoy. "My companion seems to have forgotten that we're escaped felons."

"We'd better get to the ship," said Shenoy.

"Right," said Jaemu. "We'll discuss my fee later."

"Your fee?"

"I'm the one who knows where to find what you're looking for."

"So what do you want for your services?"

"Half," said Jaemu.

"Half the Old Ones' artifacts and secrets?" demanded Shenoy. "That's outrageous!"

"Okay, you don't want half, so be it," said the Vitunpelay. He paused for a moment. "I'll take sixty percent."

"Out of the question!" growled Shenoy.

"Up to you."

"May I make a counter-offer?" said Tabor.

"Go ahead," said Shenoy disgustedly.

"We'll be happy to give you sixty percent," began Tabor.

"Deal!" said Jaemu.

"But we're going to charge you fifty percent for your passage to and from the Mank home planet."

"To quote your employer, out of the question!" said Jaemu.

"Fine," said Tabor with a shrug. "We'll find someone on the planet who can help us. Have fun dealing with the posse, which figures to be along any minute now." He turned to Shenoy. "Let's go."

"Just a minute!" said Jaemu urgently.

"Yes?"

"I've reconsidered your offer."

Tabor smiled. "I thought you might."

"But for ten percent I'm just a guide. Murder, mayhem, and revolution cost more."

"We'll take that under advisement," said Tabor.

"Of course," continued the Vitunpelay, "if you could supply me with some weaponry before we land I might under the proper circumstances add mayhem . . . "

"We'll consider it," said Tabor.

"If you're all through with your high-level negotiations," interjected Shenoy nervously, "can we please be going? I see a lot of activity over at the jail."

Tabor nodded, gestured Jaemu to follow him, and fell into step behind Shenoy, who led them through unlit streets and back alleys to the spaceport. Two hundred credits caused the guard to look the other way, and a moment later they were aloft and streaking for the stratosphere.

"What have we got to eat?" asked Jaemu.

"Nothing a Vitunpelay would like," replied Tabor.

"Any kind of dead flesh will do," said Jaemu. "I stopped being fussy eight or nine incarcerations ago."

Tabor shrugged. "There's the galley," he said, pointing.

Jaemu walked over to it, and Tabor sat down in the copilot's chair.

"Was it rough?" asked Shenoy.

"I was only there for a day," replied Tabor.

"I've read about alien jails."

"That's probably a level or two better than experiencing them," said Tabor.

"They didn't beat you?"

"I'm sorry to disappoint you, but you could make an incredibly boring ten-minute holo about it."

"I didn't mean to intrude," said Shenoy.

"There's nothing to intrude on. They locked us up, we sat there for a day, and we escaped."

"But—"

Tabor smiled. "You've been reading too many cheap adventure stories."

Shenoy sighed. "I'm a scientist. I spend most of my time with computers, and the rest of it finding and examining things that most people would walk right past. I've led a . . ."

"If you say 'cloistered,' I may laugh," said Tabor.

"An uneventful life."

"You won the damned Sagittarius Prize," replied Tabor. "I'd call *that* an event. And then you did it again."

"But you lead such an exciting life!" said Shenoy.

"Well, cheer up," said Tabor. "If half of what I've heard about the Mank Empire is true, we're about to experience a little more excitement than any sane man"—he glanced at Jaemu—"or crazy Vitunpelay wants to handle."

CHAPTER 24

✸

"Get us out of here!" shrieked Rammadrecula. The swarm of huge insects was now very close.

Ju'ula's eyes popped open again. "What does she think I am? A chauffeur?"

Occo ignored everything except the problem immediately at hand. "How do I wake up the Teleplaser?"

"Skerkie? Don't worry about him. Dumber than a crate of rocks, but he's conscientious."

As if that were the cue, the Teleplaser suddenly came to life. As Occo had seen it do before, the Teleplaser unfolded rapidly into a derrick-like structure whose many extensions sprouted weapons.

Not the same weapons, though. These were more like flat grids with a meshed structure.

"GALLING APPROPINQUATION!" the Teleplaser boomed. "REBARBATIVE INSULT! OBLOQUY IMPENDS!"

The grids began flying about with unerring precision, swatting away the oncoming insects. The blows were powerful enough to shatter the monstrosities and turn them into disassembled pieces of . . .

Something. It didn't look like protoplasm or body parts, though. More like shards of dull metal or perhaps plastic now hurled into the oblivion of deep space.

"Go, Skerkie, go!" cried Bresk.

"That is still irregular!" complained Proceeds-With-Circumspection. Dutiful as always, however, the Ebbo recorded the proceedings in its tablet.

Rammadrecula finally broke off with her pointless screeching and tried to do something useful. She scrabbled at a pouch around her midsection and drew forth a weapon. Then, began firing at the still-distant gigantic figure of Yuyu the Unfortunate.

Which was pointless. The weapon was a match-grade target pistol, shooting unbihexium rounds. Fired in empty space, the projectiles could theoretically reach their target before their half-life expired—except Occo was pretty sure they were being deflected by the transition from the atmospheric shell that somehow surrounded them into the vacuum beyond. In any event, given the relative masses involved, this was like tossing pebbles at a behemoth. Even if they hit they wouldn't do any significant damage.

Occo was doubtful if even the Teleplaser could damage the monstrous godling. No, their only hope was escape. And that meant providing Ju'ula with a different image. Perhaps . . .

Yes . . . adjusting for scale . . .

She brought to mind the memory of a noxious amphibian she'd once encountered on one of the moons of Kladda Kta.

Rammadrecula started screeching again. The great tongue of Yuyu the Unfortunate was lashing out toward them, looking like the approach of a fleshy tidal wave. Nothing could possibly withstand—

❦ ❦ ❦

The noxious little amphibian just had time to look up before the conveyance the Warlock Variation Drive had become landed on top of it and drove its now-jellied flesh into the swampy muck—

—thereby awakening the ravenous vegetation below the scummy surface which Occo had forgotten about in the press of the moment. Palps of monstrous size, shape and stench sprang up all around the lip of their peculiar vessel, waving about as if they were the tongues of a multitude of giant amphibians.

Finally, Rammadrecula's weapon came into its own. Say what you would about the eccentric heterochthonatrix, her marksmanship was excellent. One palp after another was torn to pieces.

"I cannot properly record the shots!" cried Proceeds-With-Circumspection. "The records will be highly inaccurate!"

These words of dismay jogged Occo's memory. She now recalled that the swamp vegetation on this planet— what was it called? Flaod? Floud? Something like that—was actually comprised of a single organism about the size—

Their vessel heaved upward as if it were being lifted by a muddy volcano.

—of Yuyu the Unfortunate.

❦ ❦ ❦

Happily, thoughts of muddy volcanos brought to mind the great spas on Wulk Tressor, where Occo and her husbands had once spent a pleasant vacation. In a moment, the gigantic vegetation vanished, replaced by a soothing landscape of softly bubbling ooze.

❧ ❧ ❧

Sadly, her memories had been skewed by nostalgia. She'd forgotten that the ooze of Wulk Tressor, as balmy and relaxing as it might be, also produced deadly fumes which required the use of breathing apparatus—which, on this occasion, were completely lacking.

Rammadrecula tried to screech but managed only a rasping cough. Proceeds-With-Circumspection tried to complain but managed a mere wheeze. Bresk farted grandiloquently and proceeded to hold his breath, which the little familiar could do for quite a long time.

Much longer than Occo could. What now?

Bresk—holding breath—suffocation—

The solution was obvious. Occo imagined themselves trapped in a submerged wreck on the ocean-girdled planet of Duik, as she and her familiar had once been.

❧ ❧ ❧

She sucked in a great breath. So did Rammadrecula. So did Proceeds-With-Circumspection, in the sibilant, wing-clicking manner of Ebbo respiration.

Bresk farted. "Oh, marvelous! Back on Duik. You couldn't think of anything better? I remind you that the reason we were in that submerged wreck was because the not-wrecked vessel we began our voyage on was wrecked along the way by one of the ravenous shipwrecking predatory leviathans for which Duik is notorious in that portion of the Sagittarius Arm. And—oh, look, here comes one now!"

Bresk's gaze had moved to the submerged wreck's viewscreen—no, that was an actual physical window, Occo remembered—beyond which could be seen the hideous form of exactly such a leviathan, gathering itself to launch an assault on the wreck which would surely and shortly result in the shattering of that window, thus removing their protection from the crushing weight of the deep sea water beyond.

A window which, Occo noted, was already cracked.

And which was immediately shattered when Rammadrecula, screeching in her by-now-familiar manner, fired several shots through it at the figure of the leviathan beyond.

The window disintegrated. A mangling, obliterating surge of water under immense pressure smashed in upon them—

❋ ❋ ❋

—in a manner somewhat similar if more instantly lethal than the cascade of flower petals on the fourth moon of Jhowall's World with which the famed and feared carnivorous plants of that moon immobilized their prey. Falling upon Occo and her companions in exactly the cascading manner she remembered, the flower petals extruded the venomous nematocysts which would paralyze them all within less than two minims—

❋ ❋ ❋

—thereby triggering her memory of the cataracts on Nanna-charadaum—

"Don't you have *any* pleasant memories?" demanded Bresk.

—up which leapt the migrating swarms of arthropods seeking their ancient spawning pools—

—which migration invariably drew swarms of ravenous predators, not one of which was particularly fussy about what it ravened upon and were perfectly willing to turn aside from the cataracts to feast upon the occasional Nac Zhe Anglan or Ebbo passing by.

Especially the Ebbo, whose physiognomy did bear a certain resemblance to that of the cataract-leaping arthropods, at least if you were near-sighted pale-colored carnivores like the ones even now rushing toward them—

❖ ❖ ❖

—in a manner that was, in its own way, uncannily reminiscent of the avalanches to which the slopes of Mount Ou on Shreamath were prone and which accounted for the extraordinary casualty rate among those climbing enthusiasts who hoped to conquer the inhabited galaxy's third-most-famous peak.

Rammadrecula fired a fusillade of shots at the oncoming avalanche. The whipcrack of the supersonic transuranic rounds, echoing in the steep valley where they found themselves, triggered two more avalanches. Now three swelling, tumultuous masses of snow whose weight could not possibly be calculated were plummeting upon them, soon to add their corpses to those of the untold number of sportsentients who had met their doom on these slopes in years, decades, centuries and millennia past. It was said that if the snows of Mount Ou ever melted, the decomposing bodies of the multitude thus exposed could be smelled for thousands of leagues.

※ ※ ※

Much like the stench of the world-girdling swamps of Horgva, upon one of the floating lily pads of which they now found themselves.

"You are the wildest Mama *ever*," said Ju'ula, her eyes appearing from the surface of the shallow platter she'd turned herself into.

"That's a Warlock Drive!" cried Rammadrecula. The heterochthonatrix's expression exuded good cheer. "And here I thought we'd descended into madness!"

A huge, squatly built amphibian hopped onto the platter, extending its monstrous tongue toward Occo. But three shots by Rammadrecula sent the unsavory beast flying back into the muck from which it emerged.

The sound of the shots, however, immediately drew the attention of every creature lurking beneath the scummy surface which was inclined toward either aggression or predation. Within minims, a horde of creatures was swimming/hopping/flying—and in one particularly unsettling case, sliming—its way toward them.

On a more positive note, the Skerkud Teleplaser— which had for whatever reasons impelled its simulacra of consciousness ignored plant palps, oceanic leviathans, spawning arthropods and that which predated upon them, came to life again. Unfolding into the now-familiar derrick shape—

"MINACITIES UNVEILED! REPREHENTS POLLUTE! EXTIRPATION UNFURLS!"

—the Teleplaser soon transformed the swamp around

them into a bubbling stew of shredded animal and plant parts.

Which, unfortunately, drew the attention of those monstrosities for which the planet Horgva was most famous, the aerial Great Grazers of the Mire. Occo could already see four—no, five—of the enormous blimp-shaped things coming toward them, their grapnels and clapperclaws skimming the surface of the swamp and drawing up whatever they found into the belly-maws above.

*   *   *

Much as she remembered the still-more-stupendous shape of the Colossus of Saint Bracco of the Maelstrom approaching her from the storm clouds of the giant gas planet Xazzay over which Occo and Bresk flew in a dilapidated and now sadly dysfunctional spacecraft which she'd purchased from a now-revealed-to-be-dishonest vendor on Rhoste in a moment of incaution.

"Not this again!" cried Bresk. "Ju'ula, you can't possibly be as decrepit as that miserable tub!"

The Warlock Variation Drive's eyes came up and fixed a baleful glare on the familiar. "That's Ju'ulkrexopopgrebfiltra to you, fartboy. And I'm whatever the image brings to mind. Don't blame me if Mama's got a creepy mind."

The dorsal maw of the Colossus gaped wide, exactly as Occo remembered. But thankfully—

*   *   *

—also as she remembered the carapace of a tiny parasite opening up to discharge effluvia on the planet Qif, as the larger parasite upon which it fed swelled with the ichor it was sucking from the still-larger parasite upon which it nestled, which in turn was being plucked from its host by the needle-shaped beak of the choek whose much-prized pelt was sought by hunters from all the nearby systems, including the notorious Fourth Fraction Liquidator of the Plussi Chancellex whom Occo had tracked across a swath of the Sagittarius in order to wreak vengeance for the selfsame Liquidator's murder of the Naccor Jute's junior novitiant administrator.

Her retribution had been glorious. The Liquidator liquidated—quite literally. She'd castigated the miscreant with a Newoo emulsifier. Fondly, she recalled the Plussi melting all over the dorsal armor of—

❖ ❖ ❖

Which, alas, called up the image of the lava flows on—

"Link! Link!" shrilled Bresk. Occo raised her earflaps.

—the most magnificent volcano within forty light-years if one allowed for—

Her familiar started making the neural connections.

—truly ghastly fatalities, even worse than those inflicted by the Llagad Schism before their rampage was cut short—

❖ ❖ ❖

Bresk transmitted the image of a world that looked sort of like a gwendgee, but with extra pustules.

<Focus! Focus!> The familiar's thoughts were a bit shrill. *<This is a world, not a creature. Those are extinct—well, mostly extinct—volcanos. The darker coloring is from congealed lava flows.>*

❖ ❖ ❖

An instant later, they were on the surface. The

Warlock Variation Drive's form returned to normal. So did the Teleplaser's.

"What a ride!" enthused Ju'ula. "You're the best Mama ever, I'll say it again. But you should probably get some therapy. You're pretty disturbed."

CHAPTER 25

❋

"So are we getting close?" asked Shenoy anxiously.

"It's not that simple," answered Tabor.

Shenoy frowned. "Why not?"

"We know we're at the outskirts of the Mank Empire," replied Tabor.

"Then what's the problem?"

Tabor turned to the Vitunpelay. "You tell him."

"The Empire covers twenty-seven parsecs and has eighty-two inhabited worlds," said Jaemu. "And they don't like visitors."

"We'll just explain that we're friendly, and on a scientific mission."

"They'll never believe it," said Tabor. "That's why we're approaching so cautiously and circuitously. Just to be on the safe side, in case we get caught, I disabled all our weapons systems after we took off."

"You did *what*?" demanded Shenoy.

"How far do you think we'd get against a military fleet?" said Tabor.

"He's got a point," admitted Jaemu.

"All right, all right," muttered Shenoy. "So how far are we from . . . I don't know . . . Mank Prime or whatever they call their homeworld?"

"They call it Mank," answered Jaemu. "They also call their star Mank. And they call their empire Mank." He paused and shook his head. "They are very unimaginative."

"On the other hand, we know who we're dealing with."

"But we're not dealing with *anyone*," complained Shenoy. "We're here. We've entered their empire. We're not trying to hide. Why haven't they contacted us?"

"Maybe they're waiting to see what we plan to do, where we're going," suggested Tabor.

"Or maybe they're so powerful—or so unperceptive—that they can't imagine that a single unarmed ship is a threat to them."

"Of course we're not a threat. But they should want to know our registry, and who or what's aboard, and what our purpose is."

"Maybe they're so secure that they don't care," suggested the Vitunpelay.

"You're just a bundle of laughs," remarked Tabor.

"My mother always said so."

Tabor stared at the Vitunpelay. "I find it hard to believe that you had a mother."

"She was the ugliest, meanest, most self-centered, greediest female in the galaxy," said Jaemu.

"Yeah, I can believe that," said Tabor.

"But she loved me."

"Oh?"

"In her own way," said the Vitunpelay.

"And what way was that?"

"She ate my three littermates the day we all hatched," answered Jaemu.

"Yeah, I guess that's a kind of love," agreed Tabor. "Or at least good taste." He walked over to the instrument panel. "That's damned odd."

"What is?" asked Shenoy.

"They know we're here. They probably know we don't represent a threat. But they *are* a military empire, and as far as our instrumentation can show, no one's even tracking us."

"What do you make of that?"

Tabor smiled. "It means we've come to the right place."

"I don't follow you."

"The fact that they're not using any technology known to us to track us doesn't mean we're not being tracked," answered Tabor. "And if they're not using technology we're familiar with . . . "

"Ah!" said Shenoy with a smile. "The Old Ones' technology!"

"Or their magic," agreed the Vitunpelay.

"So they're not hindering us," continued Shenoy. "What do we do now?"

"Same thing we were always going to do," replied Tabor.

"It gets tricky," said Shenoy, frowning. "I mean, I know that we want the Mank Empire, but there are so many worlds."

"We've got a guide, remember?" said Tabor, jerking a thumb in the Vitunpelay's direction.

"Say, that's right!" replied Shenoy enthusiastically. He turned to Jaemu. "Which world do we want?"

"I have no idea," said the Vitunpelay.

"I thought you knew how to find what we're looking for."

"Once we're on the planet," confirmed Jaemu. "But I was fleeing for my life. I don't know *which* planet it's on."

"I think you're lying."

"No, he's not," interjected Tabor.

Shenoy turned to him. "Oh? What makes you think so."

"If he knew which planet we wanted, he'd be asking for a bigger share."

"Then what do we do?"

"Let's assume that it's not on Mank Prime or whatever the hell they call their homeworld," said Tabor. "Now, if we were dealing with a normal problem, I'd say that we should hunt up the most-fortified world in the quadrant and that'd be what we want. But since they don't seem to be the least bit worried about our presence, that means the world we're looking for can take care of itself."

"Of course!" exclaimed Shenoy, snapping his fingers. "So what we really want is a world where the Old Ones would be comfortable, since they were clearly a starfaring race and could set up shop wherever they wanted. And *that* means we're looking for the world that is closest to Cthulhu in terms of atmosphere, temperature and gravity!"

"Makes sense to me," agreed Tabor. He turned to the Vitunpelay. "How about you?"

"Land there and I'll tell you."

"Well, at least that's not a negative," said Shenoy. He began fiddling with the control panel. "Okay, I'll eliminate the populated chlorine and methane worlds." He studied a small screen. "That leaves fifty-seven worlds. Now those with the wrong gravity." Pause. "Down to thirty-one. Now those with the wrong climate." Pause. "Seventeen." He turned to Tabor. "What else?"

"I don't know. Check and see if any of the seventeen has had a catastrophic disruption. Like, did any of them collide with a comet, and have a huge volcano blow, or undergo a climate change in the past couple of millennia where the oceans or lakes all dried up?"

Shenoy entered the data and looked at the screen. "Fourteen."

And it was still fourteen an hour later, as they kept trying to come up with more disqualifying conditions.

Finally the Vitunpelay spoke up. "I have a suggestion."

"Oh?"

He nodded his massive head. "Yes. Do you know when the jail on Cthulhu was built?"

"I can find out," answered Shenoy. "Or at least get an approximation."

"Do."

Shenoy consulted with the computer for a moment. "Approximately two millennia ago, give or take."

The Vitunpelay's mandibles gaped wide. "There you have it."

"There we have *what*?" said Tabor.

"If you were the Old Ones, would you leave your secrets on a world that was part of a military empire?" said Jaemu. "I suggest that you eliminate every one of those fourteen worlds that has a native sentient population, and consider only those worlds that were colonized in the past two millennia."

Shenoy frowned. "What if Cthulhu was just an outpost and had nothing to do with the world we're looking for? They could have been here for ten thousand years."

"Anything's possible," said Jaemu. "For instance, it's entirely possible that you'll have to land on all fourteen worlds—or possibly even three hundred unpopulated worlds, should it turn out that the Old Ones were insubstantial creatures who were impervious to heat and cold and poisonous atmospheres, or indeed no atmospheres at all. But it's a starting point, and if you can eliminate half of those fourteen worlds, at least the initial phase will seem less daunting."

Tabor turned to Shenoy. "What do you think?"

"It couldn't hurt. We've got to start *some*where."

And five minutes later they had narrowed their field of potential worlds down to five.

"One's in the Manks' home system," noted Tabor. "I'd leave that for last."

"You think it's less likely that they'd have set up shop in the Manks' system?" asked Shenoy.

Tabor smiled. "I think it's less likely that we won't be harassed and hindered if we don't try to land in the Manks' home system."

"Makes sense," admitted Shenoy. "All right, what's left are Badreimusch II, Milchbradt IV, Morgan III, and Pwaxtit IV."

"I wish you'd have read them off earlier," said Tabor.

"Why?"

"You've got three alien names and one that was clearly named by or after a human."

"Well, I'll be damned!" said Shenoy. "You're right!"

And a moment later the ship's course was adjusted so that it would land on a totally alien world named Morgan in seven hours.

        ❊ ❊ ❊

"We touch down in three minutes," announced Shenoy. He turned to the Vitunpelay. "I think it's time you told us exactly what we'll be confronting."

"The people who guard the Old Ones' secrets, of course," answered Jaemu.

"You're not being very helpful," complained Shenoy. "What do the Mank look like?"

Jaemu shrugged. "I really couldn't say."

"You want to reconsider that answer?" growled Tabor.

"I would love to reconsider it," answered Jaemu, "but it is the truth."

"Explain!"

"This is not Mank, but the Mank Empire," said the Vitunpelay. "Since it is not their home planet, I assume that it is not populated by Manks, but by their partners, slaves, or subordinates. For what it's worth, they all speak a common language—at least, all the races I met here."

"How many races?" demanded Tabor.

"Five. But then, I was on seven worlds in the Empire."

"And what language do they speak?"

"Mank, of course."

Tabor turned to Shenoy. "Shall I kill him now?"

"Let me ask a question first." He turned to Jaemu. "How did you communicate with them?"

"I used a universal translator, of course. Please don't tell me you humans are so stupid you learn alien languages one at a time. If so, I need new partners. Or I'll be spending all my time teaching you how to feed yourselves."

Shenoy turned to Tabor. "If universal translators work with Manks and their subordinate species, that suggests they still haven't uncovered the secrets of the Old Ones."

"Huh? How does that follow?"

"It should be obvious. Surely one of the accomplishments of a master species would be to develop a universal language and impose its use upon all other species. Did Romans go around translating all the barbarian languages? Of course not. They required the barbarians to learn Latin."

Tabor thought about it. There did seem to be a twisted kind of sense involved.

But he didn't ponder the subject for long. They had more pressing matters to attend to. "We've landed," he said.

"Let me get a rifle and I'm ready to go," said Jaemu. "I can modify it to suit me well enough."

"Leave it here," said Shenoy.

"Let him take it," said Tabor, removing his own weaponry and tossing it on the copilot's chair.

"But . . ." began Shenoy.

"Think it through, Rupert," said Tabor. "If we get spotted and they feel at all threatened, who are they going to kill first?"

"Ah!" exclaimed Shenoy with a smile. He turned to the Vitunpelay. "Would you like Russell's weapons too?"

Jaemu stared at him for a moment, then stared at the rifle, and then set it down. "I have reconsidered the issue."

"All right," said Tabor after a moment. "We're on the planet. What are we near?"

"I thought it best not to set us down near a heavily populated area," answered Shenoy, "so we're in the middle of a desert."

"Wonderful," muttered Tabor.

"But we're near some ruins."

"Old Ones' ruins?"

"We won't know until we get there," said Shenoy.

"Oh, we'll know before that," said Tabor.

"We will?"

Tabor nodded an affirmative. "If no one tries to stop us, it's got nothing to do with the Old Ones."

Shenoy sighed. "Why didn't *I* think of that?"

"Because it wouldn't have made any difference."

Shenoy ordered the hatch to open, a ramp descended, and the three of them walked down to the sandy surface.

And suddenly found themselves facing a squat being who hadn't been there five seconds earlier. It had two owl-like eyes, a very short beak, a wide mouth, and was covered with growths about fifteen centimeters long which were somewhere between fur and the spines of a sea urchin. Other than boots, the only clothing it wore was what looked for all the world like a diaper and a harness with two shoulder straps upon which were appended various unidentifiable objects which might be tools or weapons—or cosmetic kits.

"Good afternoon," it said, speaking in perfect English

without the need for a UT. "And welcome to the world of Morgan."

"Would I be correct in surmising that your name isn't Morgan and we're not conversing in your native language?" said Shenoy.

"Totally correct, Sir Rupert."

"He's not really a 'sir,'" remarked Tabor as Shenoy glared at him.

"He is for as long as he is our guest on Morgan," answered the creature.

"And have you a name?" asked Shenoy.

"What name do you like?" it asked.

"Given that we've just come from Cthulhu, and we're looking for anything the Old Ones left behind, I think Nosferatu might make a fitting name," responded Shenoy. "But I suppose it would be more convenient for you to just tell us your real name."

"You're quite perceptive, Sir Rupert," replied the creature. "It just so happens that my name *is* Nosferatu." It extended a claw. "Pleased to meet you."

Shenoy took and shook what passed for its hand. "The feeling is mutual."

"Uh . . ." said Tabor. "If we can put this mutual admiration society on hold for a few minutes, we've got a lot of questions to ask you."

"Certainly, my dear Russell," said Nosferatu.

"Good. And my name is Russ."

"Fine. And you can call me Nosfer."

"Is this your real appearance?" asked Tabor.

Nosferatu frowned. "Don't you like it?"

The Vitunpelay laughed at that.

"You have an ill-mannered pet, Russ," said the creature.

"I'm no pet!" growled Jaemu.

"My mistake," said Nosferatu. "You have an ill-mannered lackey, Russ."

Vitunpelay uttered an obscenity in his own language.

"As it demonstrates again," noted the creature. "But where are my manners? Are you hungry?"

"Not right now," said Shenoy.

"You're sure? I have a feeling that duck in orange sauce might change your mind, while Russ would love some veal parmesan. As for the lackey, I'm sure we could find some scraps for it."

"Before we eat, I should really like to just talk with you," said Shenoy.

"You are guests on my planet," answered Nosferatu. "How can I say no?" He pulled a lighted cigar out of the air, brought it to his lips, opened his mouth and revealed some serious-looking fangs, inserted it, and took a deep puff.

"I'd offer one to you, but it's bad for your health."

"But not yours?"

"It's even worse for ours, but then we know how to protect ourselves."

"Or at least you know who can protect you," said Tabor.

"That goes without saying," replied Nosferatu.

"No it doesn't," said Shenoy. "In fact, it's what we're here to talk about."

"About the effects of cigar smoke?" asked the creature, frowning. "You could have gotten your answer out of any textbook or medical journal."

"No," said Shenoy. "About why you are protected from cigar smoke."

"Ah!" said Nosferatu. "Of course. You must excuse me. I was chosen to make first contact with you because I am quite the simplest member of my society, and my death would cause the least problems for it."

"You're the dumb one?" blurted Tabor.

"Certainly. We couldn't risk any more valuable members until we knew your intentions. With ignorant, primitive races such as yourselves, one can never be sure."

"But you know it now," interjected Shenoy.

"Yes, I'm reasonably sure of it now, though of course one never knows what your lackey might do," he answered, jerking what passed for a thumb in Jaemu's direction.

"Can we please get back to the subject?" asked Shenoy quickly, before the never-too-predictable Vitunpelay might respond in an untoward manner.

"Certainly," said Nosferatu. "We were on the subject of cigars, as I recall."

"Actually, it was the Old Ones."

Nosferatu frowned. "You're not supposed to know anything about them."

"But we do," said Shenoy. "And we'd like to learn more."

"Did the Manks send you here to test us?" demanded Nosferatu.

"*Never mind,*" said an immaterial voice. "*I'll take it from here.*"

An instant later Nosferatu vanished and another member of the same race popped into view.

"I apologize for my confederate," said the new creature. "But as you can easily see, he was much the most expendable of us."

"No harm done," said Shenoy. "Have you a name?"

"None of us do, actually," came the answer. "Call me anything you like."

"Well, the planet is Morgan, so why don't we call you Morgan?" suggested Shenoy.

"Fine by me."

"Who *was* Morgan, by the way?"

"I suppose he was the member of your race who first mapped or set down on the planet."

"Yet the name stuck."

"It stuck on *your* maps," replied Morgan. "We call it—" He uttered a word no human or Vitunpelay physiology could pronounce. The UT made it out to be "Oijrapopoth," for whatever that was worth.

"But for the purpose of this conversation," Morgan continued, "and indeed for the duration of your visit, we shall be happy to refer to the world as Morgan and ourselves as Morganites."

"Did the original Morgan land here before or after the Old Ones?" asked Shenoy.

"Yes."

"Yes before, or yes after?"

"Yes, one or the other," said Morgan.

"I thought you were going to help us?"

"Within reason," came the reply. "I told you about Morgan, didn't I?"

"We want to know about the Old Ones."

"I just knew you were going to say that." Morgan then

sighed—or perhaps that deep breath-followed-by-exhalation was simply part of its normal respiratory pattern. Trying to decipher the body language of new alien species was always a chancy proposition.

"What did you expect?" said Tabor. "But first, I have another question. Since you're loaded down with all the Old Ones' secrets, why aren't you the rulers of the universe?"

"Therein lies a story."

CHAPTER 26

"We are not native to this world," said Morgan, "as you may well have guessed by now. Like you, we became aware some millennia ago of the Old Ones and their accomplishments, which seemed little short of magic. And of course we wanted to learn what they knew, to join them at the apex of what I shall call the galactic food chain.

"But the Old Ones were a very careful race. They left behind some examples of the miracles they wrought, those actions that seemed to turn the established principles of Science on its ear, but they left no trace of where they had gone to, or even if they were still alive.

"Naturally, finding them—or what had happened to them—became a priority of my race, and soon became its obsession. Not only to discover the secrets to their miracles, but also to learn the answer to a question that seemed to grow in importance with every passing day: if such a race had indeed become extinct, exactly what kind of force could have put an end to them? To put it another way, what unknown danger lurked in the universe?

"So we began by examining every world in our sector of the galaxy, both inhabited or theoretically uninhabited, looking for any trace of the Old Ones or their incredible achievements. Some planets resented our presence, and tried to prevent our search. Naturally we could not allow this, not with the stakes so high. World after world fell before our military might, and were shortly incorporated into our Federation. We brooked no resistance; tolerated no abstention.

"We spent many fruitless centuries in that quest. Eventually, a sizeable portion of our Federation felt that the search was a waste of time and resources. No one doubted that that the Old Ones had existed, because we had ample proof that they had. But the suspicion grew that they had left behind no key to their incredible powers.

"And then, on an obscure planet some two hundred parsecs from where I am standing now, we found . . . Not the secrets, but a hint to their location. Was it a true hint, or a false trail? We were unsure the day we found it—but we were dead sure, and I use the term advisedly, one stellar day later. The planet, which all our instrumentation told us was totally stable, exploded, killing our entire landing party, and seriously damaging the ship, which had remained in orbit rather than landing on the uneven, rocky surface.

"There was nothing left of the planet, not a single clue to its destruction, which itself was a major clue, because worlds don't explode simply because a single six-person landing craft touches down on them.

"We devoted all our efforts to determining what had

caused the destruction of the world, because the only conclusion to be drawn from the episode was that the Old Ones—or *some*one—didn't want us to find whatever was there on the surface.

"In the end, we had to conclude there were no remaining clues, but the episode doubled our already firm resolve to continue our quest.

"Now, while we were scouring the galaxy, looking for any sign that might lead us to the Old Ones or their secrets, we were not the only race, or even the only federation of races, to do so. Indeed, dozens, perhaps hundreds, were voyaging through the galaxy, each upon an identical quest. At first we were resentful, because after all our centuries of searching, all our sacrifices, we didn't want some other race to come upon our goal first. Then we thought about it more deeply, and realized that with more than two hundred billion stars in the galaxy, including a multitude of G-type stars, we could use all the help we could get—and when we decided that one of them was getting close to the secrets or the creators of the secrets, well, that would be time enough to take action and assure our primacy.

"Two centuries after the episode of the exploding planet, after we'd gone so far afield that some of our vessels became generation ships—military and scientific ships where two and even three generations were born, grew to maturity, and eventually died without ever touching down on their home planet—we finally found hard evidence that the Old Ones had indeed left their secrets behind."

"And what was that compelling evidence?

"The planet Mank. The fourth planet of this very system.

"We knew from the reports of others that the Mank had a complex society, that they had created colonies on their two moons and on the fifth and sixth planets. And yet the sensors of our probes showed almost no neutrino activity, no fission, no power surges of any kind, nor could we even detect a single, solitary spaceport on any world they controlled. Clearly this implied a power source—or a method of avoiding power sources—that was unknown in the galaxy. That implied that the Mank had learned their technology—some portion of it, at least—from the Old Ones.

"We then approached the Mank system openly, communicating that we planned to land on Mank—we called it Mank IV, since we had no idea what they called all the other planets and moons in the system. To show that we came in peace we said we had disabled all our weaponry.

"That was a lie, of course. But we thought it would get us close enough to Mank to observe its power sources more closely.

"And suddenly a voice, not coming through the speakers, but right there on the command deck, said 'That's a lie.'

"We turned to see who or what had spoken, and found ourselves confronting the first Mank anyone had ever seen. Its outlines were blurred and indistinct, however, so we could discern nothing beyond a bilateral, bifurcate being approximately our own size.

"'We had high hopes for you,' the creature said,

speaking our own language with absolutely no accent. 'But the very first words out of your mouths were a lie.'"

"'Who are you?'" demanded the head of our security team, drawing his weapon and aiming it at the Mank's head.

"'Don't threaten me with your toys,' said the Mank, waving what seemed to be a hand through the air—and the pistol disappeared. 'Now,' it continued, 'are you ready to speak honestly and peaceably, or do you choose the alternative, which is that I will destroy your ship?'

"'Not while you're on it, you won't,' said another security officer.

"'How do you think I got here?' the Mank asked—and suddenly everyone was silent. Presumably, it could remove itself from the ship at the moment that it destroyed it.

"The Mank seemed to look around for a moment. 'An adequate vessel,' he said. 'You'd be well-advised to keep it intact until our business is concluded.'

"'And what *is* our business?' asked the captain.

"'You have distinguished yourselves from among all other races save one, which is to say, only you have figured out that the Mank Empire houses the secrets that you seek.'

"'What other race?' demanded the captain.

"'A member of the race of Man, an entity named Morgan, crashed on one of the planets of this system. Before he died he realized that the Old Ones had spent some months there.'"

"Which planet?" asked Shenoy eagerly.

"Calm down," said Morgan. "That is *not* the world you

seek. It is just a world in the Mank system, more important than any world beyond the system, of course, but not the world you have come to explore.

"The Mank then explained to us that the Old Ones were *not* immortal, that indeed the last of them had died more than a thousand years ago. Facing some sort of catastrophe, which they implied was natural, the Old Ones emigrated to the Mank system seeking refuge—and were exterminated by the Mank.

"You see, the Mank had thought they had learned all of the Old Ones' secrets before killing them, but in that they were mistaken. The Old Ones realized that the Mank could be as vicious, selfish and foolish as any race, so they hid the key to their secrets on the larger of Mank's two moons before landing on the planet and befriending the Mank.

"The Mank learned many things from them—what you call teleportation and telepathy, for instance. But the major secrets, those that would allow a race to rule the galaxy, even the universe, as completely as the Old Ones once did, these they hid so thoroughly that even with the Mank's enhanced powers and perceptions, they remain hidden.

"This was explained to that first ship of my Federation, and a bargain was made. Since the Mank do not yet have what they want from the Old Ones, they have some vulnerabilities—less than any planet, but *some*. They know more about the Old Ones, their secrets, and how to reach and utilize them, than any other race. They do not intend to share those secrets—but if we were willing to create outposts on Morgan and a few other outer worlds and moons and help defend the system against potential military invasion, when the Mank finally discover the major secrets of the Old Ones, we would be favored among all other races. We would receive positions of power and prestige when the Mank Empire includes millions of worlds in the galaxy rather than the mere handful they have now.

"When we considered the powers a single Mank already possessed, it was an easy decision. You and your party clearly do not represent a military threat to the Mank, so now that I've satisfied your curiosity as best I can, I will take you to whichever location you choose: Mank or its larger moon."

❖ ❖ ❖

"That's an interesting story," commented Shenoy. "It's not what I expected, but it doesn't contradict anything I know or that we've discovered."

"So what's in it for *you*?" asked the Vitunpelay.

"I just told you," replied Morgan.

"I know," answered Jaemu, "but surely you want to be more than the Manks' lackeys."

"We don't view it quite that way," said Morgan. "I notice you don't mind being under the command of humans."

"I'm free to come and go and do anything I please without clearing it with them," replied the Vitunpelay.

Morgan seemed about to reply, thought better of it, and merely grunted something unintelligible.

"All right," said Morgan to Shenoy. "I've told them you're coming."

"When?" asked Shenoy.

"Just now."

"Let's go, then," said Tabor. "Do you teleport us there?"

Morgan shook his head. "Even if they approve of you, which is to say, they decide to let you live, it will take a week before you're ready to teleport."

"It's a wonder that the Old Ones didn't set foot on every world in the galaxy," remarked Shenoy.

Morgan looked amused. "What makes you think they didn't?"

"I wonder that anything—disease, old age, physical attack, *anything*—could kill them."

"It *is* surprising," agreed Morgan.

"Well, shall we go?" suggested Tabor.

Morgan nodded his agreement. "Yes, we might as well."

Tabor led the way to the ship, and a few minutes later it was streaking through the atmosphere of Morgan and heading toward the inner planets.

"How many populated worlds are there in this system?" asked Tabor.

"I suppose it depends on what you mean by a populated world," answered Morgan. "Only Mank itself has a native population, but there are fortresses, colonies, outposts, whatever you wish to call them, on three other planets and four moons."

"What was it that caused the Old Ones to seek refuge on Mank?" asked Shenoy. "Was there something of value in the planet, or . . . ?"

"I believe I will let the Mank answer that."

They were all silent for a few moments. Then, as the

ship was passing the fifth planet out from the sun, Morgan suddenly frowned, seemed to be concentrating on something for a moment, then looked up.

"It seems that I am taking you to the larger moon of Mank."

"They can read your minds and ours from that far away?" asked Tabor.

"Of course," answered Morgan. "That's how we knew you were coming to my planet, and why we were prepared to converse with you."

"So what's on the larger moon?" asked Tabor.

"Our destination."

"I know that. I mean, why are we landing there instead of on the planet?"

"Because that's where I have been instructed to take you," answered Morgan.

"You're not being very helpful," growled Tabor. "Why are we *not* going to Mank?"

"Because I have been instructed that until your intentions are clear, you will not be allowed on Mank itself."

"Relax, Russell," said Shenoy. "They may be annoyed with us for entering their system, and they may not like some of our attitudes, but"—he flashed Tabor a triumphant smile—"they're not going to hinder us or do us any damage."

"What are you talking about, Rupert?"

"They *need* us!"

"The guys with the Old Ones' secrets don't need anyone," replied Tabor.

"I fully agree," said Shenoy.

"Then what the hell are you talking about?"

"I wish I could whisper it to you, or somehow write it down and transmit it to your pocket computer, but Morgan could hear or see or otherwise know what message I'm trying to impart to you." He looked at alien. "Wouldn't you?" he concluded.

"Of course I would."

"So I might as well just tell you directly," continued Shenoy.

"Go ahead," said Tabor and Morgan in unison.

"Think it through, Russell," said Shenoy. "Whoever possesses all of the Old Ones' secrets would rule the galaxy. Nothing would be beyond their abilities. Think of the things they could do!" enthused Shenoy.

"I know," replied Tabor irritably. "We've already seen them. Teleportation, telepathy, probably telekinesis as well."

"Party tricks!" said Shenoy decisively.

"What the hell are you talking about?" demanded Tabor.

"I'd like to know too," said the Vitunpelay, frowning.

Shenoy smiled. "Shall I tell them, or would you rather?" he asked Morgan.

"You tell them. I'm interested to see what you come up with."

"So far we've been concentrating on what they *can* do," continued Shenoy. "And it's been so impressive to us that we've not paid any attention to what they *can't* do!"

"Such as?" said Tabor.

"Why does the most powerful race in the galaxy have such a small empire?" Shenoy shot back. "Why do they need another race—Morgan's race—to act as guards to their system's outer perimeter? They're telepaths. They know why we've come. Why didn't they threaten us if we entered the system, or better still, push all thoughts of the Old Ones out of our minds? Do you think we're here just for their amusement?"

"They didn't sound very amused," admitted Tabor.

"They're not amused," said Shenoy. A triumphant smile crossed his face. "What they are is *desperate*."

"Now I'm confused," said Tabor, frowning. "Desperate for *what*?"

"For what we've come for," answered Shenoy. "For the true secrets of the Old Ones. Not the party tricks, but the things that will turn them into virtual gods and allow them to rule the universe!" He paused, and looked at Morgan. "And that means that the secrets, or the doorway to secrets, or the access to the secrets, lies not on Mank but on Mank's larger moon, doesn't it?"

"You will not find what you seek on Mank," said the alien. "If we let you live, you—rather, we—may find it on the moon."

"Of course you'll let us live," said Shenoy. "You've spent more than a millennium searching for the key. You're not going to find it without us."

"Correction," said Morgan. "We are not going to find it without *someone*."

"I just said that."

"What an ego you possess! Do you think no one else in the entire galaxy would figure out that the answers to the ultimate questions lay within the Mank Empire?"

"Who else?" asked Shenoy curiously.

Morgan gestured in a way that indicated the ship's surroundings. "Even as we speak, a Nac Zhe Anglan vessel has entered our system, as selfish and self-centered as you. They, like you, were certain no one else had ever thought that the secrets might lie within our Empire, whereas you are the seventh and eighth expeditions to hit upon the truth in the past millennium."

"That many?" said Tabor.

"That few?" said Shenoy, frowning.

"They, like you, will be allowed to land only on the moon." Morgan paused. "Then we will decide what to do with you, whether to allow you to help us find the key to our treasure or to terminate you."

* * *

Within an hour they were orbiting the moon. It looked like any other barren world in their viewscreen, but their instruments reported that it possessed a breathable atmosphere and acceptable gravity.

"Well, here we are," announced Morgan. "We'll be setting down near that structure up ahead." He indicated a structure that clearly was not natural but created by intelligent design.

"I've been wondering . . ." began Tabor.

"What?" asked Shenoy.

"Should we even bother? I mean, if we can find something that they've been unable to find for a thousand years, they'll just take it away from us, and probably kill us into the bargain."

"Not necessarily," said Shenoy.

"You're thinking about this Knack ship that Morgan mentioned," said Tabor. "I don't see how that can help."

Rupert shook his head. "Not the Knack ship."

"Then what?"

"Two things." He turned toward Jaemu and pointed at Morgan. "The first one is—kill that annoying creature, would you, Jaemu?"

"Be my pleasure," said the Vitunpelay, in a tone that sounded like a cross between a snarl and a chuckle. The huge alien swept one of his great palps around Morgan's neck.

Tried to, rather. The palp seemed to pass through thin air. It was hard to tell who seemed more surprised—Jaemu, Russ Tabor, or Morgan himself.

The alien squawked—and then vanished. The Vitunpelay studied his palp with what seemed to be either great chagrin or great satisfaction, or both. Chagrin because he'd failed to slay Morgan; satisfaction, because at least he'd made him disappear.

"Thought so," said Shenoy, with considerable satisfaction. "It's all smoke and mirrors. They don't have teleportation *or* telepathy."

Tabor frowned. "Then how . . . "

"Call it astral projection, for lack of a better term." Shenoy waved a hand. "Magic, of a sort. Which leads me to the second thing. Or perhaps I should say cluster of things."

"Which are?"

"There is no Mank Empire, and there are no Manks. Not living ones, anyway—they may have existed at one time, I'm not sure yet. And Morgan's folk are a bunch of posturers, poseurs and charlatans." The scholar paused for a moment. "Well, mostly."

Despite himself, Russ Tabor was a little shaken. "For Christ's sake, Rupert! You took one hell of a risk there!"

Shenoy shrugged. "Not really. If the Morganites had just claimed the ability to teleport, I wouldn't have done it. Mind you, teleportation's extremely unlikely—the theoretical obstacles are immense and the technological ones even worse. But it's not actually precluded by science. Whereas telepathy is simply impossible. So when they claimed that ability, it cast all their claims into doubt."

Tabor frowned. "Why? It would seem to me that from the standpoint of physics, the ability to project thoughts wouldn't be any harder than the ability to project material objects. Probably easier, in fact."

"Physics has nothing to do with it. Telepathy is precluded by biology. To be precise, the theory of evolution."

"Huh?" Jaemu's contribution was to clack his mandibles, which might be the Vitunpelay manner of expressing confusion.

"But it's obvious! Well, perhaps I misspoke. Telepathy as such—depending on how you define the term—is certainly possible. You could even argue that it's omnipresent. What produces a thought in your brain other than telepathic communication between neurons?"

"That's not—"

Shenoy waved his hand airily. "Yes, yes, you can argue that those are electrochemical impulses. What's the difference? The critical point is that telepathy is counterposed to the evolution of *intelligence*. One can postulate the existence of telepaths, certainly. There are giant fungi, for instance, whose mass and physical dimensions dwarf those of even the mightiest trees. Somehow those fungi manage to maintain enough internal communication to survive indefinitely. Call it electrochemical, call it telepathy. But they're also as dumb as—well, as fungus. Which is exactly what you'd expect."

Tabor scratched his head. "I'm still not following you."

"Think it through, Russ. Intelligence is impossible without being mediated through an elaborate and extraordinarily complex symbological system. You could even argue that's what intelligence is in the first place—a shared system of symbols. But that sort of system would never evolve if communication between separate organisms wasn't *difficult*. Let's use the three of us here as an example. If you and I and Jaemu could express our thoughts to each other as easily and immediately as two cells in our bodies—or two cells in a giant fungus—then we'd have no need for language or, indeed, for any kind of thinking at all. Any more than we need to have a discussion with our digestive system to eat.

"The idea of telepathy is simply twaddle. The math involved gets tricky in places, but there's no doubt about the result among evolutionary biologists, neurologists, developmental linguists—anyone who studies the issue." Shenoy shook his head. "You really should try to keep up with the literature, Russell. It's obvious the Morganites didn't bother to, or they wouldn't have tried to pull this swindle on us. Well. On me, anyway."

"But . . ." Jaemu grasped the essence of the logic first. "Hoo!" he exclaimed. "In other words, you couldn't develop telepathy unless you were too stupid to use it!"

"Ah . . ." Shenoy looked a bit cross-eyed. "That's one way of putting it, I suppose. I think it's more appropriate to say that the evolution of intelligence presupposes the need to overcome the *lack* of telepathy."

"That's just what I said. If you're a telepathic species, you're too stupid to think."

Russ shook his head, as if he were a dog shaking off rain water. "Never mind. I have to assume that you're right, since otherwise it's unlikely Morgan would have been immaterial and just vanished when he was attacked."

"I'm not sure it's actually a 'he,'" cautioned Shenoy.

Russ ignored that caveat. The savant might well be right, but when in doubt Tabor found it safer to assume an opponent was probably male. Granted, that was just a product of his own species gender bias. A Knack would assume the exact opposite.

But he had worse problems to deal with at the moment. "What did you mean when you said that the Morganites were *mostly* a bunch of posturers, poseurs and charlatans?"

"I should think that would be obvious as well. First, if they weren't basically faking their nature and the whole setup here, they wouldn't have had to go through that rigmarole in the first place."

"Yeah, I got that. It's the 'mostly' business that I'm worried about."

"Well, they can't be *entirely* posturers—or they'd have long since been displaced by other posturers. What I mean is, there has to be *something* left by the Old Ones down on that moon or they wouldn't have tried to swindle us. But if that's the case, why hasn't someone else elbowed them aside and tried to grab what's down there?"

The Vitunpelay's smaller tentacles bunched into knots. Whatever emotion that gesture signified was unclear to the two humans. "Hoo!" he boomed again. "There can only be one of two answers. Either they're more powerful than anyone else who's come across this secret, or the secret is so well-guarded that more powerful beings who try to take it are destroyed."

"I suspect it's a combination, but mostly the latter." Rupert's expression momentarily bordered on admiration. "They're basically hucksters who try to swindle someone else into taking the risks while they wait to snatch the gains."

"Which is just another way of saying that whatever's down there is so dangerous that everyone the Morganites have so far conned into trying to get it have gotten fried."

"Starting with the Manks themselves, I suspect," said Shenoy. "The most likely scenario is that the Morganites' researches led them to believe that there existed a repository of the Old Ones here in the Mank Empire— what was once the Mank Empire, I should say—and they somehow persuaded the Manks to do the direct investigation of the site. I'm not sure how, though."

Tabor grunted. "If you're right, they probably used a reverse twist on the B'rer Rabbit ploy."

Shenoy frowned. "I'm not familiar . . . "

"It's an old folk tale from the American south. A rabbit caught by a fox pleaded with the fox not to throw him into a briar patch. The fox did so—thereby enabling the rabbit to escape."

Jaemu clacked his mandibles loudly. "Hoo! Yes, that's how they would have done it! 'Please, O Mighty Mank, do not force us to investigate that Vile Vault of Unknown Powers.' The Mank would have assumed the Morganites were trying to trick them and so they went and investigated it themselves—thereby triggering whatever immensely destructive force lurked within the repository."

Shenoy nodded. "Something like that."

Tabor rubbed his jaw. "So what you're suggesting is that the Morganites are now trying to trick us into investigating the Old One secrets they think are hidden somewhere on this moon. How many times do you think they've done this?"

"More than once, most likely. They must hope that someday one of their patsies will uncover a way to use the secrets without being destroyed."

"That doesn't make a lot of sense. In that case, the patsies wouldn't be patsies any longer. *They'd* be the ones empowered by the Old Ones' secrets."

"Yes, I know. The Morganites must have some reason to think they could seize the secrets before those they tricked could use them."

"Which would be . . . ?"

Shenoy shrugged. "I don't know yet. We'll have to figure it out as we go."

"So what now?" asked Russ. "Do we head straight down there?"

Shenoy pursed his lips. "I think . . . not. It's unlikely the Morganites lie about everything, after all—and why would they bother to lie about the arrival of other aliens anyway? So what don't we start by seeing if we can form an alliance with whatever party of Nac Zhe Anglan has arrived in the system?"

Russ nodded. "All right. Since we're not going to land right away, let's assume a polar orbit. We can use the time to get a full picture of the moon's surface."

Slightly less than seven hours later, the two humans and the Vitunpelay stared at the bizarre alien craft which their ship's sensors had spotted as it approached the planet.

"Please tell me that's not a flying carpet," said Tabor. He squinted at the object on the screen. "Or flying saucer, or whatever the hell it is."

"Worse," said Jaemu. The word sounded like a cough. "Much worse. That's a Warlock Drive. Got to be."

Shenoy clapped both hands. "You're right, it has to be—and a variation drive, at that! They're mad! They're utterly mad! What an incredible opportunity!" He turned his head. "Ship," he commanded. "Follow those lunatics!" Then he scratched his jaw. "Or . . . what's the proper term for deranged Nac Zhe Anglan? Luknacktics, perhaps?"

"Vitunurpo," supplied Jaemu. "It's one of the terms that Human—what did you call him? a Finn?—used to refer to us. But since we settled on Vitunpelay there's no reason I can't bestow the title on them."

The Vitunpelay studied the progress of the Knacks as they approached—using the term so very, very, very loosely—the moon below. "It means 'fucking idiots,' by the way."

CHAPTER 27

The Warlock Variation Drive touched down on the moon—literally. Just before landing, Ju'ula extruded what looked like nothing so much as a huge hand whose digits probed the surface for a moment before the Drive settled on it.

That done, Ju'ula's eyes swiveled to study Rammadrecula. The heterochthonatrix was engaged in reloading its weapon. Or perhaps "recharging" it was a more apt description of her activity. From what Occo could tell, the process seem to involve incantations more than anything else—although she might be mistaken. Occo had no personal experience with that type of esoteric target pistol. The weapons used by a castigant were of necessity more rugged and less finicky.

"There's something problematic about her," Ju'ula stated.

"I'll say!" chimed in Bresk. "The human colloquialism is 'fishy,' although I have no idea why a bilateral, torpedo-shaped water-dweller is any more dubious than any other phylum."

Occo had already reached that conclusion herself. She brought to her mind the image of the dungeon they had once found themselves in. An instant later, they were there. The same harness-clad large mammal was staring at them.

"Back again?" it demanded.

Expertly, Occo disarmed Rammadrecula. Before the heterochthonatrix could do more than squawk a protest, Occo thrust her into the paws of the dungeon-keeper.

"I need answers," she said.

※ ※ ※

"They disappeared!" said Jaemu. "Just like that!" The huge Vitunpelay stared at the screen.

Russ scratched his jaw. "You think that was teleportation, Rupert?"

Shenoy, also peering intently at the screen, frowned for a moment. Then, shook his head. "No, I don't think so. I think the Warlock Variation Drive did that. However it did it. Nobody really knows much about any of the Warlock drives and the Variation is reputed to be the weirdest of them all."

"So what we do?"

Shenoy hesitated for a moment. Then said, "Let's just wait for a bit. They might come back."

※ ※ ※

"There's a good start," said the mammalian torturer, with considerable satisfaction. "D'you want its knees broken or just wrenched?—or I can tear the lower legs off entirely."

Occo contemplated the setup, for a moment. Rammadrecula's upper body was immobilized in a cross between a harness and a cage, while all four of her knees were encased in impressively massive . . . what to call them? Kneecuffs? Joint-twisters?

"I believe we can leave outright dismemberment as a possible later option," she said. "Let's just start with some simple agony."

"Coming right up." The mammal worked at a small control console and the heterochthonatrix immediately began screeching.

"I'm innocent of all wrongdoing!" she cried. Then, added threat to protest: "Are you mad? I am an official of the Envacht Lu! The penalties for even threatening me, much less harming me, are horrible to contemplate!"

"So they are," said Occo. "But I am by now quite certain that none of your recent actions have either the sanction or support—or even the cognizance—of the Envacht Lu. Whatever you're up to, it's got nothing to do with your status as a heterochthonatrix."

To the torturer she said: "Twist the other way, if you please."

The creature worked at the console again. Rammadrecula's screeching grew louder and more frantic. At this point, Proceeds-With-Circumspection began to get restless, which the Ebbo indicated by an annoying rubbing together of its hindmost legs.

"Record everything," Occo said. That familiar task seemed to settle the bureaucrat. Within minims, the Ebbo was scritching away at its tablet.

Occo returned her attention to the torturer. "And now back again," she commanded.

"I'll talk! I'll talk!" yowled Rammadrecula.

Occo raised a hand. "Hold a moment," she said to the torturer.

"You can't trust them to tell the truth until they've had at least one limb properly mangled," he protested. "At this stage they'll say anything."

"Torture is actually not a very useful interrogation technique," said Bresk. "Whatever delusions"—here a loud fart—"this furball might entertain."

"Hey!" protested the torturer. "Are you going to let that thing insult me like that? I'm a highly qualified professional!"

"Bresk, shut up," said Occo. As a rule, she agreed with her familiar's assessment. She'd never found torture particularly helpful herself. But that was because the sentients she normally subjected to interrogation were enemies determined to thwart her purpose.

She did not believe that to be the case here, however. Whatever Rammadrecula's motives might be—which Occo thought were probably not very clear even to the heterochthonatrix herself—her behavior had the earmarks of someone trying to extricate herself from a predicament without having thought through all the possible ramifications and consequences.

To put it more simply, Occo was fairly certain that Rammadrecula *wanted* to confess what she was about. But she wouldn't do it unless she was provided with a reasonable excuse for doing so—an excuse that she herself would accept.

For that purpose, what better than torture?

"Again," she commanded.

She let the torturer ply his trade for a bit. That didn't

amount to much more than twisting one knob back and forth, whatever the mammal's own delusions of grandeur might be concerning the "professional qualifications" involved. As skill levels went, this was on a par with a simian-analog poking at an insect mound with a stick.

"*I'll talk! I'll talk!*"

"Keep at it," Occo said.

A reasonably short time later, she said to the torturer: "All right, desist for the moment."

"Talk," she commanded Rammadrecula. "Why did you come on this expedition? And please spare me the silliness that you needed to prove your lack of continuing affiliation to the Flengren Apostollege. If the Envacht Lu had any doubts on that subject, they never would have permitted you to join their ranks in the first place."

The heterochthonatrix dissolved into lachrymosia, fluid gushing from her eyes and lower mouth.

"This is what Humans would call 'blubbering,'" said Bresk. "Don't ask me why, since their adipose tissue is concentrated around their midsection and is generally inert. I suspect the reason may be that when they flense each other in the course of formal duels—"

Occo ignored the familiar's pointless chatter. "Talk!" she commanded.

"It's true! It's true!" Rammadrecula cried out. "I lied! No one suspects me of anything except incompetence! And it's not fair!"

Occo gestured toward the torturer. "Loosen the device."

"That's not a good idea," he cautioned. "The moment they start finally talking is the most perilous of all.

Falsehoods and fabrications will pour out like water through a sluice. You can't believe any of it."

But despite his protests, the torturer obeyed her command.

"Keep talking," Occo ordered the heterochthonatrix. "Why and how did I get involved in your problems?"

Rammadrecula burst into lachrymosia again. "I've been stuck on that wretched planet ever since I joined the Envacht Lu. Did I say 'joined'? Am I guilty of such a misstatement of fact? Say rather that I was impressed into Envacht Lu! All but forcibly marched into it!"

"Forced by whom?" Occo demanded. "And for what reason?"

There followed a long and lachrymosic tale of woe, which wobbled back and forth between accusations (on the part of Rammadrecula) of envious resentment of her brilliance on the part of her peers; sullen and cynical malice toward her on the part of superiors mortified by that selfsame brilliance; accusations (on the part of her superiors) of duplicity when it came to examinations; and (on the part of her peers) of sordid conduct motivated by ambition which was simultaneously insatiable and impossible to satisfy because (so said her peers and superiors alike) Rammadrecula had neither the talent nor discipline nor self-control nor ability necessary to satisfy that selfsame ambition.

"Lies! All lies!" she concluded.

The torturer gave Occo a look which she interpreted as quizzical. Hard to be sure, of course, when dealing with mammals. The fur which covered their bodies obscured their features as well.

"She's probably still lying," he said.

Occo didn't think so. Rammadrecula's *interpretation* of the events related was questionable, to say the least. But the story taken as a whole had the ring of truth about it. This would hardly be the first time that an overly ambitious and insufficiently capable scion of a powerful sect ran afoul of the sect's authorities. Some of the more rigorous denominations would have culled her outright, but apparently the Flengren Apostollege was more inclined toward the ancient method of expulsion and exile.

"But why the Envacht Lu?" she asked the hetero-chthonatrix. "And perhaps more to the point, why would the Envacht Lu agree to accept you?"

There followed an even longer though less lachrymosic tale. The gist, extracted from the great pile of allegations, denunciations and recriminations which half-buried it, was that the official within the Flengren Apostollege who was in charge of Rammadrecula's disposition owed a favor to the official of the Envacht Lu who enrolled her in their ranks.

"What a pile of nonsense!" said Bresk. "I'm willing to bet that stands everything on its head. The Flengren in charge probably had a grudge against the Envacht Lu and chose this method to inflict a petty injury."

Rammadrecula managed a glare, despite being immobilized. "You really ought to discipline that familiar of yours," she said.

"As a general rule, that statement has merit," Occo replied. "But not, I think, in this case."

She suspected that Bresk had the right of it—certainly

more than Rammacredula's own version. But it didn't really matter either way. By now Occo was satisfied that the heterochthonatrix did not have any ill-intent toward Occo herself and her purpose.

Which did not mean she would be of any use for that purpose, of course.

"What to do . . ." she mused to herself.

She felt Bresk's neural connectors probing under her earflaps and raised them to assist his goal. The familiar's advice was usually worth listening to.

<She's annoying and a dullard—not to mention a buffoon—but she's also got one indubitably valuable quality,> came his thoughts.

Which is . . . ?

<She's rich. However much she irritated the Flengren Apostollege, they chose to simply exile her. They didn't strip her of her assets. Her not inconsiderable assets, I would point out—that ship of hers is literally worth a fortune.>

True, but I don't see what good that does us. We left her ship somewhere behind. All she has in her possession now is that idiotic target pistol.

<I wouldn't be so sure of that. Ask Ju'ula where the ship is.>

Occo looked down at the Warlock Variation Drive, who to all appearances had fallen asleep.

"Ju'ula?"

Her eyes opened. "Are we done with this silly business yet?"

"Almost. Where is the heterochthonatrix's ship? The one we—ah—flew away from."

Ju'ula's eyes rolled. "There are so many things wrong with that one short sentence that it's hard to know where to start. First, we did not 'fly' away from anything. That implies travel from one point in spacetime to another, which is not what happened. Second, the term 'spacetime' is gibberish anyway. Third, the ship is where it is. Fourth, 'where it is' would be more accurately stated as 'where it wants to be' except—we're up to point five, now—it's a brainless piece of machinery which doesn't actually 'want' anything but that's as close as I can get using this crude instrument you call a 'language.' Which—point six—is actually not a 'language' at all but just an arbitrary set of mutually accepted symbolic reference points. Which, finally, leads me to point seven, which is that I can't answer the question because—don't take this personally, it's just a fact—you aren't nearly bright enough to understand the answer."

Occo wasn't offended. She thought the Warlock Variation Drive was probably right and she was feeling especially dimwitted because the question she really wanted an answer to wasn't the one she had asked but—

"What I meant was, can you bring it back?"

Ju'ula squeezed her eyes shut as if in pain. "That sentence is no better. No, I can't bring it 'back' because it never went anywhere. It's right where it always was, which is where it's supposed to be."

"But—"

<Visualize it. However it works, the Warlock Variation Drive doesn't use the same sort of coordinate reference system we call—>

Occo visualized the interior of Rammadrecula's ship.

An instant later—if the transition even took an "instant"—they were in the luxurious central chamber of the vessel.

Relieved of her restraints, the heterochthonatrix collapsed to the floor.

"You should have tipped the torturer, Mama," Ju'ula said reproachfully. "He'll be cranky next time you visit."

Occo had no plans to revisit that dungeon. Still . . .

She visualized the dungeon.

Surprised, the torturer looked up from his implements.

"Good job," Occo said, handing him a credit chit.

He gazed down at it dubiously. "Not sure where I could spend this, but I appreciate the gesture. Glad to be of service."

She was back on the ship. Or perhaps she was just where she was supposed to be again. Who could say? Travel by Warlock Variation Drive was epistemologically challenging.

※ ※ ※

"Where the hell did that ship come from?" demanded Tabor.

Shenoy scratched his jaw. "I think it's them. The Knacks on the magic carpet, I mean. It's on the same spot on the moon where they were before they vanished."

Russ and Jaemu stared at the new image on the screen.

"Are you sure?" asked the Vitunpelay.

"Of course not. But it hardly matters since certainty is an epistemologically challenging notion to begin with."

He turned his head, which was a pointless gesture since the ship's AI was in no particular direction. "Ship, we want to rendezvous with that vessel."

CHAPTER 28

❊

"There's good news, middling news, bad news and execrable news," Bresk announced, after a quick scrutiny of the ship's sensor suite. "I'll start with—"

"Bad news first," Occo commanded.

"—the good news because the bad news doesn't truly show its colors without that positive nimbus."

"I *said*—"

"The atmosphere's breathable. On the middling side, it's awfully thin—as you'd expect given the weak gravity. The bad news is that while it's barely breathable it's poorly suited for winged air travel—"

"I command you on pain of—"

"Which undoubtedly explains why the alien craft approaching us will be here in less than ten medims. It's landing directly on its jets. A somewhat risky maneuver that does not speak well for the aliens' sense of caution and prudence. Which in turn suggests the possibility of hostile relations."

By then Occo had pushed Bresk aside and was studying the sensor suite herself.

"It doesn't seem to be a warship," she said.

"Not even close," Bresk agreed. "Which—again—suggests the aliens, whoever they are, are possessed by no great ability when it comes to risk assessment. A characteristic which, need I remind you, is often associated with belligerence. I recommend unfolding—or whatever you call it—the Skerkud Teleplaser."

Ju'ula eyes popped open. "Skerkie won't wake up inside this ship unless I tell him to. If you want him, you need me to go into action."

Her eyes closed. "Which is preposterous. I'm tired. Mama is a lot of fun but she's not what you'd call restful. I'm going back to sleep. Deal with the problem yourselves."

Occo was unsure of the course to follow. The approaching ship had the appearance of a Human-made vessel, but that didn't really indicate very much. Several species, including a number of sects among the Nac Zhe Anglan, were known to purchase and use Human spacecraft.

"Let me negotiate with them," said Rammadrecula. "No matter who they are, they're unlikely to want to get at cross-purposes with the Envacht Lu."

She had a point. The main focus of the Envacht Lu was inward, not outward. For the most part, the military order simply ignored alien species. Nonetheless, there had been enough clashes with such in the past that few if any aliens would be willing to antagonize an Envacht Lu official.

Unless they had a pressing reason to do so, of course—which these oncoming aliens might very well have, if they were also seeking the hidden repository of the Old Ones.

The *reputedly* hidden repository of the Old Ones, she cautioned herself. There was still no hard evidence that the repository existed on this moon, or even existed at all.

"Very well," she said.

❀ ❀ ❀

"You stay here," Tabor told Shenoy. "Let me go talk with them first."

"What if they prove hostile?"

"I'll go with him," announced Jaemu. "Most sentients are reluctant to get at cross-purposes with a Vitunpelay." He clacked his mandibles loudly. "Being, as we are, sometimes hard to distinguish from homicidal maniacs. Just let me get the rifle."

❀ ❀ ❀

By the time the alien spaceship landed, not far away, Rammadrecula had exited the airlock and was coming down the ramp onto the moon's surface. The heterochthonatrix was wearing respiratory equipment. The moon's atmosphere wasn't so thin as to be unbreathable, but it was too close for comfort.

A short time after Rammadrecula reached the surface, an airlock in the alien vessel opened, a ramp extruded, and two aliens emerged.

❀ ❀ ❀

Tabor was also wearing breathing apparatus, and for the same reason. Jaemu wasn't, because there was no equipment on the human vessel that could be adapted to his needs.

"Not a big problem," he'd assured everyone. "I can hold my breath quite a while unless I'm forced to exert myself."

Which he might be, if the aliens proved to be hostile. But Jaemu didn't seem to be very concerned about the matter and Russ saw no reason for him to be either. If a stray Vitunpelay came to a bad end, what did he really care?

※ ※ ※

"The big one's a Vitunpelay," said Bresk, studying the images in the viewscreen. "This could get a little hairy, as humans would say."

The expression made no sense at all, so far as Occo could determine. Humans were already hairy, so what difference could it make if they got a little more so? It would be like a Nac Zhe Anglan warning that things could get a little knobby-kneed.

But this was no time to be pondering the vagaries of human intelligence. Regardless of whatever expression one used, having a Vitunpelay included in the situation automatically lowered the chances of a sane outcome. The creatures were quite unpredictable.

"Does this vessel have armaments?" She was feeling more than a bit foolish that she hadn't thought to ask the question before the heterochthonatrix left the ship.

"Several varieties," said the Ebbo. "Beginning with the thermonuclear arsenal, we have—"

"I think we can skip over the weapons of mass destruction for the moment," said Occo. "What is available that might be described as a targetable weapon?"

"The thermonuclear devices on this ship *are*

targetable," said Proceeds-With-Circumspection. "Within a circular error probable of—"

"Targetable on the aliens emerging from *this* ship." Occo pointed at the vessel in the viewscreen. "Without damaging the heterochthonatrix."

"In that case, you have a choice between a muon lance and a retromolecularizer."

A muon lance was only "targetable" if one had no concern for anything in line of sight beyond the target. Given that Occo had no idea what might be out there, its use was contraindicated.

"Ship, extrude the retromolecularizer."

A faint whirring sound was heard.

❋ ❋ ❋

"They're bringing some sort of weapon to bear," said Jaemu. "Shall I fire?"

"No!" exclaimed Russ. "Are you crazy? That's a thirty-exabyte retromolecularizer. It'll turn us and everything around us into primordial ooze."

"Threatening us with it is an outrageous act of aggression," complained the Vitunpelay.

"It's neither aggression nor outrageous," said Russ. "It's common sense on their part, just as"—he pointed over his shoulder with a thumb—"what Rupert's doing is common sense."

The Vitunpelay *Bauplan* was poorly suited for head turning, so Jaemu had to maneuver himself halfway around to see what Tabor was referring to.

"That's quite an impressive . . . whatever it is," he said.

"It's a Jadlay deimager."

"De*imager*? What kind of idiot counters something

that'll turn us into slime with something that just ruins our enemy's image?"

Russ smiled. "Like Rupert says, you should really try to keep up with the literature. It destroys an image by rotating the thing imaged into the twelfth dimension. Which is just an antiseptic way of saying that it makes it impossible, since there are only eleven dimensions to begin with."

For a moment, the Vitunpelay looked cross-eyed. "That . . . sounds nasty."

Russ shrugged. "For all we know, it sends its target into heaven and eternal bliss. Nobody has any idea what happens to something that's been hit by a Jadlay deimager. Except that they go away and never ever ever come back."

As they'd been speaking, Russ had kept advancing on the aliens—slowly, though. He didn't want anyone getting nervous.

Once they were within ten meters, he held up his hand in what was generally accepted as a gesture of peace throughout the known galaxy. Well . . . accepted by everyone except Vitunpelay. But since the Vitunpelay was on his side at the moment, he wasn't going to fret over that.

"We come in peace," he said.

"That could be a lie or a half-truth, though," added Jaemu. "I wouldn't trust my partner if I were you."

Russ tried not to snarl. "You can ignore him. He's a fucking clown. *I* come in peace." He now jerked his thumb in Jaemu's direction. "Him, who knows? You can always point the retromolecularizer at him—*after* constricting the focus. Which you have to do anyway as close as you are to us, or you'll get caught up in the blast yourselves."

In the distance, he could see the retromoleculizer's aperture narrowing. It seemed to shift a little also, to point more directly at Jaemu, although he wasn't sure about that.

The Knack they'd come to meet now spoke up. "Be warned! I am a puissant figure in the Envacht Lu! To offend or insult me is perilous, to threaten me risks calamitous result, to harm me in any manner is tantamount to self-destruction!"

Russ reached up to scratch his jaw, but the breathing apparatus was in the way. He had to satisfy himself with plucking at one of the straps holding it in place.

"What level of official?" he asked. "Planetary proconsul? System surrogate?"

The Knack's posture stiffened, causing it to rise up a few centimeters. "I am Heterochthonatrix Heurse Gotha Rammadrecula."

❈ ❈ ❈

"But that's bizarre!" exclaimed Shenoy over the comm. *"What is a member of the Flengren Apostollege doing in the Envacht Lu? And a heterochthonatrix, to boot!"*

Russ was wondering the same thing himself. Those officials the Envacht Lu titled "heterochthonatrixes" were the ones dealing with aliens. It was something of an oddball rank in the Envacht Lu hierarchy, since the Knack military order rarely dealt with aliens at all—and then, usually, only to threaten them in a manner that was about as sophisticated as one dog in an alley growling at another.

He'd once heard a human ambassador refer to a heterochthonatrix as the Knack equivalent of a criminal street gang appointing one of their members as a chief of protocol when dealing with other gangs. "About as useless as tits on a bull," he'd concluded.

"This is getting interesting," Shenoy added. *"Hold on, Russ. I'm coming out."*

"Dammit, Rupert—" But Shenoy had already left the comm, and Russ could do nothing but fume. If there was any one thing that could drive a security specialist half-insane, it was a client who refused to listen to his advice. What was the point of hiring a bodyguard if you insisted on throwing your body into harm's way?

A short time later Shenoy was coming down the ramp. Once on the surface, he hurried toward the small group gathered between the two ships. Naturally, the damn fool wasn't wearing any respiratory equipment.

At least the Knack ship's retromolecularizer didn't shift its aim from Jaemu. Of course, no one in their right mind, presented with a choice between a human sage and a Vitunpelay, would target the human. Well, unless the shock of wild and unruly white hair confused them and they decided it was a peculiar weapon system of some sort.

As soon as Shenoy reached them he extended his hand toward the Knack. "Greetings!" he said.

The Knack stared down at the hand. "What are you offering me?" it demanded. "I see nothing there. Is this a trick of some sort? If so, I warn you! Attempting to defraud or otherwise mislead an official of the Envacht Lu is a foolhardy enterprise that is sure to—"

Russ took hold of Rupert's arm and pulled it back

down. "Relax, o puissant official. My associate is unfamiliar with the ways of the Nac Zhe Anglan. Extending a manipulative appendage is an ancient human custom to indicate amity and a desire to avoid causing harm."

The Knack stared at him, its mustard-colored eyes now reduced to slits. "How bizarre."

* * *

On board their ship, Bresk said to Occo: "If you don't want this parlay to dissolve into a pageant of misapprehension and semi-comic misunderstanding, I suggest you—"

But Occo was already making for the airlock. What sort of fumble-witted heterochthonatrix wasn't familiar with the basic customs of the galaxy's major species? Occo had never had any dealings with Humans herself, prior to this point, but she'd known perfectly well what the human hand-extension gesture had signified.

In essence: *to prove I come in peace I show you that I hold no weapon.*

It was just the sort of silliness you'd expect from a species that suffered from an absurdly optimistic view of the universe. In all the millennia of Nac Zhe Anglan history, Occo could not recall a single incident of record in which a betrayal had been committed by a weapon held openly in hand. Ridiculous! A sane plotter used poison spread on surfaces beforehand, weapons wielded by confederates cunningly hidden from view, missiles fired from ambush—the list went on and on.

She needed to get out there and take charge of the situation or it would rapidly become chaotic.

* * *

"Heads up, Rupert. Here comes another one." Russ had caught sight of the new Knack as soon as he—no, more likely she, judging from the huge knees—started down the ramp.

Interestingly, this one didn't seem to be carrying any weapons at all. Granted, it was impossible to be sure. The harness that Knacks all seem to wear had various items attached to the straps or carried in pouches whose functions were usually indeterminate. One of them might be a microgrenade. But Russ didn't think the Knack was carrying any sort of sidearm.

As soon as the Knack arrived she extended her hand. "Greetings, Humans. I am Occo Nasht Jopri Kruy Gadrax, formerly of the Naccor Jute. Am I correct in my surmise, that you are on this moon because you seek to uncover the secrets of the Old Ones?"

"Bingo," said Russ.

"Would that be your surname or given name?" asked the Knack. "If I understand human naming conventions properly."

Russ shook his head. "'Bingo' is just an expression. It means more-or-less 'I've won the prize.' My actual name is Russ Tabor."

He nodded toward Shenoy. "And this would be Rupert Shenoy."

"Ah!" The Knack did her own stiff-necked version of a nod. "The famous savant. As Humans reckon such things."

Bingo again. But Russ didn't say it aloud. He smiled at Shenoy and said: "I believe we're in the right company."

"So it would seem."

CHAPTER 29

❋

"So there you have it," Shenoy concluded. "You can see now why I placed no credence in the Morganite tale."

Occo stared at the Human.

Bresk farted. "You ordered this Morgan killed because you didn't believe his story on account of *evolutionary theory*?" The familiar farted again. "You're either insane or much smarter than any Human is supposed to be."

The larger Human's face twisted oddly. Occo thought that expression indicated amusement—a "grin," the aliens called it, if she remembered correctly—but she wasn't sure.

"He's not crazy," he said. "Rupert really is that smart. It's a little scary sometimes. Though not as scary as he is when he's forgetting where he is on account of he's somewhere nobody has any business being even if it's just in his own head."

Occo tried to make sense of that statement and gave up halfway through. She wondered if all Humans were a little insane. It could be hard to tell with alien species.

Shenoy had ignored the interchange entirely. His attention was now fully occupied in an examination of the central chamber of Rammadrecula's ship.

"Pretty plush," he commented. Then, rose to his feet and moved toward the inert form of Ju'ula. As was usually the case when the Warlock Variation Drive was dormant, she looked like a very large cruciform vegetable.

"This is an odd-looking piece of furniture," Shenoy commented. Before Occo could intervene, the alien leaned over and poked Ju'ula with a finger. "Doesn't look too comfortable, although that might just be—*yah!*"

Ju'ula's eyes had popped open. "What is this Human doing in here and why is it bothering me? Skerkie, wake up!"

The Teleplaser emerged from the alcove where Occo had placed it and began its familiar unfolding. Given the limited height available in the chamber, it was extending outward more than upward.

Bresk farted loudly. "Not in here! We'll all get killed!"

But the familiar had misestimated—or perhaps it would be better to say, underestimated—the degree to which the Teleplaser's behavior was guided by the Warlock Variation Drive. Instead of its extensions producing weapons, they produced a variety of restraints. An instant later, the Shenoy Human was completely immobilized—and when the larger Human named Tabor tried to intervene, it found itself likewise ensnared.

"Good move, Rupert," complained Tabor. He gave Occo a look from under lowered brows over its tiny eyes. "You see what I mean? He's even scarier when he's up and about. Doesn't pay any attention to anything."

Occo decided to intervene—or try, at least. It was hard to know how the Warlock Variation Drive might react.

"He meant no harm, Ju'ula. And I'd rather keep him alive and unhurt. He seems to know a great deal that may be relevant to my purpose."

Ju'ula swiveled one of her eyes to look at Occo while the other remained fixed on the figure of Shenoy. "A *Human*? That seems most unlikely. As a rule, Humans are even dumber than you folk."

"Not this one, apparently. He has the reputation of being quite intelligent."

"Oh, that's nonsense." Ju'ula brought both eyes to bear on Shenoy. "But it's easily determined. You—Human. Do you agree with the proposition that the ontological significance of the hexadecimal neuroanalysis of—"

The ensuing sentences—or perhaps it was all one sentence—were completely incomprehensible. And Ju'ula never finished whatever she was saying anyway because the Human interrupted before she was done.

"Oh, that's blithering nonsense!" exclaimed Shenoy. "How can any creature sentient enough to use mathematics in the first place be so stupid as to think that—"

The rest was just as incomprehensible as the original statement by the Warlock Variation Drive.

By the time Shenoy was finished, Ju'ula had extruded four more eyes and was staring at the Human with all six of them.

"Ha!" she exclaimed. "It turns out you were right, Mama. She *is* smart. I didn't know humans were capable of that much in the way of reasoning."

"I'm male, actually," Shenoy said.

Ju'ula closed all six eyes. "You really don't want to annoy me, Human."

"You really don't," chimed in Bresk. "But don't take it personally. She's—yes, she insists she's female, even though—"

Ju'ula eyes popped open and all six swiveled toward Bresk. "Watch it, fartboy!"

"Which no doubt she is, seeing as how she says so, even though—never mind—she's got me pegged for a male even though as you can see"—Bresk floated up and slowly spun around—"I've got no—"

He broke off, seeing that the Teleplaser was starting to unfold more appendages. "Well, never mind that either."

The sage's big Human companion cleared his throat. "Rupert, just accept that you're now female and be a man about it."

Shenoy frowned. "That statement is even more ridiculous than the one—" He broke off and brought the frown to bear on the Warlock Variation Drive. "Female, is it? All right. It's all in the interest of science, I suppose. Although someday I'd like to know how you came into existence in the first place."

Two of Ju'ula's eyes were withdrawn. "Don't get above yourself. You're bright but you're not *that* bright. Not your fault, though. You can't be that bright without abandoning mortality."

"Oh, come on," said Tabor, in a tone which Occo took to be scoffing. "Are you seriously claiming you're *immortal*?"

Ju'ula's eyes closed. "That statement is actually painful."

"Russ, the notion of 'immortality' is just a meaningless noise," said Shenoy. "What the Warlock Variation Drive means is that the relationship to mortality required to understand its—"

All six eyes popped open.

"Excuse me, *her* origins, is consubstantial rather than transubstantial."

"Nicely put. The pain eases," Ju'ula said. "Mama, you'd do well to hang onto this Human. She really is much smarter than average."

Occo had already come to that conclusion herself. "Agreed. So now, Rupert Shenoy, tell me what you propose that we do."

The Human sage made an odd little noise. "Before we get into that, could you . . . ah, these manacles? Not to mention shackles, handcuffs, chains, fetters, trammels . . . "

"Oh, sorry," said Ju'ula. "Skerkie's a little slow." She emitted a sort of high-pitched little squeaking noise and the Teleplaser immediately released the two Humans and began folding itself back up.

"Thank you," said Shenoy, rubbing his arms with his hands. "I believe our first course of action should be to seek out this reputed repository of the Old Ones. Unless the Morganite tale was a tissue of lies from top to bottom, the repository should be located somewhere on this moon."

"Rupert," cautioned his companion, "it might just be a complete fabrication."

Simultaneously, Occo and Shenoy shook their heads.

Seeing his gesture mirrored, Shenoy gestured toward Occo. "You explain it."

"It makes no sense for the entirety of their statements to be lies," Occo said. "They wouldn't have interacted with you at all unless they wanted something from you."

Tabor rubbed his face. "Okay, that makes sense."

"And what would it be, except to persuade you to search the moon in their stead?"

The Human's peculiar face-rubbing became more vigorous. "Which means there's something dangerous about finding the repository."

"So we may presume," agreed Occo. "Something exceedingly dangerous, at that. I agree with Sage Shenoy—"

"I prefer Sir Rupert, actually."

"Sir Rupert, then, when he opines that while the Morganites are clearly not as powerful as they claimed to be, they could hardly be powerless. Apparently they were mighty enough to destroy the Mank, whose military prowess has been a legend in this arm of the galaxy for millennia."

"Although one has to wonder if that legend was not itself at least partly fabricated," Shenoy cautioned. "But either way, we arrive at the same conclusion. Whether the Morganites were able to slay the Mank of legend or they simply *thought* they were, they must have possessed great power—and at least some of that power must still remain."

"Yet not enough to overcome whatever it is that guards the repository of the Old Ones," Occo concluded. "It will be a perilous undertaking indeed."

Silence fell in the chamber. The six sentients in the room—seven, counting Bresk; eight, if you included the Warlock Variation Drive; nine if you stretched the definition and added the Skerkud Teleplaser—looked back and forth at each other. (Excluding the Teleplaser, who had no visible ocular organs, and the Warlock Variation Drive, whose eyes were still closed.)

"A problem remains," Occo said.

Shenoy smiled. "Indeed. How can we trust each other—which we must, in order to form an alliance."

The two Nac Zhe Anglan and the Ebbo stared at the Human. The Ebbo began scribbling on its tablet. Occo and Rammadrecula now looked at each other.

"As I told you, they are a species with only the feeblest grasp on reality," said the heterochthonatrix.

"So you did. I had not truly understood, however, the full extent of their unsanity."

Bresk farted sarcastically. "You still don't. It's not just trust—the Human languages all have a multitude of similar fantasies. In English alone, we can count confidence, faith, hope, reliance—"

"Enough," commanded Occo.

Shenoy looked at Tabor. "I seem to be missing something."

Russ chuckled. "Knacks aren't exactly famous for their rosy outlook. As you might expect from a species which has several thousand religious denominations and sects—not one of which believes in a benevolent deity or deities—they pretty much consider 'trust' a synonym for 'crazy.'"

"Oh." The savant frowned. "But how do they get anything done, then?"

"More often than not, they don't," said Russ. "Knacks are like humans, in that they favor old saws and precepts. Just to name a few I can remember off the top of my head, and translating them into the English equivalent:

"If it's not broken, it will be soon. Don't fix it, though, because someone is sure to break it again.

"Don't count your chickens after they hatch because some are bound to die right off.

"Leap before you look since it's probably a mirage anyway.

"A penny saved is a penny about to be stolen.

"I could go on, but you get the point."

Shenoy shook his head, not in a gesture of negation but simply to clear it. "Goodness. I knew the Nac Zhe Anglan had a culture that changed very slowly. Now I understand why."

"Yep. They don't make any deals until and unless they can be sure that no one involved in it can stab anyone else in the back—not 'won't,' mind you, but 'can't.' They assume that if treachery is possible it will happen."

"But . . . "

Occo almost felt sorry for the pitiful creatures. "We cannot possibly form the alliance you propose until we have assurances that when you contemplate betraying us the penalties will be so severe that you will be reluctantly forced to refrain from natural behavior."

Silence fell upon the chamber again, as the various sentients present tried to imagine a suitable arrangement.

Ju'ula extruded one eye. "This is tiresome. Just have Skerkie make whatever guarantees you need."

All eyes now turned toward the Teleplaser in the

alcove. The device—creature?—had resumed its normal quasi-tureen appearance.

"But . . . how could it do that?" asked Russ.

Ju'ula extruded a second eye. "Tiresome! Skerkie, wake up. These parasapients need to form a hexagonal concordaunt."

The eyes swiveled to study Bresk. "Better make it heptagonal."

The Teleplaser unfolded. Within minims it had produced seven extensions that resembled . . .

"Hey!" said Russ. "Those look like hypodermic—"

The extensions flashed and the needle tips reached and penetrated their marks. Seven sentients—counting Bresk in the mix, which was a dubious proposition—emitted a variety of cries and squeals of pain and outrage.

The extensions were withdrawn. Folded up. Within two minims, the Teleplaser was dormant again.

Russ rubbed his shoulder. "What the hell—?"

"You have all been implanted with concordaunt sureties," said Ju'ula. "Any betrayal by any of you will hatch the surety. What would occur next is too ghastly to relate."

The heterochthonatrix reached for the pistol on her harness. "I ought to—!" she began to bellow. But before Rammadrecula could get another word out, she clutched one of her rear legs and half-collapsed to the deck.

"Ah! The pain!"

Ju'ula studied her dispassionately. "The surety is beginning to wake since, by threatening mayhem, the Nac Zhe Anglan hemisapient has jeopardized the concordaunt.

Not quite a betrayal, no, but close enough for the brain simulacrum of the implanted horror to stir restlessly. I recommend a rapid embrace of philosophical and spiritual tranquility."

"Calm down, Rammadrecula," said Occo. "As the old adage has it, what's done is doomed anyway. Since we seem to have solved the problem of guaranteeing the pact, we may as well get about our task."

She turned to the Human sage. "What course of action do you propose?"

Shenoy combed through his bizarre tuft of white fur—no, they called it "hair," didn't they?—with stubby digits. "Well, the first thing we need to do is find the repository. But I have no idea how to go about doing that. It has to be extraordinarily well-hidden, I would think. We had our complete sensor suite deployed as we approached the moon, and we maintained a polar orbit for more than three cycles before we landed, and we didn't spot anything that looked promising."

"We can't do a direct search of the surface," said Tabor. "This moon is bigger than Mars. We're looking at an area somewhere in the range of two hundred million kilometers squared."

Occo steeled her resolve. "The solution—I should say, the method needed for a solution—is clear. Bresk, link up. Everyone else, gather closely around. I will probably need input from all of you."

Her companions moved toward her. Bresk did as he was told, but not without producing an alarmed fart.

"What do you have in mind?" he demanded. "Surely you're not contemplating—"

"Ju'ula," said Occo. "I'm afraid your rest is over."

Her eyes popped open. Two, then four, then six.

"*Noooooooooooooooo . . . .*" Bresk moaned.

CHAPTER 30

✴

Occo started with as general an image as possible of what she imagined the universe's most hidden repository might look like.

Blackness. No—not even that. Black is still a color. This was a void so complete as to negate all color.

Wait! Was that a red gleam in the distance?

No—two gleams. Growing larger by the minim.

Resolving into two eyes. Huge, glaring, angry eyes. The eyes of a deity—demon, it hardly mattered—swollen both in might and madness.

"Not many of my Mamas were bold enough to invade the realm of The Disheartening One," Ju'ula said cheerfully. "Six all told—counting you. Let's see how long you last. The record is seven minims from first gleam. You're up to four. Oh, look—the third eye is starting to open."

Sure enough, between and slightly above the existing two eyes a third was emerging. Still more huge, more glaring, and utterly enraged.

"Counting down . . . five minims."

Bresk's thought intruded. **<Remember those nasty creatures on the sixth moon of—>**

❋ ❋ ❋

The moon's surface was just as Occo remembered it. Stony, almost barren of vegetation. Its most notable feature were the narrow mounds rising up everywhere, each about the height of a Nac Zhe Anglan—and each with multiple apertures from which the nasty creatures were even now emerging. Hexapodal, pincered, mottled-brown in color except for the three red eyes.

Rammadrecula came into her own here. Her pistol was already out and producing a great slaughter among the oncoming horde. Say what else you would about the heterochthonatrix, her marksmanship was phenomenal.

Still, there was no chance Rammadrecula could slay all of the creatures—and for whatever reasons motivated the Skerkud Teleplaser, it was remaining inert and would apparently be of no help at all.

❋ ❋ ❋

Happily, the three-eyed creatures reminded Occo of the similarly occulated denizens of the gorges of Tokorori Sto known as drogonxollos. Which, though much larger, were also more timid in their disposition, which was not surprising given that their flesh was tasty beyond measure and greatly prized by all manner of hunters.

Among whose number Occo herself had once been included in the course of a rare vacation with her husbands. Down into the hiding holes they'd gone, armed with the traditional tridents used to hunt drogonxollos.

Where they'd gotten hopelessly lost and eventually stumbled into a grotto which turned out to be the nest of one of the giant limbless predators for which the biota of Tokorori Sto was also famous.

Their tridents flashed—struck and struck again. But to no avail! Where the serpentine reptiles that the limbless predator superficially resembled had scaly armored skin, this ghastly creature's integument was slime incarnate. Their tridents were soon stuck. The slime oozed up the handles and they were forced to relinquish their weapons lest they themselves become glued fast to the monster.

Down the narrow tunnels and corridors they fled. Down ever downward, as the cunning horror cut off their escape routes. It moved no faster than they, but it knew the labyrinth far better.

Down even downward—

❋ ❋ ❋

Much as Occo imagined the search for the repository of the Old Ones would lead them as well.

Down ever downward . . .

Into what? A cavern? A pit? And if a pit, might it be . . . Bottomless?

❋ ❋ ❋

Down and down they plunged.

Down and down they plunged.

Down and down they plunged.

The illumination from the lamps on their harnesses provided only the faintest lighting—until Russ Tabor drew forth some sort of handheld device which emitted a much brighter beam.

"Jesus H. Christ!" he bellowed. "What the hell have you gotten us into?"

The beam from his device showed a featureless wall on all sides. The pit's diameter was roughly five times the height of a Nac Zhe Anglan.

Featureless—and oddly colorless. Not even gray, so much as a vague translucence.

Down and down they plunged.

Down and down they plunged.

"I can't see any bottom!" Tabor shouted. He now had the beam of light aimed directly below them—but nothing could be seen, beyond more featureless and colorless wall rushing past them.

Down and down they plunged.

"Everyone please calm down!" said the sage Shenoy. "We are quite safe from any harm. Well, until we perish from thirst. But that will take a while yet. Ah . . . for we humans, at least. I'm not sure how often Nac Zhe Anglan and Vitunpelay need to hydrate."

"I can go for days without water," said Jaemu, sounding quite cheerful. "Of course, I start getting grumpy."

"How are we *safe*?" demanded Tabor. "This thing has to bottom out at some point!"

"No, it won't," said Shenoy. "I assure you it's quite bottomless. We could stay in it without striking any bottom until our protons decayed some, oh, quattuordecillion years from now, thereabouts. That's if protons decay at all, which is still not established."

"Oh, bullshit!" said Tabor. "There's no such thing as a bottomless pit."

"Well, of course not. But we're not in a bottomless pit. We're in a Moebius wormhole."

"A *what*?"

"Moebius wormhole." Shenoy made an odd clucking sound. "As I've said before, Russ, you really should try to keep up with the literature. No one's ever seen a Moebius wormhole before, but this is actually a rather close match to what was predicted. It's the intersection of the branes, you know. They produce all sorts of peculiar effects—one or more of which, I suspect, is what explains the magic of the Old Ones."

He now looked at the Warlock Variation Drive, which had resumed its normal cruciform shape and was falling not far from Occo. Ju'ula didn't seem especially concerned herself about the situation, Occo realized. She did have one eyestalk extruded, but the eye itself was only half-open.

"If I might make so bold," Shenoy said, "I wonder if your Warlock Variation Drive would be willing to—mindmeld? whatever you call it—with me for a moment or so."

Ju'ula's eye opened fully. Then, an instant later, was joined by three more.

"You propose to have me engaged with two Mamas at once?" she asked. "That's a little kinky."

Two of the eyes swiveled to look at Occo. "But if Mama has no objection, I guess it's okay with me."

Occo had no objection at all, since she was quite at a loss to figure out how to extricate themselves from their predicament.

"Go ahead," she said.

Two more eyes came out. All six were now peering intently at Shenoy.

"There's one condition," Ju'ula said. "You have to change your name. I'm okay with kinky but I draw the line at depravity."

Shenoy frowned. "Change my name? But . . . to what?"

Tabor made a booming sound which startled Occo.

\<Humans call that laughing,\> Bresk explained. **\<It's their way of expressing humor.\>**

"Isn't it obvious, Rupert?" said Tabor. "Or should I say, Rupert-who-was. I now proclaim you . . . oh, let's make it Prudence Shenoy. Or would you prefer Primrose? Or better still—I hereby name you Ronnette Shenoy."

"That's preposterous!"

All six of the Warlock Variation Drive's eyes grew slitted. "You're not going to piss me off, are you? To use that crude Human idiom."

Shenoy stared at her.

"I really, really, really, really, really, really, really—add another quattuordecillion 'reallys' to that list—recommend that you not piss me off."

Shenoy cleared his throat. "Ah . . . would you settle for Robin?"

"No."

"Leslie, then?"

"No."

"Taylor, Randy, Stacy, Daryl—?"

"Cut it out, Mama. *No cheating.*"

Shenoy exhaled loudly. "Very well. Ronnette it is."

"Okay, then," said Ju'ula. "What did you have in mind?"

"It seems—correct me if I am in error at any

point—that when Occo here visualizes a location, which is what stimulates your—"

"Don't be gross, Mama Ronnette. I hate gross stuff."

" . . . Ah, very well, then. Let me say instead that Occo's visualizations engage your attention—"

He paused for a moment, warily studying the Warlock Variation Drive for any signs of irritation, insofar as "signs of irritation" could be detected on something that looked like a cruciform vegetable.

Seeing nothing amiss, the Human sage proceeded. "What is really happening is that one of many possible symbological systems—what we might also call 'languages'—"

"What we most certainly may *not* also call 'languages,'" interrupted Ju'ula. "Languages are stupid. Stick with symbological systems."

"Ah . . . yes, certainly. One of many possible symbological systems is mutually acknowledged—but each party in what we might call the arrangement is actually regarding it differently."

"Well, sure. I understand it correctly. Occo's kind of sweet, but she's a dimwit so she imagines it in pictures. Which is okay, even if it's primitive. I just draw the line at language stuff. I am *not* going to work myself to death trying to figure out what a mishmash of sounds and spittle is supposed to mean."

"No, of course not. Perish the thought. But what I am leading toward is the proposition that mathematics would be a better way of effectuating that same mutual acknowledgment of a shared—no! no! say rather, compromised upon—humbly and diffidently on our part;

benevolently, on yours—symbological system. Am I mistaken?"

Ju'ula studied the Human sage for a moment. "Allowing for the fact that what you call 'mathematics' isn't what you think it is . . . yes. It would probably work better."

She swiveled her eyestalks toward Occo. "Meaning no offense, Mama Occo, but you're pretty sloppy about it."

Bresk farted. "Which explains why her visualizations always get us into so much trouble."

"Don't be disrespectful, fartboy," said Ju'ula. "And it's not true, anyway. The symbological system that Mama Ronnette wants to use will probably get you into just as much trouble. Won't be as sloppy, though."

Bresk farted again, this time with alarm. "Wait a mimim! Maybe we should think this over—"

But Shenoy's eyes were already closed. "Um . . . Yes, I think this will do," he said.

※ ※ ※

The vista was just as bland and featureless as the Moebius wormhole, but had even fewer referents. Gray everywhere, that same translucent lack of color, but with nothing at all to provide any sense of scale.

Slowly, nodules began to coalesce. Then, began assuming form and shape.

But then . . .

Eventually, Occo realized that she was looking at mathematical symbols of some sort—well, symbols of some sort, at any rate—not one of which was in any way familiar to her.

She looked around. None of her companions were visible any longer, although she could somehow sense their presence.

Bresk was still neurologically connected—but she couldn't see him either.

Human mathematical conventions, I assume, she thought.

<Not . . . really> came her familiar's response. **<None of these symbols have any referents in human mathematics that I'm aware of. It's as if . . . Hard as it is to believe, I think Shenoy is just making it up as he goes along.>**

That's impressive, I take it?

<It borders on lunacy, but, yes, it's impressive. The problem is that with no established referents or—call them boundaries, if you will—all Shenoy has to do is lose concentration and we're all likely to—ahhhhhhhhhhh . . . .>

His thoughts faded away. And as they did, Occo began to realize that everything else was starting to fade away as well. The featureless surroundings became . . . unfeatured, as it were. She could see right through parts of her own body. Then, as impossible as it seemed, she could see right through her own thoughts

as if they barely existed at all

and were

becoming   farther   apart

what was her name

* * *

Suddenly, everything crystallized around her again. She was Occo!

Occo Nasht Jopri Kruy Gadrax.

She was standing on a flat plain. Almost featureless, but solid. There were colors, too. Not many, and those all pastels. Still, they were indubitably colors.

And life! A little octopodal creature sidled out from behind a small rock and—

Attacked her. Tried to, rather. Was it mad? She outweighed it by at least three orders of magnitude.

As she demonstrated by stepping on the creature and crushing it into the rocky soil. When she withdrew her ped, only a shapeless mass in a tiny puddle of ichor remained.

Odd—but also reassuring, in its way.

Suddenly, Bresk appeared, floating just above her and still neurally attached.

<That was unsettling. To put it mildly.>

Rammadrecula appeared, as did the two Humans and the Warlock Variation Drive. A moment later, the Ebbo and Vitunpelay did likewise. All that was missing was the Skerkud Teleplaser.

Which emerged from . . . . wherever . . . an instant later.

Ju'ula was looking up at Shenoy. It was hard to tell, but Occo thought her gaze was reproachful.

"Don't ever do that again, Mama Ronnette," she said. "We barely made it out of . . . well, I can't call it 'there,' of course. Which is why we barely made it out."

The Human sage smiled a bit crookedly. "It *was* a bit more on the edge than I'd intended. However, as the bard said, all's well that ends well."

Shenoy turned to face the rest of them. His smile

widened. "I have found the Repository of the Old Ones."

"No kidding?" asked Tabor. Without waiting for an answer to that clearly rhetorical question, he asked a real one: "So where is it?"

"Well . . . 'where' isn't exactly the issue. Or, um, the problem. As I suspected, the Old Ones folded the location of their repository into a supra-spacetime dimensional reality. It does not actually exist anywhere in the usual sense of the term."

"Then . . . where is it?"

Shenoy made a clucking noise. "'Where' is a meaningless term, in this context. It would be better to say 'how is it?' Or, more precisely, 'how is it gotten to?' Well . . . being absolutely precise, I suppose I should say 'how *hard* is it to get to?'"

<I have a bad feeling about this.>

So did Occo. But there was nothing to do other than press forward.

"So how hard is it to get to?" she asked.

"As hard as we can possibly make it," was Shenoy's answer.

"What?" demanded Tabor. "Why should we make it as hard to get to as we can?"

Shenoy frowned at him. "But, Russ, I just got through explaining that the Old Ones hid their repository by folding it into a supra-spacetime dimensional reality."

"Wherever the hell that means!"

"I would think it was obvious. The only way we can get there is by making it as hard as possible to get there. The harder it is, the more likely we will succeed."

"That's nuts!"

"Well, of course. What part of 'supra-spacetime dimensional reality' are you having the most trouble understanding?"

CHAPTER 31

Seeing that every being was still staring at him, Shenoy smiled. "None of you are thinking this through properly." He nodded toward the Warlock Variation Drive. "As it— ah, she—just said, referring to the location of the repository, we can't call it 'there,' of course. That's because it has no actual location, in the normal sense of the term. One cannot *get* to the place because it isn't a 'place' at all. Instead, one must *attain* the repository. Which can only be done by tricking it into revealing itself through what one might call search-by-desperation."

More silence. Then Tabor said: "Huh?"

"Search-by-desperation. We imagine places that are increasingly more dangerous and increasingly more difficult to escape. As we do so, we come—well, I can't really call it 'nearer' but that's a reasonable poetic depiction of the process—to the repository. Not 'nearer' in terms of spacetime topography, but more proximate in terms of the repository's willingness to reveal itself."

"Huh?" Tabor repeated.

"How could a location be 'willing' to do anything?" Occo demanded. "That's nonsensical."

Shenoy peered at her as if examining a peculiar object. "But—didn't I just get through explaining that the repository is not a location in the first place?"

"Then what is it?"

"Well . . ." Shenoy peered at the Warlock Variation Drive, as if seeking help.

Ju'ula immediately retracted all six of her eyestalks. "I've got nothing to do with this. I see nothing, I hear nothing, and I'm certainly not going to say anything. Maybe this will all turn out to be a bad dream."

Shenoy nodded his head. "That's actually not too bad a depiction of the repository of the Old Ones. It is indeed something of a nightmare—that you can only attain through reverie. Which, of course, is the underlying mechanism of the Warlock Variation Drive."

Ju'ula's eyes popped open again. They seemed to glare with red rage.

"Using the term 'mechanism' very loosely," Shenoy added hurriedly. The redness in the Warlock Variation Drive's eyes faded into a sort of luminous pink-orange. She swiveled them toward Occo.

"You're really in deep trouble," she said. "And I'm not going any further until one condition is clearly established."

She swiveled her eyestalks back toward Shenoy. "*She* doesn't do the driving. You're pretty wild, Mama, but *she's* downright crazy."

"Then why should we follow his—her—advice at all?" Occo wanted to know.

Ju'ula seemed to shiver for an instant. "I didn't say she was wrong. I said she was crazy."

Rammadrecula now spoke. "But if the Human is insane—"

Ju'ula's eyes clenched tight. "When did I say she was 'insane'? I said she was *crazy*."

Hearing the silence around her, Ju'ula's eyes opened again. "How can you creatures feed yourselves? Do you really not understand the distinctions between insane, unsane, deranged, mad, irrational, senseless, psychotic, unhinged, demented, barmy, unbalanced, unhinged, aberrant and crazy?"

The silence continued until Tabor said: "Uhh . . . ."

The Warlock Variation Drive closed her eyes again. "Never mind. You wouldn't understand if I explained. Humans have an expression for it."

"'Purls before swine,'" Bresk offered.

Ju'ula's eyes popped open and she goggled at the familiar. "Not useless after all, if one allows that the possession of useless information is not itself useless."

"But what does it mean?" asked Jaemu.

Bresk answered: "'Purls before swine' is a colloquialism dating back into Human prehistory. Nac Zhe Anglan scholars think that it's a reference to the inability of nonsentient foragers to use any sort of uniform resource locator, much less persistent ones."

Tabor rolled his eyes. Shenoy started to say something but the bigger Human restrained him. "Don't bother, Rupert. Talking about pearls before swine."

He now looked at the Warlock Variation Drive. "If I've got this straight, you're willing to help us find—locate, uncover, discover, whatever-damn-term you want—this repository. On the condition that Rupert isn't the one who . . . Ah, what's the right term? I've got a feeling 'operates you' won't cut it."

Ju'ula's eyestalks grew in number to eight, all of them tipped with orbs so red with fury, so incandescent with rage—

❊ ❊ ❊

That Occo could not help but be reminded of the Octuplets of Gelle Bas, the regents of the secretive polity known to the galaxy at large as the Pontificate of Good Fortune but understood by all Naccor Jute castigants to be, in reality, a criminal enterprise devoted to the acquisition and sale of the tonics, narcotics and potions used by the assassins of 73 Kaych to work themselves into the frenzy needed to assault the fortresses of Kaychan antagonists. Among whom was prominently numbered the Envacht Lu, explaining the great care with which 73 Kaych had kept the location of its sect hidden from sight—

Until Occo herself had uncovered it and exchanged the galactic coordinates to the Envacht Lu in return for various favors, thus enabling that mighty military order to launch a campaign to finally rid the galaxy of the constant nuisance of assassination attempts, which would have earned the Naccor Jute the thanks and amity of a goodly portion of the Nac Zhe Anglan species despite its heretical theology had not the ruling officials of Occo's sect kept the secret to themself in the hopes of shielding Occo from the wrath of the now-bereft-of-their-best-customers Pontificate of Good Fortune. A hope which proved fallacious, undone by the cleverness of the Pontificate's own castigants, who captured Occo and brought her before the assembled Octuplets of Gelle Bas—

Who, in their fury, ignored the dictates of good sense and had Occo turned over to the care of their torturers instead of executing her immediately, thus enabling the Naccor Jute to appeal to the Envacht Lu who, not sated with the imminent destruction of 73 Kaych, now turned their dread attention to the Pontificate of Good Fortune, whose desperate attempts to placate the implacable military order caused their attention to be diverted from Occo—

Thus enabling her to escape by suborning the Octuplets' torturers, an eventuality which the Octuplets should have foreseen given that any number of scholarly studies of the proclivities of torturers had demonstrated them to be, as a rule, corrupt beyond measure. In that respect, being quite unlike the castigants and inquisitors among whose ranks Occo herself was numbered, whose fidelity and adherence to principle was a byword among all sects and denominations of the Nac Zhe Anglan—

Except for the Dassir Sorority, whose conviction that the Old Ones and their ancient nemeses had both been devoted to malfeasance and license had led them to exalt all manner of dissolute conduct, which, sadly for themselves, had brought down upon them the frenzied hordes of 73 Kaych assassins who had been the Sorority's undoing—

But also, oddly enough, had been the proximate cause of Occo's escape from the clutches of the Octuplets because, once she was free of the Octuplets' torturers by dint of bribery, the Pontificate had lacked sufficient assassins to track her down again because most of them were even at that very moment engaged in the annihilation of the lamented-by-none Dassir Sorority.

❊ ❊ ❊

Clearly, however, the Octuplets had not forgotten the incident.

"*YOU!*" they cried as one, their rage growing as Occo and her companion drew nearer on the Warlock Variation Drive's newest incarnation, which—

Occo glanced around quickly.

—resembled nothing so much as the fabled Bench of Undoing upon which the legendary mage Jio Lawr Kammion had been conveyed to her doom at the hands— using the term loosely—of the ghastly Nebular Specters—

—who, Occo now realized, were also numbered eight in number, in that respect—

"I'll take it from here," said Russ Tabor.

❊ ❊ ❊

Occo couldn't make any sense of what was approaching, at first—or what they were approaching, perhaps. A cluster of serpents?—no, it was more like the writhing nest of a jajallaw on the outer moon of Svath, as the hermaphroditic monster gave up its flesh to be consumed by its own offspring. Except—

"It's Cthulhu!" cried the Human sage Shenoy. "In the very flesh! I didn't think the ancient god was real!"

"It's not . . . exactly," said Tabor between clenched teeth. His forehead was beaded with some sort of peculiar moisture.

<It's called "sweat,"> explained Bresk. **<It's really**

disgusting stuff. One of the ways Humans maintain their internal temperature in a state of homeostasis is by liquefying their own flesh. That's what you're seeing now.>

Occo was dumbfounded. Partly because of the inefficient—not to mention revolting—nature of the mechanism, but also because the ambient temperature was not at all torrid. It seemed rather cool, in fact.

<Their internal temperature seems to be affected by their emotional state as well. They have all sorts of expressions for it. For this, they'd say he's "sweating bullets." "Cool as a cucumber" more-or-less indicates the opposite.>

What is a cucumber?

< From the context, I'd guess it was a synonym for an ice cube. Maybe one that was degrading due to a rise in temperature. Probably it was "cube-under," originally. On the other hand—>

But Occo ignored the rest of her familiar's prattle. She could now see that the object they were approaching was indeed the gigantic monster whom they'd encountered in their first voyage on the Warlock Variation Drive—insofar as the prosaic term "voyage" could be applied at all to this form of transport.

They were close, now, and it was obvious that the malevolent deity wasn't going to be fooled again into allowing them to escape by plunging through its gullet. That gullet was no longer open, kept shut by an immense and horny beak.

"Russ, be careful!" cried Shenoy.

Again through clenched teeth, Tabor hissed: "Keep it

down, will you? This is going to be tricky. I don't need any distractions."

He cocked his head toward Occo, without taking his gaze from the nearing form of Cthulhu.

"Get ready," he said.

Get ready for what? Occo wondered.

Suddenly, just as Cthulhu's mighty tentacles were closing around them, the scene—

—reality?—

—illusion?—

—provisional continuum?—

Changed utterly. The Warlock Variation Drive had been transformed into a sort of huge blubbery ring of some unknown substance, gripped between two enormous but smoothly polished logs and being hefted toward—

—in the distance—

What looked for all the world like the open mouth of a Human grown to the scale of a leviathan.

"Take that, Cthulhu!" Tabor boomed. "Evil ancient god turned into calamari! Am I good or what?"

His face was distorted by that grotesque expression Humans called a grin. He turned it upon Occo.

"Your turn," he said. "And I wouldn't dawdle. That guy looks pretty hungry."

❁ ❁ ❁

Again, Occo was dumbfounded. What was she supposed—

<The cenotes of Battenkuluk!>

❁ ❁ ❁

The seemingly interminable plunge into the greatest

of the cenotes of Battenkuluk was much as Occo remembered it. Down and down and down, the fungi-covered walls racing past, the fingers and claws and tentacles and extremities and digits and otherwise indescribable tactile members of the many sentients from many species who had been trapped by that same fungi seemed to grasp at Occo and her companions as they sped by.

An illusion, of course. They were all as dead as the most ancient black dwarf in the universe. The fungi of the cenotes of Battenkuluk are justly renowned for their mortiferous nature.

Which, sadly, was no more malignant than that which awaited them at the terminus of their precipitous descent. For there, nestled among the bones, chitin and shrunken exoskeletons of those who had somehow evaded the fungi, lay the creature considered by many exobiologists of several species to be the most savage and lethal ambush-predator in the known portions of the galaxy.

The cenotroll of Battenkuluk!

To say that Occo was exasperated by her familiar did not do justice to the term "exasperate."

You idiot! Why did you bring up this memory—which, I remind you, is actually not a memory at all but merely a recollection of an episode in a training simulator. You cretin. You—

<Haven't you figured it out yet?> Bresk's tone was inappropriately derisive, for a familiar addressing its mistress. Occo was now determined to—

<The whole point of this exercise is to approach as closely as possible to the most perilous of all

*hidden dangers. And what could be worse than the
cenotroll lurking at the bottom of the greatest cenote
in Battenkuluk?>*

The annoying creature . . .

Had a point. But—

How are we supposed to survive the encounter?

*<How should I know? But it's not our problem.
At the last minim, hand control over to the Human.
Tabor, I mean—not Shenoy! Never Shenoy!>*

But . . .

There was no time left. The bone-, chitin- and
exoskeleton-covered base of the cenote was now visible,
rushing toward them. Some great though still invisible
creature could be seen stirring below the surface. Any
moment now—

"I'll take it from here," said Tabor.

CHAPTER 32

⁂

They were at the event horizon—at the very edge. Already Occo could feel the great tidal forces pulling her apart. The Human imbecile had delivered them from the cenotroll only to hand them over to the greatest peril in the known universe. A black hole!

And no ordinary black hole. From the edge of her sight—what little was left of it as her eyes were also being pulled out of shape—Occo could see the entire sidereal universe stretching in all directions, which—

Made no sense at all because they were neither at the center of a galaxy nor—

"Unveil yourself!" she cried out furiously. "Or we'll drag you down with us!"

❖ ❖ ❖

The plain was featureless in all directions. Perfectly flat in all dimensions, too.

As was Occo herself. And, glancing around—never up; never down; that being quite impossible—she saw the same to be true of all her companions.

Flat—flat—flat. The Warlock Variation Drive, Rammadrecula, the Skerkud Teleplaser, Jaemu, the Ebbo and both Humans—all were like so many blobs of paste smeared across the landscape—if it was "land" at all, which she doubted. Soil had texture. This surface . . .

Was a pure abstraction, she thought.

<Oh, good move,> groused Bresk—who was smeared so thin he was almost transparent. **<Humans call this leaping from the frying pan into the fire. Now what do we do?>**

Occo was wondering the same herself. But, by now, she thought she had a sense of how this all worked.

"Your turn, I believe," she said to Tabor, who was smeared next to her.

"Indeed so," he replied. His voice sounded as flat as he was, which was hardly surprising given that his universal translator had also been smeared into a two-dimensional . . .

What to call it? "Paste" wouldn't really do. Paste also has texture, which was quite impossible in their new two-dimensional universe.

"Repository!" Tabor called out. "Five more seconds and we're going where no man or sentient of any type has ever gone—into the One Dimension! Get ready to squiggle, you string-theory-about-to-become!"

Suddenly, Occo felt herself—what to call it? Shrinking?

But the sensation was over almost as soon as it began. An instant later they were all standing on a real surface—three-dimensional, again—which—

She looked around.

Was evidently the surface of the moon they'd been on. She could see the orb of the planet Mank in the sky above.

And, perched on short stilts before them, was a cubical structure about twice the size of Jaemu.

Who, Occo suddenly realized as she looked around, was no longer with them. Where had the Vitunpelay gone?

"Is that it?" asked Tabor, nodding toward the structure in front of them. "And if so, how do we get in? I don't see a door or any kind of entrance."

Shenoy was frowning at the cube. "I don't know," he said. "There are no features I can see. Hardly any color, for that matter."

That was true, which suggested that Humans and Nac Zhe Anglan had approximately the same visual range. The cube was a sort of dull beige, which made it blend in quite well with the moon's surface. Had it been made of the same sort of rock?

But that seemed unlikely. Occo couldn't be certain without a close investigation of the structure's surface, but she doubted that it had been made of any sort of normal construction materials.

"Bresk, investigate," she commanded.

The familiar's mantle flared outward and the probes sped toward the cube.

As the probes approached, a semi-transparent shell seemed to pop into existence around the structure. The first probe to touch it vanished. So did the next.

The rest veered aside. "Now what?" complained Bresk.

"Did the other probes record anything?" Occo asked.

"Nothing. There was no energy pulse, nothing. I have no idea what happened."

The probes returned to the familiar and nestled within his mantle again. There was obviously no point in wasting them.

Tabor looked at Shenoy and repeated Bresk's query. "Now what?"

The Human sage ran fingers through his mass of white head fur. "I'm not sure. At a guess—"

"*Hands and forelimbs up!*" cried a shrill voice. "*And any other appendage or digit we may have overlooked due to our limited familiarity with your several species!*"

Turning, Occo saw that a number of Morganites had appeared behind them, as if out of nowhere. There were eight of them, all of whom were holding peculiar-looking devices that Occo suspected were weapons. Several of them were also carrying large backpacks.

She couldn't help but wonder if they were real. Appearing out of nowhere like that, perhaps they were— what had Shenoy called them?—astral projections. Her hand moved toward one of the microgrenades attached to her harness. There was an easy way to find out.

But then Jaemu popped up out of nowhere also, right next to one of the Morganites.

"You still owe me ten percent of whatever's in there," he said, pointing at the cube. "Now all we have to do is figure out how you can collect before these Morganites butcher you all. Which they'll do, of course, as soon as they're sure this is the actual repository. They've had mixed results in the past when they tried to trick sentients into doing what you just did."

He turned to the Morganite he was standing next to. "And remember our deal—the ten percent you owe me is based on gross, not the net after the Humans and Knacks hand over their ten percent."

The Morganite waved its hand in what Occo took to be an assenting gesture.

"You betrayed us!" she accused Jaemu.

The huge alien's mandibles spread wide. Occo couldn't tell if he was amused or offended—or possibly both, given the Vitunpelay's quirky nature.

"I did *not*," Jaemu insisted. "My deal with Tabor and Shenoy was that I'd lead you to the repository. Which I did. More or less. We had no deal after that—and I never had any deal with you two Knacks of any kind."

His smaller tentacles writhed for a moment in what might be a Vitunpelay analog to a gesture of apology. "Sorry about that, Russ. Nothing personal, it was just business."

Occo glared at the Skerkud Teleplaser. "Do something!" she demanded. But the weird alien device made no response.

She now turned to the Warlock Variation Drive. "Ju'ula, can he get away with this? I thought you said the Teleplaser would prevent anyone from committing treachery."

Ju'ula had two eyestalks extended. She peered at Occo, then at Jaemu, then at the Skerkud Teleplaser, then back at Occo.

"That's within the limits of Skerkie's understanding, Mama," she said, sounding mildly reproachful. "I *told* you he worked in security. He's pretty easy to confuse—and nobody in the galaxy is more confusing than a Vitunpelay. So, yes, I'm afraid you're in a bad place."

Shenoy spoke up. "I admit to being a bit curious, Jaemu. How did you get hold of the Morganites in order to arrange your betray—ah, let's just call it your stab in the back?"

"Oh, I've never *not* been in touch with them. You were quite right, Rupert."

"*Ronnette,*" said the Warlock Variation Drive, almost hissing the word. "Don't irk me."

"You were quite right, Ronnette," continued Jaemu breezily. "The Morganites don't have telepathy or teleportation but they do astral projection extraordinarily well. One of them was in touch with me not long after you had me try to kill the one on the ship—or, I should say, the one not on the ship."

Tabor's jaws were clenched, which Occo thought was a human mannerism expressing anger. But when he spoke, his tone of voice seemed calm enough. "If the Morganites don't have teleportation, how did they appear out of nowhere?"

All the Morganites started barking. That seemed to indicate amusement, because after a few minims the one standing next to Jaemu broke off and said: "We were here all the time." He pointed behind him. "That's an astral hatch, leading to an astral hideout. We've known for more than a century where the repository of the Old Ones existed in terms of the moon's coordinates. The problem was getting it to appear out of whatever continuum it hides itself in. Which"—*bark! bark! bark!*—"you morons just did for us."

He brought his weapon up to bear on them. "Now stand to the side so we can open it."

"How do you do that?" asked Shenoy.

"Don't worry," said the Morganite who seemed to be the leader. Occo thought he might be the one—or whose astral projection—had been on the ship. "You'll see it happen."

"Because we're bait," said Shenoy, nodding. "There's something in that repository that you're afraid of."

The Morganite ignored him and looked at one of his companions. That one set down his weapon and withdrew another odd-looking piece of equipment from his backpack. It looked like some sort of illuminating device.

He pointed it at the cube and pressed a button.

Nothing happened.

The Morganite hissed something under his breath and made some sort of adjustment to the device. Then, pressed the button again.

Nothing happened.

The Morganite, still hissing, made another adjustment before pressing the button a third time.

The stilts holding up the repository began to shorten. An iris-shaped opening in the cube began to dilate.

"Okay, twenty-two percent," said Tabor. "On the gross."

"Twenty-five," said Jaemu.

"Twenty-three and not a damn penny more."

"What's a penny?" Jaeme asked. But before he finished saying *penny* both of the Vitunpelay's great gripping tentacles lashed out and seized the Morganites on either side of him by the shoulders. He smashed them together. Blood and bone and brains flew everywhere.

Then, he cast them aside, bowling over two more Morganites in the process.

The three Morganites still holding weapons began to bring them to bear on the Vitunpelay. Russ snatched out his pistol and aimed at the one closest to Jaemu.

But Rammadrecula was already firing. *Tchaa! Tchaa! Tchaa! Tchaa! Tchaa! Tchaa!* The three Morganites were—

Pretty much shredded from the chest up. At this close range, the unbihexium rounds made an incredible mess.

Tabor shifted his aim and shot the two Morganites whom Jaemu had sent sprawling.

Only one was still alive—the one opening the repository. He stared at them, eyes very wide. Then, flung down the device and started to race away. But before he could take more than three steps—

Something came out of the repository and brought him down. Occo couldn't really see what it was, exactly. It was as if the *thing* had the same powers possessed by a Gawad murkster of obscuring vision.

But if she couldn't see the *thing* clearly she was quite able to see what it was doing to the Morganite. A chunk of his midsection vanished, as if a great bite had been taken out of him. Then another.

"It's the monster from the prison!" shouted Tabor. He brought his pistol to bear.

But Shenoy grabbed his shoulder and pulled him away. "It won't hurt it, Russ! Come on!" The white-furred sage pointed at the cube, whose iris was still open. "We have to get in there! Quickly!"

Occo didn't know if the Human was right, but she figured he was more likely to know what to do than anyone else. So she snatched up the Warlock Variation Drive and ran toward the cube. Bresk had already attached himself to her hard points and was pulled along.

Rammadrecula, on the other hand—the fool!—was now firing at the *thing*. Glancing back, Occo saw that the unbihexium rounds which had slaughtered the Morganites seem to be having no effect at all on the *thing* from the repository.

Tabor seized the heterochthonatrix around the waist, more-or-less hoisted her onto his back, and raced for the cube. Rammadrecula seemed oblivious to what was happening to her. Still screeching with fury, she kept firing at the monster—which had by now devoured about half of the Morganite.

Perhaps it would take the time to devour the rest of the corpses, Occo hoped.

But . . . no. She hadn't really thought it would. The thing seemed to swell, and then came speeding toward them. They wouldn't make it to the iris before it arrived.

Then—for whatever reason impelled the device, which Occo had never really understood—the Skerkud Teleplaser suddenly began unfolding. Within two minims, it had interposed itself between the cube and the oncoming *thing*.

"OPPROBRIOUS DISCOURTESY!" it boomed. "SANCTIONS AND FORFEITURES MUSTERED! MORTIFICATIONS ENHAN—"

The *thing* smashed into the Teleplaser. Everything was obscured except the Skerkud's flailing extremities.

The fracas slowed the monster enough, however, that everyone was able to make it into the cube.

Looking back through the iris opening, Occo could see that the Teleplaser was being ripped to shreds. Pieces of it flew everywhere, only to be seized by extensions of the *thing* and dragged back into the oiling melee.

Then—silence. The *thing*, still obscured, seem to slouch toward the repository.

"Now what?" asked Tabor.

❀ ❀ ❀

"Oh, bother," said Ju'ula. "I can't believe this is happening. For the first time in—what is it?—almost fourteen half-lives of Iodine-129, I have to really exert myself. Mama, you've got a lot to answer for."

Looking down, Occo saw that the Warlock Variation Drive had now extruded twelve—no, fourteen—eyestalks. One of the eyes was giving Occo an accusatory look. The other thirteen were studying the oncoming *thing*.

"Well, there's no help for it," Ju'ula said. "If I don't entangle time's arrow, we'll wind up spending the next eighteen half-lives of technetium-98 contemplating the innards of a charm quark—and don't let the name fool you. The innards of any kind of quark are *borrrrrrrrrrrrrrrrrring*."

Shenoy was frowning. "Techtetium-98? That'd be . . ." He paused very briefly. "Almost forty-seven million years. We couldn't possibly survive."

"You *wish*," said Ju'ula. "Never been inside a quark, I take it? Well, you'd stay alive—but you'd all be what you

Humans call dingbats long before it was over. Even the Ebbo."

The *thing* was now only two meters or so from the open iris, but it was still impossible to determine any features. The formless monster seemed to crouch down a little, as if getting ready to spring.

"Come on," said Ju'ula impatiently, apparently addressing the *thing*. "Stop dawdling."

The *thing* leapt at them!

"About time," said the Warlock Variation Drive.

Everything around Occo seemed to swirl into chaos.

"Which is not exactly an illusion," Ju'ula continued. "But you'll wish it was."

CHAPTER 33

✷

They seemed to be rushing down a corridor of some sort—allowing for a "corridor" having more-or-less circular dimensions which were:

a) indeterminate in size;

b) indeterminate in structure;

c) resembled the inside of a kaleidoscope;

d) apparently designed by a lunatic.

Occo had no great hope this was going to turn out well—and the next words from the Warlock Variation Drive lowered that hope still further.

"We've got some control over the casualty figures, Mama," she said. "Keeping your species from going extinct isn't a big problem, since we were lucky enough to ingurgitate a daimōn formulated by the Fiends. If it'd been one formulated by the Old Ones or the Unfriendlies or the Estrangers or the Hoar Ghosts—not to mention They-Who-Must-Not-Be-Named—it'd be a lot trickier. But the Fiends were so maniacally savage that their daimōns haven't got the patience to carry out really effective genocide. Still, it's going to lust for a high body count. So where do you want to start?"

Occo didn't know what to say. The Human sage Shenoy spoke instead:

"What are the . . . ah, rules?"

"There are no *rules*," replied the Warlock Variation Drive. "That's a construct from your superstitions."

"What are the guidelines, then? Or should I say apothegms?"

"Apothegms'll work. The best one is 'what goes around, comes around.' But you can't ever ignore 'a stitch in time saves nine.' Not to mention that 'little thieves are hanged but great ones escape.'"

"What is a stitch?" Occo demanded.

Ju'ula swiveled one eye to gaze at her. "The Human asked the question, Mama, so the answers are all Human ones. And I really think you'd be smart to let her do the navigating. Don't take this personally, but Mama Ronnette can think rings around you."

Occo decided that advice was probably worth following.

"So navigate then, Shenoy," she said.

The Human sage had his lips pursed and was running digits through his head fur. "'What goes around, comes around.' And 'a stitch in time . . . '" He muttered. "Ah! Of course! Warlock Variation Drive, set a course—"

"You don't do the driving!" Ju'ula said sharply. "Tell Mama where you want to go."

Shenoy turned to Occo. "I think we should start back on Cthulhu. The planet, I mean, not the god-monster. At the prison."

Occo brought the image of the Human prison to mind. Shortly thereafter, the bizarre corridor they'd been in was replaced by a crudely built and rather dirty hallway. Heavy metal doors were set into the walls at regular intervals. She recognized them as the entrances to the cells she'd seen in her earlier visit.

One of the cell doors was open. Occo's vision of it was obscured, as if she were looking through a peculiar lens—or from inside a vehicle which had a distortion in its viewscreen.

The view swept into a cell. It was empty, showing no traces of anything except the same ichor stains she'd seen on her earlier visit.

The stains seem to brighten. Then—

"Oh, dear," said Shenoy. "I hadn't foreseen this, although I should have. We're in a causal loop needed to avoid a time paradox."

A Human form appeared, its mouth wide open. It—no, it was probably a he—was undoubtedly screaming, for the view retreated slightly and Occo could now see that the Human was being devoured by—

By them, apparently. Glancing around, Occo could see the distorted faces and figures of her companions, as if in a dream. They weren't inside a vehicle, she now realized. In some manner she couldn't imagine, they were inside the *thing*.

"We're cohabiting, aren't we?" Shenoy said. "In some sort of commensal relationship with the monster."

"You'd better hope it's more than that," said Ju'ula. "The daimōn has no patience with freeloaders. From our standpoint, it's symbiosis or death. Well—death or eternal madness for you. For me, it'll just be a really long, really really boring interlude."

Another Human came into view, also screaming. After a short time, a third one appeared and was likewise consumed.

The view seemed to race off. They were back in that bizarre corridor. Then they entered another cell. A Human was standing there and turned to look at them. His eyes widened, his mouth started to open.

"Basil!" exclaimed Shenoy.

"Look out!" cried Tabor.

The Human fell out of sight. The view widened, as if—

As if—

"It's going to eat him, Rupert!" Tabor shouted. "Do something!"

Shenoy looked confused. "But what am I supposed—"

Occo wasn't sure exactly what she did, but she sensed that she was able to restrain the monster. The view shifted again.

The corridor—and then another Human appeared, standing on the deck of a vessel. Occo thought she was female.

"Andrea!" exclaimed Shenoy.

"Get us out of here!" said Tabor. "Or it'll kill her too!"

Occo was getting a better sense for how the process—worked, wasn't quite the right term. *Negotiated* would be better.

Not this one, was the message she sent out, by a process she decided to call "telepathy" even though she was fairly certain it wasn't.

The Human female vanished. They were back in the corridor. Racing—somewhere. Or should she say, *somewhen*?

"Can I stop it, Ju'ula?"

"You've got a better chance of stopping a neutron star from spinning," was the Warlock Variation Drive's answer. "The moment you coalesced with the daimōn, you unleashed the thing. You can control it—within limits— but that's about all, until it runs its course."

"And what is the end of that course?"

Ju'ula brought four eyes to bear. "Are you really that dumb? It ends when all of you are destroyed—but not before all of your kith and kin are destroyed as well."

"That explains the death of Basil," said Shenoy. His brow was oddly crinkled. "It also explains the attack on Andrea—which she did survive, by the way, so apparently you pulled the daimōn off in time."

"But why did it start by killing the prisoners?" asked Tabor. "They're no kith and kin of yours."

Shenoy looked down at the Warlock Variation Drive. "This daimōn, Ju'ula . . . It's not all that bright itself, is it?"

The Drive looked back at him with no fewer than ten eyes. "We're discussing a being that spends most of its existence—what's that gross expression you Humans use? 'Stewing in its own juice.' You figure it out."

"Dumber'n a box of rocks, in other words," said Tabor. Even Occo could tell that the alien's tone of voice expressed deep satisfaction. "So there you have it, Rupert. It ate the prisoners because it figured they must have been important to you—seeing as you went all that way to visit them."

"But that's—"

Tabor help up his hand. "Please! Let's avoid terms like 'nonsense' and 'ridiculous,' shall we?" He twirled his finger, indicating their bizarre surroundings. "Little pitchers have big ears."

Occo tried to make sense out of that last statement. Feeling Bresk's neural connectors probing beneath her earflaps, she decided not to ask the Humans themselves. Bresk seemed to be a treasure trove of information on the bipedal aliens.

<That's a reference to spawn absorbing more than you think,> he explained. **<In context—>**

Tabor doesn't want the monster to start thinking about this subject. Namely, its none-too-great intelligence.

<Because he thinks we could play tricks on it— and he may be right.>

Tabor clapped a big hand on Shenoy's shoulder. "Sorry about that, Rupert. The sudden death of all three of your brothers and your parents that we just witnessed must have been devastating."

The sage's brow crinkled still further. "What are you . . . ? Ah. Yes. Indeed. Horrible." He placed the back of his hand to his forehead and made a bizarre face. "Woe is me! Now totally bereft of family and all friends! Well, except you, Russ, but you're doomed anyway."

"Good thing I don't have any family left myself, them all having died years ago," said Tabor loudly. "And I'm such an asshole I never had any friends at all, not since Tommy Hancock slugged me when I was six years old. The rotten bastard got what was coming to him, though. On the way home after slugging me he collapsed from childhood coronary disease, rolled down a hill onto the tracks and got run over by a freight train. There wasn't enough left of him to do an autopsy to figure out whether the blunt force trauma or the heart attack was what killed him."

<I think that's what Humans call "laying it on thick.">

"You once had a *friend?*" demanded the Vitunpelay. Jaemu's mandibles were gaped wider than Occo had ever seen. "I never did—and no siblings, either, after I ate all of them in the crèche. My parents were furious. I don't think they would have ever forgiven me. No way to know, of course, since I poisoned them not long afterward. That's when I was exiled. Banished from Vitunpelay space forevermore. Haven't seen a single member of my species since."

Unwittingly—and despite her attempts to resist— Jaemu's words stirred up Occo's memories of the Naccor Jute and her husbands. She could sense the corridor racing off again.

The viewed shifted and a distorted image of Flaak appeared. In what seemed like a mere instant the view was skimming the surface of the planet, racing toward—

The shallow valley where the Naccor Jute had established its cloister. They had sped back in time to the moments just before her order and her husbands and all those close to her had been destroyed.

By Occo herself, as it turned out. When she and her companions unleashed the daimōn, they had doomed all whom she held dear.

<Get off a signal—and then stall as best you can.>

That was—

Worth trying. She still had the emergency beacon attached to her harness.

"Ju'ula, can signals penetrate"—she waved her hand about, indicating the weirdness that surrounded them—"whatever we're inside?"

"Insofar as I can make any sense out of that gibberish, yes. But we're not *inside* anything, Mama, we are—using the term very loosely—what Mama Ronnette calls 'consubstantial' with the daimōn. That means if you want to send a signal you have to do it before you do it."

"Of course!" exclaimed Shenoy. "'A stitch in time saves nine'!—or rather, time itself. If I might navigate for a moment . . ."

The Human did—or thought—or whatever—something Occo could not analyze. For lack of any other referent, it felt as if they were spinning around wildly, except there was neither disorientation nor any sense of centrifugal force.

"Mama Ronnette doesn't *ever* get to drive," Ju'ula said. "She's bad enough just navigating."

The spinning sensation was replaced by a sense of . . . stasis, perhaps?

"Send your signal now," Shenoy said. "And hurry—before the notion of 'hurrying' gets defined by the daimōn. Right now, it's pretty confused."

Occo took the beacon off her harness, set it to indicate *maximum peril* rather than *assistance needed,* and then pressed the trigger.

She felt nothing, and was a bit relieved. She hadn't expected to, since by one of the provisions of the

Dessetrai Pact, beacon signals were exempt from the prohibition on faster-than-light mechanisms. But the means by which the Fiend-designed daimōn operated were completely unknown to her, and she hadn't been sure it would not somehow interfere.

So far as she could tell, it hadn't. But she could sense the daimōn slipping from the stasis and she could only hope her warning signal had gotten out in time.

Whatever *time* might mean in this context.

The view shifted and now they were looking down on the edifices which made up the Naccor Jute's cloister. There was no sign of movement anywhere, though, which she took to be a positive sign. And—

<There are hardly any ships left! It worked! They fled in time!>

So it seemed. Somewhere in space, her husbands and all those whom she had once held dear—and not, in the case of her wretched mentor—were voyaging toward a destination she did not know and never would.

She would never see any of them again. But that had already been true. At least now she had the satisfaction of knowing they were all still alive, where she had thought them all dead.

She watched as the daimōn, using whatever mysterious and immense powers were at its disposal, transformed the planet's surface below into the horrid landscape that she remembered. So, she had the further satisfaction of being proved right, after all—the destruction *had* been the work of weapons designed and wielded by deities (or demons, the distinction was meaningless). One of their creations, at least.

Yet not by the Old Ones, apparently. If the Warlock Variation Drive was to be believed—and Occo thought that disbelieving her was probably foolish in the extreme—the daimōn had been forged/bred/spawned/???/ by those ancient powers who called themselves or were known by the name of Fiends.

Who were they? More to the point, did Occo even want to know?

Probably not. She recited to herself the three prayers of the Naccor Jute:

May ignorance and obscurity preserve us.

Seek not revelation lest you be revealed.

Leave unto others what you would have others expose.

The reminder of her order's wisdom brought some comfort. Immediately undone by her wretched familiar.

<Nice try, but I don't think it'll work. Unless I miss my guess, we're about—>

The view shifted again, replaced by the transmaterial corridor.

<What I thought. Humans would say, "we're off to the races.">

What races? What are you prattling about?

<A figure of speech. Who's left who needs kith and kin destroyed and who hasn't had the wits to do it themselves?>

Occo turned to look at Rammadrecula.

<Don't forget Proceeds-With-Circumspection. Although Ebbo probably don't have enough emotional attachment to anything to stir up a homicidal monster. But however it works, between a dull-witted heterochthonatrix and an Ebbo-witted

Ebbo, I'd say there's no way to avoid a war with the Envacht Lu.>

Occo now looked at the Ebbo, who was once again scritching away at its tablet.

<Which you just started. All right, we started— but I'm going to claim innocence by reason of being a hapless familiar.>

"What's happening *now*?" queried Rammadrecula, sounding peevish.

CHAPTER 34

❋

The view had already shifted. They seemed to be speeding through the void—but only for a moment, before the image of a revanship appeared. Occo wasn't certain, because all revanships looked essentially alike, but she could only suppose that this was *Suffer and Die, Execrable Ones*, to which she had been summoned at the start of this adventure.

Bresk confirmed her guess. *<That's definitely the same revanship we were on before,>* he said. *<You can always tell by the minor details of the fuselage's superstructure, if you have an eidetic memory. Which I do and you don't, so just take my word for it.>*

"The monster means to destroy it!" Rammadrecula exclaimed. The heterochthonatrix had finally figured out what everyone else had.

But probably not the solution to the problem, so Occo spoke up. "A pity that none of your kith and kin are on that ship, though. Nor any friends or associates. Nor any kith and kin of any of your associates. Nor any associates of your kith and kin nor any of *their* associates."

Rammadrecula stared at her. Clearly, she had still not come to understand the workings of the daimōn's mind— or whatever passed for its mind.

Proceeds-With-Circumspection didn't seem to understand the nature of the peril either. But, for once, the Ebbo's obsessive record-keeping and attention to detail came in useful.

"Indeed so," it said, studying its tablet. "The closest consanguinity between Heterochthonatrix Rammadrecula and any sentient on Revanship *Suffer and Die, Execrable Ones* is so remote that there is no term to describe it even in the kinship lexicon of the Vlaxo Levirate."

The view shifted away from the revanship and seemed to vallicate, as if the daimōn were uncertain or confused.

Unfortunately, having produced that desired result, the single-minded scribe pressed onward.

"Quite unlike the situation on Heterochthonatrix Rammadrecula's home planet of Flendic," the Ebbo continued, "where she has a multitude of kin. Both of her parents are now deceased, having been culled some years ago for producing an excess of substandard offspring, and the same is true of most of Rammadrecula's siblings. Still, at least four sisters and brothers were alive as of the last recording received by Revanship *Suffer and Die, Execrable Ones,* as well as—"

The Ebbo droned on, but Occo ignored the rest. The damage had already been done. The view had steadied and once again they seemed to be racing through the void.

If void it actually was. There was no way Occo could

determine the nature of the medium through which they were passing—or even if "passing" was the proper verb to describe their mode of travel.

The Human sage might know, but Occo was unwilling to ask Shenoy. By now, she'd come to share the Warlock Variation Drive's aversion to Shenoy's method of navigation.

Leave unto others seemed a generally useful guideline.

But however they were voyaging and through whatever medium, there was no doubt of their destination. The daimōn was headed for Rammadrecula's home planet, upon which it would presumably inflict the same bizarre and hideous damage it had already wreaked on Flaak.

Finally, Rammadrecula's slow wit caught up to what was transpiring. The ensuing reaction, however, was not what Occo had foreseen.

"By all means!" screeched the heterochthonatrix. "My siblings and cousins—each and every one! There was not a single exception!—testified against me during my canvass! I had not a friend nor a sponsor in the world. No confederate, no colleague, not even an accessory. I was alone! All alone! Defamed by all!"

Rammadrecula had worked herself into something of a frenzy, stooped over and beating her foreknees with her fists. "Slay them all, o puissant daimōn! Spare none—not a one! Boil the whole planet, turn bedrock into ruin, ruin into paste, paste into primordial undifferentiated ooze!"

Once again, the view began to jiggle.

Rammadrecula's knee-pounding grew more frenzied still. "No! No! Waver not in your righteous course! Falter not in your resolve!"

The view oscillated still more. Occo and Tabor—simultaneously, as they must have both realized the truth at the same instant—began to aid and abet Rammadrecula in her sororicidal fury.

"Keep it steady, Great Daimōn!" boomed the big Human. "He who hesitates is lost!"

For her part, Occo cried out: "Maintain the course for Flendic! Bring justice and psychic surcease for the much-wronged heterochthonatrix! Turn the planet into a magma stew!"

Tabor picked up the train of thought effortlessly: "Better still—scramble the whole orb! Mash basalt into iron, granite into air!"

"And bacon! And bacon!" exclaimed Bresk.

Occo and Tabor both stared at the familiar. Occo, because she didn't understand what bacon was in the first place. Tabor . . .

"How the hell does he know about bacon?" the Human demanded. Then, recalling his purpose: "But it doesn't matter—because he's right! Can't have a scrambled planet without bacon!"

By now, the view was wobbling badly.

"No! No!" shrieked Rammadrecula. The heterochthonatrix drew her pistol and aimed it at the distorted view in front of them, presumably because the dullard had no idea where else to point it. "Continue or I'll shoot!"

Shoot what? Occo wondered. *Does the daimōn even have a material corpus? And if so, where is it?*

She'd been thinking to herself, but she was still neurally linked with Bresk so the familiar replied.

<I don't think so—not, at least, in any usual sense of the term "material." But you might ask Shenoy. I wouldn't be surprised if he's figured it out. That Human is extraordinarily intelligent. We'll probably have to kill him, sooner or later. Or do what Humans themselves do—lock him up and throw away the key.>

Before Occo could decide whether or not asking Shenoy was a good idea, the Human sage made it a moot point.

"You're wasting your time and energy, Hetero-chthonatrix," he said. Pointing his spindly Human forefinger at the view before them he added: "That's not actually something we're seeing with our own senses. It's what the daimōn sees—or I should say, senses. It's probably not using sight at all, we're just translating it that way in our own minds."

Looking confused and uncertain, Rammadrecula waved the pistol about in a manner that was simultaneously comical and alarming. The Envacht Lu official was definitely not possessed of the keenest intellect. It was no wonder the Flengren Apostollege had decided to exile her.

"Where is the daimōn, then?" she demanded.

Shenoy now used his forefinger to make a twirling motion. "Insofar as its presence can be situated in our four-dimensional spacetime, it's all around us. Or I should say, we are resident within its *geist*. The language involved is imprecise and ambiguous, although I think with some effort I could depict it accurately in mathematical terms."

"Don't you dare, Mama Ronnette!" said the Warlock Variation Drive.

Shenoy gave her a wary glance. "Perhaps not a good idea. Suffice it to say, Heterochthonatrix Heurse Gotha Rammadrecula, that there is no way to harm the daimōn that would not involve our own psychic self-destruction. We are now of its flesh, immaterially speaking."

Rammadrecula lowered the pistol and began another undignified lachrymosic display. Fluid spilled out from her eyes and lower mouth.

"My one chance at requital—negated!" she wailed. "All those who wronged me will go unpunished!"

Shenoy did that odd little shoulder heave that Humans called a *shrug*. "I'm afraid you went about it the wrong way," he said. "What you should have done—"

"Rupert!" his companion Tabor said sharply. "Leave off. I've done some things in my life I'm not too proud of, but so far I've managed to avoid committing genocide. I'd like to keep it that way, if you don't mind."

The sage's brow crinkled again. "Genocide? What're you—? Oh." He gave another wary glance, this one aimed at Rammadrecula. "Yes, well. I suppose there's no need to go into the tactical issues involved."

Fortunately, although she was probably too dimwitted to understand it anyway, Rammadrecula had paid no attention to the last exchange between the two Humans. She was still leaking profusely.

The view produced by the daimōn began to flutter about wildly.

"Somebody better get this thing under control," said Bresk. "And *quickly*." The ensuing farts were a veritable aria of alarm.

Which was understandable—the view was now

dizzying, as the scene quivered and quavered and rippled and sometimes seem to vibrate like a string. They were caught inside—consubstantial with, whatever that meant—an ancient malevolent force that was rapidly losing its temper. And Occo was fairly certain the daimōn had been ill-tempered to begin with. Created, born, shaped, fabricated, tailored—however it had been brought into existence by the Fiends, whoever they were. But the name itself did not bode well for the future of those ensnared in their schemes.

Shenoy was currying his head fur vigorously—and using both hands in the process, which Occo had never seen him do before.

The sight was comforting. Occo had come to realize that the Human sage was probably an order of magnitude smarter than anyone else in their party. Smart didn't necessarily mean wise, of course. But at the moment she'd settle for smart.

"Ju'ula," said Shenoy, "correct me if I'm wrong, but I've come to the conclusion that there's no way to shut off—de-energize, cancel, annul, whatever the proper term might be—the daimōn once it's been activated."

The Warlock Variation Drive closed her eyes and twisted all her eyestalks, as if she was momentarily inclined to tie them into knots.

"That is so . . . well, not 'wrong,' I suppose," she said. "But every part of that statement is an affront to metaphysical elegance."

The eyestalks relaxed. "To start with, you don't 'turn on' a daimōn, so you can hardly 'shut it off.' If you insist on a simple term to describe an eleven-dimensional reality, use 'launch' instead. I assume the end point of that process is obvious, even to you."

And with that, she closed her eyes and retracted all the eyestalks except one, which moved slowly back and forth as if it stood on guard.

"Indeed!" said Shenoy. He turned toward the rest of them. "As she says, the conclusion is obvious."

Tabor said: "How so? It may be obvious to you, but it isn't to me."

"Nor me," chimed in Occo.

"Hoo!" boomed Jaemu. "That's because you're not eccentric enough! It's certainly obvious to *me*."

Occo's knees stiffened. She could see that Tabor's jaws were tight and felt a momentary kinship toward the Human. The Vitunpelay irritated both of them.

"Explain, if you don't mind," said Tabor. The words came out hissing a little.

"Simple! What gets 'launched'? A missile, that's what! And how do you 'shut off' a missile once it's launched?"

The great mandibles opened and clacked a couple of times. "You don't! You just hope you aimed it right so it hits something that you wanted destroyed. And whatever you do, make sure it doesn't come back down on your head."

Again, he clacked his mandibles. "Hoo! I'd love to meet one of these Fiends! Practically Vitunpelay, they must be."

"I'm afraid it's not quite that simple, Jaemu," said Shenoy. "The daimōn's not a machine. It has volition and purpose of its own. Whatever it's aimed at—using the term 'aim' very loosely—has to be something it *wants* to destroy. And so far . . ."

He went back to rubbing his head fur, although only with one hand. "So far the only things we know it wants to destroy are, well, us. And our kith and kin. We've just been able to forestall it by—"

Tabor interrupted hastily. "By carefully and unequivocally and positively making clear that none of us has any kith and kin left." He glanced at Rammadrecula. "Well, except for the heterochthonatrix, but once she made clear she'd be delighted if her kith and kin were destroyed that took all the fun out of it for the daimōn. So . . . "

"What about the Morganites?" Occo suggested. "I would think the daimōn might feel some animosity toward them."

"It's worth a try," allowed Shenoy. He got a peculiar expression on his face, as if his mind was wandering elsewhere.

Ju'ula's guarding eye popped open. "Mama Ronnette doesn't drive! Under any conditions!"

Shenoy was startled. His gaze regained focus. He looked at Occo.

"It's up to you, then," he said.

Occo brought into her mind the image of the moon orbiting around the planet Mank.

She was expecting the instantaneous transfer that the Warlock Variation Drive had done on all previous occasions. But instead, the distorted view settled down and seemed to race off.

"Interesting," mused Shenoy. "Ju'ula, why are we moving like this, instead of the way you usually do it?"

Three eyestalks emerged and swiveled to look at

Shenoy. "Are you under the impression that I got out of this mess you created? Well, I didn't. Thanks to you"—the eyestalks waved about—"that would be all of you except maybe the Ebbo, I am what you Humans call screwed. We're all in this together, at least for now and maybe forevermore—and isn't that a horrible thought?"

"Ah," mused Shenoy. "I see. You are now yourself consubstantial with the daimōn, in other words. So everything needs to be mediated through it. Is it an 'it,' by the way?"

"Are you kidding?" replied Ju'ula. "The daimōn is dimwitted, emotionally unstable, and controlled at all times by passions and caprices. Of course he's male."

While the daimōn mode of transport was not instantaneous, it was fairly close. At that moment the view around them shifted from formlessness to a distorted but still unmistakable image of Mank's larger moon.

CHAPTER 35

"Just as featureless as before," Shenoy mused. "But perhaps . . ." He started to turn toward Occo but she'd already figured out what he wanted. She brought the image of the once-hidden cube to mind, from whence the daimōn had emerged.

Less than two minims later, the view refocused and they were looking down on the cube from what appeared to be a very close distance. But the cube had changed drastically. It was now a ruin of its former self, hollowed-out and badly charred.

Struck by another thought, Occo imagined the view—

Shifting, in a slow circle, as it was already doing. However great might be the daimōn's hostility toward them, it reacted promptly and efficiently to any visual stimulus.

The corpses of the slain Morganites were gone. There were no traces of them except for a couple of dark patches where the Vitunpelay had crushed the skulls of the first two who'd been slain in the fracas.

"Interesting," said Shenoy. "And most illuminating as well."

"How is this 'illuminating'?" Tabor asked. Occo thought he sounded a bit peevish, although she was still unsure how to interpret the subtleties of Human gestures and tones of voice.

She certainly felt a bit peevish.

"But it's obvious, Russ!" said Shenoy. "The fact that the daimōn's former residence is now a ruin indicates, first, that the malevolent spirit requires no physical domicile or even residue of one; and, second, that there were no other secrets in the repository except whatever is bound up with the daimōn himself. Or perhaps I should say there never was a repository of secrets other than the daimōn. We think of the 'daimōn' as a being simply out of superstition."

Tabor emulated Shenoy's head rubbing. "If I'm following you properly, what you're saying is that the repository of the secrets of the Old Ones was the daimōn itself."

Ju'ula's watchdog eye opened slightly. "The daimōn *him*self. Just because he's not a being doesn't mean he isn't as dumb as a male."

Tabor stared down at her. "Wait a minute . . . in other words, you're agreeing with Rupert. Ah, sorry, with Mama Ronnette. The daimōn *is* a repository of the Old Ones."

Ju'ula's eye opened wider. "No, he's a repository of the *Fiends*. If you want to discover the secrets of the Old Ones, you're going to have to work a little harder than this."

The eye closed again. "That's assuming you survive.

Which gets more and more unlikely the longer you keep annoying the daimōn because you haven't provided him with anyone on whom to vent his spleen. I suggest you concentrate on that problem and stop worrying about the Old Ones. As the saying goes, 'when you have a Fiend for a friend, you don't need any enemies.'"

"Good point," said Tabor. "Rupert, give me—us—your best guess. Where do you think the Morganites live? What's their home planet?"

"I very much doubt if they have one anymore," replied Shenoy. "Their behavior suggests they are an ancient race which long ago settled into being what amounts to sapient parasites. They befriend alien species only to feed off of them afterward. That being the case—"

"Hoo!" boomed the Vitunpelay. "Of course!" He moved forward and said to Occo: "If you don't mind, I'd like to run the daimōn for a moment."

The view shattered, as if the image had been shaken by a mighty earthquake.

Ju'ula extended eight eyestalks, all with the eyes wide open.

"Now you've done it, you moron. You don't 'run' the daimōn. Even suggesting such a thing brings out his fury."

"My apologies!" said Jaemu. "I misspoke. What I meant to say was that I'd like to suggest a different perspective. To be specific, the planet of which this is a moon."

The view seemed to steady a bit, although it still hadn't coalesced to anything recognizable.

"He's like a little kid in a tantrum with his eyes closed," muttered Tabor. Then, more loudly: "Keep going, Jaemu. I think you may be making some progress."

"Hoo! Great Daimōn, I'm willing to bet that planet is infested with Morganites. The rotten nasty creatures who entrapped you—"

Ju'ula's eyestalks fluttered for a moment. "No, they didn't. Those clowns? Capture a *daimōn*? In their dreams, maybe."

"I think it far more likely that the daimōn was placed in that cube by the Fiends themselves," said Shenoy. "It was not a trap laid by the Morganites but simply one they discovered—and then lured others to open and take all the risks."

Jaemu clacked his mandibles and then rubbed them against each other, producing a quite unsettling noise. Occo thought the mannerism was a Vitunpelay way of indicating irritation—or maybe embarrassment—but she wasn't sure. Given the nature of that weird species, any mannerism of theirs could indicate almost anything at any given time. She was coming to share Rammadrecula's assessment, given at their first meeting, that someday they'd have to exterminate the pests.

But not today. "It's also possible, Jaemu," she suggested, "that the planet Mank harbors your long-missing kinfolk. Perhaps they resettled here after your banishment and exile."

"Most likely indeed!" exclaimed Jaemu. "Overcome with shame at my disgrace, they would have fled into exile themselves—and what better place for Vitunpelay to find obscurity than the dread planet of the reputedly mighty and malevolent Mank? Especially since they don't actually exist any more."

His tentacles writhed about, as if he were gripped with

fevered excitement. "Oh, to be reunited at last with those I hold most dear!"

<Are the two of you mad? It's a hell-monster created by ancient deities! It can't possibly be stupid enough to fall for this silly charade. More likely, it will turn on you and then—>

The view steadied. An instant later they were rushing toward the planet.

<Ah . . . Never mind. Akh! What is it doing?>

The familiar's startled exclamation was caused by the daimōn plunging directly into the planet. A moment later they had penetrated the surface and were . . .

Burrowing, for lack of a better term. Judging from the view they now had, the daimōn was charging back and forth through the soil of Mank—sometimes even burrowing through bedrock—in his frenzied search for Jaemu's kinfolk.

Fabled kinfolk.

Of which, needless to say, the daimōn uncovered not a one—but he did expose several lairs of Morganites. The treacherous sentients seemed to be plentiful beneath the planet's surface.

The expressions on their faces when the daimōn burst through their nests were rather amusing, Occo thought. She wondered what the daimōn looked like from the outside, to Morganites. Did it have the same formless shape they had seen when it emerged from the cube?

Eventually, the daimōn seemed to grow weary of the search. Or perhaps the monster was simply frustrated by his failure to uncover anything below the surface other than Morganites, in whom he seemed to have no interest whatsoever.

The view emerged from the surface. They were looking at the smaller of the planet's two moons.

The view rushed toward that moon. And a moment later . . .

"Oh, great," said Tabor. "Congratulations, Jaemu. You've made the daimōn so mad he's gobbling up the moon."

"Not exactly," said the Warlock Variation Drive. "A daimōn feeds more like one of those little beasts on your planet—what're they called?—starfish, as I recall. The ones who extrude their stomach and digest their prey on the outside. That's more or less what's happening here. When he's done, the moon will still be there—in a manner of speaking—but he'll have extracted all its nutrients."

She retracted her eyes. "It's pretty gross so I'm not watching. I suggest you figure out something else because once the daimōn finishes with the moon—the *little* moon, I remind you; this won't take long—you dummies are in real trouble."

"Not really," said Shenoy. The Human sage had a smile on his face which Occo thought was more peculiar-looking than usual. "I've been working through the math and the conclusion I've reached is the only one that seems to make sense."

Ju'ula's eyes remained hidden. "I'm not listening to this," she said. "I can't hear you."

"Don't be foolish. You don't really have any choice, if I'm not mistaken. We've had this all wrong from the beginning. Sentients call you a 'warlock variation drive,' Ju'ula. But that's not the correct description, is it?"

The Warlock Variation Drive made no response. To all outward appearances, she was nothing more than an inert object that looked like a large cruciform vegetable.

Shenoy shook his head. "No, of course not. One of those three terms is wrong. Not 'warlock,' since whatever powers you possess are clearly . . . what to call it? *Un*natural is begging the question, *super*-natural may or may not be accurate—for all we know these power are subnatural—and while *para*normal has some validity—"

One of Ju'ula's eyes extended, though not far. "Excuse me!" she snapped irritably. "The accepted term in polite company is metanormal."

Shenoy stared down at her. Then, cleared his throat.

"Indeed. Metanormal it is. The term 'variation' also seems appropriate—as we have all borne witness to. That leaves 'drive,' and I have to admit I'm feeling rather stupid at the moment. Which is an unaccustomed sensation and certainly not one I'm enjoying."

"What's wrong with 'drive'?" asked Jaemu. He snapped his mandibles in a manner that would be quite alarming if there were any rhyme or reason to Vitunpelay mannerisms. For all Occo knew, that indicated geniality.

"A 'drive,' no matter its specific mechanism, is an engine—a machine, if you will. It has no volition of its own. And while Ju'ula often uses the term 'drive' when she refers to one of us—well, Occo; she has a particular distaste for my methods—choosing the way and place to go, I suspect she's just being polite."

The Warlock Variation Drive's eye opened again.

"Way I was brought up—but you're right. The term's silly. None of you 'drives' me. In fact, if that notion weren't so utterly ridiculous that I can't take it seriously, I'd be quite peeved. None of you wants to see me get peeved."

And the eye closed again.

Tabor laughed. "I'll be damned. She's a Warlock Variation *Conductor*. Like on a tram or a bus."

Shenoy shook his head. "The word's right but your connotation is wrong. She's indeed the conductor—but what she's conducting is more like an orchestra than a bus. And we're the players."

Ju'ula's eye reopened and was joined by seven others. Then another seven. It was the first time any of them had seen her extend fourteen eyes. All of them gazed at the Human sage with what seemed to be approval.

"At last. At long, long last," she said. "I had given up hope that this day would ever come. I didn't think there were any sentients left capable of doing the math."

All fourteen eyes suddenly squinted at Shenoy. "You *can* do the math, yes?"

"Oh, certainly." The Human looked around. "If there were a blackboard . . . "

"Ebbo!" said the Warlock Variation Drive—no, Conductor. "Give the Human your tablet."

With obvious reluctance but no overt protest, Proceeds-With-Circumspection obeyed. Shenoy took a moment to figure out the operation of the device, and then began jotting formulas with his finger. After a short time, he held up the tablet so that Ju'ula could see what he'd put there.

Occo could see the screen also, but the inscriptions on

it were just gibberish to her. They didn't even look like mathematical symbols, at least as she understood them.

The Warlock Variation Conductor didn't read for more than a minim before it shut all its eyes and exclaimed: "Put that away! No, erase it! No, give it to me."

Something that vaguely resembled a tentacle with a bifurcated tip at the end shot out from Ju'ula's torso, snatched the tablet, and withdrew it into the torso itself. Peculiar sounds could be heard, as if the tablet was being consumed in some sort of enormous gizzard.

"The records!" squealed the Ebbo.

Ju'ula made a burping noise. "Be quiet, officious scribe. I still have possession of your records, in the unlikely event they're ever needed. What is important is that a potentially disastrous security breach has been averted."

Her fourteen eyes studied Shenoy. With considerable respect, insofar as any expression could be determined on the Warlock Variation Conductor's form.

"I hadn't really expected you could do it," she explained. "All right, I don't think any harm was done. You now have a Caliber Twadda Grade 14 Margrave clearance—but you still don't have a need to know all that much."

She bestowed on the others a gaze which seemed considerably less respectful. "The rest of you . . . Caliber Herzog Grade 3 Marmot clearance should do well enough for the time being, I think."

Rammadrecula stiffened, clearly offended. "I am an Envacht Lu Heterochthonatrix! I have no idea what those silly security rhymes indicate, but you should know that the Envacht Lu considers me—"

The rest dissolved into a squawk of confusion.

Again, the view had shifted. But, this time, they were not traveling through the bizarre corridor produced by the daimōn's mode of transport. Nor did they experience the instantaneous shift produced by Ju'ula when she'd still been operating as the Warlock Variation Drive.

Instead, to all appearances, they were suspended on an invisible platform and racing through interstellar space at an incredible velocity. They could actually *see* stars and nebulas and even distance globular clusters and galaxies shifting positions.

"I prefer the view," Ju'ula explained.

Tabor groped around with his hands. "Okay, the atmosphere seems stable—but I don't understand what's keeping it in place."

"Skerkie is. Environmental control is one of his functions. Now that I put him back together."

Looking behind them, Occo could see that the Skerkud Teleplaser had indeed been reassembled. So far as she could determine, he had suffered no permanent damage from his brawl with the daimōn.

Speaking of the daimōn . . .

"Where'd that Fiend thingie get off to?" Tabor asked.

"Hold on," said Ju'ula. They were now swooping between what looked like two huge gaseous columns. It took Occo a moment to realize that they were passing through the branches of a nebula that must have measured several light years across.

"Good Lord!" exclaimed Shenoy. "Those are the Pillars of Creation!"

"The navigation here's a bit tricky," Ju'ula said. "I need to concentrate. Won't take long."

Indeed, it didn't. A few minims later she turned a pair of eyes on Tabor and said: "I incorporated the daimōn into our collective essence. You ingested about four and half percent of it. The rest of you, about the same, except the Vitunpelay got six percent and the Ebbo only two and a half. Mama Ronnette and I split most of it, of course."

Everyone stared down at her.

"Huh?" said Tabor.

"Oh, my," said Shenoy.

"This is most irregular," said Proceeds-With-Circumspection.

"Hoo!" boomed Jaemu. "I'm part Fiend! My childhood dream come true at last!"

"Get it out of me!" shrieked Rammadrecula.

Ju'ula swiveled the eyes from Tabor to the heterochthonatrix. "You don't have any part of the daimōn, actually. Because you're not going to be with us much longer."

Their incalculable speed seem to slow, and then suddenly they came to a stop. Occo saw that they were now positioned a short distance from a revanship.

"*Suffer and Die, Execrable Ones*, I presume."

"Indeed," replied Ju'ula. "This is where you get off, Heterochthonatrix Heurse Gotha Rammadrecula."

CHAPTER 36

✳

"Why am I getting off here?" Rammadrecula demanded. Clearly, the heterochthonatrix was simultaneously aggrieved, insulted, angered and resentful.

Judging from the pinkish hue of Ju'ula's eyes and the rigidity of its eyestalks, the Warlock Variation Conductor was about to explain matters to Rammadrecula in blunt terms which would do nothing to assuage her hurt feelings. Occo felt a moment's sympathy for her.

Not much, no—but enough that she intervened.

"We need you to explain to the Envacht Lu where the perilous situation stands. Not only with regard to controlling the daimōn"—Occo waved a hand about, indicating their peculiar circumstances—"but also the ongoing menace of the Morganites."

"You can explain that yourself," Rammadrecula said sulkily.

"To be sure. In fact—we will!" She said that quite forcefully, it having just dawned on her that any explanation of the events they'd undergone coming from the heterochthonatrix would be garbled and confused at best. "But we need you there to confirm the veracity of the tale."

Glumly, she now realized that she'd just committed all of them to boarding the revanship, something she'd intended to avoid. But . . .

"Guess we have no choice," Tabor murmured. "Damn it."

He was standing right next to her so she was the only one who would have heard the words. It struck Occo for the first time that she had developed a lot more respect for the big Human's competence that she had for most members of her own species. Tabor lacked his companion Shenoy's frightening intelligence, granted, but like Occo herself he was practically minded. He'd have made quite a good castigant, actually.

From somewhere, a voice manifested itself.

"*Bizarre object in space which we tentatively categorize as a vessel, this is Envacht Lu Revanship* Suffer and Die, Execrable Ones. *You are required to make your identity and purpose known immediately. Failure to follow our instructions will make you subject to Level Buerth-Nog-Vlo chastisement.*"

<That doesn't make any sense at all!> protested Bresk. **<Buerth-Nog-Vlo? That would mean . . . >**

His thought broke off, for the same reason Occo's own thoughts were wandering aimlessly. As a chastisement, the combination was . . . effectively impossible. How would you dematerialize entrails, especially ones which had already been burnt to a crisp?

"There is no such chastisement!" protested Rammadrecula.

"*Who is speaking?*" demanded the same voice.

"This is Heterochthonatrix Heurse Gotha Rammadrecula."

"*One moment.*" There was a pause of several minims. Occo had no difficulty imagining the Envacht Lu officials on the ship consulting with one of their Ebbo scribes.

The voice came back. "*You are assigned to an outpost more than one hundred and thirty light-years distant, Heterochthonatrix Rammadrecula. What are you doing here? Without permission recorded, we note ominously. The chastisement for abandonment of a post by a heterochthonatrix without the express authority—*"

Occo intervened again, before Rammadrecula could say something stupid. "This is Occo Nasht Jopri Kruy Gadrax speaking. Ours is a long and convoluted tale which we will be glad to provide you in person. To summarize, pursuant to the instructions of Amerce Imposer Vrachi, given to me on this very revanship some time ago, I am reporting on the possibility that the destruction of my home cloister transgressed the bounds of propriety."

"*One moment.*" Again, there was a pause, this one considerably longer. Eventually, a new voice manifested itself.

"*This is Amerce Imposer Vrachi. What do you have to report, Gadrax?*"

"My home cloister was indeed destroyed by means which transgressed the bounds of propriety."

"*Who were the perpetrators?*"

"Therein lies the length and complexity of our tale— as well as explaining the presence of Heterochthonatrix Heurse Gotha Rammadrecula." After a moment, she added: "Who has played an essential role in uncovering the malefactors."

Technically, that wasn't a lie. Not quite.

There was another pause. Then: "*Come aboard.*"

Occo looked around. "Our party is quite varied, Amerce Imposer, and I would not wish any untoward incidents."

"*Who is among you?*"

"Two Nac Zhe Anglan, myself and Heterochthonatrix Rammadrecula. Two Humans, one Ebbo, and one Vitunpelay."

Another pause. "*The Humans and the Ebbo may accompany you. Not the Vitunpelay. The creatures are well known to be unsane.*"

"Hoo!" boomed Jaemu. "Even the mighty Envacht Lu tremble in our presence!" He waved his tentacles about. "But they need not fear. I shall magnanimously remain behind. No doubt Ju'ula and I will enjoy a long and animated conversation."

"In your dreams," said the Warlock Variation Conductor.

"Who is that speaking?" demanded the Amerce Imposer. His tone was suspicious.

"Ah . . . That was just the vessel's AI."

Judging from the slitted dimensions of the three eyes Ju'ula had peering at her, Occo might wind up paying a price for that remark. But that was a problem for later. At the moment, she was concerned to avoid any confrontation between the Envacht Lu and the Warlock Variation Conductor. The end result of such was likely to be . . .

She realized she had no idea what it was likely to be. Except—not good.

"*Come aboard,*" the Amerce Imposer repeated.

※ ※ ※

Occo had been wondering exactly how they'd make the transfer to the revanship from . . . whatever "vessel" Ju'ula had created. As it turned out, the process was accomplished by Ju'ula extending from the platform what looked for all the world like a very large and very long tongue that licked the side of the revanship, causing one of the hatches to open.

Across the tongue they marched. Thankfully, the surface was neither wet nor slimy.

As it turned out, the hatch that Ju'ula had opened was not a personnel transfer hatch. It was the airlock for an inspection hatch which led into a compartment just barely large enough to hold them all. The compartment was completely empty and featureless except for a multitude of instrument displays on the walls. There was a smaller hatch at the opposite end of the chamber but it was locked.

And . . . there they remained, for several medims, until the hatch on the far side of the chamber opened.

Amerce Imposer Vlachi came in, looking exceedingly displeased.

"How did you get in here?" she demanded. "The security protocols controlling that airlock are extraordinarily imposing. I demand an answer!"

Occo had been expecting this awkwardness, and had already settled on a response. She drew herself up as stiffly and haughtily as she could manage—which was quite stiffly and haughtily indeed; she was an accomplished castigant with many years of successful missions behind her—and snapped: "Be serious! It was mere hatchling's play. I now have Caliber Twadda Grade 14 Margrave security clearance."

The Amerce Imposer stared at her. "There is no such clearance level!"

Occo pointed at the airlock behind her. "Then how do you explain the ease with which I penetrated your protocols?"

Tabor spoke up, his tone of voice—at least, as transmitted via the universal translator—full of good cheer and reasonableness. "Wouldn't this all be much easier to discuss in the Amerce Imposer's office?"

Vlachi eyed him. "I have no office. It is a *suite,* as befits one of my stature."

"Indeed so!" said Tabor. "Let us to your suite, then."

After a moment's hesitation, Vlachi turned and passed back through the hatch. "Follow me," she commanded.

❈ ❈ ❈

The tale was long in the telling, with many interruptions and questions by the Amerce Imposer. But, eventually, it was done.

Now with respect rather than suspicion in the way she regarded them, Vrachi said: "I will need to discuss these matters with the High Council of the Envacht Lu, before I can authorize any further action. You will be required to wait here until I do."

Occo and Tabor looked at each other. By now, at least when it came to practical issues, the two of them were beginning to function as the joint leaders of their little . . . what to call it? Task force, perhaps.

"How long will it take for you to consult with the High Council?" asked Tabor. "Quite some time, I would imagine, given the limitations you Knacks—ah, Nac Zhe Anglan—place on supralight travel."

"Approximately two and half solar cycles. That would be the actual travel time. To which we would need to add whatever time is taken by the High Council in its deliberations. Which are never quick and likely to be of especially great duration given the nature of the subject. My estimate is that the total time which will elapse before I return will be three solar cycles."

"That would be Mellan solar cycles, am I right?" asked Tabor.

"Yes, of course."

He did that lip-puckering thing that Humans did when they were pondering something they found distasteful. By now, Occo had gotten quite good at deciphering the habits of the species.

"About eight and half Terran years, in other words," said Tabor. "I'm afraid that's not—"

Occo interrupted him. "I am of duly recorded gadrax status, Amerce Imposer," she pointed out. "Therefore not under your jurisdiction. And the Humans certainly aren't."

Vrachi rose from her bench, her posture now very stiff.

"The circumstances are exceptional—no, extraordinary. Even unparalleled. I therefore have no choice but to expand my authority—"

A very loud voice manifested itself in the suite. Occo realized it was that of the Warlock Variation Conductor.

"OH, PIFFLE. I HAVE NEITHER THE TIME FOR THIS NONSENSE NOR CERTAINLY THE

INCLINATION. AND *I* HAVE SECURITY CLEAR-
ANCE CALIBER TWADDA GRADE 51 DUKE."

An instant later, they materialized back aboard the
bizarre vessel that Ju'ula had created—or perhaps
expanded outward from herself.

Amerce Imposer Vrachi erupted in protest. But before
she had spoken more than a few words, Ju'ula turned three
eyestalks around to look back at the Skerkud Teleplaser.

"Restrain the loudmouth," she said.

The Teleplaser immediately unfolded its extensions
into a shape quite similar to that it had used to restrain
Tabor and Shenoy. Within two minims, the Amerce
Imposer had been likewise immobilized.

"What are the coordinates of this High Council of
yours?" Ju'ula asked. "You may use any notation system
you prefer."

Vrachi's response was not entirely coherent. Most of
it consisted of curses, imprecations and fierce vows to
maintain silence at all cost.

Ju'ula now looked at Occo. "Your job, this."

Occo visualized the dungeon . . .

❋ ❋ ❋

And there they were again. The fur-covered torturer
seemed to be expecting them.

"I knew you'd be back," he said, sounding quite cheerful.
"Good tippers always make for regular customers."

He now studied the Amerce Imposer, who had in
some way exchanged the Teleplaser restraints for those of
the mammal's dungeon.

"What are you looking for?" the torturer asked.
"Answers, or just the pleasure of a leisurely torment?"

Occo was tempted to respond with the latter of the options. By now, she'd grown almost as irritated with the Amerce Imposer as she'd become with Rammadrecula. What was it with Envacht Lu officials, anyway?

But . . . duty called.

"Answers, if you would. We need the galactic coordinates of the High Council of the Envacht Lu."

"Of what universe?"

That peculiar booming voice that Ju'ula had used earlier came into the dungeon.

"DOESN'T MATTER. I'LL TRANSLATE."

"As you wish."

❧ ❧ ❧

The torturer went to work. Occo had been expecting the furball to apply hot pokers, pincers—all matter of horrid pain-inflicting tools and machines.

But, instead, the torturer began by squeezing a few drops of water onto Vrachi's head and standing back.

Before too long, Vrachi began squirming. "Dry it off! Dry it off!"

The torturer shook his furry head. "No, no. I think we'll let nature take its course."

And so he did. He just stood there doing nothing while the drops of water slowly evaporated—and Vrachi's squirming intensified.

Eventually the drops dried and the torturer brought forth a small bowl of what looked like . . .

Dirt?

Apparently so. He sprinkled the soil on various portions of the Amerce Imposer's torso.

And, once again, stood back and waited.

It didn't take long before Vrachi was flinging herself back and forth in the restraining mechanism and shouting: "Clean it off! Clean it off!"

Again, the torturer shook his furry head. "No, no. You'll manage yourself. Eventually."

And eventually the Amerce Imposer did manage to get all the dirt off herself, although it took a lot of effort.

The torture now brought forth a small dish full of what looked like . . .

Food?

Apparently so. Rather old and somewhat rancid food.

He began spooning portions of the food onto Vrachi. "This should do it, I think," he said.

"I'll talk! I'll talk!" shrieked Vrachi. "The coordinates are—"

She began rattling them off frantically.

Tabor shook his head admiringly. "Damn, you're good," he said to his fellow furball.

The mammal torturer's face creased into a smile of sorts. "Always works with the right sort of officials. Everything must be in order, you know."

Belatedly, Occo realized she hadn't thought to bring anything with which to tip the torturer. But Tabor reached into a pocket on his lower garment and brought forth a small pouch from which he extracted a couple of peculiar-looking slips of what looked like plastic of some sort.

"Fortunately, I keep these bills as souvenirs," he explained, handing them over to the torturer. "Unless you'd prefer a credit transfer . . . ?"

"I don't hold with these newfangled customs," said the

torturer. "Cash is fine." He held up the plastic sheets and studied them curiously. "Don't recognize the currency, though. What is it?"

"Procyon *Deutsche Marks*," replied Tabor. "The planet was originally settled by German emigrants who were still holding a grudge about the Euro. It's something of a collector's item."

"Well, thank you. I look forward to seeing you again."

Occo was about to explain that was hardly likely, but cut the words short.

It might not be, after all. Who could say?

❋ ❋ ❋

A moment later, they rematerialized aboard Ju'ula's vessel.

"Hey," said Tabor to Shenoy. "I thought you said teleportation was all but impossible. So what do you call this?"

Shenoy, unusually, looked uncertain. He ran digits through his head fur again. "Well, I'm not sure, but I don't actually think Ju'ula—"

"Don't bother, Mama Ronnette," said the Warlock Variation Conductor. "He wouldn't understand the explanation anyway, even assuming you manage to figure it out."

She swiveled two of her eyestalks toward Tabor. "No, it wasn't teleportation. The whole idea's twaddle. Almost as silly as telepathy. All I did was jiggle the branes a bit at the edges. Think of it as flipping a bug from one sheet onto another. Teleportation would be instantaneously moving the bug all the way across one of the sheets. Twaddle."

She now swiveled the eyestalks toward the rear of the vessel—or, it might be better to say, toward that portion of the bizarre platform in what appeared to be empty space that Occo had arbitrarily designated as "the rear"— and examined the figure of Amerce Imposer Vrachi. Who was, once again, immobilized in the Teleplaser's restraints.

"Will you behave yourself now?" Ju'ula asked.

Vrachi glared at her but managed to keep her tone of voice reasonably civil. "Let me go," she demanded.

Ju'ula's eyes moved away.

"Please," Vrachi added.

The restraints fell away. A moment later, the Teleplaser folded itself back up into the tureen shape it assumed when it was dormant.

"I'd say brace yourselves and hang on," said Ju'ula, "but that would be silly false modesty."

And off they raced, through the void of interstellar space.

Not long thereafter, staring at the sight they were passing by, Amerce Imposer Vrachi spoke. Her tone was now awe-inspired.

"That's the Kall Xe Nebula," she said, almost whispering.

Tabor nodded. "Yeah, sure is. We call it the Orion Nebula. Looks even more impressive up close, doesn't it?"

"Do you believe us now?" said Occo. It was a statement, not a question.

※ ※ ※

It didn't seem very long at all before they came to a halt alongside the largest space station Occo had ever seen. The immense structure was orbiting a gas giant in a solar system which, so far as she could determine, had no other planets. Of course, she only had the instruments available to her which were portable enough to carry on her harness. There might be a few small rocky planets somewhere about she hadn't spotted.

"Here we are," said Ju'ula. They were very close to the station—close enough that Ju'ula reached out that weird tongue again and licked open the nearest entryway.

"Over you go, Amerce Imposer," she said. "Take the heterochthonatrix with you. And tell those fussbudgets over there not to take long. My time is valuable and my patience is miserly."

Hurriedly, Vrachi and Rammadrecula crossed over to the space station. By then, Occo could see a multitude of turrets and apertures holding a wide variety of weapons—some of them instruments of mass destruction—being pointed in their direction.

"Oh, piffle," said Ju'ula.

CHAPTER 37

✸

The space station vanished. They now seemed to be in orbit by themselves.

"Where'd it go?" asked Tabor.

Shenoy made a peculiar little sound that bore some resemblance to a laugh but wasn't loud enough.

<Humans call that a "chuckle,"> explained Bresk. **<I don't know of any species that makes as many peculiar noises as Humans do. Their farts are pretty pathetic, though, according to the records.>**

"I don't think it 'went' anywhere, Russ," said Shenoy. "I think Ju'ula just . . . what would you call it? Dimensionally rotated the station?"

"Pretty close," agreed the Warlock Variation Conductor. "Except I didn't fiddle with any of our eleven dimensions, I just borrowed some from another brane. If you were on board that space station, you'd think you were floating above an enormous ocean made of something that obviously wasn't water. If you were really, really, really stupid you'd try to find out what it was. But

429

I don't think anybody on that space station is *that* stupid. We'll know soon enough. If the Amerce Imposer isn't back in—what's that time frame you Humans use?—five minutes, I believe, then we'll know they were that dumb. Since there won't be anything left of them. Just as well, if you ask me. I'm willing to spend a little time dickering with these Envacht Lu nuisances, just to keep peace in the family, so to speak. But not much."

"*Are* we a family now?" asked Shenoy.

"Closest term I can think of," replied Ju'ula. "The fancy way of saying it would be that we are now a close-knit band of spiritual kin bonded by purpose as well as—oh, I forgot—Skerkie, wake up. I don't want another slipup like the last one and we both know what Vitunpelay are like."

The Teleplaser unfolded. A moment later—

"Oh, hell!" said Tabor.

The same hypodermic-like instruments flashed and plunged into the flesh of every being on the vessel.

Or corpuses, if might be better to say—because one of them penetrated the Warlock Variation Conductor also.

"That hurts," she complained.

"Sure does," said Tabor, rubbing one of his upper arms. "What'd you do that for?"

"We have all been implanted with concordaunt sureties," said Ju'ula. "But this time—pay attention, Jaemu!—there won't be any loophole for Vitunpelay whimsy to take advantage of. Be warned! Any betrayal by anyone of our unity and/or our purpose will hatch the surety. What would occur next is too ghastly to relate but I'm going to anyway—"

And so she did. Proceeds-With-Circumspection fainted about halfway through.

"Silly bugger," commented Ju'ula, when she was finished. "Ebbos are incapable of treachery so it had nothing to worry about anyway. Except the perils of our enterprise, of course."

Tabor scratched his cheek. "I don't recall volunteering for this," he said. "I was just on a job"—he pointed a thumb at Shenoy, standing next to him—"protecting this fellow."

Ju'ula brought five eyes to bear on him. "Surely you aren't contemplating the abandonment of our concordaunt and its mission? Now that I've explained the consequences of doing so."

"What part of 'volunteering' are you having the most trouble with?" Tabor asked. His tone was becoming rougher.

"'Volunteering' has nothing to do with it. It's your fault, anyway. You and Mama Ronnette"—Ju'ula's eyestalks waved about—"along with this gadrax maniac and the big fucking clown—took it upon yourselves to arouse the ancient powers. *All* of them, because when you wake up one the rest start stirring too. The Old Ones, the Fiends, the Hoar Ghosts, the Unfriendlies, the Estrangers—even They-Who-Must-Not-Be-Named!"

It was the first time Occo had ever seen the Warlock Variation Conductor get really agitated.

"Talk about morons!" Ju'ula continued. "Did *I* volunteer? Mr. Disgruntled So-called Security Expert who was dumb enough to dance into a deific-or-demonic—there's no difference because that's one thing the Naccor Jute got right—nightmare that everyone thought or at least hoped had been fossilized. To use a Human quip, 'Hell, no!' I was drafted just like you were. Except my conscription happened so long ago your ancestors were still trying to figure out how to crawl up out of the sea. I was on reserve duty, damn it—until *you* showed up. My last gig, I was a museum guard. Talk about an easy assignment!"

As she'd spoken, Occo had found herself getting more interested than aggravated. "Then why did you say 'At last!' As if you were pleased about it all."

Ju'ula fell silent. All her eyestalks withdrew for a moment.

"Well . . . "

The eyestalks re-emerged, slowly.

"Okay, I was bored. Reserve duty sounds pretty good—and it is, too! But five hundred million years of it . . . I was even starting to miss playing what Mr. Security here would call 'tic-tac-toe.' Which is the most boring game ever invented by any species."

She brought seven eyestalks to bear on Tabor. "So quit grousing. There's a war on—will be soon, anyway—and you're draft number came up. Way it goes. If it makes you feel any better, you'll be getting a big raise in pay."

Tabor seemed to perk up. "I will?"

"Well. Not 'pay,' exactly. But the perks are pretty terrific. Speaking of which . . . "

A moment later, the vessel was radically transformed. Where before they had seemed to be standing on a plain and unadorned—if gauzily mysterious—platform exposed to vacuum, they were now inside what appeared to be an enormous luxury liner. There was even a string quartet playing in a nearby alcove.

Which, admittedly, pleased no one.

"What are those bizarre instruments?" asked the Vitunpelay.

"And what is that racket they're making?" chimed in Tabor. "Please don't tell me that's supposed to be a melody."

The string quartet vanished. "Sorry," muttered Ju'ula. "I'm still working out some of the details. It's a little tricky since I have to work with the raw materials at hand, which are the spirit—no, call it the *noumenon*— of the Fiend daimōn and what's left of Heterochthonatrix Rammadrecula's spacecraft after I cannibalized it."

"She might get cranky about that," said Shenoy.

"Ask me if I care. Ah, there—that's better." The alcove was now filled with a bizarre-looking mechanism.

"A jukebox!" exclaimed Tabor. He hurried over and examined the control panel. "Look at this, Rupert! It's even got 'The Great Pretender' by the Platters. God, that tune's ancient."

He pushed a button and began crooning along with the horrid noise that emerged:

"Oh oh, yes I'm the great pretender,
"Adrift in a world of my own . . ."
<Make him stop! Make him stop!>
But Occo decided that putting up with the caterwauling was better than putting up with the Human's grousing about being conscripted. Besides, she was more interested in the nature of the task for which they'd been conscripted.

So she turned back to Ju'ula. "What's this you're saying about a 'war'? A war with whom? And over what?"

Ju'ula stared up at her. "A war with the ancient powers, of course. More precisely, a war *between* the ancient powers that we'll be doing our best to stay out of. Fat chance of that happening, though. They don't call them devils and demons for nothing, when they aren't calling them gods and goddesses."

That's what Occo had been afraid of. "What possible role can we play in such an affair?"

"What do you think? We'll be the reconnaissance team, Occo. What Humans would call the Mata Hari. Or is it the Hara Kiri? I can't remember."

"The space station's back," said Shenoy.

Turning to the viewscreen that now adorned one side of the huge chamber, Occo saw that the Human was right. The Envacht Lu fortress had returned from whatever bizarre continuum the Warlock Variation Conductor had sent it into.

"That was quick," she said. "I wouldn't have thought they'd come to a decision that quickly."

"Oh, they've been discussing the matter for half a solar cycle," said Ju'ula. "Time passes more slowly where they were. Which is why I sent them there. I wasn't about to waste our time waiting for them to finish wrangling."

The figure of Amerce Imposer Vrachi appeared on the screen. "We have reached our conclusions," she announced. "First, we are dispatching an Uttermost Reproach to smite the Morganites on the planet Mank. They pose an intolerable peril to galactic tranquility. I am pleased to report that former Heterochthonatrix Rammadrecula has volunteered for the mission."

Vrachi turned away to look behind her. "She would like to say a few last words to you."

Rammadrecula now appeared on the screen, looking immensely pleased with herself.

"Comrades! I must leave you now—but not before bestowing upon you my best wishes and bequeathing to you all my material possessions. My ship, my Gawad murkster, my vast collection of Human curios—all yours, now! I go on a mission from which no heroine ever returns."

She held up a hand, forestalling any possible protest. "But grieve for me not, comrades! Ours is the best of times, and the worst of times. It is a far, far better thing that I do, than I have ever done; it is a far, far better rest that I go to than I have ever known. *Adieu!*"

And she left.

What does "adieu" mean, Bresk?

<It means literally "to God" in one of the Human tongues. It's a term used in times of separation to indicate that the speaker goes to join the beneficent deity in whom they believe.>

Occo hadn't liked Rammadrecula, to be sure. But this . . .

She's gone mad.

<Too much time studying Humans. What do you expect?>

Tabor had been shaking his head. Now he said: "Jeepers. I can't say I cared much for the numbskull, but I didn't wish her to commit suicide."

"Oh, I shouldn't fret much over that, Russ," said Shenoy. "The planet Mank is so far away from here—they're restricted to sublight travel, remember?—that the revanship can't possibly get there for . . ." He faded into silence, his eyes unfocused, as he tried to work through the math.

"Help me here, would you, Ju'ula," he said. "I'm not sure of the exact distances involved."

"By the time Rammadrecula and her revanship get to their target," replied the Warlock Variation Conductor, "your great-great-grandchildren—in the event you have any, which is unlikely given the soon-to-be-encountered desperate perils of your own lifespan—will be decrepit with age if they are not already dead. That's assuming any of your species is still alive. Which is no more likely than your own survival if we don't stop dawdling and get about our mission."

"Indeed." Shenoy looked back at the screen, in which Vrachi had reappeared. "You implied that there was at least one more conclusion you had reached. What is it?" he asked.

The Amerce Imposer seemed a bit abashed. "Well, ah . . . This is more in the way of a suggestion—perhaps we could call it a proposal—than an actual conclusion, as such. We were thinking it might be a good idea if you—all of you—went out there somewhere—far from here; very far from here—to see what you might discover. Concerning . . . whatever."

"I see." Shenoy nodded. "And I assume you will want us to report back at regular and frequent intervals."

"No need! No need! Do report back, by all means.

But . . . it needn't be often, or soon, and certainly not at any set intervals."

Vrachi fell silent. Her expression strove to convey amity and goodwill. In this effort she failed—failed wretchedly. But Occo would allow that at least she tried.

There was no point in wasting any more time. She glanced at Tabor.

He nodded. "Might as well, I suppose."

"Ju'ula, let's be off," she said.

Instantly, they were racing through interstellar space. This time, though, they could enjoy the sight through the relative stability of a viewscreen rather than the unsettling experience of being completely surrounded by the void.

"Where *is* the Gawad murkster?" queried Bresk. "I don't see it anywhere—which by itself isn't surprising, of course. But I don't see any of its usual surrounding murkiness."

"I cannibalized it also," replied Ju'ula. "Or incorporated it into our combined essence, if you prefer. Our entire vessel is now murked, you will be pleased to learn. Not even the Estrangers could spot us now, unless we choose to reveal ourselves."

That *was* cheery news.

"So where are we going?" Shenoy asked.

"How am I supposed to know?" demanded Ju'ula.

"Well . . . Because you're the Warlock Variation—"

"*Conductor*, remember? I'm just a grunt." Ju'ula swiveled six eyes to gaze at Occo with not much in the way of friendly regard. "The AI, I believe you said."

Tabor's brow crinkled. "But—You're the conductor. You lead the whole orchestra."

"That is putting the matter far too categorically. I lead

the orchestra in playing the *piece of music*. Which I did not compose. Someone else did."

"Who?"

Now, fourteen of Ju'ula's eyes emerged and she swept her gaze over all the sentients assembled in the chamber—Occo, Bresk—using the term "sentient" a bit loosely—Shenoy, Tabor, Jaemu and Proceeds-With-Circumspection.

"You, of course. Like, I said, I'm just a grunt. It's time for you officers to get to work for a change. I don't do composing. I just conduct. Although, if you'll take a bit of advice from someone slaving away in the pit—I'd start with the Fiends. They're more murderous than a collapsing Type O supergiant but they're not exactly what you'd call keen-witted. Whatever you do, stay away from They-Who-Must-Not-Be-Named until and unless you're finally ready to name them."

She fell silent. All her eyestalks withdrew.

Everyone looked at each other. Then Tabor said to Shenoy: "You're the brain, Rupert. No, no—I misspoke! *Lord Shenoy*, I should have said."

The Human sage's face was split by a huge smile. "Well! If you insist, I suppose . . . "

Tabor turned to Occo and clapped a big hand on her shoulder.

"As for you," he said, "I think this is the beginning of a beautiful friendship."

"We are not friends," she protested. "The notion is ridiculous."

Why is he saying that? she demanded of Bresk. *Is it a trick?*

<Give me a moment to consult the records. Ah— here it is. No, it's a reference to an ancient Human legend named Casablanca. I'm not certain, but I think Tabor wants you to be his partner in founding what they call a "casino.">

And what is that?

<Brace yourself, this gets truly weird. It seems Humans take great pleasure in playing a game—they call it "gambling"—based on the belief that if you subject your destiny to random chance, the outcome might be favorable.>

For a moment, Occo was too dumbfounded to speak. But . . . that's insane!

<I can see now why Rammadrecula said it wouldn't be necessary to exterminate Humans. They'll do it themselves. Of course—since we're now conjoined to them—I can also see why Ju'ula foresees no great prospects for us, either.>

"We're doomed," Occo said aloud.

"Don't be so gloomy," chided Tabor. "With a bit of luck—a little helping hand from the Good Lord, as they say—we might come out of this okay."

<Stark raving mad.>

"Doomed," Occo repeated.